LETHAL LADDER

A middle-aged woman run down on a New York Street.

An elderly gentleman with his head blown off in Boston.

An elegant adultress butchered in her Connecticut mansion.

A voluptuous co-ed seduced and slain in a swank Colorado ski resort.

Now Markham had just one more step to reach his goal—and only one worry as he boarded the plane for Washington, D.C. The final man he meant to murder knew even better than he how to kill. . . .

STALKING

"Keeps the adrenaline flowing!"
—*Publishers Weekly*
"Strong!"—*Kirkus Reviews*
"Chilling and convincing!"
—*Santa Barbara News-Press*

Big Bestsellers from SIGNET

- [ ] **SPHINX by Robin Cook.** (#E9194—$2.95)
- [ ] **COMA by Robin Cook.** (#E8202—$2.50)
- [ ] **LOVE IS NOT ENOUGH by Ruth Lyons.** (#E9196—$2.50)*
- [ ] **LET THE LION EAT STRAW by Ellease Southerland.** (#J9201—$1.95)*
- [ ] **STARBRIAR by Lee Wells.** (#E9202—$2.25)*
- [ ] **BLOOD RITES by Barry Nazarian.** (#J9203—$1.95)*
- [ ] **SALT MINE by David Lippincott.** (#E9158—$2.25)*
- [ ] **SAVAGE RANSOM by David Lippincott.** (#E8749—$2.25)*
- [ ] **ROOMMATE by Jacqueline Wein.** (#E9160—$2.25)*
- [ ] **WINE OF THE DREAMERS by Susannah Leigh.** (#E9157—$2.95)
- [ ] **GLYNDA by Susannah Leigh.** (#E8548—$2.50)*
- [ ] **CLAUDINE'S DAUGHTER by Rosalind Laker.** (#E9159—$2.25)*
- [ ] **WARWYCK'S WOMAN by Rosalind Laker.** (#E8813—$2.25)*
- [ ] **THE MONEYMAN by Judith Liederman.** (#E9164—$2.75)*
- [ ] **SINS OF OMISSION by Chelsea Quinn Yarbro.** (#E9165—$2.25)*

* Price slightly higher in Canada

Buy them at your local bookstore or use this convenient coupon for ordering.

THE NEW AMERICAN LIBRARY, INC.,
P.O. Box 999, Bergenfield, New Jersey 07621

Please send me the SIGNET BOOKS I have checked above. I am enclosing $_____ (please add 50¢ to this order to cover postage and handling). Send check or money order—no cash or C.O.D.'s. Prices and numbers are subject to change without notice.

Name _____

Address _____

City_____ State_____ Zip Code_____

Allow 4-6 weeks for delivery.
This offer is subject to withdrawal without notice.

STALKING

TOM SELIGSON

A SIGNET BOOK
NEW AMERICAN LIBRARY
TIMES MIRROR

NAL BOOKS ARE AVAILABLE AT QUANTITY DISCOUNTS
WHEN USED TO PROMOTE PRODUCTS OR SERVICES. FOR
INFORMATION PLEASE WRITE TO PREMIUM MARKETING DIVISION,
THE NEW AMERICAN LIBRARY, INC., 1633 BROADWAY,
NEW YORK, NEW YORK 10019.

Copyright © 1979 by Tom Seligson

All rights reserved. For information address
The New American Library, Inc.

A hardcover edition of this book was published by Everest House,
Publishers, and simultaneously in Canada by Beaverbooks,
Pickering, Ontario.

SIGNET TRADEMARK REG. U.S. PAT. OFF. AND FOREIGN COUNTRIES
REGISTERED TRADEMARK—MARCA REGISTRADA
HECHO EN CHICAGO, U.S.A.

SIGNET, SIGNET CLASSICS, MENTOR, PLUME, MERIDIAN AND NAL BOOKS
are published by The New American Library, Inc.,
1633 Broadway, New York, New York 10019

First Signet Printing, May, 1980

1 2 3 4 5 6 7 8 9

PRINTED IN THE UNITED STATES OF AMERICA

For Leah Madrid

Prologue

Weather permitting, Wilson left the house at nine o'clock sharp. Two buses later, followed by a brisk walk through the closest thing in Chicago that resembled a field, and he was at the Lincoln Park courts. At that hour of the day there was never any problem picking up a game. Cabdrivers taking exercise between fares, mailmen extending their routes, as well as students, retired seniors like himself, along with the professionally unemployed. There was even a regular named Mickey, who, though he looked like an accountant, was said to be a hit man for the mob. Supposedly carried his heat packed in an attaché case with his racket and balls. All Wilson knew was that the guy had a serve like a .38, and punched his volleys like he was knocking you across a room. Wilson had played him more than he cared to remember. Whether rallying from the baseline or charging to the net, the senior citizen never took a game.

He fared little better with the others. "Wilson the Winner" they called him behind his back. Indeed he was sure his string of defeats deserved placement in some kind of book of records. He had not won a victory since moving from Maryland a year before.

But today was going to be different. Wilson had sensed it as soon as he and McNulty took the court. Wilson was playing as he had never played before. Like an A-number-one *pro*. And he had only one more game to go.

He could see McNulty waiting impatiently on the far court. His Hawaiian shirt was untucked from his shorts, his knee socks bunched at his ankles. Even his ever-present cigar was now unlit, McNulty working it back and forth like a metronome.

Wilson won the first point on a passing shot as McNulty came to net. The second was his after a long rally, his opponent's backhand just missing the line.

Grunting with determination, McNulty double-faulted. "Shit!" he yelled, loud enough to turn heads six courts away. And now there was only one more point to go. Wilson won it like an expert, drawing his opponent to net with a drop shot, then sending a lob deep to the corner. McNulty made a desperate effort to reach the ball, but it was too well placed, and his feeble return landed in the alley. It was all over.

Wilson was too old to jump over the net. But he let out a Maryland version of a rebel yell and rushed forward to shake McNulty's hand. McNulty, his face as red as his shirt, mustered the most grace he was capable of in defeat.

"You know I gave up an airport fare to play with you. Some thanks you show me."

"Don't worry," said Wilson. "Just a lucky day."

They collected their towels and balls and walked off the court.

"Who knows?" the loser finally conceded. "Maybe it's good for you to get away from the game for a while. You didn't play any in New York, did you?"

"Not a stroke. Didn't even bring my racket."

"You know what I really think, Wilson. I think you've been hiding something from us. And you've done a damn good job of keeping it secret."

"What's that?" asked Wilson, touching the sunburn on the bald spot he refused to cover with a hat.

"That you've been taking lessons on the sly. *That secret.* And don't you try to deny it."

"You think that's it, huh?" said a grinning Wilson.

"Have to be. How the hell else did you get that good all of a sudden?"

Wilson laughed. "Ask me that next time. By then I'm sure I'll be back to normal."

The bus could not go fast enough for Wilson, he was so eager to tell Betty of his victory. And over a man fifteen years younger. There was life in his sixty-six-year-old limbs yet, not to mention promise in the game he had taken up only two years before. All that practice against the nearby school wall had finally paid off. It was cause for celebration. Tonight he and Betty would go out to dinner. Take in a movie. Have a couple of drinks. He just had to remember to get to bed early. After all, he now had a reputation to uphold.

It was on the second bus that Wilson began thinking of what McNulty had said. The bit about the secret. Though the cabdriver had been referring to tennis lessons, there was a real irony to his words. What had the New York trip been if it wasn't a secret? Even Betty did not know the real reason for their going. She had taken him at his word, welcoming the idea of a week of theater and shopping with as much excitement as he was feeling right now. What was retirement for, if not to play? They had kept up such a dizzying pace the whole time they were there—museums in the morning, followed by lunch and shopping, and then the theater at night—that Betty fully understood her husband's wish one afternoon to remain behind in the hotel room for a nap. She had gone to Bloomingdale's alone, looking at the new line of full-length coats and the model rooms on the fifth floor.

It was then, alone for the first time in New York, that Wilson was free to act. Not that he was hiding anything from his wife, but there was no reason for her to know. He had never told her much of what happened before, and so what was the purpose now?

As soon as she left, he changed his clothes, from khaki-colored trousers, desert boots, and an open-collar shirt, to a seersucker suit and solid dark-blue tie. He had to look legitimate if he were to be believed. His hands shook as he tied the laces on his black shoes, and though his bladder felt full, when he went to the bathroom nothing at all came. He left the room four times, forgetting in turn his wallet, his glasses, and the address of the man he was scheduled to see.

Wilson's nervousness continued on the subway downtown. Though it was so hot that the Puerto Rican next to him looked like he'd stepped from a shower, undershirt and all, Wilson felt a chill on the back of his neck. The rest of him was numb. For assurance he studied his reflection in the subway-car window. No problem, he told himself with a strained smile. He'd be able to go through with it. Lord knows, it was about time.

For Wilson this trip was like finally ending a chapter in his life. In all the work he had done in his years of service, with all the secrets he had kept to himself, this was the one that disturbed Wilson the most. It had stayed with him all this time, the kind of memory that lingered at three A.M. He wished it were gone. Now that he was retired, he wanted to put his work and his past completely behind him. That required, at least in this one instance, cleansing his guilt.

Wilson had been living with the lie for too long. So was the man he made an appointment to see that summer in New York, and to whom he finally told the truth.

And look what happened. The remainder of his stay in New York was like a second youth, a second honeymoon, and a whole new identity rolled into one. Up at seven o'clock for leg raises and *Sunrise Semester* on television, he was good for a full day of gallery-touring, people-watching, and even after-theater bar-hopping with hardly a yawn. He didn't complain while at Altman's his wife tried on five dresses in a row, but rather was attentive and helpful as she pondered the choice. For the first time in ten years he and Betty had sex in the afternoon, Mike Douglas watching from the table TV. Betty could not quite believe the change in her husband. Wilson pretended to take it in stride. He had one more test for himself, and that was today's.

He passed it beyond his hopes. Here he was, his first day back on the courts, and he goes and plays like Jimmy Connors. Well, maybe not exactly, but it sure was the best tennis of his life. Never underestimate the benefits of a clean conscience, the winner told himself.

Wilsom hopped off the bus like he was twenty-five and in love. He could not remember the last time he had been in such good spirits. Probably not since the birth of his granddaughter, Julie, more than a year and a half before, or when he learned that his monthly Social Security check was to be fifty-six dollars more than he thought.

Wilson was so caught up in his mood that he paid no attention whatever to the car parked across the street from his building. Its occupants were two men, and they paid very close attention to Wilson. With their ties undone and their shirt sleeves rolled up, they resembled salesmen or low-level city officials relaxing from the early-summer heat. They were listening to the Cubs game on the radio. While gazing out the window, the man in the passenger seat took long relaxed puffs on his briar pipe. After studying a photo he held in his hand, he nodded at the driver. He then knocked the ashes outside the window. As soon as Wilson disappeared into his building, the two men adjusted their ties, put on their coats, and got out of the car.

Betty had gone shopping, and left a note on the refrigerator door. Wilson was still in his shorts and T-shirt, and looking for a cold beer, when he heard the doorbell ring. He opened the door to two middle-aged men in business suits. One of the men was enormous and had a long crooked nose, and the other, with a crew cut, smiled from eyes so blue that for a moment Wilson was reminded of a famous Hollywood actor. The two looked like housing inspectors, and Wilson assumed they were there because of the recent trouble with the pipes.

"We're looking for Charlie Wilson," said the man with the blue eyes.

"I'm Charlie Wilson. What can I do for you?"

"You can let us in," said the Nose.

Wilson was about to ask what they wanted. However, before he could get it out, the Eyes had already pushed by him, arrogantly, as if he weren't there. They began checking out the small three-room apartment. "Anyone else here?" he asked, heading toward the bedroom, his back turned toward Wilson.

"What the hell's going on here?" Wilson had no idea who the men were or what they were after. They certainly weren't housing inspectors. That's for sure. "Hey . . ." He started to follow the Crew Cut with the eyes. But just then he heard the door lock behind him, and the next thing he knew a baseball bat smashed against his leg, knocking him to the floor. Only it wasn't a baseball bat, but a kick by the man with the crooked nose, who was now hovering menacingly above. From where he lay on his back, Wilson could see the beginnings of a double chin, and also the dark nostrils spread unevenly across his face. It was a view that inspired little confidence.

"What do you guys want? Money?"

Neither man spoke. The one with the blue eyes was obviously the brains of the two. At least he was doing all the moving. He looked down at Wilson without expression as he headed toward the kitchen.

"Let me get my wallet." Wilson reached out his arms to help himself up. But he did not get far before the man with the crooked nose, who weighed in at at least two hundred and twenty, took two steps onto his hands. Wilson could feel the knuckles threatening to crack, as well as the tears coming to his eyes, the scream building in his throat. But all of that was nothing compared to the fear that was just beginning to bud in some fiber of his brain.

"That's enough," said the other man, returning from the kitchen. He motioned to his partner to step back away from Wilson. He ran a hand through the crew-cut hair that was the color of his tanned skin. The blue eyes were wide. Wilson thought he detected a smile on the handsome face. He started to get up.

It was wishful thinking. The man's right hand came out of nowhere. The fist landed squarely against Wilson's nose, with the sound of an ax in dry wood. If he had any doubt about the nose being broken as he was flung halfway across the room, well, then he knew for a fact by the time he landed against the leg of a table. Blood was streaming from his nostrils, and breathing was out of the question except through his mouth. He looked down at his tennis shirt, which was no longer white, and for a moment he thought of Mickey, the hit man from the courts. So that's what it felt like on the receiving end of a punch. Wilson had not been in a fight for more than fifty years. Ever since grade school. However, the observation was soon lost in the fear, spreading now thicker than before, like a humid cloud dampening his skin. And with it came clarity, a regretful understanding. Wilson looked up at the blue eyes—as expressionless as before—and he knew. Undeniably. He wished he didn't. He felt a chill he was afraid he wouldn't shake.

"How was your trip to New York, Wilson?" The man wasn't wasting time.

"Fine." It was hard to talk and breathe at the same time.

"What'd you do while you were there?"

"Sightseeing. The usual stuff." Wilson leaned his head back against the table in an effort to stop the bleeding.

"Who'd you see?"

"Besides my wife, eight million New Yorkers." Wilson was surprising even himself by his defiance. What the hell? He had nothing to lose. He knew why they were there. Funny he didn't realize it sooner; he'd been around their type God-knows-how-many years. There was a time—most of his life, in fact—when he would have been afraid of guys like this. Not so much what they did, but rather what they stood for. It was the same thing in the end, and you were awed by it. After all, that's why you were there. You did your job because it was something you believed in, and you kept it to yourself. Those were the rules, and you obeyed them afterward as you had obeyed them before. Wilson's problem was that though he, like everyone else, had swallowed a lot during his career, there was just one bit of baggage that wouldn't go down. Also, he wanted a peaceful retirement, full of children and grandchildren, his stack of science journals, and an opportunity to play as much tennis as he wanted. He did not want it messed by ugly memories cropping up in the middle of a set, or while romping with five-year-old Bobby.

Why not be defiant? That's why they were here, so might as well act out the part. Besides, once again, he had nothing to lose. Somehow they had found out what he had done, and now there were no options left. Not for him, nor for them. Thinking about that somehow took away the chill.

"You betrayed confidence, didn't you?" Blue Eyes spoke while examining the roll of quarters he had held in his fist. "You broke the rules."

Wilson said nothing. Why bother explaining himself? They would not understand, even if they might have liked to. There was no room for sentiment in these boys. They were professionals among professionals. If they had originally been blessed with even one drop of kindness, well, there was no doubt it had dried up long before now. Wilson knew the high standards of their employer, and the fact that these two were here was proof enough that they had passed all the tests. Besides, he was beginning to cough from all the blood he had swallowed, so talking was even more difficult than before. Might as well just let them get on with it.

"You know our orders, Wilson. We've got no alternative."

So much for sympathy. Now it was time for business. For a moment Wilson thought of the odds on escape. There were none. Not with that gorilla standing right next to him, his blue-eyed friend no more than two feet away. And it was too late anyway, because after a slight nod from the boss, the gorilla placed a huge hand on his arm and was now yanking him to his feet. As he was led across the floor to his bedroom, Wilson wondered how it would come. He guessed it would be silent and quick.

The thoughts came like rain as he was thrown across the bed. Betty and Bobby, the books and journals he would never read, the celebration of victory that was no longer. How ironic for them to arrive on this very day. But as he saw the barrel of steel moving toward his face, felt its coldness comforting against his nose, Wilson had no regrets. Not of his life's work, nor of the decision that led to this. He had wanted to end clean, and he had. Clean, as well as a winner.

A story about Charlie Wilson's suicide appeared the next day on page six of the Chicago *Sun-Times*. It was picked up by one of the wire services, and ended up as filler on page forty-nine of the New York *Times*, right next to a half-page ad for Bloomingdale's.

1

District Attorney Frank Markham enjoyed watching a defendant squirm. It was the high point of any trial, the moment when everyone in court—defense lawyers, judge, even the jury—became witnesses to the personal confrontation between himself and the accused. He noticed Connolly shifting restlessly in his chair, gripping his fingers, viselike on the table, his tightly pressed lips drained of color. The former waterfront commissioner was obviously fearful. Staring at the defendant as he finished his final summation to the jury, Markham could barely contain his delight. He stood erect and still, his arms at his sides, the confidence clearly expressed in his dark eyes.

"I ask you once more," he said firmly. "Do not let this betrayal of public trust go unpunished. You have heard the Waterfront Commission referred to here as a 'model of corruption.' I believe Henry Connolly has the makings of a *model prisoner*."

Markham kept his eyes on Connolly as he walked slowly to his seat. The defendant glared back bitterly, his face flushed. Markham gave a slight nod. *It's all over, buddy. You're beaten, and you know it. It was just a matter of time.*

Markham had seen defendants far more defiant than Connolly. A prostitute charged with murder once whispered to him from the defense table, threatening to castrate him once she returned to the streets.

"Like you did to the sailor," he replied softly.

"With you I'll use a dull blade," she called loud enough to

be heard by the jury. Markham suppressed a smile, watching her face redden to match her Afro wig.

A Mafia loan shark once threw a punch at him on his way to taking the stand. A former college wrestler, Markham deflected the blow with an easy left hand. Though he would have loved to bury his right fist in the man's fleshy cheeks, the prosecutor did not punch back. His revenge came from seeing the defendant shackled for the rest of the trial, the metal cuffs binding through his silk sleeves.

Even the most hardened mobster lost his toughness at the prospect of years of steel bars. Markham had no doubts that was to be Connolly's future diet. No doubts at all.

From his chair, Markham glanced at the jury. He looked particularly at the woman in the middle of the second row. Mrs. Dorothy Lagana was her name. From Sullivan Street, right smack dab in the heart of Little Italy. A housewife in her early fifties, with a husband who ran a dry-cleaning store over on Mott. She had her hair up in a bun, was overweight by at least forty pounds, and wore shapeless dark-colored clothes and chunky Enna Jettick shoes. All her other qualifications were equally positive. She seemed a sure vote for conviction right down to her choice of gum (Spearmint), her favorite television show *(The Waltons)*, and the folded copy of the *National Enquirer* she carried in her oversized pocketbook.

But it had been her children that finally convinced Markham to keep her on the jury. He knew that appearances could be deceptive, especially with a woman. He had learned from the case of a student bomber, where a seemingly dyed-in-the-wool conservative had ended up voting for acquittal, not, he was convinced, out of any fault of his own, but because of the pressure she'd received from her sociologist son. Children were the key, even more than reading tastes and personal habits, and experience had taught Markham that Mrs. Lagana's two sons and a daughter made her an ideal selection. A boy in the Marines, another studying accounting at Fordham, and a daughter who was engaged to a cop. A district attorney could not do any better than Mrs. Dorothy Lagana.

Unfortunately, her broad face was now inscrutable.

Markham turned back to the defendant. Like his lawyer, Schneider, Henry Connolly was also putting on a good performance. He had evidently been very well coached. The bear of a man, who once boasted of buying judges like the less influential buy tickets for Madison Square Garden, now sat crumpled in his chair, his round face a portrait of vulnerability. He even looked to be blinking back a tear. Markham wondered out of what closet he had gotten that old threadbare suit.

As he gazed at Connolly, Markham's mind began to wander. Though he knew he should pay attention, he realized he was not listening to Schneider's summation. He'd been having that problem throughout the entire four weeks of the trial. Though he understood the reasons for his frequent lapses of attention—God knows, it was understandable, considering what was to follow the end of the trial—still, there was no excuse for being less than fully alert. His heart might not be in it, yet the prosecution still had to be completed. Besides, this Schneider was no amateur. He was one of the best criminal lawyers in town, and Markham had to be on his toes, prepared to raise an objection if he tried anything tricky. Like introducing new evidence now, during the summation. One hint of that, and Markham would be on his feet, cutting off Schneider's words before the jury could hear them. Bear up, he told himself. It's only a short while more.

But despite his best intentions, his mind seemed to have a will of its own. He momentarily succumbed to its direction, and suddenly it was like all self-restraint was gone, swept away. Anyone looking closely would have seen that his eyes were dazed and that there were faint beads of perspiration on his upper lip.

It was as if he were no longer in the courtroom. His eyes, though still riveted on Connolly, were seeing right through him. Rather than looking at a corrupt politician who had milked his position for financial gain, he was envisioning other faces, the faces of those who had preoccupied him all through the trial. The more he thought of them, the deeper became his anger, an anger that, like some nervous disorder, was impossible to contain.

But he had to try. Markham swallowed hard, and the stale taste in his mouth from too much talking reminded him where he was. He purposely caught the inside of his cheek between his teeth. Slowly and deliberately he bit down as hard as he could. As previously, the pain effectively absorbed him. The buildup, and then the sharp release of tension, helped to relax him. His head felt clearer, and his body relieved. He sighed. Pay attention, Markham warned himself. It's almost over.

The defense attorney, a florid man in his sixties, paced before the jury box. He pushed the hair from his toupee away from his forehead.

"The prosecution would have you believe that this dedicated public servant did willfully institute construction-bidding practices whose sole purpose was his own personal enrichment. 'Kickback Connolly,' the D.A. calls him." He laughed, shook his head at the apparent absurdity of it all, paused for the appropriate effect, and then continued. "Have you ever heard anything so ludicrous? Why, it's out of a B movie. A bad one. . . . And then the prosecution goes on to claim that Mr. Connolly 'borrowed' from his own budget. For what reasons? we ask. To finance a home in New Jersey, the prosecutor tells us. Yet you have heard witness after witness explain that Henry Connolly's real home was the department itself. A man doesn't steal from his own home. Certainly not a man like Henry Connolly."

Schneider stared directly at Mrs. Dorothy Lagana. It was obvious that he too considered her the key member of the jury. He extended his open hands in her direction. Pleading for her understanding, he continued. "This is typical of the farcically grandiose charges thrown about in this case, charges totally without merit."

An attentive Markham leaned back in his chair. He was not at all worried by Schneider's summation. The defense was on weak ground, and both sides knew it. Why else would the lawyer be making such sweeping statements, rather than refuting, point by point, the evidence against his client? Markham had faith in the evidence he had compiled against Henry Connolly: the testimony of three contractors with whom he'd done business, the falsified financial records supplied by a former secretary, and of course the self-incriminating tapes. Markham would not be in court now if he were not convinced he had an airtight case.

Frank Markham had not gotten to be the youngest district attorney in New York's history by bringing indictments he could not support. Even as an assistant D.A. right out of Columbia Law School, he had the reputation for painstaking preparation. He examined evidence like a surgeon over a wound, interviewed witnesses as if they were to be partners in marriage, and though he was fast on his feet, he had the habit of committing his arguments to memory while on long walks through Riverside Park.

Yet even after all this work he was cautious. Never premature. He spent more than eighteen months drawing up the case against Anthony "Nick" Nistico, the biggest supplier of heroin to Harlem and the South Bronx. Nistico drove a Rolls-Royce, wore custom-made suits, and had homes in Westchester and Boca Raton. His daughter was at Sarah Lawrence. Though numerous efforts had been made over the years to stick him with everything from murder to income-tax evasion, Nistico's private team of lawyers saw to it that he was never convicted of anything more serious than a parking ticket.

The arrogance with which Nistico eluded the law goaded young Markham. His conviction became a private mission.

He found a young pusher who was dealing for Nistico and who was out on bail following a recent arrest. Markham promised he'd see that charges were dropped in exchange for a favor. The pusher hesitated at first, afraid of Nistico's revenge. But Markham threatened him with a second conviction, one that would take him off the streets from "twenty to life." The pusher reluctantly agreed. Markham explained what he wanted him to do.

During the trial, Nistico's lawyer insisted that the drugs used as evidence against his client had been planted in his car. He also claimed that a deal had been made between the D.A.'s office and one of the prosecution witnesses. The jury chose not to believe him. That's exactly what Markham had expected. He had banked on the credibility of his office, and it paid off. He had no misgivings, no guilt whatever about fixing the case. Nistico deserved to be locked up. It was Markham's job to put him away, regardless of how he did it.

Nistico's conviction was Frank Markham's first major success. He celebrated the twenty-year sentence with caviar and champagne.

For the next several years Markham organized the prosecutions of a Vietnamese racketeer selling protection in Chinatown, a nightclub comedian whose act Markham considered obscene, and a teenage drug addict responsible for killing a prominent Columbia professor. The prosecutions were all successful, and received considerable coverage in the press.

Not all the coverage was favorable. There were articles in the *Times* about his "questionable" legal methods, his reliance on informants who themselves were under indictment, and the vehemence with which he pursued the foul-mouthed comic.

But Markham was obviously effective—there was no denying that—and therefore when his boss, Robert Sawyer, finally retired, it came as no surprise to anyone that Frank Markham was designated his choice of successor. Markham's selection was contested both because of his age—he was thirty at the time—and his hard-nosed style of prosecution. But he received Conservative-and Republican-party backing, was endorsed by the *News*, and won a close but decisive victory at the polls.

That was five years ago. The aggressive young D.A. kept the office running on the same basic philosophy practiced by Sawyer. If anything, he was even more ambitious than his predecessor. He concentrated on "quality" convictions rather than the low-level busts exercised by his colleagues in Queens and the Bronx. "I shoot first for the head," he told Barbara Walters when interviewed on the *Today* show. "They'll feel it down by the toes."

He had spent fifteen months preparing the indictment against Henry Connolly. The *Times* referred to it as his "biggest case since Nick." Today was the twenty-ninth day of the trial. Hopefully it would be the last.

Markham studied the other members of the jury. There was no telling what jurors would do once they were called upon to decide. This was especially so in trials of political figures, where the issues often became confused. Also since many jurors considered all politicians to be corrupt, they were often reluctant to single out one in particular. Nevertheless, they could be convinced, and it was for that reason Markham had directed his case at Dorothy Lagana, banking on her basic morality and capacity for outrage. Anyone whose husband spent twelve hours a day in a hot dry cleaner's would have little sympathy for a dishonest public official. Markham expected the overweight Italian housewife to be his strongest ally once deliberations began. He had the feeling she could sell someone a bridge, not to mention an opinion.

Markham wondered what she was thinking. But her face was still playing poker.

The defense lawyer concluded his plea for acquittal with the usual outstretched arms and impassioned expression. What was uncommon was the object of his closing remarks. "And so I say once again to you, members of the jury, that the only reason Henry Connolly is in this courtroom at all is that the Manhattan district attorney is out to make cheap political capital from the headlines of this case."

All eyes in the tightly packed courtroom were now on Markham. He sat calmly at the table, staring at Schneider. He was not the slightest bit fazed by the insult to his integrity. His opponent was obviously desperate, clinging to straws. Why else would he resort to name-calling? Markham felt sure the jury would agree.

Schneider continued. "By voting for acquittal, you will not only be voting for the truth, but you will also be telling the world that some citizens will not sit back and let ambitious politicians advance their careers over the backs of innocent victims. Ask yourselves. Do you want to be a party to that kind of crass exploitation? Ask yourselves that, and answer from your hearts. I think you'll agree to give Henry Connolly back his name."

There was absolute silence as the defense lawyer strode to his seat and sat down, his eyes planted on Markham. The district attorney nodded in his direction. He then turned to Connolly, and he nodded again, confidently, enjoying the defendant's discomfort. Markham kept staring until Connolly turned away.

A murmur broke out in the courtroom. It was like opening a door to a large cocktail party. It became so loud that the judge had to pound his gavel five times before order was restored and he could begin his charge of the jury.

Frank Markham wanted to avoid the reporters, so he exited through a back door near the judge's chambers. He exchanged pleasantries with his chauffeur, but was otherwise quiet as he and his assistant rode the few blocks from the Centre Street courthouse to his office on Leonard.

"How long do you think it'll be?" asked the assistant while walking from the car.

"It could be twenty minutes, or it could be two days," said Markham softly. "After a number of years in this office, you give up trying to guess. Best thing to do is just try to forget about it." He smiled at his assistant, Sherman, fresh out of law school, thinking how close they were in age. No more than ten years at the most. Still, he was as much a model to the young man in the blue blazer as Robert Sawyer was originally to him. Strangely, considering the direction of Markham's career, the thought gave him little pleasure. He no longer cared about his influence on Sherman. He no longer cared about a lot of things. Like this trial, for instance. Did it really matter whether Connolly was convicted? At one time there would have been no doubt in his mind. It was a question of simple justice. Right and wrong. No doubts at all. But now things were different. How serious was Connolly's crime, compared to others? Particularly compared to the crime he recently learned had been committed against him, the crime that now preoccupied his thoughts. Everything was relative.

Funny, he thought, how quickly your whole life can change, your goals, everything you believe in cast aside like some unneeded relic. And all because of a visit by a stranger.

He thought for a moment about Wilson, wondering if his family in Chicago suspected the real nature of his death. He wondered how his wife was taking it. And also his son. Wilson had shown him pictures of his son holding his own child when the grandchild was first born. A proud, red-haired father and a round-faced, dimpled son. The father was about Sherman's age.

He turned back to his assistant. "Don't worry," he said. "They'll call us when they're good and ready. Meanwhile, our friend Schneider is just as anxious as we are." Markham made an effort to smile. "Connolly's probably shitting in his pants."

Everyone at the office gathered around to hear the news: typists, file clerks, staff investigators, and all the other assistant attorneys. They were so enthusiastic that Markham had to raise his hands for quiet.

"The jury is out, so we came back here for a little break. When we're called back, and the verdict is read, you'll all hear about it."

They all started speaking at once, expressing their confidence and offering him the best of luck. He raised his hands once again.

"I'm tired. If Judge Winters wants me, he knows where I am."

He told his secretary that, with the exception of the call from the court, he was not to be disturbed. He then passed down the hall and into his private office. The last thing he heard before closing the door was Sherman's voice.

"I tell you, he was fantastic. Not a doubt in my mind. Connolly's finished. And after this, the boss'll be a cinch for Washington."

Markham pondered the remark as he took off his coat, loosened his tie, and poured himself a glass of tomato juice and lemon from the refrigerator in his closet. The beverage felt good against his parched courtroom throat, and he sipped it slowly while leaning back in his soft leather chair. So now even his assistants were discussing it openly, he thought, gazing out the window to the East River and the trees along Brooklyn Heights. As if his running for Congress were a surefire plan, as definite as his well-anticipated prosecution of Connolly.

He had never formally announced his interest in the seat of longtime representative Jonathan Bush. Markham had merely let it be known during a routine interview with a reporter from the *Times* that as a resident of the city's "silk-stocking" district, he believed the seventy-one-year-old Congressman was getting a little old for the job.

Everyone assumed that the trim blond district attorney had higher political ambitions. He certainly had all the qualifications. He was a Vietnam veteran, an artillery officer who'd won two Bronze Stars and a Distinguished Service Cross for his two years in the Mekong Delta. The former college wrestler and expert skier was still in good shape. He played handball at the downtown YMCA three times a week. Though he was known to sulk when he lost, his competitiveness was a political plus. What's more, he had elegant taste in clothes—suits by Cardin, and Gucci shoes—although he looked equally stylish in sweaters and corduroy. Voters wouldn't care less that he was considered a clothes horse by his staff. Markham purposely tousled his hair before going on television. He knew the hair and his dark eyes would make him popular with women.

Though at one time his marital situation might be considered a problem, modern voters were becoming accustomed to candidates separated from their wives. Besides, he and Leslie were still on amicable terms. So far there was no bitterness, no hint of scandal. And he saw his twelve-year-old son probably more than most happily married fathers.

Ultimately there was no denying that Frank Markham was a politician of considerable glamour. More important in post-Watergate America was his reputation as a tough, nononsense prosecutor, an aggressive foe of crime and corruption. Conservative voters were looking for a man with precisely his zeal for law enforcement.

Regardless of how suitable he was for higher office, it annoyed him that others had already made up their minds. Who were they to claim to know his future? That lawyer today in court, concealing Connolly's guilt behind the motives of an ambitious, thus allegedly unscrupulous D.A. Also the columnist from the *Post*, who had referred to him as a "shoo-in" in next spring's primary election. They were already speculating on his chances. No doubt the bookies were willing to give odds. He could just hear them in the back room of some bar in Astoria. "I'll give you three to one in the primary, raise it to six to one in the general, eight to one if he wins the *News* endorsement." It was his future, discussed like the point spread of the Knicks, the completions of Staubach, the knockout round of Ali's upcoming fight.

But what else could he expect. As an elected official, he was a public performer, with everyone watching, predicting his moves, anticipating his every reaction. He knew it was inevitable. The unfortunate thing was that the rumors had spread to the point where now even his assistants took his intentions for granted. Too bad. They, along with everyone else, were in for a surprise.

Markham had just shut his eyes for a brief nap when his telephone rang.

"Yes."

It was his secretary. "The court just called, sir."

"Oh, really. What can they do for us?"

"The jury is in."

"Already? It's only been, what . . . little more than an hour."

"It's hard to believe."

He stretched in his chair. "Well, the least I can do is show up."

"I'll tell them you're on your way," said his secretary.

Markham's assistant was waiting outside the door. He was beaming, and literally rubbing his hands together.

"You ready for the bad news, Sherman?" Markham said sternly.

"Bad news?" Sherman's face dropped, along with his hands. "Not if they've decided this fast."

"A verdict is always bad news, Sherman," said Markham, starting down the hall. "For us if we lose. For Connolly if we win."

"I'm sure it will be the latter, sir," said the assistant, hurrying alongside.

"Don't ever be sure of anything, Sherman. Particularly in a courtroom." Markham made himself grin. " 'Less, of course, you're the defendant, and you're guilty. In that case you damn sure better keep your mouth shut."

In New York City the trial of a major public official is like the World Series, and the reading of the verdict is the seventh game, bottom of the ninth. Consequently the courtroom was even more crowded than before. There was a hush as the judge addressed the jury. White-haired men adjusted their glasses. Women put down their knitting.

"Ladies and gentlemen of the jury. Have you reached a verdict?"

Madeleine Cook, the mother from Harlem, slowly raised her two-hundred-and-fifty-pound body. She might as well have been riding the subway for all that was revealed on her face. "Yes, your Honor . . ." dragging it out, fully enjoying the suspense. "We find the defendant, Henry Connolly, *guilty* of all charges."

Markham was oblivious to the sudden clamor in the courtroom as spectators reacted to the verdict and newsmen ran to phones. In the past he would have leaped to his feet. His enthusiasm following a conviction was characteristically more appropriate to a basketball game than to a courtroom. Now, however, he remained in his seat. *Christ, have I changed*. His only other thought was that Dorothy Lagana had not let him down. More out of force of habit than particular interest, he looked over at Connolly, curious about the expression on his face. But the convict had his back turned, and was already starting for the side door. While once that would have denied him total satisfaction, now he could not care less.

Markham had been through the ritual of victory a hundred times before. The congratulations of his assistants and friends. The respects of the judge for a well-presented case. Then the members of the jury, lining up to be received as if at a wedding or formal dance, each savoring the thrill of being part of the machinery of justice.

Armando Gonzales: "*Thees* big shot! He get what he *dee*serve. You do a good job."

Michael Dowling: "You nailed the punk. Dead to rights. Great work, Mr. D.A. You got my vote anytime."

Madeleine Cook: "Can't trust *no* politician. Stealin' the taxes of poor folks. Baby, whenever you's ready for all them other dudes, I's in the book."

And ultimately, Mrs. Dorothy Lagana: "You know, I didn't believe a word that Schneider said. Not for a minute." She leaned closer. "Between you and me, I thought Connolly was guilty soon as I set eyes on him."

Finally, Markham shook hands with the opposing lawyer, Schneider. This part he still enjoyed. It was always more fun being graciously sporting from the position of victory, rather than the other way around.

"You know I didn't mean what I said out there," insisted Schneider. "All that stuff about your unscrupulous ambition."

Markham smiled boyishly. His brown eyes sparkled. His voice was barely a whisper. "Of course you did. You meant every word, you prick."

Now that it was over, Frank Markham endured the crush of reporters and photographers on the courthouse steps. He was surprisingly patient and relaxed, considering the surrounding mass of microphones, cameras, and racing pens.

"Are you happy with the verdict?" shouted Marilyn Ricard from the *Times*.

"Yes, of course I'm happy with the verdict. I don't know about you, but I like to win. Especially after a year and a half of hard work."

"Now that the trial is over, what comes next?" asked Starky from the *News*.

"A shower, a Scotch, and twenty hours' sleep." Markham grinned like a campaigner. "Make that Scotch a double."

"What about plans for the upcoming congressional election?" This from Johnson of the *Post*.

He did not hesitate to answer. "One thing I'm sure of. I expect to vote for the candidate of my choice."

"Can't you be any more specific about your future?" insisted someone from the *Village Voice*.

"Not beyond the next two days," Markham answered politely. "I'm afraid not."

But he was kidding them, and he knew it. Of course I can tell them. I could announce it right now. Just open up and zing it right out. *Ladies and gentlemen . . . I have an important statement to make. I plan to RESIGN*. Why not tell them now? They're all here, pencils in hand, hungry for good copy. He smiled at the thought of the reaction. It sure would be a bombshell. Probably even eclipse the news of the trial. He could just imagine Jimmy Wechsler's column in the *Post*, Nat Hentoff in the *Voice*, and probably Anthony Lewis in the *Times*, all of them giving different explanations for his unexpected move. Why was he doing it? Was it for obvious reasons? Or is there some other factor at work?

They would all be wrong. Only he knew the real motivation for his decision. And of course he would never tell.

He was not sure when he would resign. Four months. Maybe five. Certainly before next spring. He did know the decision was final, as serious a commitment as his pursuit of Anthony Nistico and Henry Connolly. Who cared what the columnists would think? He knew the decision had nothing to do with higher aspirations. But obviously others would think that. They all knew that politics had always been his ultimate goal. For as long as he could remember, he'd felt irresistibly drawn to the life. Campaign trips. Speeches. Being in the public eye. However, it was all finished, through, a future now part of the past. He would never again seek political office.

Never. His dream was over, buried, like all illusions, with considerable pain. He wanted nothing whatsoever to do with the government.

While he was still speaking to reporters, he was like an actor reciting the lines, performing smoothly even though his mind was miles away, caught up in himself. The trial was over. He was thinking again of Wilson, of that afternoon visit earlier in the summer, and what the visitor had told him, what he had said.

God, how the news had hurt him! How angry and weak it made him feel. How devastated!

He felt as if the ground had crumbled beneath his feet. Everything had suddenly changed. So what if he was district attorney? Political power couldn't help him now. He had still been treated with total disregard, toyed with like some goddamn puppet.

No more. Wilson gave him the names of those responsible. Markham was going to make them pay for what they had done to him. He had no choice. How else could he live with himself? Their prosecution was all that he thought about. If the trial against Connolly were not already in progress, he would have dropped it completely. Connolly was just a two-bit punk, not worth his time, compared to those Wilson had told him about. If only he could have got them in court.

But now, with Wilson dead, that was impossible. He was on his own, left without a witness. What the hell. He had always been on his own. He'd go after them by himself. He'd get them in a way no district attorney ever did before.

It would be his last case before going into private practice, the last case of his political career.

Just then a photographer snapped a picture, which the next day appeared on the front page of the *Times*. Markham looked totally pleased with himself. He seemed to savor his glory. He seemed on top of the world. Who would guess that at that very moment he was thinking, not of victory, but of murder?

Incredible as it was, Frank Markham, the controversial Manhattan district attorney, and now the considered choice for congressman from New York, planned to commit murder. He would soon be his own enemy. No one would suspect him. That was part of his plan.

2

Central Park was gradually emptying. All the volleyball nets were down, their heavy posts disassembled and carried away, two men on each. The kites were gone, no longer medallions against a darkening blue sky. Even the picnickers who had taken advantage of the exceptionally warm October day were now on their way home. Sinking like a distant balloon behind the grand buildings on Central Park West, the setting sun cast shadows that now ran the full length of the thirty-acre meadow, all the way to the trees.

Kneading his right shoulder, Markham caught a glance of a man running past, shouting while chasing after a Frisbee thrown by a boy. The man was about Markham's age, and the boy no older than Markham's son, Billy. Another separated or divorced father, no doubt, spending an allotted Saturday with his son. They were always easy to tell. They played the hardest and made the most noise. They were the last to leave the park, staying until the lights were already shining on Fifth Avenue and Central Park South, and you couldn't tell a Frisbee from a football, or a fellow father from a mugger out for a night's work. They couldn't stand to call it quits. Markham was no different. He too hated to take Billy home.

Waiting for his son to retrieve and throw back the football, Markham looked at his watch. Seven-fifteen. Just time for a last couple of plays. He was tired and sweaty from the afternoon workout. His legs were stiff from running, and his shoulder sore from God-knows-how-many passes. Nothing was as exhausting as football with an energetic twelve-year-old. Still, he was not about to complain. This was the way he felt every week right about now. And though tired, he was content. He'd have trouble getting out of bed in the morning, but by Monday he'd already be looking forward to next Saturday afternoon.

Markham smiled as Billy approached on the run, tossing the ball back and forth in his hands. His secretary was right. The two of them did look alike. Father and son. Billy had the same fine blond hair and dark eyes, the same pencil-thin lips, and the same lithe body. Through his football jersey, Markham could see the knots of muscle in his son's upper arms. He remembered his own body at the age of twelve, and all the chin-ups he could do during seventh-grade gym. He had inherited his own looks from his father, before passing them on to his son. Now, running his hand through Billy's damp hair, he thought how his father once felt doing the same thing to him. Father and son. The comparison made him sad.

"I'm afraid we're running out of time," he said softly.

"C'mon. One more," said Billy, turning the ball over in his hand. "Please, Dad."

Markham nodded. "Okay, one more. Let's make this a long one. Straight down to that tree, then cut to your left."

"Think you can throw it that far?" said Billy, teasing.

"You just worry about catching it," Markham said with a grin. "Let me take care of the passing." He added, "Pretend this is for a touchdown."

Billy winked. "The winning one."

The snap was straight to Markham's chest. Cradling the ball from an imagined defense, he watched carefully as his son sprinted the thirty yards to the post. He raised the ball behind his ear, cocking his wrist and then letting it fly just as Billy began his move to the left. The ball came evenly off his fingertips. It was a high spiral pass perfectly aimed right into Billy's hands. Without breaking stride, Billy tucked the ball under his arm. Feinting every few yards to avoid made-up tacklers, he continued downfield. He jumped over an imagined linebacker, looking like a young Jimmy Brown. Crossing the bicycle path they had decided was the goal, he threw up the ball and raised his hands in the air.

"All right!" he shouted excitedly. "We won."

"Attaboy!" yelled his father across the meadow. "Way to go."

Markham was flushed with pride as he watched his son collect the ball and start back. Billy had caught four out of the last six passes. Much better than last week. And his running! Christ, he looked like a pro out there. Markham's coaching had paid off. Billy was improving every time they played. Soon he'd be better than Markham at his age.

The comparison was inevitable. Whenever he and Billy paused momentarily while playing football in the park, Markham could not help recalling the games he had played with his own father when he was Billy's age.

Though how could you compare the Sheep Meadow in Central Park to the backyard of a Maryland home? Markham's only obstacle while going out for a pass was his dog, Brucie, barking at his heels, or if he ran too far, the wooden fence by the road. Billy, on the other hand, had to watch out for bicycles, baby carriages, and picnickers foolish enough to spread their blankets in the middle of the thirty-yard line. However, everything else was pretty much the same: the made-up opponents, the always close score, and the long touchdown pass that invariably won the game in the last few seconds. The evening workouts were as much of a ritual for Markham and his father as the Saturday afternoons were now for Markham and his son.

They began when he was eleven, and they were the happiest times of his life.

An only child, Markham had always been closest to his father. His mother had given him no choice. His earliest memory of her was lying in bed in the middle of the afternoon, her thick dark hair uncombed on the pillow, her breath smelling like something from the medicine chest. They lived by a highway outside of Boston, and the only sound in the stale darkened room was the trucks in the distance.

"Come on outta there!" called the baby-sitters, catching him standing silently by her bed, wondering what was wrong with her. Though they differed from month to month—a skinny old lady with a funny accent and gold teeth, or a black woman with a behind the size of a door—they all said the same. "She ain't to be disturbed. The professor left strict instructions. Come on, let me fix you some cookies and milk, child."

At times there was no need for baby-sitters because his mother was dressed and downstairs. Frankie was delighted to see her feeling better. He would rush over to tell her about what she had missed—the new baseball cards he'd collected, and the underground fort he was building out back. But for some reason, his enthusiasm upset her. "Be quiet," she would say. He noticed her fingers were yellow from the cigarettes she smoked one after another, and she never looked at him when she spoke. Instead her eyes darted all over the room, or out the window, anywhere but at him. The slightest noise seemed to annoy her.

Once, after wrestling in the yard with his father, he rushed into the house, laughing.

"Shut up!" she yelled. "Must you always make so much noise?"

"I'm sorry," he said. He was always telling her he was sorry. Everything he did seemed to be wrong.

He was in the first grade when he realized his mother was different from what mothers were supposed to be. His was the only father at the parents'-day party.

"Where is *Mrs*. Markham?" asked Miss Huck, the teacher who taught him how to read.

"She's not feeling well today," said his father. "I came in her place."

Frankie kept his eyes on the floor, imagining his classmates were snickering at him. School was painful enough as it was. He was shy, and found it hard to make friends. His mother's not coming only made things worse.

"Why does Mommy spend so much time in her room?" he asked his father again that night. His mother took most of her meals on a tray.

"Frankie, you know your mother's sick."

"Won't she ever get better, Daddy?"

"Yes, but we have to be patient." His father reached across the table, and his heavy hand was comforting on Frankie's six-year-old shoulder. "You have to help me take care of her."

He drew pictures for her at school—crayon drawings of flowers and smiling suns—and each afternoon he slipped them under her door. His father said she enjoyed them, how appreciative she was, but one day he tiptoed into her room and found them, all twelve sheets of paper, crumpled in the trashcan under her desk.

His father said it was an accident. He said the drawings

must have been mixed up with the newspaper and thrown away by mistake. Of course she never would have done it on purpose, he told him. Frankie didn't believe him. As far as he was concerned, his mother just didn't like him. Why else did she yell at him all the time?

That night he dreamed he was an orphan. A man had found him, like a stray dog, and decided to bring him home. In the dream he was in the kitchen, drinking some milk, and he overheard the man and his wife arguing in the next room. "I don't want him," said the woman. When he peeked through the door, the arguing couple were his own parents. His mother turned, and seeing him, went into a rage. Next thing he knew she was chasing him out the back door.

When he woke up with a start, he was crying, his face damp as if from a fever. He ran to his father's bedroom.

"Frankie, what's the matter?"

"I hate my mommy. I wish she'd go away."

"You don't mean that, Frankie."

Yes I do, he said to himself.

Frankie had very few friends. In addition to his shyness, he was embarrassed about how his mother acted, and afraid to bring anyone to the house. However, he did not feel completely deprived. He did have his father, and his father was his best friend.

His father was home promptly at five-thirty from his job as a scientist. After a quick visit upstairs, he was all Frankie's. They did everything together. Kickball on the gravel driveway out front. Putting together the red wagon they'd taken apart the day before. Or reading stories about cowboys and pirates from the books on the shelf.

Frankie looked forward to the weekends, because then he'd have his father from morning to night. Swimming at the town pool. Shopping for new pants and sneakers, and a sleeping bag so they could camp out in the yard. Then there were sightseeing trips to Boston and to see the Red Sox play the Dodgers—hot dogs, and pennants, and Ted Williams hitting a homer with three men on base. And one Saturday Frankie's father took a different turn on the highway, and they drove for longer than they ever had before. New York City had bigger buildings than Boston, and a place called Madison Square Garden, where they watched the Harlem Globe Trotters do crazy things with a basketball. They munched popcorn and pretzels, and though he spilled a Coke on his brand-new blue suit, his father didn't get mad.

They shared a room at the Statler Hilton, and Markham's father let him stay up late to watch *Dracula* on television. When Frankie finally went to bed way after midnight, he said he was frightened from the movie, and asked if he could sleep in the same bed with his father. He wanted to be close. He thought maybe that way he would not have his usual bad dreams.

When Markham was ten, his father was transferred to a new job in Maryland. About the time of the move, his mother went away to a special hospital. "We can't help her anymore, Frankie," his father explained. He added, more to himself than his son, "Maybe I should have done this years ago. But I kept hoping she'd get better."

He remembered his father watching him, waiting for some sign that he understood. Frankie had nothing to say. Though he hated his mother for not loving him, he felt guilty about her going away. He felt maybe he was responsible, that his wish was coming true.

It was in Maryland that the football began. When Frank bought a football with money saved from his allowance, his father carried out his promise to teach him how to play. He taught him the rules, showed him how to pass and to kick, and how to hold his fingers when catching the ball. He strung a tire from a tree in the yard so that Frank could practice passing by himself. And he monitored his son's progress every evening after work. Though he worked hard all day as a consultant to a research institute funded by the government, Julius Markham was never too tired for what became his regular routine. He was soon used to being greeted at the door by a son dressed in shoulder pads and helmet, grinning from ear to ear while tossing a ball in his hands.

They played until the ball got swallowed up in the dusk. Markham could still hear his father barking out signals, and see him out of the corner of his eye, waving him across the yard. He wore tennis sneakers and madras Bermuda shorts, and if it were hot and humid, he would take off his shirt. Though forty-five years old, he looked close to thirty. His body was lean and dark from the sun, and there was not a touch of gray in his hair. His stamina was such that it was always Frank who was the first to ask about dinner.

He remembered the passes his father used to throw. Long and high, they used to drift right into his hands. What a pair they made—quarterback and end—a perfectly matched father-and-son team. Markham only wished they were real games they had played, with real opponents and honest-to-God scores. The two of them would have been unbeatable.

But one day it ended, and with the suddenness of an unseen tackler approaching from behind. Frank had spent the afternoon practicing passes into the tire. He was accurate eight out of ten passes from halfway across the yard. He couldn't wait to display his improved accuracy to his father.

He first sensed something was wrong when six o'clock came and his father had not arrived. He always called when he was going to be late. Frank was wearing his shoulder pads and spikes when Mrs. Bailey, his next-door neighbor, came to the door. Mrs. Bailey was always complaining about something, and he assumed she was there because of the long punt that had landed in her roses. "I'm sorry," he was ready to say. "But I'm still learning how to kick."

However, there was no anger in her eyes. Rather a tenderness that he had never seen before. She put her arms around him, like a father, and then she started to cry. "I'm sorry, Frank," was all she could utter between sobs. Confused and alarmed, Frank pulled away. He stood there in the doorway, feeling uneasy, waiting for her to explain.

She avoided his eyes as she stepped inside. She looked nervously around the living room, at the piano, on which he was soon to take lessons, at the football left lying on the couch, and at the pictures on the mantel, their glass catching the late-afternoon sun. Markham caught the sadness, the pity in her eyes. Despite his heavy sweatshirt, he felt a chill he had never before experienced in his thirteen years.

"Where's my father?" he said.

Mrs. Bailey kept looking at the photos on the mantel: Markham at school, his father in the yard, and one of his mother taken before he was born.

He asked her again.

"I'm sorry, Frank," she said, her voice little more than a whisper.

"What happened?" he managed, having difficulty with the words.

She took a deep breath. Then she told him about the accident.

"I don't believe you," he said angrily. "That's impossible. My father's too good a driver." She must be making it up, like one of their games in the yard. Who did she think she was, to be fooling him this way? Just wait until he told his father.

But a strange thing was happening. It was like she was slowly disappearing before him. Or were those his own eyes which made everything a blur? "I'm going to your room," she said from a distance. "I'm going to pack a bag."

It was an odd thing to want to do. "What for?" he heard himself ask.

"You're coming to my home," she said firmly. "You shouldn't be alone. It's the least I can do."

Shouldn't be alone. It was those words that did it. And the sound of her upstairs, going through his drawers. Frank suddenly felt as if sand had been poured down his throat, and six two-hundred-pound tackles were sitting on his chest. His father was not coming home. The two of them would never again play together in the yard. Mrs. Bailey was telling the truth, a truth that all the tears in his eyes would not change.

Frank was devastated. His father was his best friend.

They tried to keep the real truth from him, and for a long time they succeeded. With his mother permanently in the hospital, he moved to New Jersey to live with his aunt. For that whole first year he believed his father's death was an accident. Why was life so unkind to him? he wondered during the long afternoons he spent alone in his room. A mother who didn't love him. And a father who did, but had to go and die. He missed his father constantly, but especially every evening when they would have practiced in the yard. As if losing a father were not bad enough. But when he was also your coach, then it was doubly unfair.

Encouraged by the memory of those evenings together, Frank eventually came out of his grief. Okay, his father was dead. But *he* was alive, and the least he could do was live up to his father's dreams for his future. He swore he would become a great football player. He remembered everything his father had taught him, about all aspects of the game, and he practiced even harder than he ever had before. Place kicks, passes, and broken-field running through the bushes and trees.

He even learned to kick punts that were high, straight, and good for forty yards. He knew his father would have been proud of his exceptional progress.

Then one day he left for school, only to remember that football tryouts for the junior-high-school team were being held that afternoon. The fourteen-year-old Markham returned home for his spikes. He was on his way to the door when he heard his aunt and uncle talking in the kitchen.

"Don't you think it's time we told him?" said his uncle.

"What good would it do?" said his aunt.

His interest aroused, Markham eavesdropped for a moment. What he heard was unbelievable. There must be a mistake. They *had* to be referring to someone else. He stood quietly behind the door, his body rigid, his spikes dangling at his side. The only sound was that of the thumping in his chest. He listened carefully for a name, and when finally he heard it, he still could not believe it. Those damn liars! How could they say that? What proof did they have?

Frank burst into the room. He called them names he had never before spoken to adults. His aunt and uncle were obviously embarrassed. They were quiet, and like Mrs. Bailey, they avoided his eyes.

"Why did you say that?" he demanded. "You know it's not so."

His aunt and uncle looked uncomfortably at one another. Years later, Frank concluded that they obviously felt they had no alternative. He was now their legally adopted son, and they could not afford to lose his trust. Consequently, they told him the truth. His aunt looked out the window while his uncle quietly and haltingly explained that his father had not *really* died in a car accident. Rather, he had jumped from a bridge.

Julius Markham had taken his own life.

Frank did not speak. He turned and went quietly to his room. He remained home for the rest of the day, forgetting about school and the tryouts for the football team. He lay on his bed staring at the cracks in the ceiling, ignoring his aunt's and uncle's knocks on the door. Why did his father do it? he kept asking himself. It was just so hard to accept. If it had been his mother, he would have understood. After all, she was weak. Something like that was almost expected from her. But his father? He was supposed to be strong. He remembered the two of them talking about caring for his mother, and how, when he found his drawings in the trash, his father pretended it was an accident so his feelings wouldn't be hurt. His father tried so hard to protect him. If that wasn't being strong, then what in the world was? And strong people weren't supposed to want to die.

Maybe he was mistaken. Maybe his father *wasn't* that strong. But his father *did* love him. He was convinced of that. Or was he also wrong there?

Markham's thoughts went around in circles. Dizzy from both confusion and an overwhelming pain, he felt frightened, and more alone than ever before.

The worst part of it all was not knowing who to get mad at. Was it somehow his own fault? Had he let his father down? He tried to think of something he had done that upset him. It certainly wasn't school. He was an A student. And he'd read the report his teacher had written. "Frank is quiet. Doesn't play much with others. But very well-behaved." His father seemed pleased. Also about the football. "Keep this up," he had said, "and you'll make your high-school team."

So what could it be? Though he had never told him in so many words, his father knew how much he appreciated him. You didn't actually have to say "I love you," like they did in the movies. No, it wasn't his fault. He was sure of that.

His confusion eventually gave way to anger. Why would his father abandon him, leaving him alone? What kind of father did that to his son? Here he thought his father loved him. He was no better than his wife. All that crap about the strong and the weak. They were both the same. Neither of them gave a shit for him. But at least his mother was honest. She didn't try to fool him, like his father.

His anger grew, surprising him by its intensity. He left the room only once that afternoon, to throw his football spikes in the backyard incinerator. As he watched his shoes smolder in the flames, his heart shriveled along with them. At thirteen, he was now incapable of either trust or affection. He would no longer care about anyone except himself.

Subsequently Frank did his best to forget about his father. Through all his years of high school and college, Markham told everyone who asked that his father died before he was born. "My aunt and uncle," he told a roommate, "they raised me since I was a kid."

The lie was convincing to others, but never to himself. The bitterness was never to leave him. He was a bully in high school, picking on anyone, big or small, who annoyed him in the least. He was suspended so many times that his aunt and uncle felt compelled to send him away. They hoped the discipline of boarding school might help to control him. Even there, he continued to get into fights, often with little provocation at all. If it hadn't been for his high grades, they would have booted him right out. His housemaster said he had a chip on his shoulder, and suggested he work out his hostility on the football field.

"I hate football," Markham replied.

He chose wrestling instead, and eventually, out of necessity, he learned how to control himself. The self-discipline acquired as a wrestler later came in handy in law school, Vietnam, and as a district attorney.

But though anger is controllable, memory cannot be restrained, and over the years the thought of his father often returned to hurt him. Ted Williams, the Harlem Globe Trotters, and *Dracula* on television—all were capable of depressing him for hours. Without a doubt, it was football that pained him the most. Though Princeton swept the Ivy League during his undergraduate years, he never once went to a game. And he was always busy when asked to play in the Sunday-afternoon games between the prosecutor's office and the lawyers of Legal Aid.

Of course, all that was now in the past. His attitude about football had changed, ever since the summer visit by Charlie Wilson. Before starting these Saturday-afternoon workouts with Billy, Markham had not thrown a pass in close to twenty years.

"Great catch," he told his son, returning from across the meadow.

"Great pass," said Billy.

"Let's go home."

3

Markham bought Billy an ice-cream cone from the Baskin-Robbins on Broadway. Looking in the windows of the shops, the two of them took their time crossing Seventy-second Street. Still reluctant to end the day, Markham would have liked to take a walk down by the Hudson. But by now the sun was a mere strip of fire over in New Jersey, and the air was getting chilly. He draped his arm over his son's shoulders as they rode the elevator up to the boy's home. Billy cradled the football in his arms.

"You looked good out there," Markham said.

"Thanks."

"Just remember what I showed you about catching the ball. It's all in the fingertips. I remember my coach telling me once, 'If you got a finger on it, then it's yours.'" He spread his fingers wide to demonstrate. "Think of each of these as a claw." He was reminded of some movie from his youth, and on impulse he purposely contorted his face, opening his mouth as wide as it would go. Assuming he was then reasonably horrifying, Markham inched toward his son.

"What's with you, Dad?" said Billy, without blinking an eye. "Don't you feel well?"

Markham laughed. "I was pretending to be a monster."

Billy shrugged. "Didn't scare me."

"Can't understand it," joked Markham. "It usually works in court."

"Doesn't say much for the crooks."

Markham's estranged wife, Leslie, was in the kitchen making coffee when the two of them came in to raid the refrigerator. Seeing her now, Markham found it hard to believe he had once considered her attractive. Three years younger than he, at thirty-two she had the kind of pale dry skin that had to be watched very carefully in the sun. A half hour too much and she'd be covered with lotion for days. "Don't touch me," she'd say when they'd bump accidentally in the hallways. "Can't you see it hurts?" Without makeup, which was rare, she easily looked her age, especially around the eyes. Her breasts seemed too small. In a polo shirt they were lost. He could not remember when he'd last seen them undressed.

They met his first year out of Columbia Law School when he went to work for the district attorney's office. Leslie was one of the other lawyers. She was blond, elegantly dressed, and wore her hair cut short in the style of Vidal Sassoon.

Much of her immediate appeal stemmed from her near-total lack of sexual inhibition. On their first date, she was not the least bit self-conscious about taking her clothes off right in his living room. She undressed slowly, enjoying his enrapt attention. Her breasts were just the right size—he could cup them in his hands—and there was something deliciously inviting about the whiteness of her skin. It was like each touch would leave a mark.

She helped undress him, peeling off his socks, and grinning as she slipped down his shorts, easily, as if they were two sizes too big. She went places with her fingers and tongue he had rarely been himself. And yet, finally, when he entered her, she made quick plaintive noises from deep in her throat, and through clenched teeth told him he was good.

Nevertheless, as soon as they were done, they took separate showers, and then fell right asleep.

More than her aggressive sensuality, it was her independence that attracted Markham. Because of his experience as a child and young man, he was cynical about love. He had been hurt. He shied away from relationships of intense emotional dependence. He would not allow himself to be vulnerable once again. Though he was good in bed, there was a part of him he always kept to himself. Most women he met perceived his guarded emotions as a kind of aloofness. They considered him "distant" and "cold." Some called him "uptight." Despairing that they would ever receive the full commitment they desired, they left as readily as they came. Two nights, three at most, and that was it. So many women went through his life that Markham had difficulty remembering their names. What stuck was the size of their breasts, and whether he'd spent the night or made an excuse to go home. There were few women he didn't mind having breakfast with.

Leslie was one. She was the first woman to take him on his own terms, and that was because her needs for affection were minimal. She seemed to enjoy living and functioning alone, and saw an affair only as a means of sex and occasional companionship. She made no demands on him other than he be on time for their dates.

Their subsequent marriage was very much like a contract, and it worked for more than ten years. They were fellow professionals, lovers, and roommates, in that order. Frank prosecuted cases from the office downtown. Leslie, now in private practice, worked out of the den in their six-room apartment on Riverside Drive. She handled divorces, class-action cases, and occasional criminal matters. It was an ongoing joke that one day they would appear as opponents in court.

"You don't stand a chance," she threatened. "I know all of your tricks."

"That's what you think," he countered.

It was jealousy that eventually led to the end, a jealousy that was predictable considering both their independent natures as well as their work. Leslie became tired of what she called her "professional hobby," the living-room practice that had to be fitted in with the job of raising a son. She insisted on living alone.

"It will just be temporary," she promised. "Until I see what I can do independently of you."

Markham's primary concern was for Billy. His son was much more important to him than his wife. He loved Billy as much as he was capable of loving anyone, and he did not want the boy to suffer as he had as a child. Consequently he was willing to try anything to save the marriage. He let his wife stay in the apartment. He himself moved across town to a one-bedroom apartment at Seventy-ninth and York. Taking her at her word, he did little more than the barest of decorating. Nothing but the essentials for a "temporary" home.

"Temporary" had now lasted a year and a half. Though he missed her at first, especially the sex, he had never risked depending on her for his happiness. From the beginning he kept a vital part of himself protected. One mistake was enough.

Though disappointed, when he came to realize that the relationship was through, he was not particularly upset. As before, his major concern was for Billy, and their future together.

Leslie herded them away from the refrigerator. "Let me get it," she said, motioning toward the kitchen table. Markham and Billy sat down. "Did you have a nice day?" she asked over her shoulder while taking out ice cubes for Billy's Coke.

"I did," said Markham, "though I'm afraid the kid put me to shame."

"Dont' believe him," said Billy. "His passes were as good as ever. A regular Joe Namath, this guy."

"Oh, yeah. Then why didn't you catch all of them?" said Markham, playing dissatisfied fan.

"It's my coach's fault. The guy thinks football players should run around looking like wolfmen." Putting down his glass, Billy did an imitation of his father in the elevator. He held his spread fingers before a contorted face. "See what I mean?"

"I think the kid's sick," replied Markham, more to Billy than his wife. "Better send him to bed." Markham was anxious to be alone with Leslie. He had not spoken with her since sending the letter regarding Billy's custody. He was eager to learn her reaction.

She too was obviously impatient. "Drink up," she said to Billy. "Then, if you don't mind—"

"I know my cue," Billy answered before she could finish. He drained his Coke in one gulp, and crunched the ice between his teeth as he got up to leave. "See you both later. I'm going up to Dave's. See if his new *Playboy* arrived." He turned around when he reached the door and called to his father. "Thanks again, Dad. I really had a good time."

"Just remember what I told you. Monster or no monster. We'll practice again next time. Meanwhile," he added with a grin, "don't strain your eyes."

Leslie's smile disappeared as soon as Billy left the room. She waited for the slam of the front door before speaking. "I got your letter," she said coldly. "What's wrong? Were you afraid to discuss it over the phone? I don't know why. It's *your* side that does all the tapping."

Markham ignored the last remark. "You know as well as I

why I put it in writing. So there would be no possible misunderstanding."

"Of course. That way it's clear. And precise. Just like a brief. How *legalistic* of you." She made no effort to hide her bitterness.

"And how would you do it?" he said calmly. He was determined to handle this as amicably as possible.

"I wouldn't," she answered with a frown. "But all that's academic anyway, because it doesn't matter how you inform me. You can take out ads on the subway for all I care. The answer isn't going to change."

Markham nodded slowly. "I gather your mind's made up. You intend to insist on full custody."

Her laugh showed what she thought of the question. "Did you really expect anything else?"

"I was hoping you'd understand," said Markham, still making an effort to maintain the cordial tone to his voice.

"Understand *what*?"

"This so-called 'temporary' arrangement has gone on for more than a year and a half. All this time we've both accepted Billy's staying here with you. The point of the letter was simply to say that we now ought to consider a more permanent arrangement."

"I can read. I know what you said. What you didn't spell out was exactly what you meant."

"I was hoping we could discuss it. . . . Civilly," he added.

She leaned back against the counter, her arms folded before her. "Sure. Why not?" she said irritably. "Okay, Mr. Prosecutor. Let's hear your case."

"It's not very complicated. Since we're going to get divorced, I want to make sure I have full rights as Billy's father."

"What do you consider full?"

"I want him to live with me." He raised his hand before she could interrupt. "At least half the year."

"Oh, really? Where? In that closet you call an apartment?"

She was going to fight him all the way, and he knew it. Markham could feel his patience starting to go. "Just remember, Leslie, who's still paying for this place."

"I've got a job too, you know," she declared proudly. "I don't use any of your money for the rent. It all goes for his support." She added with a sarcastic grin, "You certainly don't have any complaints about *that*?"

"Of course not. The fact is, I want to see him more. Two evenings and one afternoon a week is not enough. . . . Not anymore."

"Why not? You feeling deprived all of a sudden?"

"Maybe."

"Funny," she scoffed. "You never cared that much when we were living together. Raising him was *my* job, remember?" The expression on her face reminded Markham of a defense attorney who had just discredited a witness and won a point. So here they were, sparring at last, and over the right to their son.

"Who says I didn't care? I can't help it your office was at home. Remember, Leslie, that's how you wanted it. Then you wanted to live alone. You wanted the apartment. I didn't like it, but I moved out anyway. You've had Billy all to yourself. Frankly, I miss him. . . . Besides, I thought you would appreciate this. Six months without the responsibility. Just think of all the work you can do."

"Don't you dare say anything about my work." Her nose wrinkled unpleasantly when she frowned. "I'm sure you're feeling tougher than ever after putting away that political hack. I read the papers. I know what they're saying. Congressman in seventy-six. Or governor in seventy-eight." The lips he once bruised in desire now twisted in contempt. "I'm not impressed." She paused, and her face brightened in a cruel smile. "How do you think your political backers will react when the story of your custody fight breaks in the papers? And it will, you know."

"Only if you make an issue of it."

"Courtroom divorces can become issues by themselves."

"But there's no reason for that. We've already settled all the other terms of the divorce. What we never agreed upon was Billy."

"It'll make quite a story," she said with a gleam. "A courtroom divorce, and one of the parties is the district attorney."

"You're right," he said evenly. Looking at the way she was nodding her head, the determined expression on her face— she was like one of his assistants, preparing a case—he now understood what his letter had done. Unknowingly he had given her something—an opportunity—she had always

39

sought. It was obvious that for her this was only a preliminary. What she wanted, what she now needed for her self-respect, as a balm for her ego, was to confront him in court, to contest him in his own arena. Apparently nothing else would suffice. Underneath the bravado, she was as insecure as they came. Strong. Independent. Bullshit! He had viewed her all wrong. If he were less involved he would have pitied her. In a way, he still did. But it was a pity now joined with loathing.

"You don't even care about Billy," Markham said bitterly. The time for politeness was gone. "All you're really interested in is proving something to yourself."

She smiled silently, as if in agreement.

"You're after my balls, aren't you?"

"How eloquent of you. Is that what you're going to tell the judge?"

"You're making a mistake, Leslie. I'll use everything in my power if this comes to court. And you know it."

"I'm really impressed," she said, reacting to his anger. "You know, I always liked you best when you lost your temper. It made you more sexy." She laughed arrogantly, then added, "Frankly, Mr. D.A., that's all I ever enjoyed about you. And even that got a little stale after a while."

"The feeling was mutual, sweetheart. Have you looked in a mirror lately?"

"You bastard!"

"Call me what you like," he said firmly, standing up. "I want Billy."

"It doesn't surprise me," said Leslie.

"Of course not. It shouldn't."

"After all, he's getting to be that age. Billy is."

"What age?" said Markham.

"He'll be thirteen next month. Wasn't that how old you were when. . . ?"

"When what?"

"When your father had his . . . accident."

Markham had told her the story early in their marriage. It had been in a weak moment which he later regretted. The regret was never as strong as now. "I don't believe you," he said, shaking his head in contempt.

"You're just trying to make up for it," she said defiantly. Her eyes were wide, glaring at him.

"Make up for it?"

"Sure. Why else this sudden interest in Billy?"

Markham could not contain himself. The sound of his slap was like a small explosion in the room. The blow from his open hand caught her square against the cheek, knocking her back against the counter. However, she remained on her feet. A sudden look of shock swept across her face, quickly disappearing into self-righteous satisfaction.

"Words suddenly fail you, Mr. Prosecutor?"

Though the edge was off his anger, he could easily have hit her again. His jaw jutted out in muted rage. "You goddamn bitch! How dare you say that!"

"You can retaliate. You've always been good at that," she said evenly, while rubbing a hand across the fast-reddening bruise on her cheek. "But I'm surprised. I thought district attorneys did all their punishing in court."

"You're gonna regret this, Leslie. Believe me."

"I doubt it."

"Don't push your luck. In or out of court. You're not so tough."

"We'll see about that."

"You're going to get hurt. Just remember. I warned you."

Before she could respond, Markham turned and stormed out of the apartment, slamming the door as he left.

"God damn her!" he said to himself while in a cab returning across town. How low could she get! How rotten! Mentioning the one thing she knew hurt him the most. Had she no limits? No sensitivity? He never should have told her about his father, revealing his most vulnerable side. But he never thought she'd go so far as to use it against him. For some reason he had trusted her. What a mistake. You'd think he'd know better. Was there anyone you could trust?

Well, maybe there was one. His thoughts shifted once again to his meeting with Charlie Wilson.

Wilson had called him from Chicago to make an appointment. Though his secretary had, as usual, run interference, explaining that the district attorney was an extremely busy man, and wouldn't one of his assistants suffice, Wilson had insisted on speaking only to him. He said that it was an "important personal matter."

"Another informer, no doubt," Markham told his secretary after hanging up. "Probably overhears two guys in black shirts and white ties talking in a men's room, and now wants to take on the Mafia. I wonder what this little bit of information will cost?"

When Wilson arrived, he acted like every other informer Markham had met. He couldn't sit still, his eyes wandering all over the room, as though looking for hidden mikes. Markham offered him a drink, hoping it would help him relax, but Wilson declined, taking a seat in front of Markham's desk.

"So tell me," said Markham, settling in his chair. "What's this important information all about?"

"Well . . . I used to work with your father at the institute in Maryland." He spoke so softly that Markham instinctively leaned forward to hear him.

"You mean Fort Detrick?" he replied, now shifting his weight back into his deeply upholstered chair. As always, the mention of his father made him uncomfortable.

Wilson sensed Markham's uneasiness. His voice was no more than a whisper. "Yes. That's where I knew him from." He paused. "Did your father ever tell you what he did at the institute?"

Markham shrugged. "He was always vague about it. Some kind of scientific research for the government."

Wilson took a deep breath, renewing his determination. "He couldn't tell you because it was classified. Absolutely top-secret. We were contracted to the Defense Department under orders not to say anything, not even to our families."

"I assumed it was something like that. I never asked him, and he never told me."

"We were working for a division of the Army. Our research was in biological warfare," he said, watching for Markham's reaction.

Markham just sat there and said nothing. He stared intently across the desk at his visitor, still uncertain as to why he was there.

Wilson continued talking, still struggling with the words. "Our research was exhaustive. We experimented with contagious germs, poisons, and other sorts of disabling chemicals. We even worked on LSD. You probably don't realize it, but your father was one of the top men in the field. But then, how could you? He couldn't talk about it."

Though Markham was always curious about what his father did, it never occurred to him that it was anything as controversial as this. He was shocked to learn that he had been involved in such a project. Despite his many questions, he could not bring himself to talk about his father. His memory was still too painful.

Markham cleared his throat. "I appreciate your having come to see me. But what my father did doesn't concern me. It was a long time ago." Nervously he glanced at his watch. "Now, if there's nothing else, I'm afraid you'll have to excuse me, Mr. Wilson. I have another appointment."

"There's more," Wilson said hesitantly, sitting ramrod straight in his chair.

"What is it?" asked Markham, now growing visibly irritated.

"It's about your father's death."

Markham shifted in his seat, crossing his legs. He noticed that his shoes needed a shine. "What *about* my father's death?" he asked, trying to compose himself.

Wilson spoke quickly now, as if to hesitate was to give up, to abandon what he had come so far to say. "As I mentioned before, one of the drugs we were testing at Fort Detrick was LSD. At the time, no one knew much about it, and so a testing program was conducted on local participants, most of whom were volunteers." He paused, before continuing. "Unfortunately, there was also some testing done on unsuspecting subjects, but believe me, Mr. Markham, I had nothing to do with that," he said defensively. "I only heard about it later."

"Go on," Markham said firmly.

"They were given the drug without their knowledge," Wilson said sadly. He paused again. "One of them was your father."

Markham just looked at him silently.

Fully expecting some kind of reaction, Wilson was unnerved by Markham's cold silence. Nervously he explained what had happened. "Since your father and I were partners, they told me all about it. He was chosen at random from among the scientists on the project. The doses of LSD were put into his coffee at lunch. Afterward, he was constantly observed, though without his knowing it. They were interested in how it would affect him, especially his work. His concentration and all that. I guess they figured the drug was only harmful for a limited time, and that its aftereffect was probably little worse than a hangover."

The impact of Wilson's secret finally hit him. While continuing to listen, without saying a word, Markham arose from his chair. Slowly he paced around the room, his back turned toward Wilson, his arms folded against his stomach. He was overwhelmed by what he was hearing. Just like when Mrs. Bailey came to the door years ago, and he refused to believe her about his father's accident. But what about Wilson? Could Markham believe him? He had to. Why else would he be here? What could he possibly gain by making this up?

"It was a terrible thing that they did," Wilson continued from across the room. "Giving him the drug without telling him. But no one on the project expected him to react the way he did. They never would have done it if they'd known it could cause such a tragedy."

Though still listening, now it was Markham's eyes that roamed the room, finally alighting on Wilson, who was sitting in his chair, staring back at him. Wilson looked relieved. Markham was stunned.

Still Wilson continued. "It was an accident. A terrible accident. None of it was planned. But they should have told you. It was inexcusable that they didn't. It only made it worse."

Wilson explained why he too had not said anything for so long. "I just did what they told me," he said sadly. "At first I agreed it was for the best. What good would it have done telling you? He was dead, and nothing would bring him back. Also, of course, there was the problem of security." He sighed, and shook his head. "At least that's what they told us. Obviously we couldn't divulge what they were doing. Believe me, I wasn't ever satisfied with that decision. I thought you should have been told what had happened."

Wilson looked down at his hands, twisting his wedding band, then turned back to Markham. "Your father used to talk so much about you. I felt like I knew you. I knew you were a football player. Quarterback, I think it was. God, did he love you!" Here he hesitated, waiting for Markham to reply.

Markham said nothing. He stood perfectly still, gazing out the window.

"You see, it was my grandson that reminded me of you," he said nervously. "His name is Bobby. I see him every chance I get. I just love that kid. If I had my way, I'd spoil him rotten. . . . Well, sometimes I'd be with him, and then for no reason at all I'd find myself thinking about you." Wilson continued softly, more to himself than to Markham. "I started wondering what had happened to you, what kind of life you had made. Call it guilt, call it whatever you want. But I decided it was wrong for me to hide it anymore. I wanted you to know the truth."

Wilson spoke to Markham with a tenderness one would use with a small child. His voice was even softer than before. "It must have been terrible, growing up thinking your father killed himself. I can imagine how abandoned you must have felt at such a young age. You must have hated him.

"You know, Mr. Markham. You look like your father. You've got the same hair. The eyes as well. I noticed it soon as I walked in."

Markham turned toward Wilson, his eyes glistening. He started to speak, but the words caught in his throat.

Desperate to relieve the guilt that had grown, like a cancer, over the years, Wilson said he would now back Markham all the way. Here were names, addresses, dates, everything he needed to sue the government for what it had done. Even the promise of his own personal testimony. "It can be the biggest case since Watergate," he said.

Before leaving, Wilson wrote down his address, promising to remain in close contact while Markham decided what to do.

That night Markham did not sleep. Nor did he for the next two nights. He kept recalling the day when he had come home for his football spikes and learned the so-called "truth" from his aunt and uncle. How readily he had believed them. Without so much as an argument, he had accepted what they said. Locking himself in his room and lying on his bed, he had done a total about-face on his father. An hour earlier he had loved him, cherishing his memory, thinking how proud his father would have been if he were chosen for the high-school team. But then, in just a matter of minutes, his love soured and turned to hate. His father killed himself. Or so he was told. And without hesitation he had believed every word.

What kind of son was he to have so little faith in his father? After all the things they had done together, didn't the memories of his father count for anything? But then again, why shouldn't he have believed his aunt and uncle? How could he know they were wrong?

He remembered now how odd his father was acting the week before he died. Twice, while going over his math homework after dinner, his father had gotten confused with a problem and become terribly upset.

"Hey, Dad," he said defensively. "What's wrong? What did I do? I'm sorry I don't understand, but—"

"It's not you, Frankie. I'm just tired, I guess. Can it wait until tomorrow?"

It was not like his father to get tired so early in the evening. And then there was the morning he came down to find his father lying on the living-room floor. He was wide-awake, staring at the ceiling, and he had the strangest faraway look in his eyes. Frank was frightened, and again he asked if anything was wrong. His father did not answer. He acted as if he weren't there. Frank did not know what to do. But suddenly his father stood up and turned to him, still dazed.

"Shouldn't you be getting ready for school?" he said, as if nothing had happened.

"Sure, Dad. I was just about to leave."

All his father's behavior made sense now. Though he had never taken LSD himself, he knew the unpredictable ways the drug affected someone. As an assistant district attorney he'd seen his share of defendants arrested for crimes committed while on bad trips. He'd seen the disorientation in their eyes. Even the occasional horror. He knew what a terrible experience LSD could be. How much more frightening, if you didn't know you had taken it.

He had been wrong all these years. His father had not abandoned him after all. Rather he had been driven to the brink by a force beyond his control. He thought he was going mad.

Though Markham was relieved to finally learn what had actually happened, the truth gave him no joy. It made him feel worse. Rather than resolving any unanswered questions about his father, it only raised new ones about himself. All that self-righteous anger and hatred he had harbored toward his father over the years suddenly dissolved into shame and remorse. How quickly he believed his father capable of rejection. And how quickly he had rejected his father in return.

His father had done nothing wrong after all. His father had not rejected him. He had rejected his father.

There were moments when he wished that Wilson had kept his secret to himself. Wasn't the old hate better than this new guilt? The guilt overwhelmed him.

However, he could begin to make up for it. At least he was determined to try. A week after Wilson's visit, Markham and Billy played football for the first time. Central Park became like his Maryland backyard. Through the feel of pigskin in his hands, and the joyous shouts of his son running for a pass, Markham sought peace of mind.

But it was not enough. Markham could not stop thinking of the men Wilson had named, the men who had murdered his father. Wilson said it was an accident. Some accident. Shit. It was murder. And the bastards never said a word. All that crap about security. They were just looking out for themselves. They didn't care if he had suffered. They didn't care about him at all. He probably never even entered their minds.

Soon he would be all they could think about. Fuck their job security. They were all going to jail.

It would be the biggest, most far-reaching civil suit of the decade. He had no doubts he would succeed. With Wilson's testimony, he couldn't lose. He planned a press conference for the announcement of the suit against the government and its former employees. The case was on his mind twenty-four hours a day.

The news of Charlie Wilson's suicide did not fool Markham for a minute. So evidently the rules were still the same after twenty-odd years. Somehow they had learned of Wilson's breach of security, and they had eliminated him with the same unfeeling contempt they had shown for his father.

He was terribly discouraged, knowing that without a witness his case now had no chance at all. What did he have for proof? A list of names. His own accusations. There was not a grand jury in the country that would bring indictments on such flimsy evidence. Especially when the people he was charging were all respectable citizens—not gangsters or junkies. In several cases they were among the most powerful men in the country.

Markham was frustrated for weeks. His case had been

snatched from his hands, and there was absolutely nothing he could do about it. His determination and frustration was like a throbbing wound that refused to heal. Though at work he went through the motions of his job, his mind was always on the one matter that consumed him. His need for justice.

Underlying that was his guilt. He was ready to do anything to relieve it. Anything at all.

The fact remained he could never win a settlement in court. There had to be another way.

The plan came to him one sleepless night. He had watched television. One of the men who was responsible for his father's death appeared on the eleven-o'clock news. He was traveling to Europe on government business, and he was interviewed at the airport. His family—wife and college-age daughter—was alongside him. The trip was also a vacation, he explained. "I don't see enough of my family. Sometimes we have to go on a trip in order to be together." He smiled contentedly. So did his plump wife and pretty blond daughter. The three of them walked arm in arm toward the airplane. They were all beaming. They had not a care in the world.

Later all Markham could think of was the man on the screen. How complacent he had looked with his family alongside him. It was hard to believe he was responsible for the death of his father. Had he no guilt? No shame? What right did the man have to be so happy, after causing Markham so much pain?

The more he thought of him, the more aggravated and upset he became. He drank two straight Scotches to help him relax. But his anxiety and rage only increased. He went out for a walk at three A.M. As if in a daze, he walked down First Avenue, from Seventy-ninth to Forty-second street, then turned the corner and walked back up Second Avenue. There was a crowd gathered around a car accident at Sixty-eighth Street. Markham passed it without breaking stride. He had coffee in an all-night diner on Eighty-sixth Street, nursing the coffee until it was cold. Later, alone on a bench by the East River, he saw the sunrise from Carl Schurz Park. The Triborough Bridge to the north and the Queensboro to the south were like spiderwebs against a manganese sky. The red beacon from the Welfare Island dock winked on and off across the empty water. A cool early-morning breeze rolled a beer can beneath his bench.

Markham was oblivious. *What right did the man have to be so happy, after causing him so much pain?* If only that man knew what it was like to lose the one person he loved best.

It was then that Markham knew what he had to do. There was no choice. He felt a racing in his chest and a lightness in his knees. He stood up abruptly, turned, and walked out of the park. Two black teenagers in white sneakers were standing by the entrance on East End Avenue. One of them elbowed the other when he saw Markham coming. But there was something in the look on Markham's face that kept them from approaching him. A glint-eyed intensity that meant he was either crazy or an undercover cop.

Markham felt the boys' presence before he saw them. He was hoping they would try something. They wouldn't have known what hit them.

He spent the rest of the day consumed by the plan. It would take considerable research, so that his method would be as effective as possible. However, as district attorney he had easy access to all the information he would need. Besides, there was no hurry. He had been waiting for more than twenty years already. He had all the time in the world. He had no qualms about his mission, and no doubts about his success.

His planning was now almost over. The research was completed. Every name had been checked and each step of the plan carefully weighed. All that remained was the final preparation, which was to come on Monday.

Stepping out of the cab, Markham realized that by this time three days hence he would already be under way. The thought pleased him, and when he saw that the fare was $1.50, he gave the driver a five-dollar bill.

"Keep the change." he said.

4

Mike thought he was playing a great Stanley Kowalski. "What are you putting on now?" he taunted, reciting the lines. He started toward the frightened blonde, now backed against the wall. He felt his eyes widen, his nostrils begin to flare, and a sudden dryness in his throat. It was all natural and spontaneous. He was feeling the role come alive. And why not? Playing the Tennessee Williams character was like acting himself. He and Stanley had the same nervous energy, an identical hair-trigger temper, and the same readiness to fight. He wondered if Kowalski, like himself, had ever been in jail. And as for Blanche, she was like every piece-of-ass cock-tease from Avenue A.

"I warn you, don't," she said. "I'm in danger." Wendy too was responding to the passion of the scene. She cried out, and pretended to strike him with the jagged piece of glass. Her idea of pretend was to go right for his neck. But an experienced Mike expertly caught her wrist. It felt small in his grasp, and he could have broken it with no trouble at all. "Drop the bottle top! Drop it!" His arm was around her waist, his face no more than an inch from hers, when he proclaimed triumphantly, "We've had this date with each other from the beginning." Just then, Miss Wild clapped her hands.

"That's enough," the drama teacher said sharply. "The rape you do on your own time. You can put her down now, Mr. Ross."

Just my luck, he thought. Right when it's getting good. "Sorry," he said to Wendy. "You heard the boss."

"That was very well done," Miss Wild said, rising from her

seat acosss the room and walking toward them. "Deliberate. Intense. And with just enough passion without being melodramatic. Excepting, of course, that business with the bottle. Miss Hunt, there is no need for actual bloodletting in the theater. Ours is an imaginative art. We leave the dependence on realism to our friends in the movies. Consider yourselves lucky."

She paused, turning around, and her dark eyes blazed as they studied the eighteen young faces in the Hudson Street loft.

"You are *actors*. Actors-in-progress, anyway. *Not* Hollywood hacks. There's a big difference." She turned back to Wendy, and she smiled. "Besides, Miss Hunt, if you wish to slit Mr. Ross's throat, there are far better ways." Miss Wild then smiled at Mike and motioned for the two of them to return to their seats.

Mike hurried back to his place. Sitting in the folding wooden chair in the large open room, he listened intently to her critique of the scene. Helen Wild had been working in the theater before most of her students were born. An actress, a director, even a producer—she was a one-woman production that had received excellent reviews and an extremely long run. Over the years she had acted with the Barrymores, and directed Katharine Hepburn and the young Brando. She was said to have been the lover of *both* George Kaufman and Moss Hart. Now in her sixties, she resembled an aging Marlene minus the legs, with the legendary eyes still as brilliant as ever, and the auburn hair kept carefully free of gray. Even in the summer she was forever in black: black jersey, black slacks, and knee-high black boots. She had more energy than any of her students.

Her strong voice dominated the room. "The sexual confrontation between Stanley Kowalski and Blanche Dubois is in many respects the climax of *Streetcar*." She paced as she talked, nervously, as though waiting in the wings to go on. "I chose this scene because, assuming you're not all illiterates—a dubious but optimistic assumption—well, the scene *should* be familiar to you."

She approached the circle of chairs. Her voice, which was deep and professorial before, now became rapidly intense. "Now, I don't want you to think. I want you merely to respond. There's a big difference. I want the men to become

Stanley, the women to become Blanche. Got it? . . . All right, that's who you are. And you're in this particular scene. When I point to you, I want to hear the first thing that comes to mind about yourself. Keep it short. Here we go."

The class responded one at a time.

"Macho," said Tommy Sheldon. "Macho and horny."

"Fragile," offered Linda Clarkson. "Fragile and afraid."

She continued around the room, pointing a slender finger in the face of every Stanley and Blanche.

Mike sat on the edge of his seat, waiting to speak. "I'm animal," he said when it was his turn to reply. "I'm defending my home and myself." He looked closely for Miss Wild's response. Was he seeing things or did she approve? He sure as hell hoped so.

"I just want to get laid," said the last Stanley in the bunch.

"Me too," agreed the ultimate Blanche.

"Darlings, there is nothing keeping you," said Miss Wild. "Class is now over. Only, please, not here."

As the students got up to leave, she explained that in the following class they would switch parts, with the women playing Stanley and the men playing Blanche. "Before we meet again, you might want to think of yourselves as the opposite sex. You men, spend an afternoon in a dress. You women, go out and beat someone up. These are just suggestions, of course. Do whatever it takes, only get yourselves into the appropriate head . . . *and* body. See you on Thursday."

Mike had an appointment, and he was in a hurry to leave. He was almost to the door when he heard her call his name.

She smiled. "Mr. Ross, I would like to see you for a moment, if I may."

"Sure. All right, Miss Wild."

She pointed to a seat by her table, and Mike sat down. He wondered what she wanted, and he felt a little strange, waiting for the other students to leave. He had never been alone with her before.

She started to speak as soon as the last student had gone through the door and down the stairs. "I asked you to stay for only one reason," she said, remaining standing. "Mr. Ross, let us not fool ourselves. The closest most people in this class will get to a Broadway stage is when they buy orchestra seats. As tough as people say this business is, believe me, it's ten times tougher. Talent is not enough. And forget what you see in Busby Berkeley movies—neither is luck. Success in the theater comes from one thing and one thing only. *Damn hard work*. Putting out for producers won't get you anything but a sore bottom."

What the hell is she driving at? he wondered.

"Forgive me for not coming immediately to the point," Miss Wild said with a laugh. "Like some of my students, I am cursed with diarrhea of the tongue."

Mike wondered what time it was. His appointment was very important, and he could not afford to be late. Still, he was reluctant to look at his watch.

"What I'm trying to say is that I believe you have something worth developing, Mr. Ross. *Talent*. That rarest of qualities. I am not sure how much of it is in your control. But I was quite impressed with the way you handled today's scene."

"Thanks." Mike smiled with pride. "I'm glad you liked it. I was trying my best." Damn straight he had talent. It was about time she noticed it.

"How old are you, Mr. Ross?"

"Twenty-six."

"I assume from your speech that you are a native of New York."

"Yes, ma'am. Avenue B." Mike added, "People *do* come from that neighborhood. It wasn't always junkies and freaks."

"You remind me of the young John Garfield. You've got the same dark eyes and hair. Your hair is longer, of course. But like Johnny, you have an extremely masculine face."

"You mean I look like a punch-drunk fighter. Isn't that it?" said Mike with a grin. He was feeling more relaxed now. He leaned back in his chair, with his hands behind his head. His T-shirt was tight against his chest.

"It must be your nose. Was it broken?" Miss Wild asked, walking over and taking her seat, which was diagonally across the table from his.

"I sure as hell wasn't born with it. Let's just say I should have picked on someone my own size. Not someone six-two." Mike was not at all sensitive about the twist in his nose. Since the fight, four years before, so many people had commented on it that it was now part of his identity. Like his wiry frame and Lower East Side accent.

"I gather then you were not a *professional* fighter?" said Miss Wild, looking over at the rip in his shirt.

"You mean, was I paid for it? No, never." He laughed. "Fact is, it usually ended up costing me plenty." Mike was reminded again of his appointment. This time he looked at his watch. He was suddenly very anxious. And less concerned about seeming rude. "Listen, Miss Wild, I gotta go."

"Just one moment, Mr. Ross. Be patient, please. . . . What I wanted to say is that I think you have potential that could be more effectively developed in a smaller class. I coach a group of *advanced* students three evenings a week. Monday, Tuesday, and Thursday. I could arrange for you to join us. Are you interested?"

"Are you kidding! I'd love it." Mike beamed. This was turning into quite a day.

"Well, then, come to the class. It's at eight o'clock, and it's held right here."

Mike started to speak, but stopped himself short. He hammered the air with his right fist. "Damn it all. I just remembered something. Afraid I can't make it, Miss Wild."

"No?" She looked surprised. "Why not?"

"Problem is, I work at night, and it's the same time as the class."

"That *is* unfortunate. But couldn't you change jobs? Or would that be too difficult?"

Mike sighed. "It's more difficult than you think."

"What is it you do, Mr. Ross?" she asked, staring at him with those incredible eyes. He had never seen them from so close up before.

"Mr. Ross . . ." she repeated.

"I . . . answer phones," he replied finally. "I work for a service. It's not much of a job, but it pays the rent, and frankly, it was hard enough getting that."

"I'm surprised to hear that," she said, pushing her chair in closer to the table. "A young man with your obvious talents. You *are* educated, are you not?"

"Sure." He laughed. "City College. Me and everybody else in New York. Trouble is, I have a couple of drawbacks that make it hard to find work. I'll tell you about them sometime."

"What is wrong with now?" Miss Wild said directly. She leaned toward him over the table. He could smell her perfume, its muskiness provocative. He could see that there were surprisingly few lines on her face, only around her eyes and the corner of her mouth. Her closeness made him slightly nervous. He had never been intimate with a woman her age. However, there's always a first time, he thought to himself.

Her leg touched his under the table. Though it might have been an accident, still she did not move it.

Intrigued, willing to stay, he had to go. He was late already. He just hoped she would not take it the wrong way. Slowly, their legs parting, Mike got up from his seat. Looking down at her, he said, "Listen, Miss Wild, I hope you understand. I don't want to sound rude, but I really gotta go."

She drew up her shoulders and narrowed her eyes in irritation. "I'm sorry you are in such a hurry," she said deliberately. "I was hoping we could have a drink together."

"I'd love to," he said. And he really did mean it. He was eating up all this flattery. He could listen to her praise him for hours. It certainly would not hurt him, getting closer to Helen Wild. In fact, he would have liked nothing better.

For the moment he skipped over what could happen at her apartment. He realized he might be getting carried away. But whether or not they went to bed, what interested him most was where the invitation could lead. From here on, their relationship might be different. He would become her protégé. That was how a lot of actors had gotten a start. The list of actors she had made went on forever. With a phone call, she could get him an audition with the biggest producers in town. With his talent, along with her help and connections, he could easily get his foot in the door. All it took was one break. And here it was, Miss Wild singling him out for special attention.

What rotten luck! Who knows when she would ask him again. But right now was out of the question. Damn it all! "Can we make it some other time?" he said, hoping he sounded sincere.

"Do I make you nervous, Mike?" It was the first time with the name. "Is that why you're hesitant?"

Mike was more worried than nervous. But it had nothing to do with her. "It's not you, Miss Wild. Like I said, I'd love to have a drink with you. But I have no choice. I just can't."

"Where are you running off to in such a state?" she asked, cocking her elegant neck. "If you don't mind me inquiring?"

And if I do, thought Mike, what then? Back to the beginners' class? Talk about being torn down the middle. "Listen, Miss Wild, don't think I'm not grateful. I appreciate your offer, and I'm gonna try to work it out. I really am. And the drink. Can you give me a rain check? Problem is, right now there's a man across town who's gonna screw me if I'm late."

"A man? What kind of man?"

"Just a man," he said with a shrug.

"Mike," she said sharply, giving him the full force of her eyes. "Are you *queer*?"

"No, Miss Wild, I'm not." That remark did it, right then and there, ended Mike's conflict. Now he was pissed off. He grabbed his sweater from the chair and started across the room. "What I *am* is on *parole*," he called over his shoulder. "I'm an ex-convict, understand, and I gotta do whatever my parole officer says. He has a shit-fit when I'm late. If I don't get down to Church Street in the next five minutes, I can kiss this or any other acting class good-bye."

"I'm sorry," she said calmly, her face lighting in comprehension. "Mike, you should have told me. Can I help you? Do you need cab fare?"

"No thanks," he called from the door. "I can manage. See you on Thursday, Miss Wild."

Mike almost tripped, hurrying down the stairs.

In a cab across town, Mike wondered if Miss Wild had meant what she said—the bit about his talent—or if it had all been a ploy to get him to go home with her. It was the kind of ploy he might have used. But coming from her? What was she—forty years older? And after that line about sex not being helpful to your career.

What the hell. So she found him attractive. So did a lot of other women. He remembered the way she kept looking at his chest. She was not bad-looking herself. She had more energy than many girls his own age. And her breasts seemed to hold up well under that black sweater. They might not be as firm as someone like Wendy's, that girl playing Blanche, but who cares? They had evidently been fondled by some of Broadway's best.

It might be interesting going to bed with a woman her age. That hat-check girl from Sardi's was the oldest so far. What was she—fifty, fifty-five? Miss Wild had an easy ten years on her. From the rumors he'd heard about her many affairs, he imagined she'd be exciting in bed.

He wondered if afterward they would lie in bed and talk, and if so, whether they would gossip about other students in class or celebrities she had known. Maybe, while sharing a cigarette, she would give him advice about his future—tell him what agents to see, and whom to audition for. He imagined her Chelsea apartment was filled with old photos and clippings, mementos of her theatrical career, and that her bedroom was probably dark and stuffy, and with a huge four-poster bed, the kind of place where you could get lost for a week.

Thinking of all he could learn from Helen Wild, how she could help him as an actor, Mike wondered for a moment how he would react, receiving her help. It might prove hard to take. No one had ever given him much guidance before, not the teachers in school, not even his father. Consequently, everything that had happened in his life—the good as well as the bad—had been his own doing. It would be quite an adjustment, having his career managed by someone else. Especially a woman.

In any case, he would think about all of it later—Miss Wild and the problems of getting too close to her. Right now it was his parole officer, Daniel McCarthy, he had to consider. Along with the thoughts that were triggered by the street they were just then passing.

5

Every time he crossed Houston Street, Mike remembered that it was here that he once almost lost his life.

In a park at the corner of Bleecker, in the summer of 1964. He was thirteen at the time, and he was running with the Angels from Avenue A. His mother had died from a tumor the year before, and without her biweekly check from the hat factory, his father had been forced to take on extra work in the evenings. The three-room tenement apartment was littered with spools of thread and assorted bolts of cloth. Mike had been bar mitzvahed that spring. He was now officially a "man." Despite what it meant both to Rabbi Schwartz and to his father, to Mike it implied he could now smoke cigarettes out on the fire escape, drink beer and cheap wine up on the roof, and stay out as late as he wanted. Why not? It was summer vacation, and there was nothing else to do.

He met Wayne Nesterenko, the warlord of the Angels, one evening in Tompkins Square Park. Mike was sitting on a bench with friends, talking about going to Coney Island, when Nesterenko walked by, commenting loudly about "chickenshit kikes." Mike jumped up and decked him with a quick right hand. The fifteen-year-old Ukrainian never knew what hit him.

"I didn't know Jews could fight," said an astonished Nesterenko, picking himself up off the ground.

"You just met one who can, punk," said Mike.

Nesterenko appreciated good natural talent. He decided to recruit the wiry, bushy-haired Jew-boy with the quick temper and respectable right hand. The Angels were all Polish and Ukrainian. Mike would be the only Jew in the gang. He agreed to join, not because it was a first for the Jews, but because it promised to be a terribly boring summer.

Mike was lucky to have made it to the fall. After firmly establishing control of the East Village, the Angels looked westward in the search for more turf. Third Avenue. Fourth Avenue. Broadway. It was as easy as picking up a rock. The only resistance was offered by the Warriors from Mulberry Street.

Thirty Angels confronted more than forty-five Warriors that night in the Bleecker Street park. They were all dressed in denim pants and dark T-shirts and carried car antennas, bicycle chains, and switchblade knives. Mike himself was unarmed. "All I need is this right hand," he bragged to the others. But to be on the safe side, he had steel-toed boots and a heavy brass buckle on a loosely fitting belt.

He did not have a chance to use either. Mike had thrown only two punches when he heard the sound of whistles and shouts, the cavalrylike arrival of the cops there to break up the fight. It was bedlam after that, with seventy-five gang members heading in all different directions. For Mike it was like the slow-motion frame of a movie: the skinny, wide-eyed boy staring at him, pointing what looked like a combined slingshot and tube in his direction. He still did not know why he was so slow to react. Frozen. Immobile. The zip gun just about to be fired.

The bullet barely missed his head. He could still feel the wind scratching his ear, and feel the panic rising from his gut. And he still had the four-inch scar on his arm from where he dived onto the open blade of a hastily abandoned knife.

It was impossible to hide the wound from his father. The emotional outpouring that followed, the weeks and weeks of being made to feel guilty because he had let his father down: "I'm glad your mother's not here to see this. Her own son a hoodlum!" That, as well as his close bout with death, not to mention the law, led Mike to abandon the Angels.

It was not until he was twenty-two and was finishing his last year of City College that Mike once again got into trouble. Like before, it was because of his temper and powerful right hand. He was still living at home with his father and sister, Marcia; driving a cab on the weekends to help pay the rent. He was reading the sports page of the *News* one afternoon when Marcia rushed into the apartment in tears. She was seventeen, very pretty, and very well built, and it was not uncommon for her to be accosted on the street. This time, however, the guy had done more than just comment. He had followed her into the building, forced her under the stairwell, and completely had his way. Her blouse and skirt were ripped, her face was badly bruised, and she was hysterical. The man had slugged her, raped her, and threatened her with worse if she went to the police.

From her description, once she calmed down, Mike thought her attacker sounded familiar. A tall Puerto Rican with a long scar on his neck. And he knew that because of New York State law, which required a corroborating witness in the case of rape, the worst he would suffer would be a charge of assault. Besides, a formal complaint would only cause his sister additional pain.

Mike found the tall Puerto Rican two nights later in a First Avenue bar. He was sitting alone drinking a beer, and Mike took a seat and ordered the same. Three beers later, he saw the man get up to leave. Mike put down his half-finished glass and followed him outside.

Their angry words lasted only a very few seconds before the first blows were exchanged. The man was roughly six-two to Mike's five-ten, and his first punch broke Mike's nose. Later Mike wondered how much of his rage had to do with his sister, and how much from the dull pain all over his face and the hot, heavy blood that gorged his throat. In any case, Mike was much faster than the Puerto Rican. He had kept up his boxing in workouts at the YMCA, and after that one lucky punch, he was literally all over him.

His nose. His ears. His cheeks. He did not stop swinging, even after the man crumpled, hitting his head against the sidewalk. He wanted to punish the damn piece of shit for what he had done to his sister.

Unseen hands eventually pulled him away, and when the guy didn't get up, Mike could not have cared less. He was leaning against the window of the bar, nursing his nose, when the cop told him what he had done. Mike went quietly.

He was calm during his arraignment, as well as all the subsequent proceedings. He was not regretful of what had happened, only over the pain it caused his father. He was always letting him down. If he could have afforded a slick uptown lawyer, he might have beaten the rap. "No chance," said the nervous young man from Legal Aid, only six months out of NYU Law School. To avoid the murder charge, he advised Mike to cop a plea. For once, Mike did as he was told. He was convicted of manslaughter, second degree. The judge sentenced him to five years in Walkill Correctional Institute, outside of Poughkeepsie.

Prison is tough in New York, especially if you are white. But the knowledge that he had killed a man with his bare hands kept away the "booty bandits," as they call the aggressive homosexuals in prison.

Mike learned right away that few people behind bars could be trusted. That included both inmates and guards. Being a virtual loner was the only way to survive with self-respect intact.

While he hated every day of his confinement, Mike tried his best to adjust. He followed the advice of the chaplain in "doing the time," rather than letting the time "do him." In several respects he benefited. He left the sports pages of the newspaper for the books in the prison library. He read more in a year and a half than he had all through high school and three years of college. Mike only wished his father had lived to see him read two books a day. At last he might have been proud.

But the most important thing that happened to Mike while at Walkill was his participation in the inmate drama program. He joined on a lark, and he was surprised to find that he really enjoyed getting into the heads of different characters, learning lines and manneristic gestures. Acting was a fantastic outlet for his ever-abundant nervous energy. And what better exercise for someone who wanted to leave his old self behind?

The former Broadway actor who conducted the program said he had talent. He gave Mike the lead in two inmate plays: the part of Biff in *Death of a Salesman*, and the part of Johnny in *A Hatful of Rain*. Mike discovered that acting absorbed him as nothing else ever had. Though he knew the life of a professional actor was as insecure as that of a stick-up man, and certainly less profitable, still he was determined to give it a try.

When he was released on parole after sixteen months (he had five months off for good behavior), Mike's second call was to the actor from Walkill, who had promised to find him a good drama coach.

Mike's first call was to the man he now saw dutifully every month. Daniel McCarthy, Mike's parole officer demanded punctuality, and Mike was now almost a half hour late.

The downtown traffic was terrible. A stalled truck blocked the intersection at Canal, and with two lanes merging to one, the cab was averaging a block to a light. Goddammit! Just my luck, thought Mike. He shouted to the cabdriver to stop at the corner of Broadway and Worth. He left a fifty-cent tip rather than wait for the change, and raced the remaining block and a half on foot. On his way into the massive redbrick municipal building, he nearly collided with two uniformed cops on their way out. "Watch yourself, Mac," said the older of the two.

"I'm sorry," said Mike over his shoulder, hurrying toward the elevator.

"There's a law against knocking people down," warned the younger partner, brushing himself off. "Take it easy."

"I'm sorry," repeated Mike. He nodded apologetically before disappearing into the open elevator. Fucking cops! That's all I need, he thought to himself as he was squeezed into the back by a crowd of secretaries, clerks, and other municipal workers. *To be arrested on some petty-ass charge.* That was the fear of all parolees, along with being tripped up by the mountainous restrictions they were required to follow.

Mike had learned from his first meeting with McCarthy, some two years before, that being on parole was in many respects like still being in prison. The list of "Do Nots" was endless. It included jobs he could not get, as well as people he could not see. For example, he was not allowed to socialize with other ex-convicts. Fortunately that posed little problem for Mike, because the few friends he had made at Walkill were either still inside, living in different cities, or keeping to themselves. Also the neighborhood boys he had grown up with—including some of the original Angels—were either already dead, so strung-out on drugs as to be virtually unrecognizable, or themselves serving sentences that would keep them off the streets for many years to come.

The most painful restriction was the ludicrous law that prohibited Mike, and all other parolees, from having sex with anyone other than his "lawfully wedded wife." He did not believe his ears when McCarthy first warned him about "sleeping around."

"You must be joking," said Mike. For Christ's sake, the parole officer himself was only in his thirties. He certainly could not expect . . .

"Hardly," McCarthy said stiffly. "Those are the rules, and they *must* be obeyed. See to it."

"I'll do that," said Mike. To himself he added: I'll see to it that I sure as hell don't get caught.

He had managed so far to avoid being accused of any parole violation. But he had almost six months left of his parole, and until then Mike knew he was less free than anyone else on the street, less free than anyone else in the elevator, before had given up auditing companies in favor of auditing less free than the girl chewing gum in his ear, and the man standing next to him who had eaten garlic for lunch.

Daniel McCarthy was a former accountant who three years one in his department who did not complain about his case load. The parole officer controlled the presents and futures of lives. He apparently liked his work, because he was the only more than seventy ex-convicts. He was thin, pale-skinned, and because of tiny eyes and a receding hairline, his face appeared to be all forehead. He was much older than his years. He was bending over his secretary's desk, signing a stack of papers, when Mike rushed through the door.

"You're late," said McCarthy, without looking up.

"I'm sorry," said Mike. "I was stuck on the subway. I would have called, but—"

"I'm a busy man, Mr. Ross," he said, unsmiling. "Go into my office."

What McCarthy called an office was a small cubicle created by frosted-glass partitions. It contained a desk, two wooden chairs, and a battered stand-up file. It reminded Mike, in its starkness, of the visiting area at Walkill. However, there he was with someone he wanted to see. Mike took the seat designed for parolees and waited for the always dreaded interview to begin.

"How is everything going?" asked McCarthy when he had taken his seat and folded his arms on top of his desk.

"Not bad," said Mike. "I'm still living in the same place, and working, and . . . generally everything's okay."

McCarthy opened the notebook in front of him. He read silently for a moment. "Of course you're still living in the same place," he said coolly, his eyes still on the page. "If you had moved, you would have told me about it, wouldn't you, Mr. Ross?" He looked up slowly with a thin, tight-lipped smile.

"Yeah, of course I would have. What I meant is that nothing's really changed that much since I was last here."

McCarthy nodded, and started in on the hair. He had a habit, which Mike noticed his very first meeting, of rubbing his fingers through the front strands of his hair. It was as if he were holding on to his hairline, trying to keep what little hair remained from literally disappearing through his fingers. The habit made the meetings even more uncomfortable for Mike. He could not afford to embarrass the parole officer, and yet it was difficult to keep his eyes from the forehead, especially since it seemed to grow every time he was there. Six months more, and McCarthy's hands would be behind his neck.

"You are working for the Acme Answering Service, are you not?" asked the parole officer.

"Yes, that's right."

"What, please tell me, do you do there?"

Mike was surprised by the question. "I answer the phone, of course. I cover the district south of Twenty-third Street and west of Fifth Avenue. That includes Chelsea and Greenwich Village."

"How fascinating," said McCarthy with obvious sarcasm.

"No one said it was fascinating," Mike tried not to let the annoyance show in his voice. "But at least it's a job. Something I'm supposed to have. Right?"

"Something you *have* to have," corrected McCarthy. "I just wonder why this particular one. A man with your intelligence. You are a college graduate. Surely there are jobs more suitable for your . . . talent?"

"Someone else asked me that today," said Mike with growing irritation. "But they didn't know any better. That certainly isn't the case with you."

"Excuse me," said McCarthy, still busy with the hair.

"I'm talking about jobs. You know better than anyone that

as an ex-convict there are very few jobs I *can* get." Despite every intention, Mike could not contain himself. "I can't work in a bank, a barber shop, a pharmacy, even a billiard parlor. Nor as an auctioneer, a junk dealer, a night watchman, or an undertaker. And I'm only scratching the surface. Assuming the job were available, I couldn't even call the numbers for bingo at a damn county fair." He sighed. It had all poured out of him in one long breath.

McCarthy removed his hands from his head and crossed them at his chest. He leaned back in his chair and was silent for at least ten seconds. When finally he spoke, his voice was lower than usual. "I've warned you before, Mr. Ross, about your temper. As no doubt you recall, it was an uncontrollable temper that got you in trouble in the first place. Now, I'm here to see that it does not happen again. I'm here to help you."

Sure, thought Mike to himself. He knew better, but he didn't dare say it.

"Now I want to hear no more outbursts," added McCarthy. "Is that clear? . . . Is it?"

"Yes," said Mike, feeling his aggravation, like a stiffness, in the back of his neck. He breathed deeply, forcing himself to calm down. "The point I was trying to make, *Sir*, is that there are very few jobs legally available for someone with a record, like myself."

"I know that. I think it's unfortunate. But surely the jobs you mentioned are not jobs you're seriously interested in? An undertaker, for example? Or an auctioneer?"

"I certainly wouldn't mind being able to work as a waiter," said Mike. "But for some stupid reason, the law says I can't work in any place licensed to sell liquor. Even beer. Not too many restaurants that don't serve booze."

"Why a waiter?" asked McCarthy. "That's not much better than answering the phone."

"The hours are more flexible. It would fit in better with my classes."

"What classes are these?" said McCarthy with the nosy interest of his profession. He was starting up again with the hair.

"I'm taking up acting. I go to classes three days a week."

"How interesting. And you're planning on . . ." He cleared his throat, ". . . making a career out of this?"

65

Mike caught the snideness in the officer's voice. He did his best to ignore it. "I thought I would give it a try. I know it's difficult, but . . ."

"You're not really serious?" said McCarthy, leaning forward across his desk, the hint of a grin beginning to form across his thin lips. "I know you did some things in prison, but . . ."

"My teacher told me today that I've got great potential. She wants me to start in the advanced class." Mike shrugged. "It's a beginning."

It started with the grin slowly expanding across his face, lifting up his cheeks, and widening his eyes. Then McCarthy removed his hands from his head and clapped his palms together as if in prayer. Seconds later came the laugh, high-pitched and breathy, like the nervous giggle of a schoolgirl in class.

Mike wanted to hit him, right then and there. Just stand up and literally lay McCarthy out. He would have done it, too, if it would not have meant an immediate end to his freedom. *Assault on a parole officer.* No way could he get away with that. Before McCarthy even arrived at the hospital, he would be picked up and whisked back inside, made to finish his original sentence and to wait for his new one to begin. For McCarthy, it would be a dream come true.

All Mike could do safely was fume. He contented himself with a cold glare—they couldn't do anything about that—along with the unrestrained bitterness in his voice. "Thanks for the encouragement, McCarthy. Now, if you've had your little laugh, I'd like to get on with this. You're the one who's supposed to be so busy."

"You sound resentful," said McCarthy, the humor still reflected in his eyes.

"You're damn right," said Mike. "I resent having to put up with this. Having to tell you where I live, where I work, how I spend my time. This whole thing is bullshit. You're not the slightest bit interested in me." He paused, then said, "You'd like nothing better than for me to do something stupid, so you could send me back. Isn't that right, McCarthy?"

The parole officer did not answer. He just sat there and stared at Mike through pencil points of eyes. "How's your sex life, Ross?" he asked finally in a voice filled with the arrogance of his power.

"You want to hear the details?"

"There better not be any," said McCarthy.

"Is there anything else?" asked Mike, hating the man more by the second.

"I hope you're obeying all the other rules."

"Don't worry about it. I'm the only one in this town who waits for the light to turn green before crossing the street."

"Good for you."

Mike slowly got up from his seat.

"Who told you to go?"

"I don't want to take any more of your time, sir." Mike's voice was as sincere as he could make it. "I know you're a busy man."

McCarthy had a love affair with his scalp before speaking. "Your hair's too long. Get it cut." He then added, "The usual warnings until next month, Mr. Ross."

"I know," said Mike. "I so much as fart wrong, and it's back inside."

"Any way you want to put it," said McCarthy. "You're the one who wants to go on the stage."

Mike left without answering back.

6

On Monday morning Markham thought about phoning in sick. He was tempted to stay home, completing his final preparation for tomorrow. However, after two cups of coffee he decided against it. Considering his reputation for rarely missing a day on the job, it was essential that he maintain his regular routine. That way there would not be the slightest hint of suspicion directed at him. Not that there would be in any case, but he was intent on leaving nothing to chance. This was his style as a prosecutor, and it remained his style now.

Fortunately the day was an easy one, given to routine meetings with his assistants, a picture-taking ceremony with the mayor at City Hall, and lunch with an old friend from law school who had recently been made a partner of his prestigious Wall Street firm. Markham coasted through the meetings and the photograph session with his mind miles away. If he had any worry that his preoccupation was observed, then his fears were put to rest by the lunch with his friend.

"You look fantastic, Frank," the new partner said with a grin. "Winning cases obviously agrees with you."

"Look who's talking," said Markham. "You haven't done so badly yourself."

"Sure. But what do I get? Money. You've got something much more important."

"What's that?"

"A political future," said the lawyer.

Markham smiled. His friend did not know the half of it.

He spent the afternoon dictating case reports to his secretary. It was a biweekly ritual which he always enjoyed, not so much because of the work itself—the compiling of perfunctory reports that no one ever read—as for the close presence of his secretary.

Jennifer had been working for him now for close to three months. Twenty-four, honey-blond, and with an aversion to bras and loose-fitting pants, she had been hired as much for her appearance as her skills. He'd felt no qualms about deliberately beautifying his drab city offices with big blue eyes, well-shaped breasts, and long trim legs. After returning from smoky conferences and drafty courtrooms, he was pleased by the sight of her outside his door, the way she smiled warmly at his approach, and the hint of South Carolina in her voice as she told him who'd called.

He especially looked forward to these scheduled afternoon sessions in his office. It was obvious that she did as well, because on the second Monday of the month, the day before case reports were due, she invariably wore one of her best silk blouses and exchanged her pants for a skirt that draped provocatively over her knees.

Markham leaned back in his chair, his hands behind his head, while Jennifer perched on her chair by the side of his desk. Her legs were crossed at the knee, and her blouse was partially unbuttoned from the top, as if by accident. She was wearing his favorite perfume—Givenchy; he had complimented her on it once before. Her light red lipstick appeared to be freshly applied.

Gazing at the whiteness of her throat, and unavoidably, down to where the swell of her breasts just began, Markham again thought of how easy it would be to take her to bed. He had considered it for some time, ever since he'd interviewed her for the job, and chosen her immediately from among the five other applicants. She had just the sort of body he liked. Tall and well-proportioned, the kind of firm though ample figure that would look as good naked in bed as it did fully clothed.

She was obviously attracted to him herself, judging from the way she dressed for these private sessions, and how she always touched him at every opportunity, helping him on with his coat, her hands caressing his shoulder, and pressing beside him when they descended together in the elevator.

Subtle she wasn't. Hardly the type to play misleading games. More importantly, she was strong and self-reliant, not the kind of woman who would demand an involvement after one pleasurable night. God knows he didn't want the burden of a relationship, especially with someone right there at work.

Though she was ideally suited for him, he was in no real hurry to succumb. He enjoyed stringing her along. Teasing her. Keeping her uncertain as to whether he was interested or not. That way she became increasingly more direct, more aggressive. Let her keep it up. Let her work for it. By the time he'd be ready for her, she'd be so wound up he could lie back and let her do all the work. She'd be uncontrollable, like some kind of animal. Just the way he wanted her.

Markham yawned. "Jennifer, these case reports can wait until tomorrow. I think I've had enough for today."

"I don't mind doing them, Mr. Markham. You know that."

"I know, Jennifer, and I appreciate it." He looked at his watch. It was four o'clock. "It's been a tiring day, and I think I'm going to go home. Matter of fact, why don't you take the rest of the day off yourself."

"That's very nice of you. But I couldn't."

"Why not?" Markham smiled. "I won't tell anyone."

Jennifer grinned. "Whatever you say."

"I'll see you tomorrow," Markham said, getting up from his chair. "I'll be in about nine-thirty."

Markham's chauffeur was waiting in the underground garage. The two of them made small talk as they drove up the East River Drive.

Arriving in front of Markham's building the chauffeur stepped out to open the back door. "Anytime special tomorrow?" he asked as Markham got out of the car.

"Thanks for reminding me, Joe. I won't be needing you at all in the morning. I've got a meeting with someone who'll be picking me up. I'll get to the office myself."

"Okay, Mr. Markham. I'll be home tonight if you need me. Tomorrow I'll be down in the garage as usual."

"See you tomorrow. And congratulate your son about getting into medical school. That's great news. Thanks for telling me about it."

Markham greeted his doorman with courtesy, and after getting his mail, rode the elevator to the eleventh floor. He listened politely to the complaints of a fellow tenant—a gray-haired businessman—about the courts' special treatment of juvenile delinquents.

"They're getting away with murder, those kids. It's not right. Doesn't matter who you are. You can't get away with murder."

"You're absolutely right," said Markham, stepping from the elevator.

He sighed with relief as he entered his apartment, closed and bolted the door. It had been a long day, and it was going to be an even longer night. He changed from his suit and tie into a sport shirt and slacks, put on his leather slippers, and poured himself a vermouth on the rocks. He would have preferred something stronger—a tall Scotch with a splash of soda—but he decided against it, as he could not afford to completely relax. He still had a lot to do before tomorrow.

He unlocked his file and took out the notebook that was wedged far back in the drawer. He opened it and placed it before him on the coffee table. Over the last two weeks he had driven tomorrow's route five times for practice, timing himself with a stopwatch and recording his time on the back page of the notebook in the form of a chart.

Sipping his vermouth, Markham studied the entries in the chart. His best time so far was twenty-one minutes, and that was from the corner of Seventy-ninth Street and First Avenue, across town via Ninty-seventh Street to the West Side Drive, up to the George Washington Bridge, and then over to New Jersey. From the Jersey side of the bridge, he had to figure on at least another six to eight minutes to the top of the hill by her home. That made it twenty-nine minutes door to door. Of course, tomorrow morning he would be going against traffic all the way. The total traveling time might actually be less. But he had to be punctual. A minute late and he would fail.

Markham had decided to use a car for this first phase of his plan because of its practicality. Its impersonality also appealed to him. All he would feel was a sharp bump. There would be no face-to-face contact. No screams. No sense of his own responsibility. He was like a passenger along for the ride.

The problem with using a car was one of logistics. The plan required perfect timing both ways. Only after weeks of practice did he feel confident. Even now he continued to study the charts. They were like transcripts to a hearing, the case report of a detective, or the testimony of a witness he would cross-examine in the morning.

He finally concluded that to allow himself the greatest leeway, in case of unexpected traffic or some tie-up on the bridge, he would leave forty minutes ahead of time. That was eleven minutes more than he needed in the middle of the day. Most probably, going in the early morning, he would have more than twenty minutes to spare. Being there slightly ahead of time was okay, as long as he didn't arouse suspicion. He would merely park the car, leave the engine running, and read the paper until he was ready. He would look like he was waiting to drive a neighbor to work.

Satisfied with his calculation, Markham ripped out the back page of the notebook and flushed it down the toilet. On his way back from the bathroom, he poured himself another vermouth. He then went to the kitchen, opened a drawer under the counter, and took out two simple devices he had made a few days before.

The first was the straight part of a metal coat hanger. It was eight inches long and was bent at one end into the shape of a fish hook. The other, a little more elaborate, consisted of three metal alligator clips connected together in a T-formation by two pieces of insulated copper wire. The ends of the clips were soldered to the wire, and the joints were wrapped in electrical tape. Just to be on the safe side, Markham undid the tape and double-checked the joints. Twisting them between his fingers, he saw that they were all still secure. He wrapped them once again in fresh tape. Confident that both devices were in good working order, he placed them on the coffee table until he was ready to go.

He undressed to his shorts and lay down on his bed for a nap. Before turning off the light, he set the clock-radio for nine-forty-five.

Markham was awakened by Herbie Mann playing "Comin' Home, Baby." If he felt a little disoriented after this late-evening nap, it vanished as he lay there listening in the dark to Mann's rhythmic flute. He felt a restless anticipation for what lay ahead, and he got out of bed and did a few quick sit-ups and stretching exercises before taking a shower.

Dressing took no time at all, as his outfit was chosen well in advance. Afterward, standing in front of the bedroom mirror, Markham studied himself, pleased at his appearance. He was glad that when planning what to wear he had remembered his old tweed sport jacket with the patches on the elbow. He had not worn it since law school, twelve years before, and he had kept it more as a souvenir than anything else. God knows he never expected to wear it again. He was flattered that it still fit. After all these years packed in his trunk, it had taken half an hour in a bathroom full of steam to get out most of the wrinkles. The few that remained added to the look he wanted. So did the narrow lapels that made the jacket hopelessly out-of-date.

His other clothes went beautifully with the jacket. The chocolate-brown corduroy trousers that he had left in the bottom of his closet for a week until they had long lost any sign of a crease. And the beige turtleneck sweater that he'd received one Christmas from Leslie but never worn because it was two sizes too big. Just like her not to know his size. Even his shoes were perfectly suited. Scuffed brown walkers with crepe soles and laces that were splitting at the ends; he had been meaning to throw them out for months. In fact, he had once actually left them by the service elevator along with the garbage, only to retrieve them at the last minute, thinking he might use them again.

This whole outfit was an inspiration. Who would ever think he would dress this way? Markham prided himself on his sense of style, and over the years his style had become part of his public image. He'd learned from past political campaigns that voters who knew him only from his pictures in the paper hardly recognized him in his casual clothes. No one would recognize him in what he was wearing now.

Markham carefully parted his usually tousled hair. He could not be any more inconspicuous. He resembled a Columbia professor, someone who taught either geology or the classics and lived on West End Avenue. He was just the kind of man you expected to see walking in Riverside Park. Day or night, you wouldn't look at him twice.

Satisfied with his appearance, Markham returned to the living room. He picked up the alligator clips and the bent coat hanger from the coffee table, fitting them both in one of his inside coat pockets. Into his outside coat pocket went a stopwatch and a pencil-sized flashlight from the desk drawer. Now he was ready. It was ten-thirty when he finally left the apartment, purposely leaving the radio on in the bedroom. It would be nice to return home to music.

Markham took the elevator to the basement so as to avoid the doorman. Returning to the building posed no problem, as the nightman was invariably so tired that he would notice nothing at all strange about his dress.

He took a cab across town to a Chinese restaurant on Broadway and One Hundredth Street. The restaurant was large and poorly lit, with faded red wallpaper and pots of imitation flowers and plants. At that hour on a Monday night there were very few diners, and they were scattered throughout the room. After a small Scotch on the rocks, he ordered hot-and-sour soup, beef with Hoisin sauce, and subgum wonton. The beef dish was a little too hot, and the wontons were a little too skimpy. But Markham didn't mind. He had not come there for the food, and definitely not the atmosphere. It was the convenient location.

He lingered over his tea and thought of his son, Billy, wondering what he was doing at that very moment. Probably reading Sports Illustrated or building a model airplane in his room. He was a bright kid, Billy was. So full of energy and curiosity. Interested in everything. He was a joy to be around. A father couldn't ask for a better son.

He in turn was a good father to Billy. He had no doubts about that. Billy knew how much he loved him, and how proud he was of his high grades in school. Well, if he didn't know now, then he was going to know soon. Markham was going to be the best damn father in the world. There was nothing he wouldn't do for that kid. After all this was over, he would get an apartment on the Drive with a view of the river. It would be just like before, except now with only the two of them. Father and son. That was how he wanted it. They would do everything together. Football in the park. Basketball games at the Garden. Late-night movies at home, and weekend trips to the country. Father and son. They'd be like best friends.

As for Leslie's interfering, he wasn't the slightest bit worried about her. Let the bitch do as she pleased, in or out of court. He was too good a lawyer to lose anything to her, especially his son. He'd use everything in his power to win custody of Billy. No matter what it took, he would succeed.

Markham was thinking of Billy's birthday coming up, wondering what he should get him, and how they would celebrate, when he glanced at his watch. That thought would have to wait, for it was time to go. It was close to midnight when Markham left the restaurant, walked the two blocks to Riverside Drive, and began his search for the car.

Considering how he was going to be using it, the car *had* to be stolen. Though he knew from actual case experience that the cars responsible for hit-and-run accidents were rarely found, he was aware that the police did occasionally outdo themselves. Armed with an eyewitness description of a car's color and make, and perhaps even a partial license-plate number, there was no telling what a patrol car might stumble on.

For that reason Markham could not take the chance of being in any way connected to the car he would use. Stealing a car for one night was much less of a risk. Especially if you knew what you were doing.

He had decided on Riverside Drive because of its isolation. From Ninty-seventh Street all the way to One Hundred and Thirteenth, the Drive is divided into two separate routes, an access road that snakes up directly in front of the buildings and a lower section that is lined with trees. In the summer and early fall, the leaves of the trees are like one long umbrella, completely covering stretches of the lower Drive. Looking down from a river view apartment, you cannot see the parked cars underneath. Nor can you see a man walking alongside them.

Markham had planned it so he arrived on the lower Drive precisely at twelve, the exact moment when New York City policemen change shifts. It is not public knowledge, in fact it is deliberately kept quiet, but as district attorney he knew that for roughly twenty minutes, as the policemen mustered for instructions, fueled up their cars, and took last-minute trips to the precinct bathroom, there would be fewer men on patrol than at any other time for the next eight hours. It was the ideal time to commit a mugging, hold up an all-night delicatessen, or steal a car. Though the street's high-intensity lights lit the park walkway as bright as day, Markham was unconcerned. Dressed as he was, he would arouse very little suspicion from dog-walkers or strollers who observed him.

It was cool for October, with a crisp breeze whipping off the Hudson. The lights from New Jersey condominiums shone brightly through the trees, as if two blocks away, and the George Washington Bridge was like an elegant necklace spanning the river.

Markham buttoned up his jacket and turned up his collar against the breeze. He walked slowly, leisurely, his hands deep in his pockets. It was like when he was an assistant district attorney and planned his trial summations while walking in the park. His concentration was now just as intense. He looked closely at every car he passed.

He found just what he was looking for at the corner of One Hundred and Third Street. It was a green 1969 Oldsmobile convertible. It carried New York State plates, had a slightly dented front end, and was badly in need of a cleaning. In the grime caked on the hood, someone had written "Wash Me" with his finger. What mattered to Markham was the car's size. It looked heavy and solid enough to crash into a tree without injuring the driver. Even more important was its design. Markham knew from his recent experience prosecuting a ring of interstate car thieves that a pre-1971 Oldsmobile is an easy car to steal.

He looked up and down the Drive. Two blocks away a man with a German shepherd was walking in the opposite direction. Otherwise there was no one in sight, and no traffic for as far as he could see. The only sound was from the cars over on the highway, and the horn of a tugboat on the Jersey side of the river. Standing alongside the car as close as he could, Markham reached down to open the door. Though he seriously doubted the door would be unlocked, it was still worth the effort. There were a lot of absentminded people in New York, many of whom surely owned cars. No luck. The handle wouldn't budge. He waited for a taxi to turn onto the Drive from a side street and continue uptown before removing the bent coat hanger from his pocket.

A 1969 Oldsmobile has small triangular windows immediately behind each door. They are separated from the windows in front by a thin strip of rubber that runs straight down from the roof to the door.

He had no difficulty at all inserting the hanger through the rubber. It offered little more resistance than cardboard. A firm push and the round piece of metal was through. He then slowly maneuvered the bent end of the hanger until it hooked around the knob locking the door. It took some doing to make it secure, but finally the hook was wedged tightly under the lip of the knob. He could feel the lip holding firm. After a quick check up and down the Drive, he pulled sharply upward on the hanger. Success. The door unlocked. Markham smiled. No wonder later-model autombiles were designed more securely.

He looked again to see that he was alone before opening the door and slipping inside. The car smelled of beer and stale cigarette tobacco. The plastic upholstery was torn across the front, and covered on the passenger side with a pile of old newspapers. Needing the room, Markham moved the newspapers to the back seat. He relocked the door and lay prone on the front seat, his head by the steering wheel, his feet against the opposite door.

Markham then took the flashlight and the alligator clips from his pocket. He leaned down so that his shoulders rested on the brake pedal and his head was underneath the dashboard. In a pre-1971 Oldsmobile, the dashboard does not curve up underneath, and from Markham's position he could easily see the exposed wires behind the instrument panel. With the help of the flashlight he located the back of the ignition.

He knew exactly what he was doing. Over the past few weeks he had practiced on no fewer than six cars on the Drive. Though they were not all Oldsmobiles, he had chosen cars whose ignitions were very similar. The wires running to the ignition were connected to two quarter-inch screws, and invariably the screws were just big enough to hold the alligator clips.

It was simply a matter of connecting the clips, thereby jumping the ignition, in order to turn over the motor. Markham was careful to see that the clips did not touch one another. He had learned during a practice run that if either clip made contact with any other metal, the system would short-circuit. The engine would suddenly stop. Fortunately, the one time it happened he was on West End Avenue at one o'clock in the morning. He was able to coast to the side of the street, then quickly lean under the dashboard to reengage the clips. But he could easily imagine being stalled in the middle of traffic, with everyone honking as he crawled down to hot-wire the car.

He tried not to think about such risks. The engine was now

running smoothly. To keep it from stalling, he depressed the gas pedal with his elbow. A good strong idle, without being loud enough to draw attention. All that remained was the problem of lights. Markham knew that in most American cars the lights, radio, and other electrical features run on a separate circuit from the ignition. In order to steal a car at night, you had to find some way to connect the lights to the ignition. That was the purpose of the third alligator clip

In took some experimentation, but by turning on the radio and then connecting the third clip to different outlets in the back, ultimately, by process of elimination, Markham was able to connect the two circuits. He knew he was successful when the radio went on.

Markham slid up from under the dashboard and tried the lights. They too were working. He was in business.

He drove the car slowly over to the East Side by way of the Ninty-sixth Street transverse. He wanted to get a feel for the way it handled, so that he would be as relaxed as possible in the morning. He tested the brakes for tightness, and was particularly interested in the car's acceleration. No problem. Judging from the way the car sped across Madison Avenue to beat the light, he would have nothing to worry about.

He was not concerned about the car being reported stolen. By the time it was missed, probably sometime tomorrow morning, he would already be through with it. Even assuming the worst, that it was discovered gone within the hour, he knew, again from his experience as district attorney, that it would be at least a day before the car's description was circulated among the police. He grinned, thinking of the advantage he had over other car thieves. He knew exactly what he was up against. He couldn't help laughing, cynically wondering who they'd get to prosecute him if he were caught.

Markham was lucky enough to find a parking place on East End Avenue, two blocks from his building. He left the door unlocked so he'd be able to enter easily in the morning. Wouldn't it be ironic, he thought, if consequently someone else stole his already stolen car? A quick backward glance at the dented green Oldsmobile allayed any fears. The car was obviously on its last legs, and no professional thief would even look at it twice. He had truly chosen well.

Using his stopwatch, Markham timed how long it took him to reach his apartment, walking at a normal clip. Five minutes, including a short wait for the elevator, during which time the doorman did little more than nod. He added the five minutes to the forty he had already allotted. Allowing an additional thirty minutes to shave, dress, and have a quick breakfast, that came to a total of an hour and fifteen minutes from when he woke up to when he should be waiting at the top of her hill.

She was expected at eight-fifteen. Markham set his clock-radio for seven o'clock. No, he decided he would give himself even more leeway. He reset the alarm for six-thirty.

Considering what he would do in the morning, Frank Markham had little difficulty falling asleep. He even had pleasant dreams.

7

At seven-thirty each morning, eleven-year-old Freddie Martinez began his rounds along the streets of Edgewater, New Jersey. The small town on the west bank of the Hudson River was dotted with modest single-family homes whose occupants were at that hour just getting up. The clang of Freddie's unoiled chain and the thump of his deliveries against doors and onto front steps served as an alarm clock to Edgewater's businessmen, civil servants from New York, and three or four bona fide Mafia members.

One of Freddie's papers went to the home of Angela Nash. Angela was sipping her coffee when she heard the thump against the door. She stepped out and waved to Freddie, who smiled and waved back. Angela Nash, in her mid-fifties, gray-haired and slightly plump, was dressed in a brown terry-cloth robe and furry blue slippers. She opened her *Times* with eagerness, because she had theater tickets for later that week to a play which had opened the night before.

She turned quickly to Richard Eder's review. "Brilliant," "Hilarious," "A memorable evening of music and laughter." She was delighted by his acclaim, his comparisons to *Hello, Dolly!* and *Gypsy*, and she was happy with herself for having bought the tickets in advance of opening night. She was reading the review for a second time, and beaming with self-satisfaction, when a quick glance at her watch reminded her she was late. She tucked the *Times* under her arm and hurried back into the house to finish her coffee and dress for work.

Twenty minutes later, at ten minutes after eight, Angela Nash left the house. She was carrying a large canvas bag. It was filled with crayons, drawings, picture books, and a new word game that she had just bought the day before. Angela Nash was an elementary-school teacher, and those items were for her second-grade class. As she walked along the sidewalk, she greeted her neighbors on their way to work.

Angela Nash knew almost everyone in her small three-block-wide town. She had lived in the same house for the last fifteen years, for the last three years all by herself, ever since her husband Walter's heart attack. Her brother, Martin, was still trying to persuade her to move. "Come to Manhasset," he was always telling her. "Then you'll be near me. I don't like you living all alone. It's not safe."

Not safe? Angela laughed to herself. What a worrywart her brother was. What else could you expect from a doctor? But just because he knew everything that *could* possibly happen, all the illnesses or accidents, that did not make *her* any more vulnerable than the next person. She suspected his real reason for wanting her to move was that he wanted her companionship now that Cathline, his wife of thirty-three years, had finally died. But she felt sure he would adjust after a while. Just like she had. And she was not that far away, if he needed her.

Besides, she liked Edgewater too much to consider moving. It was a nice community. Small. Livable. Even more important, it was accessible to her school. All she had to do was walk up the hill, and a bus took her directly to Teaneck, stopping two short blocks from Grover Elementary.

Angela Nash was on her way up the hill, thinking again of the *Times* review, wondering who she would invite to accompany her, when she first saw the car. It was headed down toward the river. She did not know much about models or years; only that it was green, and the front end looked slightly beat up. What she did know without any problem at all was that the car was going *much* too fast. Didn't the driver see the signs? Angela wondered to herself. This was no place to speed. Not with all the children around here. Especially at this hour, when they all left for school.

Angela stopped walking and looked closely at the oncoming car. She thought maybe if she could jot down the license, then she would be able to file a complaint. That's if the car were not going too fast for her to see. However, it looked like it would pass on her side of the road.

Angela did not have time to be frightened. When she realized that the car was veering across the road in her direction, her first thought was of the driver. What happened to him? she wondered. Had he lost control of the wheel? Maybe he had panicked, coming so fast down the hill. Of course, it could be something worse. A heart attack, like her husband. Or a stroke, like Mr. Atkinson, two houses down.

Angela Nash was still worrying about the driver, forgetting about herself, when the car jumped off the side of the road onto the sidewalk directly in front of her. The heavy convertible was traveling more than fifty miles an hour when it hit her, simultaneously breaking her hip and back, the separated bones puncturing her liver and kidney. She felt no pain at all, because before all of her violated nerves could scream in agony, her body had crumpled, and her head made contact with the fender. As the impact was like that of a cantaloupe dropped from a fifteen-story window and landing on concrete, Angela Nash was already dead while her body was still in the air. By the time she landed, sixty-five feet down the road, the green Oldsmobile had turned the corner and disappeared from sight.

A crowd quickly gathered around Angela Nash's body. It was Freddie Martinez who retrieved her canvas bag from where it lay untouched on the sidewalk farther up the hill.

Markham did not look back. He drove on River Road for two blocks before making a sharp right turn on Gorge Road, which took him up to Fort Lee. He drove at a normal rate of speed, stopping at every stop sign and red light. Near the site of the old Palisades Park, now a twenty-story condominium, he got stuck behind a school bus picking up children. Markham checked in the rearview mirror. There was no sign of police, no honking of horns, nor any other indication that he was being followed. He felt surprisingly relaxed, without a glimmer of fear, even when the school bus continued to stop every hundred yards to pick up its passengers.

At the intersection of Palisades Avenue and Columbia Street, Markham turned left to get away from the bus. The rest of the trip was totally uneventful. Like any other commuter into the city, he listened to the radio, paying particular attention to the reports of traffic congestion on the major arteries. He was glad, when planning his route, that he had chose to skip the George Washington Bridge for his return to New York. Instead he traveled south, parallel with the river, to Hoboken, where he took the Holland Tunnel. Just before entering the tunnel, he heard that traffic on the bridge was backed up into New Jersey.

Another advantage of the tunnel was that its exit on the New York side of the Hudson, was in lower Manhattan, directly across town from Markham's office. He purposely parked the car in a no-parking zone near the World Trade Center. He took the alligator clips with him before he left. As he was hailing a cab to take him across town, he saw that a meter maid was already approaching the car. He knew that in less than an hour the car would be towed away by the police. It would be stored, along with hundreds of other cars, in a huge city lot. The green Oldsmobile with the now badly dented front end would remain there until it was claimed.

Markham was pleased. Everything had worked exactly as planned. He was at his desk by nine-twenty-five, dictating case reports to his secretary. Jennifer looked lovelier than ever.

8

The phones would not stop ringing. They had been going like crazy since six o'clock. Hardy told Mike that it was the worst Tuesday night he could remember in months. And unexpected, too, considering this was the end of October and most of the clients were back at work and taking only weekends in the country. Seeing as if nothing of importance was opening in town that night, why the hell weren't they home answering their own phones?

Hardy worked one headset down the switchboard from Mike, and was Mike's only source of diversion during the four-to-ten shift on the Acme lines.

Hardy was in his mid-twenties, black as the Bell standard model, and every inch a princess. He referred to himself as the "fairest flower ever to blossom out of the rich soils of Macon, Georgia." Like Mike, Hardy answered phones only as a sideline. "I mean, any dummy can talk," he was quick to admit. "Just look at your operators. Baby, this is no place for *talent*." Hardy's own talent was his high tenor voice. He had arrived in New York by bus, intent on becoming the next Johnny Mathis. Indeed, his "A Certain Smile," demonstrated to his colleague one particularly quiet night, was, in Mike's opinion, as mellow as the original. However, aside from several auditions, which invariably lasted overnight, Hardy had yet to have his break. He remained plugged into the Acme console, singing scales, voice exercises, and occasional songs in between messages.

"No time for music tonight," said Mike, looking up from

his notepad after taking down a message for a Chelsea doctor.

"Baby, there is *always* time for music," said Hardy. "Especially since most of these numbers are just sittin' on their butts, too lazy to pick up for theirselves. They just gonna have to wait."

Hardy leaned his thin body back in his swivel chair, flashed a hundred-dollar grin down the line at Mike, and began to sing. Two of his lines started to ring at once. Hardy ignored them and continued singing. Now four of his phones were ringing, their lights flashing like a pinball machine.

"How's a body to practice!" said Hardy, returning to his hunched position over the board. "Tone-deaf bastards!" He plugged into one of the lights, grimaced, and then answered sweetly, "Acme Service. May I help you?"

Mike, who was enjoying the singing, could not help laughing. Yet he sympathized with his fellow operator, and was grateful that his own board was momentarily quiet. It was about time. He had already logged close to two hundred messages. And read only three pages of *Variety*. With less than an hour to go, there was no doubt that it would be a record night. Not exactly one for the books, like, say, Aaron's home runs, but a record nevertheless. What did he need? Only twenty-five more calls. Well, now it was twenty-four. His phone was ringing.

"Mike?" said the familiar voice.

"Gloria! This is a nice surprise. How are you?"

"Not bad." Her voice was soft. "What's more important, how are you?"

Mike laughed. "After tonight, I know why Ma Bell's buildings never have any windows. It's not so the operators won't get distracted. It's so they won't jump out."

"That bad?" said Gloria.

"Fortunately I only got another half an hour. After that, they can bring back smoke signals, for all I care."

"I thought I remembered you saying you were finished at ten. I would have called you earlier, but I had to wait for Arthur to leave."

"Leave? You mean tonight's the night he leaves for Dallas?"

"Don't you read the papers? It's such a big merger, this deal of his, that they even mentioned it in the *Times*."

"Guess I'll have to start reading the financial pages."

"If you want me to yourself, you will," Gloria teased. "The airport limousine just pulled out of the driveway. You know what that means. We've got three weeks."

"Three weeks. Fantastic."

"And that's at the least. It all depends on business. It's a pretty big deal for his bank."

"So it might even be longer?" said a delighted Mike.

"Could be." She drew out the words, her voice even more seductive than usual. Mike could just see her, curled up on a couch, a flimsy robe half-opened, her satiny hair hanging over the edge.

"Where are you now?" he asked. "What room, I mean?"

Her laugh was soft and breathy, like her voice. "Why do you ask?"

"I was trying to imagine someplace comfortable. Take my mind off all these red lights staring at me."

Just then one of the lights started to blink.

Mike sighed. "Hold it a second, Gloria. I'll be right with you." He plugged in the line. "Acme Service. May I help you?"

It was a woman Mike was convinced was a hooker, who gave the service number to her johns. He relayed the numbers of five men who had called earlier that evening.

"I'm sorry," said Mike after switching back to Gloria. "I'm afraid it's going to continue like this. Maybe we better—"

"I never answered your question," Gloria interrupted. "About what room I'm in." She paused, and when she spoke, her voice was little more than a whisper. "Why don't you come out and see?"

"Tonight?"

"*Why not* tonight? Arthur's gone. We'll have this whole big house to ourselves."

"I don't know," said Mike. "Don't you think it's sort of a risk?"

She laughed. "Depends on what you're afraid of."

"You know what I mean. You know why I gotta be careful."

"You call meeting at your apartment 'being careful'?"

"That's different. There's no one there but me. And no one watching. Don't you have a maid who comes every morning?"

"Tomorrow is her day off. I'm here all by myself." The sensuality in her voice communicated so well over the phone that Mike felt he was already there beside her. "Come on out, Michael. *Tonight.*"

He knew that he should say no. It was a risk he could not afford to take. Medieval though the restrictions of parole might be, they were still enforced. And that tight-ass McCarthy would love nothing better than to catch him on some violation. Seeing Gloria at his own apartment was dangerous enough. But at her husband's house—that was really tempting fate.

"There's an eleven-o'clock train. You can be here by midnight."

Then again, he really would love to see her. They had met three months before, at a cast party for an Off-Broadway play. A friend of Mike's was in the production and had invited him to the party. Gloria's husband was one of the backers of the play. He noticed her as soon as she arrived. She was wearing a tight yellow dress cut almost to the waist, and with her reddish hair and voluptuous body, she reminded him of Ann-Margret. He had kept a picture of Ann-Margret underneath the mattress in his Walkill prison cell, using it to arouse his imagination every night after lock-up. The actress was a source of inspiration for close to a year and a half. Seeing her look-alike standing across the room was like having his fantasy come to life.

Maybe he was still imagining things, but he thought she seemed bored by her considerably older cigar-smoking husband. In any case, when the man left to freshen their drinks, Mike made his move. Something about her eyes told him he should approach her with humor. He walked over and introduced himself as John Garfield.

"It's about time you got here," she said totally deadpan. "I've been waiting all night."

"I didn't catch the name," said Mike.

She smiled. "Lana Turner. You know. *The Postman Always Rings Twice.*"

They spoke briefly, feeling one another out, until her husband returned with some friends. Mike discreetly excused himself. But later in the evening he noticed her smiling at him from across the room. And as she was about to leave with her husband, she came over and shook his hand, leaving a slip of paper in his palm.

"Remember the postman," it said on the paper. Underneath was her phone number and the best time to call.

How many times had they gotten together since then? By now close to a dozen, and each date more memorable than before, what with the high-power grass she always brought as a gift, her sense of imaginative play, and her abundant energy undiminished by a husband thirty years her senior. Mike knew much of the attraction was sexual, an acting-out of his still-potent prison fantasy. But how much of the appeal was also the danger, the risk they were both taking by seeing one another? Despite his previous bad luck, Mike knew he was still turned on by risks. It was part of his nature.

Gloria's marriage made her even more desirable. Because of her husband back in Greenwich, their affair was all play and no responsibility. Mike had no interest in a more demanding relationship, the sort that included three-A.M. phone calls and heart-to-heart talks about "Who-am-I" conflicts and "Our future together." He was uncomfortable with too much intimacy, reluctant to let someone get close. It was several years since he'd been emotionally involved with a woman, a guitar player from one of his classes at City. After being in prison, where he was forced to be constantly on guard, defensively independent, he now found it hard to open himself up. He handled his problems by himself. He was not ready to share them with anyone else, much less take on any of theirs.

That's what he liked about Gloria. She made absolutely no demands upon him, other than an occasional request in bed, with which he willingly complied. She felt no necessity to tell him her innermost thoughts, or even what her day had been like. There was no past and no future between them. Just an intense and lusty present.

He was excited now, after hearing her voice, thinking of the two of them alone in that huge Connecticut home she had talked about, with its several bedrooms, sauna, and sunken bath. Remembering the games they had played in his tiny studio apartment—some of them went on for hours, utilizing costumes she brought, and different-colored wigs, the two of them acting out various roles—he could not begin to imagine what the night had in store. Strip poker in the living room? Naked hide and seek in the attic? Or a four-course meal served by candlelight in the master bedroom? With Gloria, anything was possible. She might come to the door fully dressed or in a mink coat with nothing underneath. The element of surprise was part of her charm and why he looked forward so much to seeing her.

Closing his eyes, he could see her lying sideways on the bed, one arm behind her head, the other draped languidly at her side, and him slowly approaching from across the room, eager to rub his hands over her breasts, her trim hips and thighs, the soft curve of her ass. He thought of how good she was with her lips, her hands, and ...

"Will you meet me at the train?"

"It's only a fifteen-minute walk. I'd rather wait for you here. Spend the time getting ready."

Three phones rang while Mike wrote down the directions. He ignored all of them.

Hardy guessed what was happening from the look on Mike's face. "Now *you's* the one ought to be singin'!" he called from down the line. "Let them bells ring!"

It took Mike fifteen minutes by bus to get from the Acme office over to Grand Central Station. He wanted to bring Gloria a present in return for the grass she always brought him. Deciding on a bottle of wine for a gift, he went into the package store on the main level. He was not very knowledgeable about wine, having drunk it only as a kid at annual Passover dinners and at his brother's wedding out on Long Island. The white-haired clerk saw him looking blankly at the bottles.

"Can I help you?" he said in a voice that reminded Mike of Barry Fitzgerald from some late-night movie.

"I'm trying to decide what kind of wine to buy for a friend."

"Red or white? Which do you prefer?"

"Doesn't matter," Mike said with a shrug. "It's a gift. I just want it to be good. My friend's got very good taste."

"I have just the thing for you," said the clerk, his reddish complexion suggesting he had probably tried them all. He reached for a bottle on a nearby shelf. "Beaujolais Villages-Jadot," he said. "It's from France. One of the best red wines for the price."

"How much is it?" said Mike.

"Four ninety-nine. Five forty-five with the tax. Believe me, it's worth every penny."

"I'll take it. Can you wrap it for me? Like I said, it's a gift."

"Be delighted. Will there be anything else?"

"No thanks. That'll be it."

The clerk carefully removed the price tag from the store's label on the back of the bottle. He then put the bottle in a gift box. "I know your friend will enjoy it," he said as he gave Mike his change and put the box into a paper bag. "It's got class, know what I mean?"

"Thanks again," said Mike, turning to go.

"Anytime at all," the man said with a wink. "Come back and see us."

Mike still had forty-five minutes to kill before the train. Rather than hang around the waiting room, he went out to a bar on Forty-second Street, right across from the Daily News Building. He could tell as soon as he entered that it was a clubhouse for reporters. A dozen or so middle-aged men, eyes red with fatigue and three or four Scotches, their suits wrinkled and ties undone, huddled together at the bar. They laughed uproariously at one another's jokes.

Mike took a seat at the far end of the bar, away from the noise. He was on his second beer when he felt a tap on his shoulder. He turned around to face a tall light-haired woman wearing well-cut jeans and a navy-blue turtleneck sweater. It was either because she was tired—the skin drawn on her sculptured, Indian-like face, the almond eyes less brilliant than usual—or because Mike was so preoccupied, thinking of Gloria, less than an hour away, but he did not recognize her at first.

"I thought that was you, Mike," she said, and it was the sound of New England in her voice, with its hint of boarding school, Vassar, and obvious money that made her instantly familiar. It was three years since he had seen her, but it was hard to forget one of the few women, and certainly the only attractive one, he had seen while in prison.

"Susan," he said, getting up from his seat. "Christ, I didn't recognize you."

"I'm sure I'm a mess. I just got off work. I'm across the street now, working for the Daily News."

"Is that right? A reporter, huh?"

"Been with them for more than a year. Mostly down in Washington. Finally got promoted to the big city."

"Congratulations. Sit down."

"Let me buy you a drink," said Susan.

"Let me buy you one," Mike insisted. "I promised I would. Remember?"

Susan nodded with a smile.

They sat on adjoining stools. She ordered another beer for Mike and a straight Scotch for herself.

"How long have you been in New York?" he asked.

"Actually, only a month. Soon as I got settled, I planned to look you up."

Mike grinned. "I always thought you'd end up a reporter."

"I didn't. I was planning to become a professor." She laughed. "Don't you remember? Sociology?"

"How could I forget? What with that project you were working on at college. And with us prisoners as your guinea pigs. You gave me a headache with all your questions. . . . What was the food like? What kind of training was I getting? What did I do for sexual release?" He laughed. "As if I was gonna tell you."

Susan also laughed. "You handled yourself pretty well. Yours were the best answers I got."

"You just didn't expect to find brains in Walkill. And you were right. There weren't too many."

Their drinks arrived. Mike touched his beer mug to her glass of Scotch. "It's great seeing you. And here's to the brightest reporter who ever wore pants in a New York City pressroom."

Susan looked at him strangely. "What's that supposed to mean?"

"I'm referring to your fellow newsmen," he said, motioning to the clubhouse scene down the bar. "If that's your local competition," he added with a wink, "my money's on you."

Susan smiled. "And to the next Al Pacino."

Mike lowered his mug in surprise. "How did. . . ."

"Drink up," she insisted. "It's a toast. Dammit."

She downed most of her Scotch to half of his mug.

"You're wondering how I know about your acting," she said, anticipating the question.

"It's not exactly headline news," said Mike. "Nor back-page, for that matter."

"You promise you won't be mad?"

"About what? That you've been here a month, and already you're checking up on me? I thought you finished that project at school."

"I thought I'd scout out the terrain before I came calling," Susan said with a grin.

"Well, how do you know so much about me?"

"I've got friends in court," she said, still grinning.

"You mean like that lawyer you wanted me to see?"

"That lawyer you *wouldn't* see, is more like it."

"I didn't need yours. I had one of my own."

"Louis Nizer he wasn't. I was just concerned because I thought you got screwed. You shouldn't have been there in the first place."

"No matter. I'm out now. Two years, I've been on the streets."

"I know," said Susan. "And you've got six more months of parole."

"I'm impressed," said Mike. "You don't miss a trick."

"You might say I've been spying on you. Quietly, as it were."

"Is there any other way?"

Susan smiled. "I think I've done pretty well in a week."

Mike nodded. "I hope they've given you the gossip column. You're a natural."

"Talking about gossip, how's Joey Demarko?" she asked. "Your friend in the next cell?"

"Friend? Joey Demarko?"

"You know what I mean. Didn't you tell me he was one of the few inmates you could trust?"

"That may be so, but we were hardly bosom buddies."

"What's he up to? Do you have any idea?"

"Last I heard, he was still running numbers down on Sullivan Street. Guy's allergic to legit work. He won't be long on the streets."

"Do you see him at all?"

"I'm on parole, remember. We ex-cons can't know one another."

"That's too bad," said Susan. "I always liked him."

Mike grinned. "You want his number?"

"*That* much I didn't like him."

"The only one from inside I ever miss is Stoneman."

"Stoneman? Who's he?"

"Don't you remember? I told you about him. He's the one who thought of me as his son. Always telling me prison was no place for a Jew."

"Oh, yeah. That old guy. Is he out yet?"

"We got released the same day. Far as I know, he's up in Boston with his wife." Mike sipped his beer. "How come *you're* not married?"

"How do you know I'm not?"

"I don't see a ring. Girl like you would wear one."

She made a face. "What do you mean, 'girl like me'?"

"A girl with your background, I mean. Boarding Schools. Summers in Europe. C'mon," he said with a wink. "Don't tell me you don't want a ring?"

Susan sighed. "What is this? More crap about 'postdebutante slumming'? I heard enough of that from you inside."

Mike laughed. "All I ever said was that Walkill Prison was no place to find a Yalie."

"You assumed I was looking."

Mike shrugged. "Maybe I was wrong."

It was either from the Scotch or the conversation, but Susan's face was now without its earlier pallor. Animated, her eyes bright, she looked like the energetic Vassar student he remembered. Mike had always found her attractive, and with an ingenuous sort of charm. He thought of her like a sister, and he enjoyed their weekly meetings as a rare opportunity to relax. They were held in one of the prison classrooms, and before leaving his cell he always made sure that his hair was combed and that he was wearing the cleanest of his three prison uniforms.

She was his only regular contact with the outside, and in addition to her company, he appreciated the books, magazines, and newspapers she always brought for him. And of course the cigarettes.

"Prison money," she always said, proud of her knowledge, as she handed him three packs of Camels. "Don't want you to have to borrow." She knew that borrowing in prison demanded repayment in only one way. Becoming the lender's personal "old lady," or if you refused, finding yourself cornered in the showers and forced to bend over for the troops.

Mike was grateful for all that she did. "I owe you, Susan," he told her one day. "Maybe someday I'll pay you back."

It was nice seeing her again. But of course it was different now that he was out from inside. And he was not sure what she expected from him.

"Listen. I'm invited to a party tonight. It's in the Village, right near where you . . ." She caught herself in mid-sentence.

"Near where I live," said Mike. "You really *have* been investigating me."

"I'm sorry," she said, though not really meaning it.

He patted her on the cheek. "I'd love to come, but I'm afraid I've got an appointment." He looked at his watch. "Right this minute, matter of fact."

Mike finished his beer in one gulp. He got up to go.

"Will you call me sometime?" Susan asked. "I'd love to see you. Maybe we could have dinner. I'm a pretty good cook."

"I might just take you up on that."

"I bet you don't even remember my last name."

"Draper," said Mike without hesitation. "Susan Draper. You're not the only one with a good memory."

"I see that."

"But you better give me one of your cards, because I'm sure you're unlisted."

"How did you know?" she said, opening her pocketbook. "Both about the cards and the unlisted number?"

"A lot of us are good natural reporters," said Mike, smiling. "Although some of us don't get paid." He took the card she offered, and put it in his wallet. "Take care," he said. "I'll be seeing you."

"I hope so," said Susan.

As he was leaving, Mike thought that someday soon he would call her. Why not? She looked as good as before. And she was fun to be with, even if she was a bit pushy. Maybe they would get together for lunch.

But once on the street, Mike immediately forgot about Susan Draper as he ran the block and a half back to Grand Central Station. Right now he was looking forward to being with Gloria, and he caught the eleven-o'clock train to Greenwich with not a minute to spare.

9

Dressed in a cashmere bathrobe, and sipping a Scotch, Markham was watching *Hawaii Five-O* on television. He always got a kick out of police shows. They were so totally unbelievable. After all his years as a prosecutor, working side by side with the police, he had yet to meet a cop who solved cases like Columbo, or who was as self-righteous as Baretta. The guy McGarrett in Honolulu was the worst of the lot. He never seemed to eat or sleep or to have any private life at all. Wind him up, and he bring criminals to justice. An absolutely compulsive cop. And the way he telephoned policemen in Europe and Japan for information, not only calling them by their first names, but actually receiving their assistance. What the hell world was he living in?

Markham got up and turned off the set. He had hoped McGarrett's intensity, the way he yelled "Book 'em!" after each arrest, would help him relax. No chance. He hadn't even followed the episode. He was as preoccupied as he had been all week.

Nevertheless, in many respects it had been a good week. Everything at work was going smoothly. As expected, the Connolly verdict had produced a daily barrage of phone calls that even now, several weeks later, would not let up. If it wasn't some clubhouse politico wanting to have lunch, it was a recent law-school graduate suddenly inspired to work for his office. Though the phone ringing off the hook created a nightmare for Jennifer, Markham was delighted by the response. It was gratifying, being sought after—whether by newspaper interviewers, ambitious job-seekers, or political opportunists. It didn't matter that he had no intention of exploiting his popularity in the future.

He was determined to do a good job until he resigned. Consequently his assistant Sherman's case against a West Side rapist was another source of satisfaction. The case was progressing remarkably well, with six separate victims promising to testify against the accused.

Markham was continuing to see Billy three times a week. He and Leslie were barely on speaking terms now, exchanging only a slight nod as he brushed by at the door. Fortunately, she had been out at her women's meetings the last two evenings he visited.

Still, though everything else was going along well, Markham was constantly preoccupied. Whether he was dictating a letter to Jennifer, demonstrating a correct lateral pass to his son, or watching mindless police shows on television, his thoughts were someplace else.

It had started the night after the "accident." He had never felt more alert and exhilarated. Sleeping was out of the question. It was as if he'd shot straight amphetamine in a vein. The energy pulsating through his limbs was even greater than after the Nistico conviction. Like always after a victory, he rewarded himself with the customary bottle of champagne, Dom Perignon '68, downed ceremoniously to the strains of Miles Davis on the stereo. All that was lacking to make the celebration complete was a photo of the defendant on the table before him.

Markham had gone out at midnight for a late edition of the *News*. The *Post* had carried only a brief mention of the "accident," a three-paragraph article buried inside.

But true to form, the *News* played it up big. It was a page-two story, with a picture of a newspaper boy on a bike pointing to the spot where Angela was hit. The picture meant nothing to Markham. What caught his attention, and what he underlined in red back in his apartment, rereading the sentence in between sips of champagne, was the following: "*Angela Nash is survived by her brother, Dr. Martin Greene, of Manhasset, New York.*"

Markham thought of all the people who would miss Angela Nash: her neighbors, her students at school, the women with whom she played bridge on alternate Wednesday nights.

From what he had learned, she was apparently a very likable woman, and he was sure there were many who would miss her, mourn her, and generally feel a loss in their lives. He knew all about loss. Damn right. He could match them in spades.

Markham knew it was her brother who would lose the most. He wondered how the doctor on Long Island had reacted, hearing of the death of his only living relative. Markham wondered if he cried.

The image of a doctor in tears had remained with him since, providing him considerable satisfaction. Yet its glowing effect had faded in time. Delight in the doctor's suffering was replaced in the last few days by an uneasiness he was unable to explain. He was irritable on the job. He complained to his chauffeur for driving him too slowly to work, and he even bitched at Jennifer for the way she was dressed.

"Would you mind buttoning up your blouse a little?" he said when she leaned over his desk to hand him a memo, displaying herself in the manner he had previously enjoyed.

Jennifer blushed. "I'm sorry, Mr. Markham. I didn't know it bothered you."

"This is an office," he said sternly.

Then there was the fight he had with Leslie over the phone. It was the previous Saturday evening, after spending the day playing football with Billy. Back in his apartment, he'd felt suddenly compelled to call her.

"Leslie," he said when she answered, "where were you when I dropped Billy off? I don't like leaving him alone."

"I told you. I had a meeting with a client."

"You're a rotten mother, Leslie. And you always have been."

"We'll let the judge decide that."

"If this goes to court, you don't have a chance. Billy's going to live with me."

"Why are you saying all this? What's the point? If that's all you've called for, then good-bye." She hung up.

What *was* the point? Why *had* he called? And why was he being so generally hostile to everyone around him, and feeling so nervous and depressed? It was such a precipitate change from the elation he felt following the murder, like an abrupt withdrawal from some kind of narcotic high.

It occurred to him briefly that maybe it was guilt he was

feeling, guilt for the murder of Angela Nash. *Absolutely not.* After what they had done to him, he had every right in the world. This was something he had to do in order to live with himself. The problem was, there were others involved besides Martin Greene. And he would never feel totally satisfied until all those responsible had been reached.

He would feel better again after tonight. He was convinced of that. The champagne was already chilling in the refrigerator.

His planning for tonight was by no means as elaborate as it had been for Angela Nash. He was going to wear his favorite leather jacket and corduroy slacks, as it didn't matter whether or not she recognized him. And he was going to drive his own car. Though, as before, he had driven and timed his exact route, he did not have to be as precise about his arrival. He just had to make sure she was alone when he got there, and that it was not so late that she would refuse to come to the door.

He had decided yesterday that he would leave precisely at ten-thirty, that he would take the Henry Hudson Parkway up to the Merritt Parkway, and that he would drive at a leisurely fifty miles an hour. He even knew exactly where he would park, on a dead-end road no more than a hundred yards from her house.

Markham unlocked his file and took out his gun. It was a licensed Smith & Wesson .38 Centennial, which he bought following the Nistico conviction. There had been rumors from police-department informers about a revenge contract out on his life. Markham wasn't surprised. He could easily imagine some Mafia hothead out to make a "rep" by gunning for him. Just let any of them try. He was ready for them.

The Centennial was an ideal gun to carry for self-defense. It was compact, light, and with a two-inch barrel, tapered sight, and shrouded hammer that would not snag on a pocket when hurriedly removed. It fit snugly inside his coat. The gun fired standard .38 Special cartridges which could easily kill a man at up to thirty feet.

Markham had learned to fire the gun at the police-department range. He kept up his proficiency through weekly target practice. As recently as two days ago he scored ninety-five out of a possible one hundred.

He loaded the gun with five cartridges and carried it with him to the bedroom. It occurred to him that tonight would be the first time he fired the gun at a human being. He wondered if it would feel any different.

Something gnawed at him as he was getting dressed and ready to leave. He didn't know what it was, and yet it stayed with him as he descended in the elevator and waited for the attendant to bring him his Porsche. It wasn't until he was almost to Yonkers that it hit him. He and McGarrett from *Hawaii Five-O*. There was little difference between them. They both had the same intensity, the same obsessive drive. *Wind him up and he brings criminals to justice.*

I'm as unbelievable as he is, Markham thought, looking at his reflection in the rearview mirror. "Book 'em!" he said out loud. He broke out in uncontrollable laughter, feeling a rush of self-confidence.

Gloria Thompson was busy preparing for Mike. She took shaved ice from the freezer and filled the silver ice bucket at the bar. She made two stacks of long-playing records from the collection in the den. One pile—Charlie Mingus, and Ray Charles—was for the stereo in the living room. The other assortment—Sinatra and Peggy Lee—she took to the bedroom upstairs. She selected two scented candles from a dressing-room drawer. Jasmine she placed near the sauna. Pine on a shelf by the bath. Her auburn hair hanging loosely at her back, she moved about the house with a dancer's grace. She wore ballet slippers on her feet.

Gloria was naked under her red robe. She liked the feel of silk against her body as she moved. Soft and luxurious, the way it clung to her breasts and was tight between her legs helped put her in a sensual mood. It was a trick she had learned from four years of marriage. A silk robe. Dim lights. Peggy Lee. A joint or two when Arthur wasn't looking. All these aids were helpful if your husband, just by himself, failed to turn you on.

It wasn't Arthur's fault, really. He did his best to accommodate her. What could she expect from a man old enough to be her father? She knew when she married him what she was getting herself into. Arthur had certainly made no attempt to delude her. Even from the beginning.

"I'm what we used to call a straight shooter," he said, at the party where they met. "After thirty years in the military"—he was a retired major—"and now what seems like a century in business, I've learned to speak my mind. I'm a widower. I've got two losers for sons, neither of whom would bother sending me a Christmas card COD, and frankly, goddammit, I'm lonely. Miss, I'd like to see you again."

Arthur Thompson had charm, a great deal of money, and he was gentle besides. Gloria, in turn, was tired of men who were magical in bed, only to disappear at the very mention of marriage. What's more, with the injury to her heel ending her modern-dancing career, she had no plans for the future, and she was scared. When after a three-month courtship Arthur asked her to be his wife, she agreed without hesitation. With Arthur, Gloria figured she had the best of all worlds. A dignified, companionable husband who took her traveling to Europe and bought her anything she wanted. And the time and the freedom to get for herself what little he could *not* provide.

Gloria was sure Arthur knew of her affairs. He was too bright, too realistic a man not to be aware of his own limitations. He had even hinted at it once or twice. "You make me happy, Gloria. I love you very much. I want *you* to be happy. Any way you can. Do you understand?"

Though unselfish, he was still a man, and Gloria did not want to hurt his pride. She never admitted to seeing other men—mainly because he never asked—and the afternoons in New York were always explained as shopping excursions, theater matinees, and luncheons with old friends from the dance company.

Besides, once every week to ten days, depending upon business at the bank and how tired Arthur was, Gloria did what was necessary to work up passion for her husband. She did the same things she was doing now, with the records, the candles, even the wine. The difference was that with Mike none of these aids were essential. Tonight they would serve as extra added attractions.

She turned on the sauna so it would have a chance to warm up. She then walked through the house, making sure all the blinds were drawn on the windows. Though the closest neighbor was a quarter mile down the road, some of the windows were visible from the street, and there was no sense taking a chance. It would be fun walking around naked. She pictured Mike standing before her, with his muscular arms, his tight stomach, the line of brown hair that ran from his chest all the way down to between his legs. She loved looking at him. Maybe she'd get him to do a striptease for her. She'd lie back on the couch with a glass of wine and a lit joint as he slowly, ever so slowly took off his clothes. Why not take their time? They had all night together. It was going to be fabulous.

She looked at the hall clock in anticipation. The clock said eleven-fifteen.

Gloria was listening to Ray Charles sing "Unchain My Heart," and sipping a glass of white wine, when the doorbell rang. The train must have been early for a change, she thought, putting down her glass. Either that, or Mike ran from the station. No doubt he was as eager as she. She plumped up the pillow on the couch and took a last look around the room. Everything seemed ready. She took a sip of wine before going to the door.

But it was not Mike whom she greeted. Gloria Thompson was startled by the sight of the blond stranger. She quickly closed her robe.

"I'm sorry if I surprised you," the man said softly.

"Well, I wasn't exactly expecting . . ." She folded her arms at her chest.

"I feel terrible about disturbing you. But I'm afraid my car is stuck down the road, and yours is the only house around."

"You want to use the telephone? Is that it? . . . The problem is, I'm alone here. You understand?"

"I know exactly how you feel," the man said gently. "I hate to impose on you this way. But what else can I do?" He smiled. "Believe me, it's cold out there tonight." He opened up his gloved hands for emphasis.

It was partially the man's earnest display of frustration that disarmed her. Gloria could certainly sympathize with his predicament. But even more, it was his gentleness of manner, the softness of his voice, and the kind look on his handsome face that convinced her the man was no threat. All in all, he was very persuasive.

"Okay," she said, opening the door. "Come on in. But

you'll have to make it fast." She was worried that Mike might arrive and get the wrong idea. No use starting their night on a misunderstanding. "You can use the phone in the kitchen."

"Thanks a lot. I really appreciate this."

In the bright fluorescent light of the kitchen, the man looked vaguely familiar to Gloria.

"Don't I know you from somewhere?"

"I doubt it. I don't live around here." His smile was warm and sincere. "Can I trouble you once more for a phone book?"

"Of course. I'm sorry. It's here in the drawer."

Gloria started across the room. She got halfway to the drawer.

"Please stay where you are," the man said in a voice as soft as before.

"What do you mean?" Gloria turned to face him.

"I mean turn around."

She was momentarily speechless, staring at the gun in his hand. Finally the words came. "Jesus Christ! Am I dumb!"

"Believe me, it's not your fault," he said in a controlled voice.

"All right. Let's cut the crap. What do you want?"

"I asked you to turn around."

"What for?"

"Just do as I say."

Gloria shook her head.

"Do yourself a favor, Mrs. Thompson."

"So you know my name. You didn't just pick this house because it was big."

"I'm sorry." There was a touch of resignation in the man's voice, like a father about to discipline his child.

"*You're* sorry? What does that make me?"

"I'll ask you once more. Would you please turn around?"

Whether out of stubbornness or the paralysis of fear, Gloria again refused.

The man shook his head. There was a disappointed look on his face, like somehow she had let him down. "Have it your own way."

He aimed the gun at her left breast.

Gloria Thompson had no opportunity to react. Not even a chance to say she thought she knew who he was, recognition having bubbled up somewhere amidst the fear. The last thing she could do was wonder, wonder why she was dying, and what the man she had seen on the six-o'clock news could possibly have against her.

10

Mike was one of three passengers who got off the train at Greenwich, Connecticut. The other two were businessmen commuters returning home from a late night at the office. Attaché cases brushing against the sides of well-tailored suits, they hurried off to their cars parked in the nearby lot. A solitary taxi was waiting at the foot of the platform, its engine idling. The driver eyed Mike expectantly.

Did he have the guts to risk taking a taxi to her house? It was an intriguing idea. "I'm going to the home of Arthur Thompson," he'd say from the back seat. "Over on Winding Court. Do you know where it is? . . . You do, huh? You take Mr. Thompson home from the station. . . . Yeah, he's a hell of a nice guy. . . . You heard he was out of town? One of your partners drove him to the airport?"

As if the cabdriver wouldn't broadcast it over his radio soon as he dropped Mike off. "Guess what Thompson's little lady is up to? Just wait until I tell the old man. If that ain't worth a good tip, I don't know what the hell is."

The driver was still gazing in his direction. Mike ignored him as he hurried past. He tried to look like he knew where he was going, as if he'd been here a hundred times before.

According to the directions Gloria had given him, he was to turn right at the road in front of the train station. Broadview Plaza, it was called. Half a mile on that, and then turn left onto Stonybrook Road. He'd know it from the modern-looking school straight ahead. From there it was a quarter mile to Winding Court, and another quarter mile to the house. Just a brief walk, she said over the phone. Fifteen minutes at most. *"I'd rather wait for you here. Spend the time getting ready."*

She was right. It was better this way. More exciting. Knowing she was at that very moment busy preparing for him, laying out God-knows-what sensual playthings, and planning any number of surprises—well, that made walking easily worthwhile. He wondered what she'd be wearing when she came to the door—her silky red robe, those black lounging pajamas, or perhaps that new pink camisole number with the open lace front she'd worn at his apartment the last time they'd met. Having come straight from work, he himself had no time to change. Fortunately he was wearing an outfit he knew she enjoyed. Faded tight blue jeans, brown Frye boots, and an open-collar Levi shirt. He'd undo another button just before he got there. Then he'd be perfect, with just the sort of look that always turned her on. But right now it was too chilly, and he buttoned up his old pea coat and turned up the collar against the cold.

The walk itself added to his anticipation. It was an adventure, finding his way in a town he had heard about but never seen, and then, of course, him being the only one on the street.

He thought about the people he knew who'd grown up in towns like this. Wendy, that girl from his acting class. She was from some suburb in New Jersey. And Susan Draper. She was from somewhere around here. New Canaan or Darien. He could see her growing up in a house like this one he was passing.

There it was. Winding Court. He had a quarter mile to go. It was darker here, on this private road, with fewer streetlights and houses. The only house he could see was set back far from the road behind a heavily wooded entrance and beyond a long driveway that was lined with shrubs. On the other side of the road was a stone wall in front of a huge overgrown field that went on as far as he could see. That must be the wild-life refuge Gloria had mentioned.

Maybe he and Gloria could take a walk there tomorrow. She could pack a picnic lunch and a blanket for the two of them to lie on. If it were warm enough out . . . That was one place they had never done it before—outside. Lord knows they had exhausted all the possibilities in his studio apartment. The bed, the couch, the bathtub, standing up in the hall. She had once suggested going up on the roof, but before they got up there, it started to rain. Mike was relieved. He was worried someone from a nearby building would see them and call a cop. *Indecent exposure*, along with *adultery*. That was violation enough for McCarthy to send him right back inside. The parole officer would probably try to coax Gloria into calling it rape. Nothing would surprise Mike from that son of a bitch.

He felt his excitement growing, the closer he came to the house. He stopped by the side of the road to light a cigarette, clutching the bottle of wine under his arm and cupping the match in his palm against the breeze. He wanted to be as relaxed as possible when he arrived, in a mood to fully enjoy what Gloria had planned. Nothing would spoil the night more than if his enthusiasm got the better of him. This had to be it up ahead. He took a last drag on the cigarette before grinding out the butt under his heel.

She said it was the second house on the road, and unless he'd missed one, which was doubtful, considering their size, then he was fast approaching the home of Mr. and Mrs. Arthur Thompson. Like the house he passed, this too was set far back from the road, at the end of a long driveway. A dozen or more weeping-willow trees impressively lined the drive. The house was three stories high, and reminded Mike of some of the private red-brick homes along the Promenade in Brooklyn Heights. But this was much bigger, with three chimneys, and what looked like a porch on the far side, next to what was probably the garden. He couldn't see them from here, but he knew that the pool and the guest house were around to the rear.

From where he stood on the street, Mike could see the shades drawn on the windows. There were lights on in most of the downstairs rooms, and in two rooms of the second floor. The top floor was dark.

Mike had not seen a car since turning onto Winding Court. But just to be safe, he looked up and down the road before entering the driveway. There was no one in sight. The only things moving were the branches of the trees on the far side of the road, and the dead leaves falling slowly to the ground. For someone not used to country roads at midnight, especially when an overcast sky blocked out the moon and the stars, the scene was somewhat unnerving. He was glad that he was finally here, and that Gloria was waiting inside.

Two wrought-iron carriage lamps illuminated the front door. Using the glass in one of the lamps for a mirror, Mike combed his hair. He wiped his feet on the mat and undid the next button on his shirt before ringing the bell. He held the bag with the bottle of wine behind his back.

Gloria was slow in coming.

Maybe she didn't hear the bell. He rang again, stepping up next to the door and putting his ear against the crack. He could hear a quiet two-tone chime someplace far off in the house. No strident New York buzzer for a place like this. Quiet though it may be, Gloria was no doubt used to it, and would even be listening for its sound.

So where was she? In the shower, perhaps? No, she wouldn't have waited until now to get herself ready. That was the whole point of his walking from the train. He stepped back from the door to take a look through a nearby window. The shades were drawn too tightly to see much of anything. A lamp shade. Edge of a table. Nothing to suggest what was taking Gloria so long.

Mike rang again, listening closely for her footsteps in the hall. There was something else now, besides the bell, a strange clicking noise he hadn't noticed before.

Click . . . click . . . click . . .

It was a . . . scratching of some sort.

Click . . . click . . . click . . .

But a scratching by whom? What? Or was he just hearing things? Was it his actor's fertile imagination, spurred by the darkness of the night, the wind blowing through the trees, and the fact that Gloria was purposely letting him stand out there all alone?

Purposely letting him stand there. So that was it. Another one of her games. She was obviously trying to scare him, to frighten him as best she could. Was there a better way to begin? First have him walk from the train. *"I'd rather wait for you here. Spend the time getting ready."* Getting *him* ready was more like it. She knew that a city boy would be unsettled by the midnight walk through the country. And when an undercurrent of fear started to make him nervous, add to it by not coming to the door. Leave him standing there all alone.

Click . . . click . . . click . . .

107

If Gloria thought he was going to fall for this . . . Mike chuckled. He had to hand it to her. She was as imaginative as ever, always trying to outdo herself. Here he had wondered what she'd be wearing when she came to the door. What kind of sexy outfit. Surprise. She wasn't even coming. He was obviously expected to let himself in and go looking for her. Midnight hide and seek was tonight's game, folks. And the playing field was a house he'd never been in before. With a sauna, three sunken baths, and Lord knows how many bedrooms. She could be waiting in any of them, in closets, pantries, or behind the tables or chairs. This was actually kind of exciting, now that he thought of it, even more of a turn-on than auburn wigs, black lace bikinis, and pink camisoles with unbuttoned fronts.

Gloria was some fantastic woman. Just wait until he found her.

Mike turned the doorknob. The door was unlocked, and it opened with hardly a push. Slowly he stepped inside.

The light was off in the hallway, and it took a moment for Mike to find the switch. The hallway was long and narrow, leading to what appeared to be the living room straight ahead, and to what was probably the kitchen off to the left. The kitchen door was closed.

Mike looked above him, to the gleaming chandelier suspended from the twelve-foot ceiling. It was like an inverted Christmas tree, with five concentric circles of light. He had never seen such a lamp in a private home. But nothing about Arthur Thompson's home could surprise him. Not the paintings on the wall—starkly abstract and handsomely framed, like something hanging at the Museum of Modern Art. Not the well-polished parquet floors, and not the oriental rug that ran the length of the hall and was so deeply padded that it totally muffled his footsteps.

All he could hear was the scratching noise he had heard from outside. The noise was getting gradually louder as he proceeded down the hall.

CLICK . . . CLICK . . . CLICK . . .

It was obviously coming from the living room. The closer he came, the more familiar it seemed. He knew he had heard that noise somewhere before. But where? Of course. How stupid could he be. He realized what it was as soon as he stepped into the room. The noise was a needle of a record player caught in a groove.

Mike crossed the room and began opening the teak cabinets along the far wall. He discovered a well-stocked bar, a collection of crystal, and a high-powered amplifier before finally locating the turntable. Carefully, so he wouldn't scratch the record any further, he removed the stylus from the groove. After pressing the Reject switch and bringing the turntable to a halt, he took a closer look at the record. *Ray Charles' Greatest Hits,* one of his favorite albums.

Gloria knew how much he liked it. She was apparently playing the record while waiting for him to arrive. The needle getting caught by mistake had no doubt given her ideas. Sounds a little eerie, she'd thought. Especially to someone entering a strange house. Let's give Michael a scare. He knew exactly the way her mind worked. Midnight hide and seek was the logical next step.

Now, where the hell was she? "Gloria," he called tentatively, though not really expecting her to respond. The sound of his voice accentuated the stillness of the house now that the clicking had stopped. He had never been in a place so quiet.

There was no sound at all, only his breathing, and the memory of his voice from having just called her name. The stillness made him uncomfortable, and so before continuing his search, he turned the record player back on. He kept the same record, and decided on Side A, which had "Georgia on My Mind" and "Unchain My Heart." Charles was singing "Them That Got," as Mike started looking around the room.

There was no place here for her to hide. He could see behind all the couches and chairs. Up the fireplace? No, never. The last thing Gloria would want to be was dirty, considering the game that followed hide and seek.

Rather than retrace his steps, he went out the other door of the living room into a smaller, more intimate den. Two red leather overstuffed chairs, a brown leather couch that easily cost as much as Mike spent annually on rent, and a writing desk that was dominated by a collection of pipes.

"I'm closing my eyes, Gloria. You can come out now. . . ." When he opened them, there was still no sign of Gloria's magnificent body, not even a lingering scent of her Aliage perfume.

Mike was getting a bit impatient now, and with impatience came a longing that added a certain zest to the hunt. He felt the softness of the leather couch, as though testing it for later use. Maybe this was yet another reason for the game, so that when they finally got together, he'd have already taken the grand tour of the house. Then there'd be no need for preliminaries, it was straight to the main event.

Before leaving the den, Mike took a quick look at the photos on the wall. A few were of Gloria—in a bikini on the beach, looking sexy as hell, and shopping in what looked like some Caribbean port. But most of the pictures were of her husband, Arthur. There he was with a woman, probably his first wife, and then with two teenage boys, who were obviously his sons. Mike remembered Gloria telling him that Thompson never saw his sons, at least he hadn't in the four years they'd been married. He wondered if the estrangement was because of his marriage to a woman half his age. He knew better than to discuss it with Gloria. What difference did it make anyway? It was none of his business

One more picture caught his eye. It was Arthur Thompson in a military uniform, and he was shaking hands with . . . *General Eisenhower*? He could tell it was before Ike became President, because he too was wearing a uniform. Mike knew that Thompson had been in the military before becoming a banker, but he had no idea he was this big a wheel. Christ, just look at the way Ike was grinning at him. This was not one of your everyday "pose-with-the-general" shots to hang in your office back at the Peoria National Guard. And get a load of the uniform Thompson was decked out in. He had quite a few stripes and medals of his own. Not as many as Ike of course, but he was sure playing in the same league. Thompson was without a doubt varsity material.

It made Mike a little nervous, thinking of the prominence of his absent host, and the liberties he was about to take with his not-so-absent wife. But then again, Gloria was not exactly present at the moment. There was still that one detail to worry about. Maybe in the room up ahead.

This was the dining room, and right away Mike thought he knew where she was. There wasn't much furniture here, just a big elegant table surrounded by six antique-looking chairs. Also a polished mahogany sideboard loaded with shiny silver bowls. It was the delicate silk screen in the corner of the room that drew his attention. It was painted with birds, and gave a springtime feel to the room. More important was its size. It was about six feet tall and four or five feet wide, easily big enough for a person to hide behind.

He tiptoed around the table to the side of the screen, and after poising himself, lunged behind it. "Gotcha," he yelled. But again no Gloria, only a package from the dry cleaner's and a pile of empty boxes from Bonwit Teller and Saks. The house was as quiet as before, the only sound coming from the speakers in the living room, Ray Charles' deep gravelly voice.

The far door of the dining room led back out to the hall. The stairs were straight ahead, and Mike was just about to start up. One hand was already on the banister, the other still holding the bottle of wine, when he noticed the closed door off the front entranceway, the door he had assumed led to the kitchen. There was probably a pantry, the only hiding place in a kitchen he could think of. He might as well check it out before going upstairs. Besides, he hadn't eaten since six o'clock, and maybe there were some cookies he could find. Or better yet, a bottle of beer.

He opened the door to the kitchen and fumbled for the light switch. It was inside the door to his left, almost hidden by the big two-door refrigerator.

"Gloria," he called in his best military voice. "It's me . . . Arthur. I'm home."

The kitchen was enormous. A cooking island with an exhaust fan and suspended copper hood occupied the middle of the floor. On his right was a wall of cabinets that ran the length of the room and seemed to exit out the back door directly in front of him. On the left, past the refrigerator, was a butcher-block counter, followed by the sink, dishwasher, and then an additional counter that was no doubt used as a kind of eating bar. It was a far cry from Mike's Greenwich village kitchen, which shared space with his bathtub. But did this mammoth refrigerator have as much beer as his little TV-sized model? That was the important question.

Mike put his bottle of wine on the nearby counter before opening the refrigerator door. Success. There were two Budweiser six-packs on the top shelf. That Gloria! She didn't miss a trick.

Mike pulled out a can, snapped it open with one hand, and took a healthy swig. In the excitement of the game, he hadn't realized how thirsty he was. He decided to bring the can with him as he continued the search. No, might as well start getting in the spirit of the house. In a place like this, you drank from a glass.

Mike was opening the cabinets along the right wall, looking for a glass, when he found Gloria playing dead behind the cooking island. She was lying facedown on the floor, her arms sprawled out at her sides. Her red silk robe was draped provocatively over her thighs, black ballet slippers on her feet.

"Gloria, my God! You scared me," he said with a start. "You can stop playing now, baby, before you catch cold."

Gloria didn't answer. She lay perfectly still.

What an incredible performance, he thought. She's an even better actor than I am. Lying there with her eyes closed, not moving a muscle. She must have been hiding here all this time, listening to him move around the house, waiting patiently for him to come to the kitchen and discover her. She must be awfully cold, with her bare legs against that linoleum. And yet she seemed so natural, so relaxed. She was really outdoing herself.

"Okay, Gloria, come on. Enough's enough, already," Mike said playfully as he bent down and rolled Gloria over onto her back.

Oh Jesus! . . . Mike was stunned.

He knew a gunshot wound when he saw one. He had seen a few fellow Angels end up on the wrong side of a bullet. The only difference with their wounds was that the blood had kept flowing.

But not with Gloria. The blood that had ruined her robe was just soaking into the cloth. There was no movement from her chest, no sign of flow.

Whoever had done this was obviously long gone. Mike had been in the house now for more than ten minutes, calling from one room to another. Anyone hiding there had more than enough time to surprise him, if that's what he wanted. Chances are he didn't even know Mike was coming, and had split before he arrived. But he might still be someplace near.

Without thinking, Mike sprang to his feet and rushed to the telephone. Impulsively he dialed the operator.

"Can you please connect me with the police."

"You can dial that direct, sir."

"This is an emergency, dammit. Just get me the police."

For Christ's sake, Gloria had been murdered. He had to tell the police right away. *Tell the police?* What the hell was wrong with him? Was he crazy? He couldn't tell them anything. Because if he did, how in the world was he to explain his being there? "I just came out to spend the night with Gloria. Her husband's away, you understand, and so she invited me over. I walked in and, well . . . that's how I found her. Exactly the way she is now."

They wouldn't believe a word of it. Well, maybe the part about her inviting him out there. That they might understand. But about him just happening upon her? No way. They'd grab him as a suspect faster than he could say "I had nothing to do with it." And why exactly wouldn't they believe him? Because he was an *ex-con*, that's why. A one-time loser who had served a stretch up in Walkill, and for what? Second-degree manslaughter, you say. Very interesting. Lost his temper in a fight, did he? Well, looks like he still can't control it. Just goes to show, they never should have let the guy out.

And even if they did believe him, though that certainly seemed doubtful, well, the absolute least that would happen was that he'd be declared in violation of parole. "Sleeping around, huh," McCarthy would say. "And with another man's wife. A very prominent man at that. I warned you about this, Ross. I don't have to tell you what this means."

"Greenwich Police," said the voice over the phone. "Sergeant Driscoll speaking. . . . Hello, Greenwich Police . . ."

Mike hung up the phone. He was frightened now, very frightened. He could see McCarthy's face laughing, see him scratching his scalp as he sent him back inside. He had to get out of there quickly. He had to leave this house as fast as he could. He paused only momentarily, gazing sadly at Gloria. He knew she'd understand. He turned and rushed out the back door.

It was even darker out than it had been earlier. Mike couldn't see more than a few feet in front of him. Running along the side of the house toward the driveway, he tripped on a rake handle and fell head-over-heels. Unhurt thanks to a pile of leaves, he picked himself up and continued running. He tore down the driveway and out onto the road, running almost all the way past the wildlife refuge without turning back.

He had to slow down. He had a cramp in his side, and his

lungs were aching for relief. Goddamn cigarettes, he swore to himself. *After I get back to New York, I'm quitting for good.* 'Course, he never thought he'd be running from a murder. Just his goddamn luck.

In the city there was nothing Mike was afraid of. He'd walk through the heart of Bedford Stuyvesant at two in the morning, and without carrying a weapon, not even a blade. A nighttime stroll through Central Park, just for the hell of it, didn't bother him at all. But he had to admit, these country roads really got to him, now even more than before.

Had he really walked this way earlier? And without being scared? It couldn't have been as dark then. There were no stars. No streetlights even. It was too quiet to be believed. Mike felt a sudden chill. Was that someone behind him? Someone up ahead? Calm down, he told himself. Those are your own footsteps, dummy. You're here all alone. Mike wasn't sure whether that was comforting or not. What if the murderer *were* still around? What if he'd just been waiting for him to leave?

Nervously he looked all around him. There was a car coming down the road. He could see the lights through the trees. Mike wasn't about to take any chances. He quickly stepped off the pavement into the woods. He crouched behind a tree until the lights had passed and the road was in darkness once again. Look who's playing hide and seek now. If Gloria only knew how the game had progressed.

There it was at last—Stonybrook Road. It was lighter here, which was nice in a way, but now he had to be even more on guard. He could see anybody coming, but that meant they could also see him. And face it, how many people walked the streets of Greenwich, Connecticut, at one o'clock in the morning? Not too many. He wouldn't be surprised if the cops stopped and questioned everyone they saw. That's what they supposedly did in Los Angeles, and it was probably the same thing here. Since all the residents had cars, anybody walking was obviously from out of town. And what the hell was a stranger doing here in the middle of the night? Looking to buy a house? Visiting the wildlife refuge? You gotta be kidding. Anyone on the streets was by definition up to no good. Better haul his ass in and find out what's what.

Mike couldn't afford to be third-degreed by a cop. He walked by the side of the road, remaining in the shadows as much as possible. At the first sign of a car, he darted behind a tree or a bush, whatever was handy. Fortunately, there were as few people out as there had been earlier. And if the Greenwich police were patrolling the streets, they were either invisible or on the other side of town.

Mike's big moment of panic was on Broadview Plaza, when a barking dog came bounding after him. The dog didn't seem eager to bite him. A threatening kick, and he retreated ten yards away. But he was making such a goddamn racket, Mike was sure everybody in town, including the mayor, would soon be on the scene. Luckily he spied a golf ball on someone's front lawn. The first two times he threw the ball, the dog carried it back, depositing it at his feet and barking all the louder. But when he threw the ball down the drain in the gutter, the stubborn dog stood clawing at the street as Mike hurried away.

He arrived at the train station out of breath. Despite the cool October night, his jacket was unbuttoned, and his Levi shirt was sticking to his chest.

There were four other people waiting on the platform: two sleepy railroad workers sitting on a bench with toolboxes on their laps, and a college-age couple embracing under a Marlboro sign. They were all obviously waiting for the one-twenty train to New York. Mike knew there was such a train, because he'd asked the conductor on the way out. He was concerned about the trains back to the city, just in case something unexpected happened at Gloria's. The something he imagined was her husband's flight being canceled and his returning home, at which point Mike would have headed for the nearest window. He never guessed he'd be leaving because of something like this.

Mike stood alone on the platform, smoking a cigarette. Now that he could relax, at least momentarily, it started to get to him, the impact of what had happened. Gloria was dead. Though their relationship was primarily sexual, he was extremely fond of her. He liked her humor, her spunk, her sense of life. He was going to miss her. What upset him most right now was the thought of her body lying there in the kitchen, the black ballet slippers on her feet, the red silk robe pulled up above her thighs. It bothered him that he hadn't taken the time to cover her up. That was the least he could do before leaving her there on the kitchen floor, leaving her for someone else to discover.

Who would it be? With her husband gone, it would no doubt be the maid, sometime in the morning. Oh, no, he'd forgotten. Tomorrow was the maid's day off.

Gloria was going to just lie there for two days.

After two more cigarettes, which he smoked clear to the filter, Mike made up his mind. It was the only decent thing to do. And there was very little risk for himself. The lights of the one-twenty train were approaching far down the track when he put a dime in the pay phone on the platform.

"Hello, operator. Get me the police."

"Greenwich Police. Sergeant Driscoll speaking."

"I want to report a murder," said Mike. "I have to make it fast."

Mike felt better when he got onto the train. It was fairly empty, and he took a seat by the window, lighting a cigarette as the train pulled away. He was halfway back to the city when he realized what he had done. It was the sign above the door that did it. It was an advertisement for Lancer's rosé, and it reminded him of the bottle of wine he had left in Gloria Thompson's kitchen.

11

Markham pretended to still be asleep. His hands under the pillow, his eyes firmly shut, he tried his best not to move, even now when she began rubbing his back in what she thought was a tantalizing manner. The last thing he wanted to do was to turn over and face her. She'd be smiling at him with those big blue eyes, and there'd be that look of contentment on her face. No doubt she'd want to hug him, and kiss him, and maybe even squeeze in a fast one before the alarm clock went off. He was not the slightest bit interested. All he wanted was to be alone.

The morning after was always the worst time. Waking up to a woman you didn't really care for, and having to look at her in the full light of day. It almost made the night before barely worthwhile. And it could so easily have been avoided by going to her place. Then he could always get up and leave, even in the middle of the night. Waking up alone the next day made it easy to forget about whom he'd been with.

So why had he brought her back to his own apartment? You'd think he'd know better. It was bad enough that he'd finally succumbed. The day after his trip to Greenwich he'd invited Jennifer to dinner. He had wanted her for so long, and now the timing seemed right. Gloria Thompson's murder had gone off without a hitch, and he felt like celebrating. After eating in Chinatown, they'd gone back to his place.

She looked as good naked as he'd always imagined. And the energy she displayed, whether above or below, easily matched his own. He was by no means disappointed. But once they were through, he wanted to be alone. If only he could snap his fingers and have her disappear. Why the hell had they come back here?

Her fingers were continuing, moving slowly down his back. Getting no response, she now kissed his neck and started blowing softly in his ear. She was obviously quite determined.

"What time is it?" said Markham suddenly, as if waking with a start.

"What's it matter?" she said coyly, her Southern accent painful to his ear.

"I almost forgot. I've got a breakfast appointment."

"Breakfast?" she said, surprised. "I don't remember seeing it in the book."

Markham abruptly sat up in bed. Her hand fell away from him. "Listen, Jennifer, I don't tell you everything," he said with an impatient yawn.

"What time's the appointment?" she said lazily, her hands behind her head, the sheet falling from her breasts like some *Playboy* centerfold.

"What time is it now?" He stood up and stretched, his back toward the bed.

Jennifer glanced at the clock-radio. "Seven-thirty. You set the alarm for eight."

"Dammit! What's wrong with me? The meeting's for eight. Hurry up and get dressed."

"What's the rush? I don't have to be in the office until nine." She smiled. "Remember? You work there too."

"You don't understand," said Markham, putting on his cashmere robe. "The meeting is here."

"Here?"

"Right." He turned to face her for the first time, making an effort, in spite of himself, to look affectionate. "Can you keep a secret?"

Jennifer sat up in bed. "What kind of question is that? You know I can."

He instinctively lowered his voice, as if the walls had ears. "It's another corruption case. But unlike Connolly, this one is closer to home."

"How close?" she asked.

"The police department. And it's more than a few greedy patrolmen. If what the guy coming here says is true, we may have an entire Manhattan precinct on the take. Not just lieutenants. We're talking about an *entire* command."

"My God! Which one is it?"

"I won't say. At least not yet. Wait'll I see what kind of evidence this guy brings me."

"An entire precinct! That's incredible."

"You can understand the need for secrecy," said Markham. "That's why I'm meeting the guy here rather than at the office or someplace public. . . . I hate to rush you, but you can see why it's best if I'm alone when he gets here."

"Of course," she said, jumping out of bed. "I'll leave right away. Is there time for a shower?"

"Only if you make it fast."

"You want to join me?" Jennifer said hopefully looking over her shoulder as she started across the room.

Join her in the shower? He didn't want her in the same apartment, much less the same tub. Next she'd even ask him to wash her back. "You go first," he said. "I better straighten up the house."

Markham picked up the dirty glasses and the empty champagne bottle in the living room. He was loading the dishwasher when Jennifer came into the kitchen. Thank God she finally had her clothes on. Now to get rid of her.

"Can I make you some coffee?" she asked.

"Afraid there's no time. Grab some orange juice if you want."

Jennifer poured herself a glass from the carton on the counter. She started to sit down.

"Drink up," said Markham. "This guy's going to be here any minute. . . . Come on. I'll see you to the door."

He helped her on with her coat.

"How about dinner tonight?" she asked. "I make a great chicken tempura."

"Some other time. I'll talk to you at the office."

"When do you think you'll be in?"

"Probably not much later than ten-thirty."

Jennifer smiled. "I'll see you then." She put her arms around him and kissed him on the lips. Markham politely pulled away.

"I'll see you," he said, picking up his newspaper from the mat while waiting for her to leave.

He smiled as she walked down the hall toward the elevator. He then closed and locked the door, his smile quickly vanishing. Thank God she was gone. His story had worked.

He left the paper on the hall table and went back to bed alone, setting his clock-radio for nine-thirty.

Markham was awakened by John Coltrane wailing away on the tenor sax. The radio was playing "Chasin' the Trane," and the lively piece was a perfect reflection of Markham's mood. His spirits were up, and he felt a peace of mind he hadn't experienced for months, certainly not since the visit by Charlie Wilson. He couldn't help snapping his fingers as he jumped out of bed and did a few stretching exercises before taking a shower. The hot water felt good against his chest as he washed away the traces of last night. It was like Jennifer had never been there.

After dressing and putting on water for his coffee, Markham went and retrieved the *Times* from the hall. He'd been holding off reading it until now, because he wanted to savor what he knew would be there, the public confirmation of his careful planning. He was in no hurry to be told of how flawless a job he had done. He was convinced of that already.

SLAYING IN SUBURBIA said the headline. The article was on the bottom of the front page and included a picture of the Thompson home in Greenwich. There were police cars parked in the driveway.

> Police in this wealthy suburban community outside of New York are investigating the brutal murder of a young housewife found early this morning shot to death on her kitchen floor.
>
> Her husband, retired Major Arthur Thompson, a vice-president with Citibank, had left for Dallas earlier in the evening. Informed of the murder by phone, he reportedly collapsed, and was taken to the Downtown Memorial Hospital for observation.
>
> According to Sergeant Robert Driscoll of the Greenwich Police Department, the police were notified of the murder by a "strange phone call at one-nineteen A.M." The caller, who refused to leave his name, gave only the barest of details before hanging up.

Markham reread the last paragraph with interest. An unidentified caller alerting the police? He wondered who it could be. Having learned from the newspaper of Arthur Thompson's business out of town, he'd known that Gloria would be alone. That's why he had planned for that particular night. He assumed that her body would be discovered sometime the next day by a housekeeper or neighbor. Maybe even a delivery boy. But at one A.M.? Who would be arriving at that hour?

He read further:

> The police investigation is focusing on, among other things, an un-opened bottle of wine found in the kitchen. According to Detective Sam Turner, who is in charge of the case, "the bottle appears to have been brought as a gift, and may have some connection with the mysterious phone call regarding the murder." Turner added that the fingerprints found on the front door, which are "definitely not those of the deceased," may also produce some leads.

Markham nodded to himself. The wine bottle explained it all. Why, of course. She must have been having an affair. Who else but a lover would arrive at that hour of night and be carrying a bottle of wine? Her lover must have found her in the kitchen and called the police. Considering the circumstances, he probably panicked and hung up without leaving his name.

Markham chuckled at the thought of how close he and the lover had come to crossing paths. Two hours at the most. Just went to show how even the best-laid plans could not possibly account for everything. How was he to know that Thompson's wife was fooling around? He started to laugh. He couldn't help it. If the police investigation was centering on the wine bottle, that meant the lover was the suspect. He himself hadn't left anything at the house. He was positive of that. And as for the fingerprints found on the front door? They certainly couldn't be his, as he was wearing gloves. They must also belong to the boyfriend.

Markham laughed so hard that his eyes began to tear. When the water for his coffee started to boil, he had to use two hands to pour it into the cup. Even then he spilled the cream. Why, he couldn't have planned this any better if he tried. He had succeeded in taking from Arthur Thompson the one person he was known to love best, and judging from the newspaper report, he had obviously caused him considerable pain. At the same time, someone else was taking the rap. He couldn't have wished for a better outcome. No wonder he was such a damn good prosecutor. He was an even better crook.

Markham arrived at work a little before eleven. He had a smile for everyone as he walked through the office: typists, file clerks, and other staff members with whom he never exchanged more than a few words, a "Good morning" or "Good afternoon," in the elevator, or a "Glad to see you" or "Having a good time?" at the annual Christmas party or summer picnic. He was in such a good mood that he even had a warm greeting for Roger Sullivan, an assistant who had lost his last two cases, a bank-robbery trial and an attempted-murder prosecution, to defense lawyers from Legal Aid. Markham hated to lose cases to the rival city agency. He had just yesterday reprimanded Sullivan for his poor performance.

" 'Morning, Sullivan."

" 'Morning, Mr. Markham."

"How's everything going?"

"Not bad, sir."

"Great. Keep up the good work." Markham wished he could have seen the look on Sullivan's face as he continued down the hall.

As expected, Jennifer was beaming as he approached her desk outside his door.

" 'Morning, Jennifer."

"Good morning, Mr. Markham."

He was a bit worried about her making some reference to the night before. But the crisp professional tone to her voice, without the slightest hint of undue familiarity, suggested that she knew the rewards of discretion. One was that she would keep her job, and the other was that he might invite her out again. Markham was pleased. He smiled, his eyes roaming from her face and neck to her conspicuously unbuttoned blouse.

"Were there any calls?"

"I've put the list on your desk, right next to the mail."

"Thank you, Jennifer."

"You didn't tell me how the meeting went."

"I'll talk to you about it later." Markham started for his door.

"Oh, Mr. Markham, I forgot. There are two men here to see you. They're waiting in the reception area."

"Oh, really. Who are they?"

She read from a note on her desk. "A Mr. Nugent and a Mr. Howard. They're with the Mutual of Omaha Insurance Company."

"Insurance company? Did they say what they wanted?"

"Only that it was important. They came about nine-thirty, and they've been waiting ever since."

"I see. Okay, give me about ten minutes to look over the mail, and then send them in."

Markham was reading an invitation to speak at a law-enforcement conference in Boston when Jennifer opened the door.

"Mr. Markham, the insurance agents are here now."

"Send them in," he said distractedly. He was very much interested in the invitation, and he continued reading as they entered. "Take a seat. I'll be right with you," he said, pointing to the two leather chairs in front of his desk.

When finally he looked up, it was at two middle-aged men in trim business suits. One of them had a crew cut and piercing blue eyes. He was handsome, with a lean, muscular build, and he could easily pass for an actor. The other was big and beefy, like a football lineman, and with a long nose that appeared to have figured prominently in one tackle too many. He reminded Markham of a West Side detective who, before he was transferred to desk work, was known for breaking the arms of mugging suspects on his way to locking them up.

The man with the crew cut introduced himself as Fred Nugent, and the detective look-alike was Nick Howard. Markham reached over his desk to shake both their hands. He was impressed by the firmness of their grips. Not to mention Nugent's striped Sulka tie. He didn't expect such style from a Midwestern insurance agent.

"I'm sorry to keep you waiting," he said, sitting up in his chair. "Can I get you both some coffee?"

"Your secretary already got us some," said Mr. Nugent, looking very relaxed. He crossed his legs and took out a pipe. "Do you mind if I smoke?"

"Not at all," said Markham, pushing a crystal ashtray

across his desk to within reach of the visitor. "She says you're with the Mutual of Omaha Insurance Company. Tell me, what can I do for you?"

Nugent patiently packed his pipe. He lit the tobacco and took a few contented puffs before starting to speak. "We're looking into the death of one of our policy holders. Though his death was officially ruled a suicide, his wife has contested the judgment."

Markham smiled. "For obvious reasons, I assume?"

"Of course. It was a recent policy, bought within two years, and it pays nothing in the event of suicide. We're doing a little investigation of our own in order to defend ourselves when the case comes to court."

"I understand," said Markham. "But what does this have to do with me?"

"Charlie Wilson," said Nugent abruptly. "Does that name mean anything to you?"

"Charlie Wilson . . ." said Markham. "Charlie Wilson . . ." He could see both pairs of eyes suddenly focusing on him, searching for a reaction. They expected to catch him off guard, and for him to respond without thinking. They hadn't counted on Markham's self-control, his instinct to give nothing away, whether to juries he was attempting to sway, women he wanted out of his house, or to two men who were obvious impostors, sent there to find out what he had learned.

How stupid did they think he was? He knew undercover agents when he saw them. Didn't matter who they were working for. They were always so damn agreeable. And patient. Jesus, who else would sit waiting for almost two hours, and then calmly smoke a pipe? Certainly not an insurance investigator. Few undercover agents could pull it off. There were always one or two flaws. Like that expensive silk tie that was right for the man's style, but so out-of-character for his "job." And the way they both stared as he mentioned Wilson's name. You'd think they'd be a little more subtle.

"Wilson . . . Let me think." He leaned back in his chair and gazed at the ceiling as if searching his memory. "How am I supposed to know him?" he asked, now looking directly into Nugent's penetrating blue eyes.

Nugent smiled, while puffing on his pipe. "There was a note in Wilson's diary of a meeting he had with you. On July eighteen, to be exact."

"Two weeks later he was dead," said Howard, showing for the first time that he knew how to talk.

"What did this man Wilson look like?" asked Markham, confident enough of his poker face to turn from one visitor to another. He could play the same game too, and beat them at it.

"He was in his late sixties, with thinning gray hair and a bald spot right about here," Nugent said, smiling in a too-friendly way.

"He was from Chicago," said Howard. "Maybe that helps."

Markham flashed an enlightened grin. "Chicago. Why didn't you say that earlier? Of course I remember him now. Charlie Wilson. He was here on vacation. Came in to see me. Reason I didn't remember, it was only a short social call. Five, ten minutes at the most."

"What do you mean by social?" asked Nugent with the same disarming smile. Markham could tell he was the more vicious of the two. Howard was muscle, but this one, he was the brain. If these were the men responsible for Wilson's murder, then this smiling face had been Wilson's last view on earth. Now it was here, staring at him from the very same chair Wilson had occupied only three months before. Somehow the irony amused him.

"By social, I mean precisely *that*. One of my former assistants recently moved to Chicago. He regularly played tennis with Wilson in the park. Wilson stopped by to extend his regards and to drop off an article my assistant had written. That was the extent of it."

"Can you tell us anything about his mood, his behavior, anything that might relate to his committing suicide so shortly after?" The eyes were unrelenting.

Markham didn't blink or turn away. "I'm afraid not. Like I said, I was only with him a very few minutes. I really didn't know the man at all."

"I see," said Nugent. He nodded, puffing silently on his pipe. "Well . . . I'm sorry to have taken up your time. But you understand that we have to check out every possible lead. It's the only way of closing the matter for good."

"Of course," said Markham, rising from his seat. "I regret I can't be of more assistance."

"You've been more than helpful," said Nugent, standing and extending his hand.

"Yes," said Howard, gripping Markham's hand even tighter than before, as if to hurt him for giving nothing away. "Thank you for your time."

"Not at all. Forgive me for not seeing you out. My secretary will show you the way."

With a last lingering look at Markham, the two insurance agents from Mutual of Omaha turned to leave.

"Off the record," said Markham, as they were halfway across the room. "Do you really think this Wilson character committed suicide?"

Nugent flashed another of his hundred-dollar smiles. "Not a doubt in my mind."

Howard nodded in agreement.

"A terrible thing, suicide," Markham said, shaking his head. "I feel sorry for his wife."

"I'm afraid she's going to have to face it," said Nugent. "Painful as it may be. Thanks again."

"My pleasure."

As soon as the men left, closing the door behind them, Markham stood and walked to the window. He stared blankly across to the river, and at the cars going over the Brooklyn Bridge. Now that he was alone and could afford to put down his guard, he thought about the visit.

He had known they would come eventually. He actually expected them long before now. Once Wilson's breach of security was discovered, and he was dealt with accordingly, the logical next step was to find out what he revealed. What precisely had he told Markham? Was it just the truth about his father's death, or had he also gone further, telling him the names of those responsible? He knew that's what Nugent and Howard had come to find out. He had a good idea who they were working for, the man who stood to lose most if the story of Fort Detrick ever came out.

All in all, he thought he had done a pretty good job of playing dumb. But there was no telling what they would think of his performance. They were obviously suspicious of what he knew, and eager to find out what he planned to do about it. He wondered if their boss knew of the deaths in Edgewater and Greenwich, and if so, linked them to Markham. After all, he certainly was in a position to see the connection. But then what could he do if he did know? Tip off the police? The resulting scandal would only hurt him more. Public exposure was the last thing he wanted.

Markham laughed. Who knows? Maybe they believed his story about Wilson's "social call." No reason why they shouldn't. It was pretty convincing, if he did say so himself.

Markham tried to forget about Nugent and Howard as he went back to reading his mail. But their visit obviously affected him.

Jennifer barged into the office. "I'm dying to hear. Tell me about the breakfast meeting."

"Jennifer, would you please knock?" Markham said coldly. "And how about buttoning up that blouse?"

After the meeting, Nugent and Howard took a walk through nearby City Hall Park. "What do you think?" said Howard.

"He's lying," said Nugent, puffing on his pipe. "He's a smooth one, but I'm convinced that he knows."

"What do you think he's gonna do about it?"

"I'm not sure." Nugent looked up at the building they had just left. He stared at the upper windows. "Whatever it is, we've got to stop him."

12

Mike saw the police car as soon as he turned the corner of Grove Street. There it was, blue and white, parked smack dab in front of his building. He could kid himself if he wanted, like thinking it was parked there by coincidence and the two officers were inside investigating a complaint. Maybe that Haitian couple downstairs were fighting again. But then he remembered, they had moved out week before last.

This was no time to play games. Mike knew exactly why they were there. Right this minute they were upstairs pounding on his door, and face it, they hadn't come collecting for the Police Athletic League. They had come to arrest him as a suspect in the murder of Gloria Thompson. He was probably considered "armed and dangerous," and no doubt the cops crouching in front of his door were waving .38's in their hands. They didn't take chances with an alleged murderer.

So what was he doing standing there looking over at his building? He might as well be wearing one of those sandwich signs. MIKE ROSS HERE. COME AND GET ME. Get your ass out of there.

Mike pulled up the collar on his pea coat, turned, and walked quickly down the block. He crossed Bleecker Street and went into a stationery store on the far corner. He could see his building through the window, and he pretended to leaf through a copy of *Gallery* as he stared at the front door.

In a funny way, he was relieved, now that he knew they were looking for him. At least he knew where he stood. The last three days had been a nightmare, starting on the train returning from Greenwich, when he remembered the bottle of wine left in Gloria's kitchen. He realized right then and there it would just be a question of time before the police connected him to the Thompson home. It wouldn't be hard. After all, the label from the package store was on the back of the bottle, and how many people had bought Beaujolais-Villages Jadot from Grand Central Liquors on the night of October 22? The old Irish clerk who recommended the wine would no doubt remember him. "Why, of course. Young lad. Dark hair. I can see him plain as day."

They would take the clerk downtown and have him pore over the mug books. Mike knew from prison that the books were arranged according to physical type. The red-faced clerk would be shown the section filled with young, dark-haired Caucasians. And dammit if his picture wasn't a good likeness. Even flattering in a way. He'd once thought of requesting a copy for his portfolio. The clerk would have no doubt identifying him. Then it would be just a matter of matching his fingerprints with those found at the house. And look at all the things he had touched. The front door. The telephone. The record. The refrigerator. Shit. He might as well have signed his name.

His fears were confirmed by the newspaper account. The police were indeed focusing their investigation on both the wine bottle and the fingerprints. So what was he waiting for? Before they came to arrest him, why didn't he just march into the nearest precinct and explain exactly what had happened? His date with Gloria. His finding her body. And then his panicked run from the house. "I was scared. I had to get out of there. But I swear to you, I didn't do it. Who do you think called the police? Would I have done that if I had killed her?"

He knew what they'd say. *"If you had nothing to hide, why did you hang up?"*

"Well, you see, there's this man named McCarthy, and . . ." This was the worst part of the nightmare. McCarthy grinning at him through thin lips and pencil-point eyes. And the field day he would have with his scalp as he declared Mike in violation of parole.

"This time, Mr. Ross," McCarthy would say, "you won't be going to Walkill. I'm afraid they're booked solid this season. No problem. There's lots of room in Dannemora."

Dannemora. It was as far north as you could get and still

be in New York. Some twenty-odd miles south of Canada. It was as cold as Siberia, and with conditions that made Attica seem like a luxury hotel.

For three days Mike was torn, unsure of what to do. If he went to the police, he would be sent back inside, and no way did he want that. But if he didn't give himself up . . . well, maybe he would wake up and find the whole thing was in fact a bad dream.

His uncertainty ended with the sight of the car parked outside. He was very much awake, and the cops were very much after him. That settled it. Time to keep his distance from anyone paid to lock him up.

Pretending to study the *Gallery* centerfold, Mike peered out the window at his building. There they were, the men in blue, coming out the front door. They were acting very nonchalant, as if they'd just come down from taking a bribe. Pretty slick the way they paused on his front step, one looking left, the other facing right, checking the street in case one twenty-six-year-old dark-haired Caucasian, five-foot-nine, about one hundred fifty pounds, and with a Rocky Graziano nose, alias Michael J. Ross, just happened to be around.

Instinctively, as they looked in his direction, Mike developed a special interest in *Gallery*'s Miss October. She had dark hair that hung to her waist. Fortunately he did not care much for brunettes. If he hadn't looked up at precisely that moment, he would have missed the cops across the street inadvertently give away their secret.

He was a wino sitting on a nearby bench. At least he looked like a wino. He was drinking out of a paper bag, and even from here Mike could see his dirty clothes and unshaven face. He would have thought nothing of it, if only *one* of the cops, on his way to their car, had nodded at the wino. Just a nice cop, that's all. But *two* friendly cops, both of whom showed their pleasant good natures by nodding to winos? That was stretching public relations a little too far. And on top of that, a wino who nods back? This was New York City, not some episode from *Adam-12*.

Mike was willing to bet that the wine in that paper bag tasted more like black coffee, and that somewhere under those dirty clothes was a .38 Special and a pair of handcuffs. Both were ready for a homicide suspect who lived on the block and sometime soon might want to go home.

"Hey, Mac," said a deep voice from somewhere behind him. "Mac, I'm talking to you. . . . In the blue coat, dammit."

Blue coat. That meant him. Don't tell me there's a cop in here, a fourth member of the team who had just this minute recognized him. Poised, ready to run, Mike turned toward the voice. It belonged to a round-faced man behind the counter who was all eyebrows and jowls, and unless he too was undercover, then he probably owned the store.

"What do you think this is, a library? You want the magazine, buy it and read it at home."

Mike sighed with relief. "No, thanks," he said, folding down Miss October, and putting her back on the shelf. "She's not my type. Thighs are a little big, know what I mean."

Out of the corner of his eye Mike saw the police car pass the store on its way down the street. That left only the wino guarding the fort. He wondered if he was planning on staying the night. What did it matter? No doubt he would be replaced by someone else: a Con Ed man digging a hole, a taxi driver eating his lunch, or since they were showing some imagination these days, maybe a West Village hippie seemingly stoned on quaaludes and passed out on a bench.

Mike obviously couldn't go home. That was out of the question. But right now he had to get out of these clothes and into something less recognizable.

From a pay phone in the back of the store Mike called up Honey Ferguson, his next-door neighbor. A London-born ex-vaudevillian who now worked for Avon door to door, Honey had taken a maternal fancy to Mike shortly after he'd moved into the building. She loved the fact that he was an actor. Though she'd been off the stage for years, she read *Variety* every week and still considered herself part of the show-biz world. Seeing Mike in the hall, she always asked about his career, and told him stories about her own.

They had become the best possible neighbors. Honey was forever leaving home-baked brownies in front of his door, and Mike did her shopping on the days when her arthritis kept her from going out. They were both cat lovers, and Honey had given him the pick of Samantha's most recent litter. Mike named the kitten Oliver, short for Olivier, an actor whom they both admired.

Honey had a key to Mike's apartment, so she could feed

Oliver on the evenings Mike answered phones. Mike trusted her like he would his own mother.

"Honey, this is Mike. How are you?"

"Not bad," she said, the English accent remaining, despite her forty-odd years in America. "The old joints are behaving themselves. I can't complain. Been to any auditions lately?"

"Not really. I haven't had the time," Mike said quickly. "Listen, Honey, something's come up. I'm in some trouble."

"Now, dearie, you know you can count on me. What can I do for you? Need a little extra? I've put a bit away, you know."

"No, Honey. It's not cash I need. I'm okay for now. But I want you to do me a favor. I'll explain later when I can."

"Anything you say, love. Just let me know."

"I want you to go into my apartment and pack some of my clothes. Pair of jeans. Sweater. Few changes of underwear. Enough to last me at least a couple of days. And I've got an old army jacket in the closet. Bring that too."

"You're going away, dear? Not for long, I hope?"

"I'm not sure yet," said Mike. "Listen carefully. Don't use a suitcase. There's a guy who looks like a wino, watching the building from across the street. I don't want him to be suspicious."

"Don't worry," said Honey, eager for an adventure. "I'll fix it so he won't even notice me. Just tell me where to meet you."

Mike thought for a moment. "How about Washington Square Park?"

"Sounds super. I could use a bit of a walk."

"I'll be on the southwest side of the park, near where they play chess. I'll be on a bench, hiding behind a copy of *Variety*."

"I'll find you, love. Give me about fifteen minutes."

"Take your time," said Mike. "Just make it seem natural, so the wino doesn't suspect you."

"Don't worry, love. I'll have a go at it. It will be a grand performance, I assure you."

Mike hung up the phone and bought a copy of *Variety* from the man behind the counter. "You sure you don't want to read it here?" said the owner.

"No, thanks," said Mike. "Not enough pictures."

He left the store, and with his collar pulled up high on his neck, he mingled with the late-afternoon crowds on Seventh Avenue. Slowly and cautiously he worked his way toward Washington Street, which led to the park. Everyone he passed was a possible undercover cop. That character reading a racing form in front of the OTB office. That tall black man selling incense by the subway. And even this guy in the leather jacket and single gold earring who was walking up the sidewalk, staring at him as he approached. Was he just some leather queen out cruising, or a plainclothes detective who was just this moment remembering Mike's description from that morning's station-house briefing?

And here he had worried about walking on the back streets of Greenwich. At least there he'd been alone. New York had definite disadvantages when you were running from the cops. With so many people on the streets, there was no way of knowing whom to look at and whom to avoid. Eye contact could be fatal. Inspired, he went into a Walgreen's on the corner, where he bought a pair of wire-rim sunglasses.

Mike felt better with his eyes covered. Thank God he was on his toes. If they caught him, it wouldn't be for want of trying to stay free.

The park was relatively uncrowded, with only one volleyball game being played by the fountain, and no more than two steel drums sounding from somewhere under the trees. Now that he was here, Mike wondered whether this was such a good place to meet. There were always cops patrolling in the park, breaking up fights between drunks, and trying to scare off the drug pushers who did a brisk business twenty-four hours a day.

"Loose grass, man. Speed, ludes, coke," advertised a Puerto Rican dealer who looked about fifteen and whose glazed eyes suggested he was his own best customer.

Mike shook his head and hurried past. If there was a cop nearby, he was either stone deaf or laying off pushers for the moment. Maybe he was after bigger game. Muggers, for instance. Or better yet, a murder suspect.

Mike walked quickly, his shaded eyes straight ahead. He ignored a panhandler with an outstretched hand, and a white-haired jeweler whose inventory of watches and rings was in a cardboard box on his knees. Finally he reached the corner of the park where he'd told Honey to meet him. Six old men and two students in NYU blazers sat huddled over the concrete chess tables. None of them looked up as Mike took a seat on an empty bench.

He opened *Variety* and held it close up in front of his face, turning to the Casting News in the back. There were four shows listed for Broadway, and at least twice that many for off Broadway and local dinner theaters. Usually Mike read the column with interest. But right now he was too nervous to concentrate. He read the paragraph description of the first play three times in a row before he realized that the only available parts were for women.

Where in the world was Honey? She should have been here ten minutes ago. Maybe there'd been a fourth cop hiding inside the building, and the cop had seen her enter his apartment. "Where the hell do you think you're going, lady?" Or maybe the wino became suspicious, seeing her leave carrying a bundle of clothes. "Come over here, ma'am. I want to talk to you."

He hadn't told her what *kind* of trouble he was in. Only that he couldn't go home and that he needed her help. He had implicated her in a serious crime. If anything happened to Honey, he would never forgive himself.

Mike was looking at his watch, getting more worried by the second, when out of the corner of his eye he saw someone sit on the other end of the bench. He turned his head and casually peeked over the paper.

No luck. Just another bag lady. One of those homeless New Yorkers who slept in the subways or the doorways of buildings and who carried all of her worldly possessions in the pair of shopping bags she was just now placing at her feet. Intrigued by the woman, Mike forgot about Honey for the moment. He got a kick out of how she was dressed. Torn red tennis shoes and thick athletic socks that once might have been white. Her pants were green polyester and baggy at the knees, and she had a gray sweatshirt whose hood was pulled up over her head. Her coat was limp and formless and looked at least twenty years old. Its ratty fur collar had died long ago, and its pockets were bulging with God knows what. Her final touch was a green safari hat pulled down tight over the hood, and a pair of black plastic sunglasses that covered most of her face.

Turning back to his paper, Mike stifled a laugh. Where else but New York could you see such a creature? In a small town, they would've locked her up. Still, you had to admit, her outfit was a work of ingenuity, with a style all its own. Talk about independence. She couldn't give a damn what anyone else thought.

Mike was wondering what she was carrying in the bags, when he noticed her edging closer to his end of the bench. He caught her eye, and was surprised to see her smiling at him.

"Fooled you, didn't I?" she said, taking off her plastic sunglasses. Her eyes sparkled.

"Honey? Is that you?"

"I ain't her royal highness, that's for sure."

"I don't believe it," he said, shaking his head in amazement. "I didn't recognize you at all."

"You weren't meant to, dearie. You did tell me not to look suspicious."

"Absolutely. But, Honey, I had no idea . . . You're fantastic."

"I must admit, this *is* one of my better performances, if I do say so myself. Worked like a wonder too. Your wine-loving friend is still sitting there, you know. Didn't even give me a second look."

Mike laughed. "A lot of people wouldn't give you a second look, dressed like that. I can't tell you how impressed I am. And thankful. Jesus, Honey. You're too much."

"Think nothing of it, love. We show folks gotta stick together, you know what I mean. Hope I wasn't too late. The costume girl phoned in sick, and I had to do the job myself."

"You're perfect," Mike said, reaching over and squeezing her knee. "I'm glad to see you. I was worried for a while."

"Don't worry about me, love. It's you I'm concerned about. What's this trouble you're into, that you have to go away?"

Mike looked over at the nearby chess players. Though hunched over their boards, obviously preoccupied, they could still hear him, and he was not about to take any chances. "I think it's best if we take a walk," he said. "Here, give me the bags."

"They're a mite heavy, my dear. Especially with that jacket. And I look the liberty of throwing in an extra pair of shoes."

"What's this?" said Mike, pointing to a box covered with tinfoil at the top of one of the bags.

"Nothing important, dearie. Just a little goodie I had baked up. Don't want you going hungry, you know."

Mike leaned over and kissed her on the cheek. "Honey, you're fantastic."

"Control yourself, love. I'm a lady, you know. Don't take a fancy to smooching in the park."

Mike grinned. "What can I say? You're beautiful. Can't keep my hands off you."

"You're just gonna have to learn, angel. Now, how about that walk?"

Mike took the bags, Honey took his arm, and the two of them walked slowly across the park. They were oblivious to the stares of the people they passed. Mike told her exactly what had happened, why the police were after him and why he could not risk giving himself up. She was not at all alarmed to learn that he was an ex-convict, no more than if he had told her that his middle name was John. She sympathized with his predicament, and fully understood his need to go into hiding.

"But what will you do, Michael?" she asked, stopping under the Fifth Avenue arch, a worried look on her face. "Stay in a hotel?"

Mike shook his head. "There's no way I can afford it. And thank you very much, but you can't afford it either."

"Sure I can."

"No. I'm just going to have to find someone to stay with for the time being."

"But if they're out and about looking for you, they're bound to check with all your friends."

"I know," said Mike. "I've thought about that. But there's one person they might not connect me to. At least it's worth a chance."

"This really is a terrible state. I wish there was something else I could do," said Honey.

"Believe me, you've done enough already." Mike suddenly remembered something. "There is one thing I would appreciate."

"Name it, dearie."

"It's Oliver. I'm afraid I won't be able to take care of him for a while."

"Don't you worry about little Ollie. I'm his grandmother, aren't I? I'll just tell him Daddy's on a trip, and he's come to stay with me. 'Course, he better mind his manners, if he knows what's good for him."

"Thanks a lot, Honey."

"I'll take up your mail as well. But do me two favors, please."

"Sure," said Mike.

"I want you to call me soon as you've found a place. Okay? The worry's like to drive me to drinking, 'less I know you're safe."

"I'll call you right away. I promise. . . . Listen, I better get out of here now. Standing around too long makes me nervous."

"Just a minute now, love. One more favor."

"What's that?"

"The *Variety* you're holding. Is it this week's?"

"Yes. I just bought it."

"If you don't mind, could I have it?"

"Why, sure." Mike handed her the newspaper.

"I want to see what shows are casting. Thinking of making the rounds again, you know."

Mike smiled. "I'd hire you in a minute. I think you're great."

"Shows you can appreciate talent. You'll go places, dearie."

"Thanks, but I just want to make sure it's not back inside."

"Off with you, and give me a call first chance you get."

Mike put his arms around her and hugged her close. "Thanks again, Honey. For everything."

Her eyes betrayed her concern. "Take care of yourself, Michael. See you soon."

"I hope so."

Mike turned and hurried away.

He worked his way over to University Place, trying to look as inconspicuous as possible. He was thankful that the Cedar Bar was dimly lit and that the pay phone was near the door. He managed to squeeze both bags inside the booth and close the door behind him. But after depositing a dime in the telephone, he just sat there in the darkness, reluctant to make the call.

After his worries about Honey, when she was so late, he had even more qualms about involving another person in his predicament. He really should go it alone. That's how he had done most things in his life, and it bothered him now to have to rely on someone else.

But what alternative did he have? He had to find someplace safe to stay, at least temporarily, and now that he thought of it, that wasn't asking so much. It wasn't as if he needed someone to save him. On the contrary. He was merely asking for an opportunity to save himself.

His mind made up, Mike opened his wallet and took out the card that he'd put there only three days before. He dialed the number inscribed at the bottom.

She answered on the third ring.

"Hello, Susan. This is Mike. Can I come over? I need your help."

13

Susan Draper lived on a quiet tree-lined block near Gramercy Park. Her building was a renovated five-story brownstone, with exposed brick walls, bleached wood banisters, and thick red carpeting leading up the stairs.

Mike was standing in the outer lobby peering through the etched glass door. His heart was beating rapidly, his face was flushed. He had carried the heavy bags fifteen blocks from the Cedar Bar without once stopping to rest. He couldn't take the chance. He was afraid that any minute a patrol car would screech to a halt alongside him and that a pair of drawn guns would come rushing out.

The full impact of his plight was getting to him now. It was one thing *thinking* the police might come looking for him. But it was another matter actually seeing them at his door and knowing that his worst fears had come true. He was a fugitive, just like those guys in the Wanted posters at the post office. Right this minute there were cops out searching for him, and their commendations and future promotions depended on their success in bringing him in. He was damned frightened.

He had called Susan Draper because he knew the cops would never think to question her. How would they know about his group counselor from Walkill, who had only recently moved to New York? Mike knew that Susan could be trusted.

Finding her name on the intercom, Mike pressed the button. Susan buzzed open the door without checking to see who it was. Mike lifted the shopping bags and started up the stairs.

Her apartment was on the top floor, and Mike was panting as he reached the landing. Those damn cigarettes again. How did he expect to stay ahead of the cops, if he couldn't even walk up four flights of stairs without risking cardiac arrest? Forget cancer. It was freedom he was worried about.

Susan was standing in the open doorway, a smile on her face. She was wearing French-cut blue jeans and a navy-blue V-neck sweater. Her feet were bare. "I thought actors were supposed to be in good shape," she said. "Listen to you. You sound about eighty-five."

"And I thought you were supposed to be so smart," Mike said as he approached. "You should check to see who it is before you let someone in. For all you know, there could be a rapist wandering through the halls right this minute."

She grinned. "Is that why you called?"

"No. . . . Actually I'm collecting for the Goodwill."

"Oh, really? I thought you stopped off and did a little shopping on your way over." She stepped aside so he could enter the apartment. "You should have told me. I would have had you pick up a few things."

"To tell you the truth, I'm running away from home. . . ." Looking around the apartment, Mike added, "And this will do very nicely, thank you."

It was a large one-bedroom apartment with eleven-foot ceilings and a working fireplace. The floors had been stained walnut, and a floor-to-ceiling bookcase was built along the far wall. The furniture was modern, in chrome, marble, and glass. There was a settled feeling to the room.

"How many years have you been here?" said Mike.

"Three weeks," said Susan, closing and locking the door. "I don't waste any time."

"I can see that." Mike put down his bags and took off his coat.

"Here. I'll take that," she said. "Can you stay for tea?"

"Sure."

She hung his coat up in the closet. "I'm glad that you called. What about the rest of your . . . belongings?" she said, pointing to the bags. "Anything in there going to spoil?"

"No, but there're some brownies wrapped in tinfoil in one

of the bags. Help yourself," said Mike, looking around the room.

Susan pulled out the box and placed it on the counter. "So you bake too. My, do we have talent."

"My next-door neighbor made them. She's always baking me things."

"How sweet! And what do you do for her?"

"Shop. Take out the garbage. Things like that," Mike said, admiring her books.

"Very cozy," said Susan tentatively. "Sounds like you two have a real thing going."

Mike laughed, taking a seat on the large white sofa. "If you call taking out garbage for a sixty-year-old neighbor a 'thing,' why then I guess we do."

"Let me put on water for tea," said a relieved Susan. "Or would you prefer coffee?"

"If you don't mind, I could use something stronger. Do you have any Scotch?"

"Of course. That's what I drink. But not at four o'clock. How do you want it? On the rocks or with a little water? I'm afraid I'm out of soda."

"Just the bottle would be fine. On second thought, you better bring a glass. Don't want you to think I have rotten manners."

"Be my guest. You can drink it through a straw if you like."

"Just a glass, thank you. But bring the bottle over here. I think I need a few."

"Are you nervous?" Susan said with a smile. "No need to be."

"Just tired," said Mike softly.

Susan noted the weariness in his voice. And the way he kept shifting on the couch, unable to relax. It was so unlike him to be nervous. He had always struck her as someone fully in control. Of course, other than their brief meeting in the bar, the only place she'd ever seen him was in prison. Maybe he was different on the outside. "What's wrong? Is something bothering you?"

Mike laughed. "Is it that obvious?"

Susan nodded. "I'm right, aren't I? Something's wrong."

Mike lit a cigarette. "You might say that."

Susan set his drink on the coffee table and sat down on a

chair facing the couch. She wasn't smiling anymore. Her face showed concern. "You said on the telephone that you needed my help. I thought you were kidding, and that it was just an excuse to come over. Not that you needed one, of course. But you're not kidding, are you? Look at you. You can hardly sit still. What's happened, Mike? Are you in some kind of trouble?"

Mike felt suddenly uncomfortable. With his drink in one hand and his cigarette in the other, he stood up from the couch. Turning his back toward Susan, he walked over to the window. He looked at the trees in the back courtyard and the windows of the neighboring apartments. Now that he was here, it was hard for him to face her, hard for him to tell her exactly why he'd come. He remembered all the things she had done for him in prison, the books and magazines she had brought him, as well as the cartons of cigarettes. What he remembered most was the feeling of hope she had given him, reminding him that this was but one episode in his life, and that someday he would look back on Walkill as if it had never happened. Being here now, asking for Susan's help once again, was admitting that nothing had changed. He was still in prison. He had not moved beyond it.

Susan came over and stood next to him. She put her hand on his shoulder. "Hey, Mike. You can trust me. You know that."

"I know," said Mike, still staring out the window. "That's not the point. I don't want to get you involved."

"Why not?"

"It's not your problem."

"Why don't you tell me what it is?" said Susan gently.

Mike turned and looked her straight in the eye. He wondered what she would think, learning that he was running from the cops. . . . Here we go again. Hadn't he learned by now to stay out of trouble? What the hell was wrong with him?

Susan could tell he was tormented, sensing the conflict in his eyes. It was best not to speak, not to seem too pushy, too eager to meddle. She was afraid she had appeared that way at the bar. But she was concerned about him, and she wanted him to know that whatever it was, she was willing to help.

The two of them shared a lingering look, probing one another's eyes.

"It's dangerous," said Mike finally. "You could get hurt."

"Let me be the judge of that."

Mike took a deep drag on his cigarette, turning away to exhale the smoke. When he turned back to face her, his lips were tightly compressed. "Okay." He nodded almost imperceptibly.

Susan sat in the chair, Mike on the opposite end of the couch. Somehow the distance made it easier for him to talk.

"Remember the night I saw you in the bar?" he began.

"Of course. How could I forget?"

"Well, remember I told you I had an appointment? That's why I couldn't go to that party in the Village?"

Susan nodded.

He told her everything: his affair with Gloria Thompson, their late-night date out in Greenwich, and his discovery of her body on the kitchen floor. Then his panic, his phone call to the police, and the wine bottle he had left on the table. Finally he described his fear of being suspected, the reason he could not give himself up, and today's near-encounter with the cops, who were now very definitely on his trail.

"I had to get away. That's why I called you. I didn't know where else to turn."

"I'm glad you did," said Susan. "Don't think any more about it. Of course you'll stay here."

"You know what that means?" said Mike. "Harboring a fugitive. That makes you an accessory. They can put you away too."

"Like I said, let me worry about that." She shook her head. "Of all the damn luck. And here you had only six more months of parole."

"You're telling me," said Mike, looking blankly at the far wall. "Just when it was all coming together. Like with the acting. God knows when I'll be able to do that again." He looked over at Susan. "You sure you want me to stay here? I have no idea how long it'll be."

"I invited you, didn't I?"

"But it's bound to be a problem. How are you going to explain me to your friends?"

"What friends are those?"

"Don't you have a boyfriend? Someone you see? Pretty girls like you doesn't stay unattached."

Susan smiled. "You'd be surprised."

Mike sighed. "Not that staying here's gonna do me any good. Cops'll still be after me when I leave."

"There's only one thing that will solve all of this," said Susan. "When the police discover who the real murderer is."

"What makes you think they'll look for anyone else?" said Mike sadly, using the butt of one cigarette to light another. "I'm the one they're after."

"But you didn't do it."

"Big deal. They got all the evidence they need. No reason to complicate the case. Just prosecute and get a quick conviction. Let's see. Murder One following a manslaughter rap. I should be out in about sixty years."

It bothered Susan to hear him talk this way, so discouraged, so totally without hope. "If they're not going to find him," she said, "someone else better."

"Who do you have in mind?" Mike said wearily. "Another one of your hotshot lawyers?"

"What about us?"

"What do you mean, *us*?" Mike said, frowning. "I'm no detective. I can't even walk out on the damn streets. Much less start playing Dick Tracy."

"You can't. But I can," said Susan with a determined look on her face.

Mike crushed out his cigarette. "What's this gonna be? Another one of your *adventures*? Like skipping classes at college to go visit prisoners?"

"You can say what you want," said Susan evenly. "I'm afraid you don't have much choice. I'm all you've got. Take it or leave it."

Mike started to complain. But there was nothing he could say. She was absolutely right. It was either Susan or no one.

"I'll go out to Greenwich tomorrow and talk to Arthur Thompson," said Susan. "See if I can come up with anything."

"And what am I supposed to do while you're running around playing cop."

"You're not going to like this, but you better just pretend that you're back inside. At least for a while." Susan pointed to her bookcase. "At least now you've got the library right in your cell."

"That's great," said Mike, resigned for the moment to his confinement. "Just what I always wanted."

Susan went out to buy groceries for dinner. It was only seven o'clock when she returned, but an exhausted Mike was asleep on the living-room couch. She quietly covered him with a blanket and put a pillow under his head.

Mike awoke with a start several times during the night. He had to look at Susan's bookcase to convince himself he was not in Dannemora.

14

As always, Markham's limousine was right on time, idling patiently while double-parked directly in front of his building. The sight of the sleek black car waiting there first thing in the morning never failed to please him. It was one of the privileges of being district attorney that he always appreciated, but which he would forfeit once he resigned. How quickly one became accustomed to luxury. No doubt he could easily adjust to taking taxicabs. But he was in no real hurry to try.

His chauffeur was standing beside the opened rear door. His well-polished shoes gleamed in the sunlight.

" 'Morning, Mr. Markham," he said with a nod as he touched his cap.

" 'Morning, Joe. How's everything?"

"Couldn't be better, sir. Looks like we got ourselves a beautiful day."

"That's for sure," said Markham, breathing deeply of the crisp fall air before entering the car. "What do you say we take a drive out to the country?"

Joe smiled. "How about over to the East River? I hear its lovely this time of year."

"You're on," said Markham with a grin. The East River Drive was their regular route to work.

"Did you congratulate your son for me?" called Markham through the open partition as Joe started up the car.

"I sure did. And he told me to thank you."

"You know, Joe, it's not easy getting into medical school. I hope you're proud of him."

"You better believe it. Now I'll have someone to take care of me in my old age."

"What makes you think you'll need it?" said Markham, opening his briefcase to take out his *Times*.

"Well, you never know," said the driver. "Anyway, it's good insurance."

As the car pulled off East End Avenue onto the Drive, Markham thought of his own son, Billy, wondering what he would be when he grew up. Maybe a doctor. Or a lawyer, like himself. Whatever Billy wanted would be okay with him. Right now he planned to be a professional football player. And why not, considering the progress he was making in their weekly Saturday workouts? He could now play all afternoon without dropping a pass, and his place kicks were good for thirty-five yards. Not bad for a kid all of twelve years old.

Markham smiled, thinking of Billy's birthday coming up, and the present that he had planned. He checked the date on the *Times*. November 1. His birthday was next week. He would have to make arrangements with Leslie, if the present was to be a surprise. And he would have to do it fast. He wondered if she would give him any trouble.

He watched the East River rushing by on his left, as he thought about the best way to approach her. Should he call her today at the office, or wait to reach her at home? He was considering the pros and cons of both strategies when he sensed something blocking his view of the river. It was the car in the next lane, a dark late-model sedan, a Buick or a Ford. It was traveling right alongside of the limousine, so close in fact that the man in the passenger seat couldn't have been more than five feet away. He had a woolen knit hat pulled down over most of his face. Yet his eyes were familiar.

The man opened the window. He pointed something in Markham's direction.

Without hesitation Markham dived to the floor and huddled next to the seat. He was on his way down when the shots rang out, like a string of backfires from the adjacent car. He broke his fall with his hands. With his nose pressed down against the carpet, his eyes tightly closed, and his arms covering his head, he heard the windows shatter on both sides of the car and felt the shards of glass rain onto his back. He braced himself in expectation of pain.

There were pins pricking his hands, and something heavy and sharp grazed the top of his ear. Yet, curiously, the moan he heard was not his own. It was from far away. A second passed, or maybe an hour. But the next thing he knew, the backfires had stopped and there was silence in the car. Markham thought about getting up, at least to his knees. But then he sensed what was happening. The limousine was not going straight. He could tell by the way he was pressed against the door that the car was veering off to the right. Obviously the moan came from Joe. There was no driver at the wheel.

Markham braced himself once again, tighter this time, and waited for the crash.

It was not long in coming. The crunch of glass and steel was louder than all the backfires combined. Markham was thrown forward against the rear of the front seat. It was like someone had punched him in the stomach. His breath was taken away. There was a dull pain in his head, a ringing in his ears, and then nothing....

When he opened his eyes, he was still on the floor, and a young cop was leaning over him through the open door. The cop had blond hair, crooked front teeth, and a look of worry on his face.

"Just relax, Mr. Markham. Help's on the way."

Markham shook his head in order to clear it. He noticed there was blood on the front of his shirt. His left ear hurt, as though from a burn, and the backs of his hands throbbed. He could see slivers of glass stuck in his skin. Apart from an ache in his side where he'd hit against the seat, he was fairly sure he was okay. He pushed himself up off the floor and onto the seat.

The cop with the crooked teeth gently tried to restrain him. "Stay down, Mr. Markham, please."

"Let me alone, dammit. There's nothing wrong with me."

The officer knew better than to resist. Accident victim or not, the D.A. could do as he pleased. Markham climbed out of the car, and once on his feet, took a few tentative steps, and waved his hands in the air, checking to see that everything worked. He was immediately surrounded by other policemen, some in uniform, others in plain clothes. They all began talking at once.

"Are you okay, Mr. Markham?"

"We heard what happened."

"Maybe you should sit down."

"The ambulance is on its way, sir."

"I'm fine," said Markham. "Mostly just shaken up, that's all." He gently touched his ear with a finger. The bleeding had stopped. "Where's Joe, my driver?" he said suddenly. "Is he all right?"

Without waiting for an answer, he pushed by the circle of cops. He saw Joe up ahead, lying by the side of the car, a blanket covering his chest. Two other policemen were kneeling over him.

"How is he?" said Markham.

Joe looked up at him through pained eyes. He struggled to speak. "I'm sorry, sir. . . . About the crash."

"Don't be silly, Joe."

"I told you, I'd need a . . . doctor." His voice was growing faint.

A black sergeant motioned Markham aside. "Sorry, sir. But it's best if he didn't talk. Looks like he took one in the stomach. I know how it feels," added the cop, pointing to his own midsection. "That's where it hurts the most."

Markham turned away. "Dammit!" he said quietly to himself. He hadn't planned on anything like this. He looked over at what the limousine had hit—a light pole on the right side of the highway. The steel pole was bent in an angle, like a felled tree on its way to the ground. The car had bounced back so that half of it was still on the Drive, blocking one of the downtown lanes. He could imagine what that would do to rush-hour traffic. The car's front end appeared to have been kicked in by a giant boot. The headlights were smashed beyond recognition, and the hood had folded like a paper fan.

While surveying the damage, Markham noticed that it hurt when he breathed. He was afraid that the ache in his side might be a broken rib. So what if it were. So he had a lacerated ear, a pair of pin-cushion hands, and a banged-up chest. He was lucky to be alive, especially considering he had twice escaped serious injury. First from the machine-gun attack, and then from the crash. He was leaning against the side of the car, thinking about the man in the knit hat, the man behind the gun, when another policeman approached. This one was a lieutenant, obviously top brass on the scene.

"Mr. Markham, it seems the ambulance is having trouble getting through the traffic. We're going to take you to the hospital in one of the patrol cars."

"What about Joe? He needs attention much more than I."

"They're lifting him into another car right now. You'll go in my car. And don't you worry, sir. There'll be patrol cars on both sides. Front and behind. The bastards who did this won't have another chance. By the way, sir. We got a witness who saw the car. License plate and all. The boys are on the phone to Albany right now. We'll be on to the sons of bitches before the doctor finishes patching you up."

"I hope so."

"Have you any idea who they might be?" said the lieutenant.

Markham shook his head. "Not a clue."

Lights flashing and sirens wailing, the police drove Markham the few blocks to New York Hospital, pulling up in front of the emergency entrance. A team of nurses and orderlies descended on him as soon as he stepped out of the car. Despite his protests, they insisted on lifting him onto a stretcher, and he was surrounded by a wall of blue uniforms as he was wheeled inside. Curious onlookers, even those who worked in the hospital, were discouraged from coming too close.

Markham appreciated the protection. One close call was more than enough.

While the police waited outside the emergency room, Markham was examined by the chief resident, a gray-haired man in his late fifties. First the doctor X-rayed his chest to see if the pain was in fact caused by a broken rib. Markham was in luck. There was no sign of a fracture, only a slight discoloration indicative of a bad bruise. Next the doctor cleaned the wound over his ear and patiently removed the pieces of glass from his hand. The ear required ten stitches, and both hands were wrapped in gauze. The doctor then began an extensive tapping of joints and reflexes that quickly put Markham's patience to the test.

"Is all this necessary, doctor? I told you, I feel perfectly fine."

"I'm sure you do. But whether or not you're aware of it, you had a slight concussion. That's why you blacked out. You can never be too careful in a case like this."

The doctor obviously enjoyed attending such a notable patient. He was in no hurry to quit, and he gave Markham the most thorough checkup he had had in years. Aside from minor bruises, the doctor found nothing of concern. Yet he insisted, once he was done, that Markham stay in the hospital overnight.

"It's strictly for observation," he said when Markham started to complain. "Remember, you got a bad blow to the head. We can't have you passing out at work, now, can we? I promise that if nothing develops, you can leave here first thing tomorrow."

Markham resigned himself to his unwanted stay. He was given a private room with a panoramic view of the river. Two policemen were placed outside his door. He spent the rest of the day dressed in a hospital robe and slippers, talking to the many city officials who telephoned to express their outrage over his attack.

"It's despicable," said the president of the City Council. "It makes me feel ashamed of New York."

"An absolute affront to all of us," said the district attorney from the Bronx. "Just goes to show what we in Justice are up against."

"We've got the chief of detectives himself on the case," said the police commissioner. "Don't you worry. We'll get these bastards."

"I'm sorry, Frank," said the mayor. "Any idea who it might be?"

"Are you kidding?" said Markham. "With all the people I've sent away. I've got even more enemies than you. All yours do is go on strike, or vote Republican. Mine are a little more outspoken."

"I'm glad to see you haven't lost your sense of humor."

"The day I lose that is the day I quit . . . or maybe decide to run against you."

"Seriously," said the mayor stiffly, hoping his last comment was a joke, "I'm going to make sure this never happens again."

"How are you going to do that? Lock up every one of my potential enemies? I'll be the only one left on the streets. Might get a bit lonely."

"I'm ordering police protection. Starting immediately."

"I really don't think it's necessary," said Markham. "So some asshole wants revenge and takes a shot at me. That's one of the hazards of the job, I'm afraid."

"We have to discourage it," said the mayor firmly. "Right here and now. I'm serious about this. You'll be getting protection around the clock. It's a disgrace that something like this can happen."

"I appreciate your concern, but—"

"No 'buts' about it. Soon as I hang up, I'm going to make the arrangements. I don't have to tell you, Frank. You're one of the best D.A.'s this city has had. I don't want anyone trying to scare you out of office. No, sir. Again, I'm sorry. Rest up. I'll talk to you later in the week."

Markham laughed out loud as he hung up the phone. Who did the mayor think he was kidding? The mayor would have liked nothing better than for him to get shot. What better way to lose a potential political opponent, a contender for his present office, or another one up the line. There was no charity among politicians, or anyone else for that matter. Only total self-interest. But of course the mayor had to pretend to worry for his safety. It was good politics to protect your top D.A.

Talk about pretending. Markham too was acting when he protested his need for a bodyguard. In fact, the idea appealed to him very much.

Markham knew who had tried to kill him. He'd recognized the man with the gun as Nugent, the so-called "insurance investigator" who had come to see him about Wilson. No doubt the driver of the car was Howard, his monster-sized partner. They evidently had not believed his story about Wilson's "social call," and they now intended to do to him exactly what they had done to Wilson.

Sure, Markham was worried, knowing that he was now a target. But he had no intention of changing his plans. He would just have to think even more carefully about his every single move. Not that Nugent and Howard would leave him alone in any case. They *had* to kill him. Their boss was desperately afraid of his revealing what he'd been told.

The thought of a man sitting in fear of him was amusing to Markham. After all, fear was the greatest form of recognition. If only they had thought about him years ago, before they killed his father.

The attempt on his life made Markham all the more determined to get on with his plan. And thanks to the mayor, he was now even better equipped than before. He had a policeman protecting him against future attack. What a perfect alibi for anything he did. A live-in cop.

Though his side still hurt, and his hands continued to throb, Markham contentedly lay down to nap. He couldn't wait to go to Boston next week. He was even planning to bring Billy along with him.

15

Susan arrived at Grand Central Station with ten minutes to spare. She was catching the nine-fifteen train out to Greenwich, and before leaving, she called her editor at the *News* to explain why she wouldn't be in. That feature assignment she was doing on the new housing project in the Bronx was taking longer than she had expected. It needed a little spice. A few more interviews would do it.

"All right," he said. "But I want it by Friday at the latest."

Walking through the gate to the platform, she wondered how she would get it done on time. How could she concentrate on the city's real-estate problems when it was up to her to clear Mike with the police? Too bad she couldn't explain to her editor that she was working on a much bigger story. "You know that front-page item from last week, the murder of the Connecticut housewife? I've got an exclusive angle on the case. If it pans out, we'll scoop everyone in town. All I need is time."

"And just what, precisely, is your exclusive angle, Miss Draper?"

"Well, you see, the man the police are after, the one they suspect of the crime. He says he didn't do it. He says he was framed."

"And you believe him, Miss Draper? Why is that?"

"Well, it's because . . . well, he just seems honest, I guess." Is that what it was about Mike that made her trust him? Susan asked herself as she boarded the train. Surely there must be something more. Still, she prided herself on being a good judge of character, and she knew a bullshit line when she heard one.

With Mike there had never been a hint of anything other than the truth. Susan remembered the meetings in prison, and how taken she'd been by the wavy-haired inmate from the Lower East Side. It was his openness that impressed her. Unlike the other prisoners she questioned, most of whom were quick to protest their innocence—"It was my friend who done the job, I was just along for the ride"—Mike made no excuses for himself. "After what that bastard did to my sister, I *wanted* to hurt him. Sure, his death was an accident. But that didn't make him any less dead. Soon as I saw him laying there, I knew I was gonna do time. No way could they let me walk."

Susan had tried to explain to him that with a good lawyer, and with a defense of, say, "momentary insanity," he might have gotten off. Mike was quick to respond. "I wasn't insane. I knew exactly what I was doing. And I sure as hell wasn't going to lie."

His candor was very refreshing. And it seemed totally genuine, unlike the "let-it-all-hang-out" come-on of some Columbia senior on the make. Susan had more than enough experience with men who pretentiously bared their souls as a way of getting her to bare her body. Mike was not out to impress her with his directness. He appeared to have no ulterior motive in mind. Judging from the firmness of his voice, and the way his dark eyes looked intently into hers, telling the truth was merely a question of honor.

Along with his honesty, it was his intelligence, and his sense of humor, undampened by more than a year behind bars, that attracted her to him. Moreover, he was as direct with her as he was with himself. He kidded her about her privileged "debutante" background, and insisted that she was here working with prisoners out of both boredom and guilt.

"Now that the war is over," he said with a smile, "we prisoners are the new Vietnamese. Convicts have become chic."

"I've always been interested in prison reform," Susan said in defense. "Besides, coming here is part of my work." She sensed she was protesting too much. Who was she trying to kid? She could have done her sociology research at a factory or a school. She had chosen a prison precisely because she had never been inside one before. Mike was right. It was just another adventure.

It intrigued Susan that he could see right through her. No man had ever challenged her that way before. She looked forward to their animated meetings, and she enjoyed bringing him the books, magazines, and packs of cigarettes that were so hard to come by on the inside. Mike seemed truly touched by her kindness, at times even embarrassed.

As the half-empty train now began to move, Susan stared blankly out of the window into the darkness of the tunnel. Little did Mike know how well he knew her, even more than her husband had. She had met Fred on a ferry to Greece the summer after graduation. He was tall and blond, like John Lindsay, and had the sexiest body she had ever seen, with muscular arms, and not an ounce of fat on his waist. They spent the entire two days on board locked in his cabin, and then traveled together for the rest of the summer.

It was her idea to get married that fall. Fred would have preferred that they live together without going through the formality of a wedding. But Susan thought that was cheating. If she felt ready to have a truly intimate relationship, then some halfhearted effort was not enough. She wanted to make a total commitment.

Fred was in his last year of Harvard Law School, while Susan was just beginning her master's in sociology at Boston University. They rented a small house in Cambridge, close enough to the campus so that Fred could walk to class. In addition to sharing the monthly checks they each received from home, they shared the cooking, the cleaning, even the dining-room table on which they both worked in the evenings, each with a pile of books and his own Tensor lamp.

Their life together became an unvarying routine. On Friday nights they saw movies at the Orson Welles Theater, followed by drinks at Cronin's, a straight Scotch for Susan and a vodka gimlet for Fred. On Saturdays they played tennis—Susan always won—and entertained Fred's classmates with coq au vin à la Julia Child or steaks barbecued on their backyard grill. They made love on Saturday nights and on alternate Wednesdays, if Fred did well on his biweekly exam in criminal procedure. They didn't talk much. Now that their life together was in order, there was little to discuss.

Though Susan quickly became bored, she was reluctant to

admit she had made a mistake. The same exploratory spirit that had prompted her to get married in the first place now compelled her to stick it out. No one ever said a mature relationship was all fun and games. If there was something missing in the marriage, perhaps it was her fault rather than Fred's, or the marriage itself. Maybe her expectations were wrong. Maybe all married couples soon began to take one another for granted. Maybe all sexy men eventually put on weight. Maybe marriage was meant to be dull.

Unfortunately, however, the same thing applied to graduate work in sociology. She'd been attracted by the obvious relevance of the field, the chance to do research in mental hospitals, family courts, and on problems like abortion, malnutrition, and housing discrimination. Her courses in Statistics, Research Analysis, and "The Art of the Interview" were much too academic for Susan, and she was beginning to have doubts about her chosen career.

Blinking her eyes as the train passed out of the tunnel and started through Harlem, Susan thought of the day, more than a year and a half ago, when she'd received a phone call from Joan, one of her classmates from Vassar. Joan had been one of her best friends. Like herself, Joan had been married straight out of college, to Phil, a long-haired doctor from Dartmouth, whom she had met at a dance. The two of them moved to Cleveland, where Phil was doing his internship. Aside from a rather formal-looking Christmas card, Susan had not heard from them since.

Over the phone Joan said she and Phil were separated and that she was now living in Wellesley, working as a photographer for the Associated Press, and living with a forty-year-old sculptor. Did "Suzie" want to get together for lunch?

Did she ever.

They ate in a French restaurant in downtown Boston. Right away Susan asked about Joan's separation from Phil.

"I don't know why," Joan said, pushing her hair away from her face, "but shortly after we got married, everything changed. We'd always been busy with our work before, but now it seemed we had a license to take one another for granted. All we talked about was what to have for dinner. You remember Miss Hot-to-trot here," Joan said with a grin. "Can you believe we had sex only once a week? It got so I was considering taking a lover. I mean, who the hell needs this, right? Instead I decided enough's enough. Why not split while we're still friends, before one of us starts getting bitter. And by that I mean *me*. You should've seen the look on Phil's face when I told him. Like I'd just been to bed with the Hell's Angels, and invited them all over for tea. You know, the day I left was a week before our first anniversary."

Susan could hardly believe her ears. She was listening to her own complaints spoken by her friend. "The same thing has happened to us," she confided. "We've gotten so damn used to one another. Sometimes he'll say four words over dinner."

"How can you stand that?" said Joan. "I've come to the conclusion that if a man's not interesting, then he's not worth my time. I don't care how many years we've been together. Boredom is worse than death, if you ask me. You should meet Sandy, my sculptor friend. We argue about everything: movies, books, how I should wear my hair. Life with him may not be quiet, but it sure isn't dull. Frankly, it's a challenge. That's what I like."

Susan nodded in agreement. Joan had taken the words right out of her mouth.

Two weeks later, after much soul-searching over what had ever happened to the strong-minded girl she once was, Susan told Fred of her intention to leave. There was no drama, no tears or raised voices. Fred reacted to the verdict with the composure of a lawyer. His total lack of emotion, along with his stated desire to "reason things out," convinced Susan all the more that she was doing the right thing. She got the impression that he did not take her seriously, at least until she told him she was leaving Boston.

"Leaving? But what about school?"

"I'm dropping out," said Susan. "I've decided it's not what I want."

"I think you're making a mistake, Susan," said Fred, sounding very much like her father. "What will you do with yourself?"

"I'm going to try to write," said Susan. "I wrote for the paper in college. Hopefully with Dad's connections I'll be able to get a job." She smiled. "My mind's made up. What are you worried about? You won't even know that I'm gone."

Still, it was upsetting when she said good-bye. She had hoped she could make it work.

Susan spent a year in the Washington bureau of the *News*, during which time she met no one she liked. Finally she decided it was time to transfer to New York. She longed for the energy of the city. It was in the car, making the move, that Susan thought of Mike, remembering the way he had challenged her during their meetings in prison. He had the kind of vitality she liked in a man. She wondered if he was released yet, and if so, what he was doing. It was over three years since she'd been at Walkill, and she would love to see him again.

As the train passed through the Bronx and into New Rochelle, Susan wondered what her parents would think if they knew she was seeing an ex-convict. And this wasn't while working for some charity, like her mother. A fund-raising dance for a boys' home, or the prison library in Attica. She was actually hiding him out from the police, while working to prove his innocence. Susan gazed at her reflection in the glass. Well, she had come to New York looking for excitement. She sure wasn't wasting time.

She took a cab from the Greenwich railroad station to Arthur Thompson's home. The driver, who had pictures of his family mounted next to a plastic Jesus on his dashboard, nodded to himself when he heard the address. He took the same route Mike had walked the night of his date.

Susan thought about what she and Mike had discussed over coffee that morning, namely that Arthur Thompson himself may have murdered his wife after learning of her affair with Mike. It certainly seemed plausible. An older man outraged by the infidelity of his young wife. She intended to observe him closely, to see how he was coping with her death. She also hoped to check out his alibi for the night of the murder.

"You can leave me right here," Susan said just before the cab started to turn into the driveway. "I'll call you when I'm ready to leave. What's the number?"

"Just ask Mr. Thompson," the driver said smugly. "He's a regular customer."

Now, why did he say that? she wondered.

Susan felt nervous walking up to the front door of the Thompson home. She felt confident of her ability to sense when someone was telling the truth. Yet never before had the stakes been as high as now. Mike's freedom depended upon her success with Arthur Thompson.

Thompson was dressed in a dark suit when he came to the door. His face was drawn, and his eyes were red. He looked every one of his sixty-eight years. Susan guessed he had just come from his wife's funeral. From the expression on his face, he was obviously in no mood to talk to reporters. This was going to be even more difficult than she had anticipated.

"Mr. Thompson," she said, "my name is Susan Draper, from the *Daily News*. I want to tell you how sorry I am about your wife."

"Is that so?" said Thompson bitterly. "You know, you reporters all use the same lines. All you really want is a quote for your goddamn stories. Go away and leave me alone." He started to close the door in her face.

"I know how you feel," said Susan quickly. "I lost a brother in Vietnam." She hated to lie, but she could think of no other way.

"I'm sorry to hear that," said Thompson stiffly, his proper military instincts overcoming his anger. "Then I'm sure you know how I feel, and will respect my wish to be left alone."

"I do, sir. But could I please come in for just a minute? If only for a glass of water. I walked all the way from the station."

Thompson's face showed his irritation. But he hadn't yet closed the door. Susan could tell that the approach had worked. Though he wanted nothing at all to do with reporters, he was too much of a gentleman to ignore a tired woman's request for a drink. Chivalry still had its uses. "All right," he said reluctantly, opening the door. "But just for a minute."

Thompson led her silently to the kitchen, where he poured her a glass of water from the tap. Uninvited, Susan carried it to the table and sat down. She drank with contentment.

"Thanks a lot," she said, putting down the glass. "Like I said, I'm very sorry about your wife, Mr. Thompson. And I hate to trouble you . . ."

"Then why do it?" said Thompson coldly, standing by the counter, his arms crossed tightly at his chest.

"We're as eager as you to catch the person responsible," said Susan.

"There's nothing I can tell you that I haven't already told the other reporters." He looked sadly down at the floor, at the police chalk marks that were still faintly visible, indicating the position of Gloria's body. "I have no idea who would want to hurt Gloria," he said softly.

"Maybe I can help," said Susan gently.

Thompson stood there in silence, staring at the floor. He sighed. When at last he spoke, his voice was little more than a whisper. "Okay," he said, resigned to the intrusion. "But I don't know why you're bothering. I understand the police already have a suspect in mind, and are close to making an arrest. As far as they're concerned, the case is almost closed."

"Could I have another glass of water?" said Susan, starting to get up.

"Sure," said Thompson pointing to the sink. Too worn out to stand, he took the seat across from her and waited for Susan to sit down once again.

Susan was driven back to the station by the same cabdriver as before. He was in his mid-fifties, balding, and with a huge paunch that probably made it difficult getting in and out of the cab.

"Tell me," said Susan lightly as the car pulled out of the driveway. "What time did you pick up Colonel Thompson the night you drove him to the airport?"

The driver smiled in the rearview mirror. He was missing a front tooth. "Are you a reporter or a cop?"

"Which do you think?" said Susan, returning the smile.

"Unless they're getting much prettier cops these days, you gotta be a reporter. Would you believe you're the eighth one I've driven out here in the last three days?"

"How do you know they were all reporters? Maybe some of them *were* cops."

"Whatever they were, they sure as hell wasn't relatives. Two minutes in the cab, and they're starting with the questions. Was Thompson well-liked in town? Did he keep much money laying around? How am I supposed to know? What do they think? I'm some friend of the family? One guy even asked me what kind of tips Thompson gave. As if his wife was killed because he stiffed some cabdriver."

"Why *do* you think she was killed?" asked Susan.

"Beats me. Why don't you ask the police?"

"You never answered my question. About what time did you pick up the colonel?"

The driver chuckled. He was obviously eating up the attention of this pretty girl. And enjoying the sparring as well. "What makes you think it was me who drove him out there?"

"The colonel told me," said Susan, maintaining a straight face despite the lie. "Is there any reason why he shouldn't?"

"I just don't want to get any more involved than I am," he said casually. "You know . . . with my *name* in the paper."

Susan nodded, taking out her notebook. "What *is* your name?"

He turned, flashing a grin. "Capella. With two L's. . . . Yeah, I'm the one who drove him out there. Delta, he was flying. See, I even remember the airline. Missed his flight, too, 'count of an accident on the Grand Central Parkway. Goddamn Stella D'Oro truck hit a pole. You shoulda seen it. Boxes of cookies all over the road, and us just sitting there bumper to bumper. People rushing out, grabbing all they could carry. Police didn't do nothing. I would have took some home myself, 'cept Miriam's on a diet."

"What do you mean, he missed the flight?" said Susan excitedly, leaning forward over the back of the front seat. "Didn't he leave for Dallas?"

"Lucky for the colonel, there was another flight in an hour. We got there so late he asked me to wait while he ran in to check. Guess he was thinking I'd drive him back home."

"What time did you get there?"

"About eleven-fifteen. Missed the plane by a good ten minutes. Lucky thing there was another."

"Sounds like a late night for you. What time did you finally get home?"

"Not until after one. Just my luck if there wasn't an accident on the other side of the highway. Goddamn jackknifed tractor-trailer. I tell you, that was quite a night. Specially when I heard Mrs. Thompson got killed. Sure as hell would like to get my hands on the son of a bitch who done it."

"You're not the only one," said a disappointed Susan, slumped back in the seat.

"By the way, what paper are you with?" asked the driver, smiling. "And when's this gonna be in?"

Though Susan had nothing encouraging to report to Mike, she decided to call him up from the telephone on the station platform. She wondered how he was getting along in the apartment.

Mike was watching television when the phone rang, and he got up from the couch to turn down the set.

"Two-nine-four-nine," he said crisply, assuming his best answering-service voice. "May I help you?"

"You can start by telling me how much you charge," teased Susan. "I had no idea you were so polished."

"I ought to be," said Mike. "I've been doing it long enough."

"That's right. I forgot. You're a pro." Susan laughed. "Any messages?"

"Only from your editor. He wants to know why the hell you're not at work."

"Oh, is that right? Didn't he tell you that I called him from Grand Central? I'm afraid you'll have to do better than that."

"I remember now. It wasn't your editor. It was your mother who phoned. We had a nice long chat."

"That's just great," said Susan, continuing to play along. "And who did you tell her you were?"

"Just some guy you met. Don't worry. I told her I was a doctor. Columbia Medical School. She was very impressed. Invited us to dinner a week from Sunday. You know how mothers are. Got to polish the silver. Send the linens out to be pressed."

"I'm glad to hear that."

"Enough kidding," said Mike, his mood changing abruptly, all sense of play gone from his voice. "What did you learn?"

Susan sighed. She was in no hurry to give him the bad news. "I'm afraid your idea doesn't work. About his taking a cab to the airport so he'd have an alibi, then getting out and taking a city cab right back to Greenwich. I spoke to the cabdriver, who told me they didn't even get there until eleven-fifteen. According to the medical report, Gloria was killed between eleven-thirty and twelve. There's no way Thompson could have gotten back there in time. The driver himself didn't get back until after one."

"Dammit!" said Mike. "It seemed like such a perfect frame. Like he just knew she would call me, and then I would discover the body and be the one blamed."

"You're misjudging him," said Susan. "I don't think he's that calculating."

"He could always have paid someone to do it. But in that case, the man was probably a pro and didn't leave any trace of himself behind."

"Forget it," said Susan. "I'm afraid we're going to have to look elsewhere. From all I could tell, he really loved Gloria. He's terribly upset, and it doesn't seem like an act."

"You're sure of that?"

"Yes. I am," she said firmly. "And you're just going to have to trust me, Mike."

"Dammit!"

Susan knew how frustrated he was. She wasn't sure what to say.

"Well, what about Thompson's sons?" said Mike. "Did you learn anything about them? A lot of people get upset when their parents marry again. Killing the new wife is a bit extreme. But who knows? Maybe one of them's some kind of wacko."

"Neither one of them was at the funeral," said Susan. "The older son evidently lives in Europe. But the younger one isn't too far away. He lives on some commune in Westchester. I'm going to go see him this afternoon."

"You're probably wasting your time," said a dejected-sounding Mike. "For all we know, Gloria was killed by some burglar she caught in the act. Right now he's on a bus to L.A."

"Come on, Mike. Nothing was taken from the house, remember. That's already been reported by the police. And as far as my time is concerned," added Susan, "I'll be the judge of that, thank you. . . . What have *you* been doing all morning?"

"Not much," said Mike sarcastically. "Took a walk. Gave a few interviews to the press. I've invited some cops over for tea this afternoon."

"Be my guest," said Susan, trying to humor him. "The pot's in the cabinet above the refrigerator."

"Actually, I've found a great way to forget about all this mess."

"What's that?"

"Daytime television," said Mike. "I had no idea what great shows they have on. *Ryan's Hope* is just ending. Now it's time for *All My Children*. No, maybe I'll watch *The Gong Show*. Which do you think is better?"

"Cheer up," said Susan. "At least you're not alone. You know how many housewives are doing the exact same thing right this minute?"

"Gee, great. That really makes me feel better. At least they've got a choice in the matter," said Mike bitterly. "That's more than I can say."

"Try reading a book," said Susan. "I'll be back as soon as I can. Is there anything I can bring you? Like something special for dinner?"

"How about a signed confession by Gloria Thompson's murderer? And him along with it? You know, a little dessert with the coffee."

"I'm afraid that's not on special this week, but I'll see what I can do. Okay? Just sit tight. I'll see you later."

16

"Bunch of weirdos," said the cabdriver, shaking his bald head. "Wait'll you see 'em."

"How many people live there?" asked Susan.

"Fifty. A hundred. Who the hell knows? Too many, if you ask me. It ain't healthy. They ought a close the place down."

It was after two o'clock, and Susan was being driven through Bedford Hills, on her way to the address given to her for Arthur Thompson's son.

As the cab passed along the rural back roads of this affluent suburban town, Susan wondered if Mike could be right, and that it was Thompson's son who was responsible for the murder. Children often acted irrationally when a mother or father married again.

You'd have to be pretty screwed up, a "wacko" in Mike's words, to want to kill your father's new wife. Susan was eager to learn whether Russell Thompson might just fit the bill.

"How long have they been here?" Susan asked the cabdriver.

"Little more than a year. They're in the old Lawrenceson house. You know Sam Lawrenceson. Film producer in the thirties. Did all them Bette Davis movies. His wife lived here till she died back in seventy-one. House has been on the market ever since. Quarter of a million they were askin'. Who knows where these nuts came up with that kind of money." The driver laughed. "Word is they all belong to some kind of church. One of them Indian religions." He smiled. "Maybe you're thinkin' of joinin'?"

"No, thank you," said Susan. "I'm just here to see a friend."

They entered a long gravel driveway leading to a large white Tudor-style mansion. The house reminded Susan of some of the grandiose homes in New Canaan, where she grew up.

"That's how you'd be spending your time if you stayed," said the cabdriver, pointing to a group of people on the grass. There were about fifteen of them, walking in various directions, their legs stiff and their arms straight at their sides. Eyes glazed, they looked like they were in some kind of trance. "What'd I tell ya? Just look at 'em. Bunch of zombies."

Susan paid the driver and got out of the cab. She was struck by how quiet it was, once the car had left. The only sound was the occasional crunch of a leaf underfoot. She looked closer at the people walking on the lawn. Most of them were young, in their twenties and early thirties, and dressed in blue jeans and sweaters. A few were in ponchos or serapes. They were all absolutely silent, each lost in his own little world. No one even noticed that she was there.

Susan realized right away that she had come to some kind of spiritual commune or retreat center. She knew from an article in the *News* that there were many such centers scattered around New York, most of which were open to the public.

So this was where Russell Thompson lived. She wondered if living on a spiritual commune qualified him as a "wacko" in Mike's eyes. Who knows? She had a strange feeling she just might be wasting her time. Not that she was being hasty in writing him off. But it seemed an odd place to find a murderer.

A sign on the front door said *"Enter in Search of Peace."* She opened the door and went inside.

A woman in a dark navy robe, red hair clear to her waist, was sitting on a straw mat in the hallway, the only furniture in the room. She was in the lotus position, and her eyes were closed.

"Welcome," she said softly, opening her eyes to smile as Susan approached. "I'm Sister Ruth. I'm glad to see you."

"Hello, Ruth," said Susan, clearing her throat. "Well, I'm glad to be here."

"How long will you be with us, Susan?" Ruth was in her

late twenties, and had pale, rather translucent skin and blue eyes. With a little make-up she could be pretty, Susan thought to herself. And maybe a bit more sun.

"I'm not here for a visit. I've come to speak to someone who lives here."

"Who is that?" said Ruth, still smiling. Her expression didn't change.

"His name is Russell Thompson."

"You must be referring to Brother Russell. We have no last names here."

"Whatever you call him," said Susan, returning the smile. "He's the one I want to see."

"Brother Russell is teaching breathing on the back porch. Come. I will guide you there."

"I appreciate it."

Susan followed Ruth through the house. She could easily see how it had once been owned by a producer. In addition to the fourteen-foot ceilings, there was thick wood paneling everywhere, and the floors were either old polished parquet or dark-colored marble with rich white veining. One of the fireplaces was the size of a dining-room table. She imagined that the place was once filled with the smell of expensive cigars and leather furniture, the scene of elegant parties, sit-down dinners for fifty, or cocktails for three hundred, with bars in every room.

There was now very little furniture in any of the rooms. A simple rug, a few wooden chairs, and a pile of mats similar to the one Ruth was sitting on in the hall. Mural-sized photos of a bearded Indian swami stared down from the walls. The smell was of incense.

Most of the rooms were occupied, with small groups of people who were either meditating, or practicing different positions of yoga, or, in one room, eating a simple lunch of brown rice from bowls on the floor.

Ruth opened a pair of French doors that led onto a large veranda whose overhanging roof was supported by columns. A group of twenty-odd people sat in a semicircle, holding hands while facing out toward the trees in the distance. Though it looked like they were meditating, they were evidently practicing the art of breathing.

"That's Brother Russell," whispered Ruth, pointing to a man seated in the middle. He was wearing a robe identical to

Ruth's, and he was in his early forties, with short-cropped thinning brown hair. His eyes were gentle, his face completely relaxed.

Is that the face of someone who recently committed a murder? Susan asked herself. She was rapidly developing serious doubts.

"Wait here," said Ruth. "They'll be done in a while. You might want to join them?"

"Thank you," said Susan.

She watched from across the veranda.

"Remember," said Russell, his soft voice barely breaking the stillness of the outdoors. "Remain in the upper lip area of your breath. It is the path to ultimate peace."

If only her own peace of mind could be reached that easily. Or Mike's, for that matter. Susan wished he would speed it up. She didn't want to interrupt, but she was in no mood to sit around listening to a chorus of slow breathing.

Finally Russell stood and began to move along the circle, gently patting each person's head. "Continue by yourselves," he instructed them. "We will then follow up with a chant."

He watched attentively as they practiced. Seeing her opportunity, Susan hurried across the veranda. "Brother Russell," she called.

"Yes," he said softly, turning to face her, surprised by the intrusion.

"My name is Susan Draper. I'd like to talk to you for a moment. It's very important." Unable to contain herself, it had all come out in one forceful breath.

Russell stepped away from the circle so as not to distract the group. He was a bit put off by her intensity. "Calm down," he said. "There is no reason to rush. It is bad for you. Please, take a deep breath."

Susan did as she was told. Anything to get him to talk.

Russell smiled. "There. Isn't that better? Now, what is it you would like to ask me?"

"It's about your father," Susan said directly.

"My father?" Russell looked a little confused.

"Arthur Thompson. From Greenwich. He *is* your father, isn't he?"

"The man you speak of was my physical father," said Russell calmly. "He and his wife gave me body and breath. When I learned that was all they could give, I chose a spiritual father, Baba Muktananda. His are the teachings we follow here."

"I gather then you don't see your real father very often?" said Susan.

"My physical father? Never." There was no rancor in his voice. He was merely stating a fact. "It is not that I dislike him, only that we think and live differently. He is a man of the military. I am a pacifist. He surrounds himself with material riches. I prefer a simple, more Spartan environment. There is nothing for us to share."

"Did you know that he got married again after your mother died?"

"Yes. He sent me a letter. But I have not met his new wife."

Susan believed he was telling the truth. But she wondered how he would react to the news. "Brother Russell, someone just killed her."

"I am sorry to hear that," he said without emotion. Like Ruth, his expression never changed.

"Do you have any idea who it might be?" said Susan, amazed by his total detachment. It was like talking to a wall.

He shook his head. "I'm afraid I can be of no help."

She was becoming very frustrated. "Do you have any idea who might want to cause your father pain?"

"No. I do not," said Russell slowly. "But maybe he will benefit from it. Suffering, you know, is good for the soul. Now, if you'll please excuse me, I must lead the chanting." His smile broadened. "Perhaps you would like to join us?"

"I don't think so," said Susan firmly. She actually couldn't wait to get out of there. These spiritual fanatics were giving her the creeps. Besides, this too had proven to be a dead end, and she was beginning to get worried. She had no idea where she and Mike could turn to next.

Mike clicked off the television set. He lit a cigarette and began pacing around the room. What the hell was he doing here in the first place? So he had panicked yesterday afternoon after seeing the police in front of his building. He'd come running, and Susan was nice enough to put him up. He was grateful, that's for sure. She had a lot to lose, letting him hide out here. But there was no reason for him to stay. God knows, there were lots of places to get lost in this city. They didn't call it a jungle for nothing. Those anonymous hotels in the West Thirties, rooming houses out in Queens . . .

Mike snuffed out the butt. He was kidding himself, and he knew it. How far would he get on six dollars and fifty-three cents or whatever it was he had in his pocket? You couldn't even get a room up in Harlem for that. Besides, those were the first places the cops always looked. There was probably a picture of him pasted behind the desk of every fleabag hotel in town. Some desk clerk would like nothing better than to finger him to the police, playing hero in hope of getting his picture in the *News*.

All right. He had to stay here. The question was how long. He thought of Susan running around trying to solve Gloria's murder. Remembering the meetings back in Walkill, he had no doubts she could get people to talk. The problem was, she had to know what to ask. With her background, what the hell did she know about crime? Her notion of a major offense was speeding or smoking grass. It had been his idea that Thompson himself, or one of his sons, might be responsible. Susan had agreed, and was now out doing the legwork.

Mike lit another cigarette. If it was just legwork, why did it bother him so much? Was it the thought of him relying on a woman? Damn right. It bugged the shit out of him. He should be out there himself. He had another theory about Gloria's death, and this was one that only he could pursue. What the hell was he waiting for? Christmas?

Mike threw his cigarette in the fireplace and hurried to get his coat. Sure, he was running a risk. But hopefully it would prove worthwhile.

In the top of the hall closet, where Susan had put his clothes, he spied a brown velvet hat, the floppy kind that could be shaped anyway you wanted and had a wide flexible brim. He could see Susan wearing it pulled back on her head, with jeans and high leather boots. She'd look like a rock singer, like Carly Simon or Joni Mitchell. Mike tried on the hat and studied himself in the hall mirror. It was pretty funky at that. And pulled forward, it covered much of his face. To disguise himself further, he turned up the collar of his army jacket and put on the wire-rim sunglasses he'd bought on his way to meet Honey in the park. He now resembled some Hollywood star, slumming so as not to be recognized. Fine with him. After all, the cops weren't looking for Steve McQueen.

He found an extra set of keys in the kitchen, and was just about to go when he decided he should leave Susan a note. *"This is just in case you come back before I return,"* he scribbled on a piece of typing paper. *"I have gone out to see a friend from inside, who I think may be of help. I appreciate what you're doing, but there's some things I have to do for myself. See you later. Mike. P.S. I borrowed one of your hats."*

Mike began to feel better as soon as he left the apartment. There was a spring in his step even as he went down the stairs. " 'Afternoon," he said to an old woman stopping to catch her breath between flights.

"It's windy out there," she said, assuming he was a neighbor. "Have you been out yet?"

"Not yet," he called, already halfway to the next landing. "But I can't wait."

The cold wind felt great against his face. And it made his covered-up outfit seem perfectly appropriate. The only problem was that Susan's hat was a little small on him, and he had to be careful it didn't blow away. Walking west on Twenty-first Street, Mike wasn't as nervous as he was yesterday, when everyone he passed looked like an undercover cop. Hopefully no one would recognize him, the way he was dressed. And even if they could, it was worth the risk, if only to get out of that apartment.

Still, he didn't want to take any unnecessary chances, and he walked quickly along the street, away from the curb and the view of any cruising policemen. He bought a copy of the *Times* at the entrance to the IRT at Twenty-third Street and Park Avenue. Holding the open paper in front of his face, he rode the local downtown. A transit patrolman got on at Union Square and stood swinging his club, inches from where Mike was sitting. Though Mike kept his eyes on the editorial page, he was much too distracted to read. He was sure the officer could hear the beating in his chest. The ride from Union Square to Bleecker Street, where the cop got off, had to be the longest subway ride in the city.

Mike got off at Spring Street, the next stop. He was about to throw the *Times* in a trashcan, but decided against it, thinking he might need it again. He lit a cigarette to calm his nerves before starting west across town.

Working his way along the streets of Little Italy, Mike thought of how, as a kid, he had always liked this neighborhood. The candy stores selling egg creams, and the bakeries with their Neapolitans, zabaglione, and so many other pastries that it was always hard to make a choice.

Right now what appealed to Mike most about Little Italy was the conspicuous absence of cops. He didn't know whether there were fewer assigned here or not, only that you rarely saw them around. You could stand all day on Mulberry Street without seeing a blue-and-white car. It was probably because they were unneeded, the Italians being so good at policing themselves, with their women in the windows, and the Mafia captains assigned to each block. Whatever the reason, Mike felt less worried walking these streets than he had farther uptown.

No one paid Mike the slightest attention as he continued along Prince Street, past Greene, Wooster, West Broadway, and Thompson. When he reached Sullivan Street, he turned left, going past a funeral parlor, a bar with American and Italian flags in the window, and a Catholic church where they played bingo on Wednesday nights. He stopped in front of some narrow steps leading down into a basement. The word "Pool" painted on the wall, like graffiti, told him this was the right place. After a quick check up and down the block, he went downstairs.

It was dark in the basement, with no natural light. The only illumination was the naked bulbs suspended over the six tables, one for billiards and the rest for pool. Against the side wall was a small bar with three worn stools. Mike took off his glasses so that he could see better. He also wanted to make sure he was recognized. In a place like this, it was unhealthy to be a stranger.

Two guys in loud sports shirts were playing eight ball over in the corner. One was tall and skinny, the other short and stocky, and they both looked to be roughly Mike's age. Judging from the stack of bills on the edge of the table, they were playing for more than just sport. Mike waited for the skinnier of the two to make his shot before he approached.

"Excuse me," he said, standing next to the table. "I'm looking for Joey Demarko. Do you know where he is?"

"Who wants to see him?" said the shooter, without looking up.

"I'm a friend of his," said Mike.

"Oh, yeah," said the other, heavyset one, chalking his cue. "Where do you know him from?"

Mike hesitated before answering. "Upstate. Walkill," he said softly.

The skinny shooter suddenly lost his interest in the game. He leaned back against the table and looked at Mike, studying him from head to foot. His eyes were not friendly. "What do you want to see him about?" he asked, staring at Mike's hat.

"That's between me and him," said Mike firmly. He had no patience for this bullshit. Two punks trying to impress him with how tough they were. "I told you. I'm a friend of his. Now, is he here or not? I don't have all day."

Mike saw that the fat one was ready to start trouble. He was coming around the table, holding his cue. That's all Mike needed, on top of everything else, a fight in a basement pool hall in Little Italy, and with two against his one. He was poised, ready to take off outside, when he heard a door open in the back of the room.

"Ross? Is that you?" The loud voice was unmistakable.

"No, Joey. It's Warden O'Connor," said Mike. "Who the hell else would come to see you?"

"You know this guy?" said the skinny one.

"'Course I know him," said Demarko, approaching the table. "We went to finishing school together."

"Just wanted to make sure, know what I mean?"

"Don't worry. He's okay."

Mike was relieved. Joey's timing couldn't have been better. He saw that Joey had changed somewhat since he'd seen him last back in Walkill. Though he still had the same wiry frame and thin, angular face, his dark hair, worn short, was now becoming flecked with gray. His eyes looked tired, as though from a hangover. He was wearing a brown sharkskin suit that was badly in need of a press, and his tie was undone.

"Joey, how are you?" asked Mike, extending his hand.

Joey ignored it. "Hey, don't tell me you've become a faggot?"

"What are you talking about?" said Mike, confused.

"What's with that hat? If that ain't for fruits, then I ain't got balls."

Mike saw the two punks staring at him. "Is there someplace private we can talk?"

"Just tell me. You're not a faggot, right?"

Mike couldn't help but laugh. He took off the hat. "Here, does that make you feel better?"

Joey grinned. "Yeah. Now you look like the guy I knew." He took Mike's hand and pumped it. "How the hell are ya? C'mon." He motioned with his head toward the rear. "We'll talk in my office."

The two punks resumed playing pool.

"It's good to see you," said Mike, following Joey to the back. "It's been a long time."

"Why do you think I was sounding off like that? I got out before you, remember. No telling what might have happened."

Mike accompanied him through a door in the rear into a small room just big enough for a card table and chairs. The walls were covered with centerfold nudes, and the table was littered with assorted slips of paper. Joey closed the door behind them.

"Make yourself at home," he said, pointing to a chair. "Can I get you something to drink?"

"No, thanks," said Mike, slouching casually in the chair, playing with the hat in his lap. "I see you're back in the numbers."

Joey laughed, taking a seat himself. "What'd you think? I was gonna go to NYU?"

"Not really. I just wouldn't want to see you get busted again."

"Don't you worry about me," said Joey, picking up a pile of slips, as if to show them off. "Two more months of parole, and then I'm clean. Much to our friend McCarthy's disappointment. He's been aching to stick me with a violation."

"You're not the only one," said Mike.

Joey dropped the pile of slips in front of him. His smile faded. "Hey, wait a minute. You're being here is all he needs. You trying to make it easy for that motherfucker?"

"Come on, Joey. You know I wouldn't be here if it weren't important. I got as much to lose as you."

"What the fuck do you want then?" His friendliness was quickly disappearing.

Mike wasn't surprised by Joey's reaction. After all, Mike was jeopardizing his parole. Mike only hoped his friend from Walkill would understand, once he learned why Mike had come. "I need your help," he said.

Joey nodded knowingly. "How much do you want?"

"It's not money."

"You looking for a job, is that it?"

"No. I got a job," said Mike impatiently. "Listen, Joey. I'm in trouble, but it's not my fault."

Shaking his head, Joey leaned forward over the table, studying the slips. He sat there silently, rearranging them like cards. "All right," he said finally, looking up at Mike. "Let's have it. Only make it fast. I got work to do, if you didn't notice."

Mike went directly to the point. "Did you read in the paper about that murder out in Greenwich? A suburban housewife shot to death in her kitchen?"

"I think I saw something about it. So what?"

"The cops think I did it."

"Did you?" said Joey casually, as if it wouldn't surprise him at all.

"No, of course I didn't. Goddammit! I'm not a fucking murderer."

"Weren't you in for homicide?"

"Manslaughter," said Mike angrily. "It was self-defense. You sound like a fucking guard."

"Take it easy," said Joey, putting up his hands. "If you didn't do it, then why are they after you?"

"Cops got their reasons. Point is, I'm hot. Why else do you think I wear hats like this?" Mike threw the hat down on the floor. "To be in style?"

Joey pushed back his chair and stood up from the table. "Thanks again for coming around here," he said sarcastically. "This is all I need." He walked over to a cabinet by the wall, opened a drawer, and took out a bottle of whiskey and a glass. He poured himself some, then drank it down like water.

Mike didn't say anything. He was beginning to wonder whether he had made a mistake in coming here. Just how far could you trust someone you had known only in prison? Of course, he and Joey had been fairly close. They were in adjoining cells and had shared magazines, cartons of cigarettes, even cash for the commissary, and all with no strings attached. "You and me," Joey had said one night after lockup, handing Mike a can of soda through the bars. "We gotta stick together."

He was worrying too much. Didn't Joey always sound off at the mouth, like the Mafia big shot he was so eager to become? It was all a fucking act. Mike was certain that underneath the noise he was still reliable as hell. And his connections were just what Mike needed.

Joey banged the bottle down on the table as he returned to his seat. "What do you want?"

Mike explained that he was trying to clear himself by finding out who was responsible for Gloria Thompson's death. "It occurred to me this afternoon that it's got all the signs of a professional job. Execution-type murder. No sign of robbery. Her husband's a hot-shot businessman. I wouldn't be surprised if some organization's trying to pocket him. Got to her as a way of scaring him."

"It's been known to happen," said Demarko evenly. "So what do you want from me?"

"You've got good connections. Ask around. See what you can come up with. I don't have any money," said Mike. "But I'm sure I can pay you back somehow."

Joey looked down at the table. He began playing again with his slips. Mike could tell he was thinking. "All right," he said at last, though without looking up. "I'll see what I can do."

"Thanks a lot," said Mike.

"Tell me, where are you staying?" There was a warmth now back in Joey's voice. He smiled. "So I can contact you if I come up with anything."

"Don't worry about it," said Mike, getting up from the chair. "I'll be in touch." He picked up Susan's hat from the floor and put it on his head. "I really appreciate this, Joey."

Joey shrugged. "Think nothing of it. We gotta help one another. No one else is sure gonna. Besides, I'll figure some way for you to pay me back. Maybe ask you to go out with my kid sister. You ever seen her? She's a dog."

The two of them laughed.

"Now, let's get you out of here," said Joey. "C'mon. I'll see you to the street. You walking up to Houston?"

"Why?" said Mike, putting on his sunglasses and pulling the hat down over his face.

"I gotta pay off a win. I'll walk you to the corner. See no one steals your hat."

Joey escorted Mike back through the pool hall and up the front steps. They walked silently to the corner.

"Be careful," said Joey softly.

"Thanks again," said Mike. "I'll be in touch."

Mike walked west on Houston, heading toward Sixth Avenue.

From a drugstore on the corner, Joey watched through the window. He hurried into a phone booth, deposited a dime, and dialed as quickly as he could.

He picked nervously at his lip until the call was answered.

"Hey, McCarthy. This is Joey Demarko. . . . Listen, I just saw one of your other boys. Mike Ross. . . . I know you're looking for him. . . . Five minutes ago. He's walking over to Sixth Avenue from Houston. . . . Just remember who told you, when I come to see you next week. . . . He's dressed like some kind of faggot. . . ."

17

Walking up Sixth Avenue, Mike felt relieved, now that he had gotten Joey's help. If Gloria's murder was, like he suspected, a professional hit job, then Joey was the one person who could check it out. Of course, what he would do then remained to be seen. Go after some hit man in order to clear himself? First things first. Wait until he saw what Joey came up with. He figured he'd give him two days, maybe three, before checking back with him. Until then, he just had to bide his time.

He didn't want to go back to Susan's apartment. At least not yet. He saw the Waverly Theater up ahead, and he checked the marquee to see what was playing. *Smokey and the Bandit*. Just what he needed. Pure escape entertainment. And who the hell went to the movies at four in the afternoon? What a perfect place to get lost.

Mike was just starting across the street when he saw the patrol car cruising down Sixth Avenue. Instinctively he turned back toward the sidewalk and stepped up to a nearby mailbox. Pretending to mail a letter, he bent low to study the collection schedule written in front. Mike waited until he was sure the police car was at least two blocks downtown before he looked up to face the street. Out of the corner of his eye he saw the blue-and-white car making a U-turn down by Bleecker. Don't tell me they've recognized me, he thought to himself. Not in these glasses and hat. Cool it, man. Don't do anything rash.

To be less conspicuous, he walked quickly up to Third Street and into the vest-pocket park on the corner. As always, there was a pickup basketball game in progress. Mike joined the crowd watching through the chain-wire fence. The caliber of basketball played in this park was among the best in the city. Young hot shots from Harlem and aspiring Doctor J's from the Bronx came down here regularly to compete. Mike was an avid basketball fan. He could watch these guys go at it for hours. Casually he looked over his shoulder. Who knows? Maybe the cops in that car were fans as well. Maybe that explained why they double-parked and were walking quickly across the street toward the game.

Wrong. They were looking directly at *him*. What's worse, the closest cop was quietly reaching for his gun.

Shit! Without hesitation Mike pushed through the bodies lining the entrance to the court. Knowing the police would never fire in such a crowd, he ran directly through the middle of the game, heading for the gate on the far side. He was almost in the clear when the ball changed hands. Ten giants thundered downcourt. And Mike tripped over a pair of feet wearing violin cases for shoes.

He hit the pavement hard in a belly flop, knocking the wind out of him. Though dazed, he could feel where the hot asphalt had scraped against his palms and knees as he had tried to break his fall.

"What the hell you doin', man? Can't you see we playin'?" Looking up from the ground, Mike squinted at the angry black face staring down at him. At the same time, he heard a tense voice coming from somewhere off court. "Step aside. Police. Coming through."

The black turned toward the voice, then back down at Mike. Anger gone, there was concern in his eyes. "Hey, man. They after you? Get your ass outta here."

Remembering where he was, Mike scurried to his feet and dashed through the gate. "Get out of the way. Hurry it up!" Mike heard. "Excuse me, officer. Just playing ball." He didn't have to look back. He could tell by the voices that the black had purposely blocked the cops to give him time to get away. Thank God there was still honor on these streets. No one wanted to see an innocent guy busted by the cops.

Mike turned east on Third Street, running as fast as he could. Fortunately, there was little traffic. He ran in the gutter, swerving to avoid a bicyclist, a blind man crossing the street, a girl walking her dog. Halfway down the block his hat fell from his head. Glancing quickly over his shoulder, he saw the two policemen sprinting in pursuit. They could keep the damn hat. Take it home to one of their wives. He'd buy Susan another one. Plus a coat and matching shoes. If he could only get out of this mess.

He couldn't just keep running. His arms hurt from the fall. His legs were too slow. His lungs were choked. And wasn't that the crackle of a police walkie-talkie? Any minute now there'd be cops converging from all directions, coming out of stores, parked cars, flying helicopters, for all he knew. Vying with each other for the collar. Like a loose basketball in an overtime game, he was a valuable item. And from the looks of that flashing red light only two blocks away, there was already another team of players hot on his tail.

He needed an open manhole bad. Or at least a swifter pair of legs. Mike turned the corner, his lungs gasping for air, and headed south on Macdougal, past a small coffeehouse where he used to hang out. No time to hide in there. Behind him, the sound of running footsteps, coming closer by the second, and then *"Stop! Or I'll shoot."*

If he hadn't seen the sign, Mike would've stopped. He knew when the game was over, when it was time to call it quits. Hell with pitting his legs against a .38-caliber slug. Even jail was better than getting shot. Becoming paralyzed or worse. But the fact was he *had* seen the sign. MINETTA LANE. Less than two strides away. He was already at the corner. Just as he made the turn, stepping out of sight of the .38 aimed at his back, Mike realized where he was, and when he had last been here. This was his one chance for escape.

Now, which building was it? There was no time to think. Only to act. He was approaching one he sensed was familiar. Six stories. Red brick. An "Apartment for Rent" sign posted out front. That had to be it. Sensing safety, he sprinted up the steps of the stoop, threw open the door, and ducked down in the outer lobby, out of view from the street. He waited for the running footsteps and loud curses to pass before moving. Crouched in front of the names listed on the side of the wall, he nervously ran his finger down the list, praying that he had been right. There it was. *Jones.* He pressed the button. If only it was the right one.

"Yeeeahhs?" said a heavily affected voice through the speaker.

"It's me, Mike. Let me in." He could hear the policemen returning down the street.

The noise of the buzzer opening the door was the most glorious sound in the world. Mike pushed open the door and rushed inside, taking the stairs two at a time.

The policemen were all over the building. Mike could hear them out in the hall banging on doors, panting from the four flights of stairs, and bitching about the loss of an important arrest.

"Where the hell did he go?" said one.

"He ain't up here," said another, calling from the roof. "He mighta jumped across. There's a building that's close enough."

"Dammit! Just our luck."

"Try these other apartments. Maybe someone saw him."

Mike heard them knock on the door. He inched closer to the wall, accidentally knocking a hangar to the floor. He hoped they didn't hear it. He tried to keep perfectly still. The smell of camphor made it hard to breathe.

"Open up! Police."

Mike heard footsteps in the foyer, approaching the door. *Don't tell me he's letting them in. I thought he was going to pretend to be away.* He heard the lock being turned. *Oh, Jesus!*

"Yes?" said a yawning voice. "What is it?"

"We're looking for someone who was seen entering this building. Did you hear anyone running in the halls?"

"Only you, handsome. Waking me up."

"Don't be cute, fella," retorted the cop impatiently. "How long you been asleep?"

"What time's it now?"

"Four o'clock."

"Two hours then. My beauty nap. Take it every day."

"Listen, you little creep. I don't got time for this shit. Did you hear anything or not?"

"My, you're tough. Anyone ever tell you, you got beautiful eyes?"

"C'mon," said another voice. "We're just wasting time."

"Tell me, Blue Eyes. This man you're looking for. Was he my type?"

"You mean a fucking queer? I wouldn't be surprised," grumbled the policeman faintly, continuing down the hall.

Mike heard the door close and lock. Footsteps, and then the closet where he was hiding slowly being opened. A grinning black face peered behind the hangers. "You can come out now," Hardy whispered. "I scared them away."

Mike saw that Hardy was naked except for a sheet wrapped around his waist. "Scared them, huh. Dressed like that? Blue Eyes will probably come back for a visit."

"Lot you know about it," said Hardy teasing. "Look at you. You're still in the closet."

Mike laughed.

"C'mon out. The boys are all gone. I'll make you a drink."

"I sure as hell could use one." His heart was pounding like a tin drum.

It was a small, sparsely furnished studio apartment. The shades were drawn to keep out the sun. Pictures of Johnny Mathis, Johnny Ray, and Ruth Etting lined the walls. Hardy poured two vodkas on the rocks, then sprawled out on the bed. Mike collapsed into a nearby chair.

Over sips of his drink, Mike told Hardy what had happened and why the police were after him. "Thank God you were home and were quick to answer the door. Otherwise, you'd have to come visit me upstate."

"You shouldn't be walking around, dummy. That's just asking to be picked up."

"I was coming back from seeing someone I thought might help. A friend of mine from Walkill."

Hardy nodded knowingly. "A friend, huh. And five minutes later the cops are on your butt. Just a coincidence, right?"

Mike put down his drink. "Jesus, I hadn't even thought of that."

"Why not? You so trusting all of a sudden?"

"I was too busy running to think about it. Dammit! You're right. That fucking Demarko! That son of a bitch! Boy, would I like to kick his ass."

"He'd probably love it. I know those Italians. Baby, looks like you gotta stay off the streets. You want to stay here, it's fine with me. Problem is, I only have one bed."

Mike smiled. "Save it for Blue Eyes. I think he's more

your type. Thanks anyway, but I already have a place to stay."

"Oh, yeah? With whom?"

"A woman friend. I don't think you know her."

"Figures." Hardy sighed. "Don't say I didn't try." He sipped his drink. "Seriously, though, whatever I can do to help, just let me know. This is terrible, baby. Absolutely terrible."

"You're telling me," said Mike.

"Call me on the job if there's anything I can do." Hardy smiled. "You know the number."

"Too well. Can you believe I actually miss working? Anything's better than this. What did the boss say when I didn't show up?"

"Same old crap. How irresponsible show-biz people were. How if he had his way, he'd never hire any of us."

Mike laughed. He was feeling more relaxed now. And appreciating what a good friend he had in Hardy. "What'd you say to him?"

"Nothing. I started singing 'Maria.' Drove him out of the room. Fucking guy wouldn't know talent if he fell on it. Talk about talent, you should see the dyke he brought in to take your place. Short hair. Boots, pants, the works. Someone ought to teach her how to be a lady. I'd do it myself, 'cept I'm afraid she might beat me up."

Hardy had given Mike an idea about how he could safely get back to Susan's. "You wouldn't know where I can get some women's clothes?" he asked.

"Women's clothes? What you want with them?"

Mike shrugged. "I'm out of the closet, right? Maybe it's time to really take the plunge."

Hardy grinned. "Baby, you came to the right place. They don't call this downtown Bendel's for nothing."

Susan was worried. Where in the world was Mike? She'd been home for over an hour now, and there was still no word from him. Was he crazy, leaving the apartment? That was just asking to be locked up. She wondered if she had misjudged him. Maybe he wasn't so smart after all, but instead was out looking for trouble. Maybe taking serious risks gave him some kind of thrill. If so, then he was stupid, and deserved whatever happened to him.

Take it easy, she told herself, looking out the window at the street. She was just angry because he wasn't there to greet her. What did she expect? Gratitude? Did she really think he'd stick around, waiting patiently for her to clear him with the police? She was acting like those civil-rights workers in the sixties, expecting the blacks to fawn over them in thanks. It was Mike's life.

Still, the least he could do was call. She was worried. She wondered who the friend was he was seeing for help. Joey Demarko, of course. He said it was someone from "inside." Susan rushed into the kitchen and pulled the phone book out of a drawer. She turned quickly to the D's. Maybe Mike was still there. If not, she could find out what time he had left. Joey would tell her. Of course he'd remember her from the meetings.

There was a Joseph Demarko jewelry store on East Fifty-second Street, and a J. Demarko on Upper Broadway. She knew that wasn't it. Mike said he lived somewhere in Little Italy. There it was. Jos Demarko. Thompson Street. Susan dialed the number.

She was pacing in the kitchen, trailing the telephone cord, waiting for Joey to pick up, when the doorbell rang. Maybe that was Mike now. But he had taken the keys, so why would he ring?

Susan hung up the phone and went to open the door.

The woman standing there looked like she just stepped off the pages of *Vogue*. She was wearing red pants and a matching jacket on top of a celery-green cowl-neck sweater. Her hair was hidden beneath a polka-dot Hermes kerchief, and her aviator sunglasses were so darkly tinted that you couldn't see her eyes. She had on a great deal of makeup, lipstick and rouge, all of which looked freshly applied. A brown leather Gucci bag dangled from her shoulder. Susan assumed she had just moved into the building, and perhaps wanted to borrow something.

"Sorry I'm late. I stopped off to do a little shopping."

Susan did a double take. "Mike?" she asked.

"Who else did you expect? I would've let myself in, but I couldn't reach the keys."

She stepped aside so he could enter the apartment, then quickly closed and locked the door. "I didn't even recognize you."

"You weren't supposed to. That's the point of all this. Wait'll I tell you what happened," he said in one breath.

"Why didn't you call me?" she said angrily. "I was worried silly."

"Didn't you see the note I left?"

"That was hours ago. You could've been arrested, for all I knew. Thanks a lot."

"I'm sorry," said Mike, irritated and surprised by her reaction. "There just wasn't time." As he walked over to the couch, he took off the glasses with one hand and the kerchief with the other. He had some trouble unhooking the pants in the back. "Hey, give me a hand with this, will you?" he asked, looking over at Susan, standing across the room. Still angry, she had turned her back to him.

"What's wrong? You never seen someone undress before? Don't worry. I got shorts on underneath. My own. I mean, there's a limit."

Reluctantly she turned to face him. The sight of him in makeup, struggling with the pants, made her forget her anger. "Look at you. I'm surprised someone didn't try to pick you up."

"They did. Some guy on the bus asked me out for a date."

"Oh, yeah? What'd you tell him?"

Mike imitated a woman's falsetto voice. "Thank you, but my husband is waiting."

Susan couldn't help laughing as she helped him with the pants. "You're very good at that. Did you ever think of becoming an actor?"

"I'd rather be a fugitive," said Mike sarcastically, taking off the jacket, the sweater, and the bra that was stuffed with a pair of socks. "It's more fun."

"I'm glad you're okay," said Susan with a deep sigh of relief now that the anger had passed.

"You and me both," said Mike. "Can you help me take off this makeup? I feel like Mae West."

"I really should let you do it yourself. Serves you right for going out in the first place."

Mike shrugged. "Okay. I'll do it myself." He started for the bathroom.

Susan sighed. "Knowing you, you'll ruin the towels. Wait a second, I'll give you a hand."

As Susan used a cloth to scrub his face over the bathroom sink, Mike told her about his going to see Joey Demarko.

"I figured that's who you meant. Fact, I was trying to call him when you arrived."

"Thank God you didn't. Then we'd really be screwed. Fucking guy ratted on me. I'm convinced of it. Five minutes after I leave him, two cops are after me. There's no other way they coulda known it was me, 'less someone squealed. I was wearing glasses, a hat. By the way, I lost your hat. I'm sorry. I'll get you another one."

"Forget about it," said Susan. "I'm really surprised about Joey."

"I'm not. I should've known better. See what kind of friends you make in prison? Most of them ain't worth shit."

Susan removed the face powder that was under his chin, covering his whiskers.

"Dammit," said Mike. "I said I was sorry. Do you have to be so rough?"

"Pipe down. I'm almost done. Whoever put this on did one hell of a job. Where'd you go? Elizabeth Arden?"

"Friend of mine's house. Hardy. Guy's got lots of talent. Made that pantsuit I was wearing. Weren't for him, I'd be locked up in some precinct right now."

He told her about the chase through the basketball court and the streets of the West Village. "Fortunately Hardy lived right there on the block. I had a drink there one night after work."

"Lucky he was home," said Susan.

"Lucky he was awake is more like it. He's out all night long. Sometimes he sleeps clear past five. Hey, did you see Thompson's son?"

"I saw him, all right. But it wasn't much help. He's deep into spiritualism. Chanting. Meditation. All of it. The guy wouldn't hurt a cockroach. He never even met Gloria."

"You believe him?" said Mike.

"I'm afraid so."

"Shit!"

"It's been a rotten day for both of us. But at least you're safe." Susan efficiently rubbed his face dry. "That's the best I can do for you. See what you think."

Mike looked at himself in the mirror. "What do you mean, what do I think? I look like me."

"That's the point," said Susan, smiling. "I think I liked you better the other way."

"That's your problem," Mike teased, turning the tub faucet on. "I need to take a shower," he said, waiting for her to leave.

"I'll start dinner. I did a little shopping myself on the way home."

Susan was opening a bottle of red wine when Mike came in from the bathroom. He had shaved and washed his hair, and he looked sexy drying his hair in his cowboy shirt and tight jeans. "We're almost ready to eat. I just have to set the table."

"I hope you didn't go to any bother. Anything is fine with me," he said, flinging the wet towel over the sofa.

"No trouble at all," she said, forgetting, as he sat down at the table, that she had gone blocks out of her way to the best butcher in the neighborhood, and had spent close to ten dollars on the wine. "But hang up the towel first."

"Oh, yeah, sure."

Susan served the broiled sirloin steak, toasted garlic bread, and the fresh spinach salad with mushrooms and chives.

"This is fabulous," said Mike, cutting into the steak. "Remind me to come to you for help more often."

Susan enjoyed watching him eat so heartily. Sitting there at the glass-top table, Mike seemed almost relaxed. It was as if this was a regular date, and that after dinner they would go out for a movie or a stroll, a drink somewhere in the Village before ending the evening back at his place. She preferred not to think, at least for the moment, of why Mike was here.

However, there was little else on his mind. "I was saying before, I wouldn't be surprised if Thompson was being pressured by some mob. Big businessman like that. Happens all the time. They might have got to Gloria as a way of scaring him."

"He didn't say anything about it," said Susan.

"No way he would of. He's probably too scared to admit it, even to himself."

"I'll check tomorrow with the crime reporter at the *News*. Maybe he knows something. Do you have any other ideas?"

"What about the military?" said Mike, biting into his third piece of garlic bread. "I told you about those pictures of him with Eisenhower."

Susan poured him some more wine. "I really doubt that has anything to do with it. I asked Thompson about his military career, and he was perfectly straightforward. Ran through all the posts he was on, the action he saw during World War Two, all of it. Besides, he retired so long ago, back in the early fifties. According to him, his last assignment was totally inconsequential. He was stationed on some minor post in Maryland."

Mike stood up from the table. "We're just guessing anyway. What the hell's the use?" he said. "We're never gonna find out what happened." He walked over to the couch and lay down, staring at the ceiling. "I might as well just turn myself in and be done with it."

"Don't be silly," said Susan, coming over and standing in front of him. "Besides the crime reporter, there are lots of other people I can talk to. Don't worry. We'll break this thing."

"I don't know," said Mike. "I think we're kidding ourselves." He was feeling very discouraged.

"C'mon, finish your dinner. I got a special dessert. If you don't watch out, I'll eat it all myself."

Susan got up and went to the kitchen. Mike could hear her open the refrigerator and then return to the table. "Wow, does this look good," she said. "It'll be worth every pound I gain."

"What is it?" said Mike tentatively.

"Nothing you'd like. 'Less of course you like Miss Grimble's cherry cheesecake with graham-cracker crust. Not to mention some Haagen Dazs rum-raisin ice cream on the side, along with French roast coffee from Balducci's, followed up by Drambuie or cognac, or . . . But you're not interested in any of this, so might as well just lie there."

"Boy do you know how to torture someone," said Mike, getting up and returning to the table. "You'd make a great prison guard."

"I've got to learn to be tougher," said Susan, dishing out the dessert. "Can't expect me to go to bat for an inmate, if the inmate's gonna go looking for trouble."

"How many times do I have to tell you I'm sorry? What the hell do you want from me? Blood?"

"I want you to *stay* here," said Susan. "I expect to find you when I come back tomorrow."

"It's damn hard," said Mike. "I can't tell you how boring it is. One day, and I've had enough of the soaps. And I must've read every single word in the *Times*. Even the obituary page."

"Start in on the books. I've got enough to keep you busy for weeks."

"That's encouraging," said Mike sarcastically. "By the way, I hope you don't mind, but I took a look at your photo album. Who's the blond guy in all the photos?"

"You must mean Fred."

"Who's Fred?"

"My husband," said Susan casually.

"Your husband? You didn't tell me you were married."

"You never asked. You just noticed I didn't have a ring. Besides, I'm divorced. Aren't you glad? Where would you be now, if I weren't?"

Mike grinned. "Guess I'd just have to find me another divorcée."

"They're certainly enough of us around," said Susan.

"Seriously, why did you split up?"

"Irreconcilable differences. He liked apple pie. I preferred cherry cheesecake. It was the beginning of the end."

"That makes sense," said Mike. "How about another piece?"

Susan suggested that they take their coffee over to the couch.

"Good idea," said Mike.

"Go sit down. I'll bring it over."

Mike leaned back on the sofa, his feet flat on the floor, his hands on his thighs, staring straight ahead at the books. Susan sprawled at the other end, her legs curled under her like a cat. The coffeecups were on the marble table in front of them.

"It's been quite a day," said Susan.

"That's for sure."

She drained her cup. "Would you like some more?"

"No, thanks. This'll be enough." He sipped the coffee, cradling the cup in his hand.

Susan saw how Mike's jeans bunched at his thighs. She leaned forward to return her cup to the table, then sat back down closer to him on the couch. Their knees were an inch apart.

Mike finished his coffee. Now he leaned forward to place the cup on the table. Susan took the opportunity to move even closer. When Mike leaned back, their legs were touching.

"Can I get you anything else? Some Drambuie or cognac?"

"No, thanks. This is fine. Help yourself, though."

Susan smiled. "I guess I can live without it."

Mike reached into his shirt pocket for a cigarette.

"Let me light it for you," said Susan. She took a match from the table, struck it, and moved it slowly to the end of the cigarette. She stared in Mike's eyes as he took a deep drag. Still looking at him, she blew out the flame.

"Thanks," he said casually.

"You're welcome," she said softly.

Mike smoked his cigarette in silence. They were now so close that Susan could feel his chest rise and fall with each puff. She was waiting for him to put his arm around her. But when he finished the cigarette, tapped it out in the ashtray, then folded his arms in front of him, she sensed that she could wait all night.

Of course, she didn't have to wait for him. She could start in herself. But there was a limit to Susan's boldness. And she didn't want Mike to think she was pushy.

Mike was nervous being so close to Susan. He could tell that she was waiting for him to make the first move. He rarely needed encouragement, especially from someone as attractive as she. Yet each time he considered putting his arm around her, he found himself strangely inhibited. He was still uncomfortable being so dependent on Susan. He felt that by making love he would be somehow giving in, confirming his need for her. No doubt the sex would be good. But with his last bit of independence gone, he would wake up tomorrow feeling more depressed than ever.

"I'm tired," he said at last. "I think I'll go to sleep."

"Okay, Michael," said Susan, unsure whether or not she should feel hurt. As she slowly stood up from the couch, she impulsively reached over and mussed his hair.

Mike looked up at her. "Thank you, Susan," he said softly. "For everything."

Susan smiled. "Sleep well. I'll see you in the morning."

18

"Is that Boston?" said Billy, his nose up against the airplane window.

Markham loosened his seat belt so he could lean over for a better look. He pressed close to his son. "That's it, all right. We're lucky it's so clear. You really get a good view."

"Sure didn't take us very long. Seems like we just left New York."

"Look, there's the Custom House Tower," said Markham, draping his arm around Billy's shoulder. "Right along the water. It's one of the tallest buildings in Boston. We'll go up in it later."

"Is it as big as the World Trade Center?"

"Not that big."

"Dad, where's Schaefer Stadium?"

"It's in Foxboro. You can't see it from here. Don't worry. You'll be there tomorrow."

"Yeah. When the Jets destroy the Patriots."

"I wouldn't be so sure. The Patriots are favored."

"The Jets *better* win," said Billy. "I didn't come all this way to see them lose."

Markham kept his arm around Billy's shoulder as the two of them stared out the window. He could tell it was going to be a marvelous trip. Look at how everything had fallen into place. First there was the invitation to speak at the New England Law Enforcement Conference. Though he normally turned down most out-of-town speaking engagements, this one he eagerly accepted. He liked going back to Boston. He had to go there in any case, and here was a ready-made alibi.

Somehow it seemed right to bring Billy along. Maybe because the conference coincided with his birthday. What a perfect present. They could go sightseeing together, even take in a football game. What luck that the Patriots were playing a home game, and against none other than Billy's favorite team.

When Markham revealed the surprise present one afternoon, right in front of Leslie, Billy was so surprised, jumping up and down, that his mother had no choice but to agree. "Pretty damn manipulative," she said later, when Billy ran upstairs to tell a friend.

"Oh, really? You ain't seen nothing," said Markham with an unpleasant smirk. "Just try me in court."

"Bastard."

"You better believe it, Leslie. And I wouldn't forget that if I were you."

Markham now had Billy to himself for two full days. He intended to take him all over Boston, to the places he had gone with his own father so many years before. He could hardly wait. What did it matter that his bodyguard, sitting across the aisle, would be tagging along? The guard, assigned by the mayor since the attempt on his life, would not interfere. And when the time came to go about his business, Markham would slip away with no problem at all. Here too everything was planned. He knew exactly where to go, and when to get there. It would be a piece of cake.

"Dad?" said Billy.

Staring blankly out the window, Markham still had his arm around his son.

"Dad?" Billy repeated.

"Yes?"

"You better fasten your seat belt. We're about ready to land."

They took a cab from Logan Airport to the Colonnade, on Huntington Avenue. Markham had chosen the new hotel both for its elegance—the derby-hatted doorman and plush orange-and-gold lobby with potted palms and crystal chandelier—and for its convenient location across from the Prudential Center. The Prudential subway station was on the Green Line of the MBTA, the line Markham would use later that night.

He had reserved two adjoining rooms, one for himself and

Billy and the other for the guard, Patrolman Peters, who was out of the Sixth Precinct downtown. Peters was built like a side of beef. His deep-set eyes were constantly alert, and the safety strap on his shoulder holster was always undone. Markham couldn't have asked for a more suitable bodyguard. Peters never crowded him, preferring to hover close but removed. Better yet, he rarely spoke, which was unusual for a cop. Markham could easily forget he was there.

"All set, Billy," said his father eagerly after they had unpacked their bags. "Let's go sightseeing."

"Where to?"

"Leave that to me." Markham picked up his camera. "Are you ready, Peters?"

The guard smoothed his sport coat down over his piece. "Yes, sir."

They started at the Boston Common, which, Markham explained, was the oldest public park in the country, "a place where cows once grazed, and witches were hanged." From there they followed the "freedom trail" through downtown Boston, stopping in the "new" State House, the Park Street Church, and other historical sites along the way. Markham maintained a running commentary throughout. Billy was impressed by his father's knowledge.

"How do you know so much, Dad?"

"You forget. I grew up near Boston. I was taken here many times when I was a kid."

They visited Faneuil Hall, the site of the Boston Massacre, and the Granary Burying Ground. "Goddammit!" said Markham when he couldn't recall the date of the massacre, and whether it was John Adams or Paul Revere buried in the graveyard.

"You can't remember everything," said Billy.

"Yes I should," said Markham, intent on recalling every single fact he had shared with his father. "There's no excuse."

Billy soon became bored with his father's crash course in colonial history. He asked if they could go to a movie. Markham was insistent that they continue. "You can see a movie anytime at home. You're here with me, Billy, and you have to learn everything."

They had lunch at Durgin Park, waiting a half hour in line for the roast beef, cornbread, and Indian pudding that Markham remembered as being so good. Fortunately, it still was.

Then it was off to the site of the Boston Tea Party, *Old Ironsides,* and the Bunker Hill Monument.

Billy asked if they were in some kind of race.

"There's so much to see," Markham replied pensively. He was staring out the window as the cab crossed the Charlestown Bridge toward the monument. "We only have this one day, and then it's all gone."

Billy suppressed a sigh. Peters massaged his aching calves. Markham was oblivious.

It was coming back to him now, fleetingly at first, but with growing clarity, the sights, the sounds, the memories from his youth. Wasn't it right there, in front of the monument, that he had posed for a picture? He could almost see his father standing nearby, aiming his camera, smiling, the afternoon sun playing on his dark blond hair. Markham positioned Billy where he himself had stood, then took the picture from the exact same spot.

Peters offered to take a picture of father and son. "Good idea," said Markham, recalling that a stranger had once done the same. "We'll stand over by that tree." He put his arm around Billy, holding him as he had been held.

"How 'bout it, Dad?" said Billy. "Can we go back to the hotel now? I'm really tired."

"One more stop," said Markham. He was feeling exhilarated, flushed by the memories he had once tried to lose, but was now so compelled to regain. "And then that'll be it."

They took a cab to the Custom House Tower, which Markham had pointed out from the airplane. Riding the old elevator to the top, he remembered coming here at nine years old, just before they moved to Maryland. His father had brought him into Boston to see the Red Sox play the Yankees. It was a night game, and the two of them spent the afternoon sightseeing. The tower was the very last stop.

On the observation deck, facing the wharves, the aquarium, and across the harbor to the North Shore beaches, Markham recalled the previous visit. Like now, the air was cool and crisp, and the sun was low in the sky, casting dark shadows over the water. He squinted at Billy, standing by his side. He saw himself at nine, wearing the gray flannel pants that always itched his legs, and the camel's hair coat Daddy bought for him two weeks before.

Daddy was wearing a dark blue suit and Frankie's favorite

striped tie. He had on bay rum after-shave. He reached down and ran his hand through Frankie's hair. Frankie felt loved and protected. He couldn't have been happier.

As if nothing had changed, Markham now stroked Billy's hair. He smiled. "We'll have fun in Maryland," he said softly. "You'll like it there."

"Maryland?" said Billy. "What are you talking about, Dad?"

Slowly Markham's smile faded. Painfully he sensed his mistake. "Bastards," he said to himself. "All of them." He was anticipating tonight.

He wished they'd put down their damn hands. It was bad enough having to speak to five hundred small-town D.A.'s and criminal lawyers about "The Post-Watergate Jury." But then to have to concentrate on their questions, when his mind was so far away. It was maddening. How much longer was this going to last?

Thank God his host was finally joining him at the podium. It was about time. "I'm afraid that's all the questions we have time for," he announced. "I want to thank Mr. Markham for so kindly coming to be with us tonight."

Markham nodded in appreciation of the applause, while discreetly glancing at his watch. He was going to have to hurry. He politely excused himself from the host, and motioned to Peters, who was sitting alongside him on the stage. "C'mon," he said. "Let's go back to the hotel."

Billy was watching television when Markham and Peters returned to The Colonnade. He yawned. "How was your speech, Dad?"

"I'll tell you tomorrow. You look as tired as I feel. Let's go to bed. You want to be in good shape to enjoy the game."

"That's for sure," said Billy, turning off the set.

"Good night," said Markham to Peters before closing the door between their rooms. "Any trouble, and I'll knock."

"Don't worry, Mr. Markham. I'm a light sleeper. Good night, sir."

Markham waited until the breathing in the next bed was steady and slow. He then quietly got out of bed and put on the clothes he had unpacked and placed deep in a drawer. Black corduroy pants. A brown turtleneck sweater. And a suede leather cap, which he pulled down close to his ears. His

.38 Centennial was wrapped inside a scarf. The gun went into the side pocket of his trench coat, the scarf around his neck. Markham carried his shoes in his hands as he tiptoed to the door. He was so quiet that not even a light sleeper would have heard him leave.

As he resembled a typically dressed Boston professor, no one in the lobby gave Markham a second look as he passed through to the street. He hurried to the nearby subway station, where he caught the Green Line in the direction of Brookline. He checked his watch. Eleven-fifty. He was ten minutes ahead of schedule.

James Nelson stood up from the card table and stretched.

"I'm afraid that's it for me. It's already past my bedtime."

"Here I was hoping to clean you out," said Sam Schwartz, still grinning from the last hand.

"What makes you think you haven't already?"

"I'll loan you a couple of bucks. C'mon. Just a few more hands."

"No, thanks," said Nelson. "It's time to quit. See you next week."

"I'll walk you to the car," said Nelson's brother, Frederick. "Get a breath of fresh air."

Frederick put his arm around James's shoulders as they walked along the driveway. "How much did you lose?" asked Frederick.

James shrugged. "Sixty. Sixty-five. These Saturday nights are getting to be pretty expensive."

"Don't worry," said his brother. "Your luck will change."

"When? When I'm seventy?"

Frederick smiled. "That's not so far off."

"Thanks a lot," said James, opening his car door. "Listen, what time shall I come by tomorrow?"

"Try to be here by ten so we can beat the traffic. You know the game is sold out. Half my department is going."

"Tearing themselves away from the labs, are they?"

"That's right. We're giving the white mice a holiday. Anything to beat the Jets. Drive carefully, now. I'll see you tomorrow."

Driving through the streets of suburban Brookline, James berated himself for losing so much money. These weekly games were becoming an extravagant form of entertainment.

Well, what of it? Didn't he deserve a little relaxation? He had worked hard all his life. And what was fifty or sixty dollars a week out of his Social Security, his substantial pension from the Boston school system, as well as all his savings? His expenses were next to nothing. Food. Electricity. Gasoline. There were no children to support, and no greedy ex-wives.

Poor Frederick. He sometimes wondered how his brother made ends meet, what with three separate alimonies to pay, along with a step-daughter who always had her hand out. Good as his position at MIT was, it was not *that* well-paying. Frederick was the last person who should waste his money gambling.

But his brother was obviously lonely, and used the card games as a pretext to have people around. Why, a day didn't go by without Frederick calling up on the phone, inviting James for dinner, cards, or to a football or basketball game. James was flattered. It was only in recent years, since Frederick's latest divorce, that they had become so close. And he remembered how hurt his brother had gotten when he'd turned him down twice in a row, once to go bowling, and then to some faculty party.

"You're the only family I care about," Frederick said. "The only one who's not ripping me off."

As he drove into the driveway of his small ranch-style house, James reminded himself to ask Frederick tomorrow if he needed some money. What were brothers for, if not to help one another? Frederick always took such an interest in James's problems, his high blood pressure, and the arthritis in his hip, and it was the least he could do to reciprocate.

James stopped the car, and with the engine still running, he got out to open the garage door. He realized he had forgotten to lock it in his haste to get to the game. And with three burglaries in the neighborhood within the last month. Oh, well. There wasn't much a burglar could get from the garage. Spare tires. His broken outboard motor. Nothing that couldn't be easily replaced.

Returning to the car, James drove slowly into the garage, his headlights picking out the motor and the tires. See. He was worrying too much. He turned off the engine and was just about to get out, when something moving in the rearview mirror caught his eye. He looked up, to see the garage door closing by itself.

What in the world was going on? Had the supporting chain snapped? He turned around. It was dim in the unlit garage, only a muted light from the street penetrating the windows. The outboard motor, the trunk of the car, his hand on the back of the seat. All were swallowed up in the dark.

James sensed something was wrong. Out of the corner of his eye he saw a dark form move from the side wall slowly toward the car. Oh, my God! There was a burglar here after all. He must have surprised him in the act. James was frightened, unsure of what to do. But he had the presence of mind to reach for the button to lock himself in.

He was too late. Before he got to the lock, the door opened beneath his hand. James quickly recoiled across the seat. He huddled tightly on the other side of the car. He wasn't sure which was worse—the total silence in the garage, or not seeing who was standing by the open door.

"What do you want?" he called in desperation. "Take anything. It's yours."

Silence.

"Please. Just leave me alone."

Suddenly a light shone in his eyes. James instinctively raised his hands.

Markham held the flashlight in one hand, his gun in the other. He saw the fear on James Nelson's face. The wide eyes and twisted mouth. It was beautiful. He could have enjoyed it for hours. But he had to get back to the hotel. "Bastard," he said before he slowly pulled the trigger. He smiled, watching the body jerk as he fired three times.

Markham was still smiling when he woke up the next day. He felt at peace with the world. Boston. Billy. James Nelson. Now, if only the Jets would win.

19

Mike slammed the book shut. Still sprawled on the couch, he tossed it onto the table, next to the others. It was getting so he could not read a thing without getting upset. *The Autobiography of Malcolm X*, Tennessee Williams' *Memoirs*, or *Live and Let Die*. Didn't matter what he had taken down from Susan's shelf. Rather than helping him to relax, everything reminded him of his predicament. Malcolm X, himself shot to death, made him think of Gloria. Williams' anecdotes about the theater reminded him of the acting lessons he was missing. And the way James Bond took care of business made him feel absolutely helpless by comparison.

He had already read *Newsweek*, *New York*, and *People*, cover to cover. He skimmed through the *Times*, checking whether there was any new mention of the police investigation. Thank God there wasn't. With a sigh of relief Mike lit a cigarette and reached once again for the paper to concentrate on the news.

There was a photo on the front page of the district attorney giving a speech out of town. He was obviously running for something to warrant that kind of attention. Mike thought of how he too would make it up front if he were arrested.

Compulsively Mike continued through the *Times*. On the obituary page he saw that a famous actress had died. He looked to see if anyone else of note was listed.

JAMES S. NELSON, 69, FORMER BOSTON SCHOOL CHANCELLOR

James S. Nelson, who served the Boston school system

for more than four decades, as classroom teacher, principal, and for fifteen years as chancellor, was found shot to death Saturday night in his suburban Brookline home.

Just his luck! Here he's beginning to get out of himself, starting to relax, when he picks an article that brings him right back. Another goddamn murder. Mike was about to turn to the editorial page when one line of the half-column obituary caught his eye.

> Nelson is survived by his brother, Frederick, a professor of biology at MIT and former Defense Department official under both Truman and Eisenhower.

Mike put down the paper. Distracted, he lit another cigarette. *Eisenhower.*

It was hard to think of him as a war hero. He looked so common in a business suit. He should have stayed in uniform, with a hat covering his head, and a chestful of medals. Mike thought of the picture in Gloria's den. Arthur Thompson standing alongside the general. Thompson's medals were nothing compared to Ike's.

He never did find out where that picture was taken. Some military base Ike was visiting. What did Susan say Thompson had done in the service? That's right. She didn't know. But she was sure it had nothing to do with Gloria's death.

Mike slowly puffed at his cigarette, watching the smoke curl upward and disappear. Shit! Here he was thinking of Gloria's death once again. If it's not a murder in Boston that reminds him of her, why then it's a . . . next of kin to the victim who once served in the military.

Served in the military. Just like Thompson. How's that for a coincidence.

Out of curiosity Mike picked up the paper and reread the obituary. Intrigued, he read it again. What was he thinking? Was he crazy? You know how many people get murdered in and around New York. In and around Boston. In and around every major city. Some of them are bound to have the same professions. But here it wasn't the victims who were similar. It was their relatives. Arthur Thompson and—what was his name?—Frederick Nelson. They had both served in the military. Well, so did millions of people. Still, this was long after World War Two. Okay, then thousands.

Both of them lost their next of kin, and about a week apart. So what? Well, if it was true that mob muscle had killed Gloria as a way of hurting Thompson, then might not the same thing be true in Boston? Sure. But that still didn't mean they were related. What could the mob possibly want from a retired military man who now taught biology? Again, it was his damn one-track mind refusing to make sense.

Disgusted with himself, Mike put down the paper and walked to the kitchen for a glass of orange juice. Opening the refrigerator, he forgot what he was looking for. He slammed the door and went back to read the article once more. He carried it with him to the window, as if the sunlight would reveal something he had missed.

It was a simple coincidence. Nothing more than that. No way were the murders related. Well, then, why couldn't he put the paper down? Was it because he had discovered this by himself, without Susan's help? Was he so desperate to assert himself that he would cling to something as farfetched as this?

What did he have to lose? he asked himself. Anything? No. Nothing at all. And he sure had a lot to gain. His mind made up, Mike picked up the telephone. He called Susan at work.

"City desk. Draper here."

"My, don't we sound professional?" said Mike.

"Of course. What else did you expect?" she said. "So tell me, how are you making out?"

"Half blind. I've been reading everything in sight."

"It's good for you. Keeps you off the streets." She lowered her voice to a whisper. "I talked to the crime reporter about Thompson. He's gonna see what he can dig up."

"Great. Listen, Susan, there's something else I want you to check out."

"Oh, really. What's that?"

"See what you can find out about both James and Frederick Nelson. They're brothers, living up in Boston. James was the former school chancellor. He was sixty-nine years old, and he was murdered night before last. Shot in his home. All I know about Frederick is that he's a professor at MIT who used to be in the Defense Department. They're both pretty prominent, so there might be something in your files. Otherwise, call one of your correspondents up in Boston. Can you do that?"

"Sure. If you think it's important. What's this all about?" asked Susan.

"I'll explain when you get home. It's just a hunch, but do as I say, okay?"

"On one condition," said Susan. "That you keep your nose buried in those books."

"It's a deal. What time will you be home?"

"About six. What shall I pick up for dinner?"

"Anything. Just hurry it up."

"I'll make it as fast as I can. I expect to find you when I get there."

"Don't worry. I'll be here."

"You better be. If you know what's good for you."

"I gotta get off now," said Mike.

"Oh, yeah? What's your rush?"

"I gotta get back to my reading."

Susan laughed. "See you later, Michael."

When she arrived home at six-thirty, grocery bag in hand, Mike jumped up from the couch to greet her.

"What took you so long? I was worried half to death."

Susan smiled, shaking her head. "Sorry. It won't work. That's my line."

"What'd you find out?" he asked eagerly.

"Mind if I take my coat off? And put these groceries away?"

"Here. I'll take them."

"Which? The groceries or the coat?"

"Both. You just go sit down. And take out your notes."

"What's your hurry?" said Susan, handing him the bag and laying the coat over his arm.

"Guess."

"You think there may be some connection to Gloria's murder?"

"I don't think anything yet. Wait'll I hear what you have."

Susan sat on the couch, Mike on one of the chairs. She placed her notebook on the coffee table in between them.

"Some of this stuff we had right in the files. But most of it I got from our man up in Boston."

"I hope you didn't tell him what you wanted it for," said Mike.

"Are you kidding? And let him steal my story? Not on your life."

"Good. Let's have it."

Susan leaned over the table to read her notes. Mike leaned forward to hear. "James Nelson was born in 1908. He attended Boston University, majored in education, and graduated in 1928. Went right to work in the city school system. Taught math and science on the high-school level before becoming a principal in 1940. Pretty dull, if you ask me. You sure you need this?"

"Just keep reading," said Mike.

"Yes, sir!" Susan saluted. "He was appointed assistant chancellor in 1951, then full chancellor in 1955, remaining there until his retirement in 1972. He lived for the last thirty years at 528 Lawrence Road in Brookline, and . . . what else do I have? Oh, yes. He never married."

"What about military service? Anything on that?"

"Let's see. A punctured eardrum kept him out of the Army. But he served as an air-raid warden during World War Two."

"Very good," said Mike, sitting on the edge of his chair. "Now, what about his brother, Frederick?"

Susan turned the page in her notebook. "Frederick was born in 1917, which makes him nine years younger than his brother."

"Any other kids in the family?"

"Not that I know of," said Susan. "I didn't ask. But Boston would have told me if there were."

"Go on." Mike chewed on his lower lip.

"Frederick graduated from Harvard in 1938. Played varsity football and was on the dean's list twice. He got his Ph.D. in biology in 1941, after which he enlisted in the Army. He saw action in the Pacific during the war, rose to the rank of major. He later became an associate professor at MIT and contributed widely to academic journals, which led to his being recruited by the Defense Department in 1950. Frederick Nelson served in the department until 1956, when he returned to MIT. Married and divorced three times, he has a stepdaughter from his second marriage. He lives at—"

"That's enough," said Mike, interrupting. "Did you find out exactly what he did for the Pentagon?"

"No. Only where he was. He was in Washington, D.C., for

a year and a half. But most of the time he was stationed at a place called Fort Detrick. Does that name mean anything to you?"

Mike shook his head. "Where is it?"

"Someplace in Maryland," said Susan.

"Wait a minute," said Mike, rising to his feet. "Didn't you say Arthur Thompson was also stationed in Maryland?"

"That's right. But I don't know where."

"Find out, will you?"

"You really think there's some connection between Gloria's murder and the murder of this guy Nelson?"

"Let me put it this way," said Mike, pacing slowly in front of the couch. "We have two civilians, both of whom once served in the military at roughly the same time. Both of them lose a very close relative, again at roughly the same time. Both of those relatives are murdered. I admit the whole thing may be farfetched. God knows, I'm desperate to find something. But then again, that makes three similarities."

"I hate to say this," said Susan. "But couldn't it all just be a coincidence?"

"Like I said, that makes three similarities. I read a line in one of your books today. *'The first time it's coincidence, the second time it's happenstance, the third time it's enemy action.'*"

"Who wrote it?"

"Ian Fleming."

Susan couldn't help herself. She started to laugh.

"What's so funny?" said Mike, stopping his pacing.

"Nothing, Mr. *James Bond.*"

"Go ahead and laugh. Laugh all you want. We gotta start somewhere. You know, I'm looking to take a walk once in a while."

Susan stopped laughing. "I'm sorry. Come sit down," she said, pointing next to her on the couch.

"Why? So you can make fun of me some more?"

She shrugged. "All right. I won't tell you, then."

"Tell me what?" said Mike.

"My secret," said Susan.

"What kind of secret?"

Susan's eyes were bright. "You'll never know, will you? 'Less of course you come sit down."

Sighing, Mike sat next to her. He was aware of her nearness. "There. I'm sitting. You happy?"

Susan looked at his long eyelashes, and the hair on his chest that was visible through his open shirt. She smiled. "The secret *is* . . . that maybe I *like* keeping you prisoner. Have you ever thought of that?"

"It's crossed my mind."

"Do you approve, or not?"

"What's my sentence?" said Mike.

"That all depends," said Susan.

"On what?" Mike was feeling more comfortable being so close to Susan. He felt better about himself. After drawing that connection from the *Times*, it was like he was once again taking charge.

"On how you behave," she said.

"Oh, yeah? What do I have to do?" Mike noticed the softness of her skin, the fineness of her dark blond hair.

"Nothing. Just be nice."

He looked her straight in the eye. "I'm always nice."

She returned the gaze. "You think so, do you?"

"Sure. Everybody likes me. I was voted Mr. Popular at Walkill."

"Is that a fact?"

"Ask any of the guards. They'll tell you."

They were side by side, staring into one another's eyes. "You make Walkill sound like a fraternity," said Susan.

"We had our own song. Our own handshake. Give me your hand. I'll show you."

Mike took Susan's hand, spread her fingers apart like a fan, and then pressed his own fingers against them. Her hand was warm.

"I get it," said Susan, studying the configuration of their fingers. "Those are supposed to be bars."

"Right," said Mike, interlacing his fingers with hers and squeezing down tightly. "And that's a jailbreak."

"Very clever," said Susan. "You want to escape from here?"

Mike smiled. "Maybe. I haven't decided yet."

Mike slowly removed his hand from hers. As naturally as if he'd held Susan a hundred times before, he reached one arm around her neck, the other around her waist. They kissed, softly at first, then with growing urgency. Susan slid over so there was room for the two of them to lie side by side. They gripped one another tightly.

"You're very strong," said Mike, rubbing her back.

"So are you," said Susan, blowing softly in his ear.

"Our bodies fit very well together."

"Don't say things like that."

"Why not? It's true."

"As your jailer, I might be tempted to throw away the key," said Susan.

Mike kissed the tip of her nose. "That's the chance I'll have to take."

"You like to live dangerously, don't you?"

"Sometimes it gets me into trouble." Smiling, Mike started to unbutton her blouse. "Sometimes not."

They were naked on the couch, their clothes lying on the floor. Susan's head was on Mike's chest. Her eyes were closed. She opened them sleepily. She noticed that Mike was staring at the ceiling.

"What's wrong?" she said.

Mike kissed her lips. "That was wonderful."

"No, really. What are you thinking?"

"Nothing."

"Don't give me that. I told you *my* secret. You tell me yours."

"What secret?" he said.

"Okay, I'll guess," said Susan. "You're thinking maybe we should go to Boston. Talk to this guy Nelson."

Mike nodded.

"Can it wait until tomorrow? I mean, do we have to go right this minute?"

"Why? What do you have planned for tonight?"

Susan ran her finger down the middle of his chest. "Give me a few minutes. I'm bound to think of something."

20

Susan drove her brown Audi Fox through downtown Boston. It was a cold gray November day, with the threat of rain or an early snowfall in the air. Shoppers bustled along Massachusetts Avenue beneath overcoats and scarves.

"Are we almost there?" said Mike, looking out the window.

"MIT is in Cambridge," said Susan. "Just over the river. We stay right on this road."

"God, I hope this isn't a waste of time."

"At least it's gotten you out of the apartment." Susan stared at the road. "Isn't that what you wanted?"

"Did get a little boring there for a while. Though last night was . . ." Mike nodded to himself.

"Was what?" said Susan casually, looking over at him.

". . . interesting," said Mike.

"Interesting? Is that all?"

"Very interesting, in fact. *Terrific,* actually. Come to think of it, last night was by far the best night I ever had . . ."

Susan couldn't help smiling.

". . . in prison," said Mike, keeping a straight face.

"All right, wise guy. Just tell me where you want to get off?"

"Anyplace around here is fine."

"I'm serious," she said, trying to look stern.

"So am I."

Susan realized he wasn't kidding. "You *are?*"

"I think you should go to see Frederick Nelson by yourself. It'll be easier to get him to talk if there's only one of us.

And being a woman isn't going to hurt any. Especially if the guy's been married three times."

"But what are you going to do while I'm there?"

"Don't worry about me. I'll go to a movie. Give you a couple of hours, case he's out of his office. Just tell me where I should meet you."

She thought for a moment. "Why don't you meet me at Casablanca. It's a bar right on Brattle Street, near where the subway lets out. Ask anyone. They'll tell you where it is."

"How do you know Cambridge so well?" said Mike.

"I ought to know it. I lived here for a year when I was first married. My husband was in school at Harvard."

"Oh, really? What was he studying?"

"Law," said Susan casually. "He's a criminal lawyer."

"Any good?"

"Matter of fact, he is. For someone just starting out, he's already handled some pretty good cases."

Mike shrugged. "Maybe I'll go see him."

Susan looked perplexed. "I thought you didn't want to use a lawyer?"

"I don't," said Mike with a grin. "Just want to see your taste."

Susan pulled to a stop in front of a subway station. "Get out of here before I call the cops."

Mike put up his hands. "Yes, ma'am. I'll go quietly."

"I'll meet you about three o'clock. And do me a favor. Be careful."

"Hey, listen, I'm just going to the movies," said Mike.

"Make sure it's a long one. I don't like the idea of you wandering around the streets."

Mike got out of the car and headed for the subway station. Susan blew him a kiss through the window. He waved back.

She parked near the MIT campus and asked a security guard for the location of the Biology Center. It was a massive gray building whose long corridors smelled of formaldehyde. Susan took the elevator to the fifth floor, passing several large laboratories on the way to Frederick Nelson's two-room office.

"May I help you?" asked his elderly secretary, looking up from the typewriter.

"Yes. I'd like to see Professor Nelson, if he's in."

"Are you one of his students?"

"No. My name is Susan Draper. I'm with the *Daily News* in New York."

"I see. What is it you'd like to see the professor about?"

"It's a personal matter," said Susan. "You can tell him it won't take but a few minutes."

"Have a seat," said the secretary, getting up from her chair. "I'll tell the professor you're here. You can hang your coat on the rack."

Susan was leafing through a science journal, thinking of the best way to approach Nelson, when his secretary opened the door to his office. "The professor will see you now, Miss Draper."

Susan put down the magazine. "Thank you very much."

Frederick Nelson was standing in shirt sleeves and tie behind his cluttered desk. He was a very young-looking sixty, his thick dark hair dotted with gray only around the temples, and his trim waistline obviously the result of regular exercise. His brown eyes were penetrating, though not particularly warm. Susan could see why many women might find him attractive. He was very distinguished-looking, and probably quite vigorous in bed.

"Miss Draper," he said. "Please, won't you have a seat."

"Thank you, professor. I'm sorry to barge in on you this way."

He smiled, leaning back in his chair, his hands behind his head. "It's quite all right, I assure you. What can I do for you?"

"I may as well come right to the point," said Susan. "I'm here concerning your brother, James. First of all, let me tell you how sorry I am."

Nelson's expression darkened immediately. His eyes narrowing, he sat upright in his chair, his hands dropping to his lap. "Miss Draper, you can forget the formalities. What *about* James?" he said coldly.

"I have reason to believe there may be some connection between his death and a recent murder in New York."

"You do, do you? I'm delighted to hear that," he said sarcastically.

"I know this isn't easy to talk about, professor—"

"But that shouldn't bother you. You'll still come sailing in here for your damn newspaper."

Susan took a deep breath. "Who do the police think killed your brother?"

"If you had bothered to check, you'd know they suspect James was killed by a burglar he surprised in the act."

"And you believe them?"

"What difference does it make who did it?" shot back Nelson. "It's not going to bring Jimmy back."

"What if I told you I think your brother may have been killed as a way of getting to you? Possibly to scare you."

"Who's after me?" he said caustically. "The Mafia or the Soviet Union?"

"I don't know yet," said Susan.

"What is this? Some sick joke?"

"What kind of work did you do for the Defense Department?" said a determined Susan.

"You tell me. You're the one with all the answers."

"I know you were stationed in Washington, and at some place called Fort Detrick in Maryland."

"Very good. You also going to tell me what I had for dinner last night? It's probably equally important."

Susan sighed. "Professor Nelson. This may seem like some kind of game to you. But I'm trying to find out what may be behind your brother's murder."

Nelson slammed his hands down on the desk. He stood up abruptly. "Let me tell you something, miss. I don't know what in the world you're after, and frankly, I don't care. I have no idea why anyone would want to hurt my brother. Or me, for that matter. What's more, I have no interest in speculating about some wildly imaginary plot for the benefit of your newspaper. What scandal sheet did you say you worked for?"

Susan could see she was getting nowhere. And was not about to. "Thank you for your time, professor," she said coldly, getting up to leave. "I can find my way out."

"Do that. And tell your editor that next time he sends someone up here to bother me, I'm gonna call the security guard."

Susan deliberately slammed the door behind her as she hurried into the outer office. Her face was flushed. Dammit! she said to herself. What was she going to tell Mike? Here he'd put so much hope in this new lead, and she'd gone and blown it with her lousy interview. But how else could she have approached him but directly? What did it matter now, anyway? There was no going back. She just hoped Mike would understand.

Susan retrieved her coat from the rack. Putting it on, she noticed Nelson's secretary speaking to a woman who was obviously not a student. The woman seemed to be in her late thirties, and had tangled red hair that looked like it hadn't been combed for weeks. Her trench coat was soiled, and her canvas shoes were ripped in the back. A cigarette dangled from her lips, and she was struggling in vain to light a match.

"Your father apologizes for not being able to see you, Miss Moore," said the secretary stiffly. "But he has a lecture in five minutes. He told me to give you *this*." She handed her an envelope.

"Thank you," said the woman, grabbing the envelope and starting for the door. She turned around briefly before leaving. Her voice was bitter. "Do give the professor my love."

Susan got an idea. Maybe all was not lost after all. Nodding good-bye to the secretary, she followed the woman out into the hall. Susan overtook her three doors down when she stopped to try again with her cigarette.

"Need a light?" Susan said, pulling out the matches she'd begun carrying for Mike.

"Thanks," answered the woman without looking up.

Susan lit the match and held it under the cigarette. "Excuse me, but I couldn't help overhearing. Are you Frederick Nelson's daughter?"

"What's it to you?" said the woman, looking at Susan through bloodshot eyes. Susan could smell the whiskey on her breath.

"I was hoping maybe you could help me. I came up here all the way from New York to see the professor. Turned out he wouldn't give me much of his time."

"That's him, all right. He'd just as soon write you a check as see you." She shoved the envelope into the pocket of her trench coat. "That's the only kind of generosity he knows."

"Can I buy you a cup of coffee?" asked Susan.

She shrugged. "Why not? I could use it. And I have nothing better to do."

"My name's Susan."

The woman nodded tentatively. "I'm Kitty. You know, like one a them cats that never grew up."

Susan smiled. "Glad to meet you, Kitty."

They walked over to a diner across the street from the campus and took a booth in the back. "Just two coffees," Susan said to the waitress approaching with menus in hand. Then, turning to Kitty: "Unless you'd like something to eat."

"No, thanks. Coffee's fine." She took out a cigarette. "Can I trouble you once again for a light?"

Susan handed her the book of matches. "Keep them. I don't smoke. I just carry them for a friend."

"Thanks."

"Excuse me for prying," said Susan after the waitress had brought their order, "but I gather you and your father don't get along too well."

"You mean Nelson?" said Kitty, pouring half a container of cream and four packets of sugar into her coffee. "He's my stepfather. Married my mother when I was a kid. Three times he's been married, and I'm the only thing he's got to show for it. How's that for striking out?"

"Why do you say that?" said Susan. This Kitty won the prize for insecurity. As well as for drinking sweet coffee.

"I ain't no bargain, believe me. I got more problems than you got teeth. Been divorced twice. Can't hold a job. You see, I take a little taste now and then. Actually, a *big* taste. And quite often."

Susan nodded, sipping her coffee. "What's your relationship like with Nelson?" she asked, trying to guide the conversation as gently as possible.

"Strictly financial. Every couple of weeks he's good for a loan."

"That's pretty nice of him, isn't it? I mean, he doesn't *have* to lend you anything?"

Kitty drained her cup. "Suppose you're right. But then, why can't he talk to me? Is that so hard? Typical scientist. All he really cares about are his damn laboratory mice. Doesn't know how to relate to people."

Susan motioned for the waitress to refill their cups. "I came up here to talk to your stepfather about his brother."

"James?" said Kitty. "Poor guy was murdered couple of nights ago."

"I know. I'm very sorry. Your stepfather seems to think it was a burglar who did it."

Kitty poured in the same quantity of cream and sugar. "Maybe it was," she said, stirring the coffee. "Who knows?"

"Do you know anyone who might have wanted to hurt him? Or your stepfather, for that matter?"

"I didn't know James too well," she said, lighting a cigarette. "But I can't imagine him having any enemies. He wasn't at all like his brother. Now, Nelson, that's different. I can think of a thousand reasons why someone might want to get back at him."

Susan put down her cup. "Any of them have to do with his work for the Defense Department?"

Kitty laughed. "Are you kidding? I wouldn't be the least bit surprised, considering what he did."

"What he *did*? When?"

"When he was down in Maryland. Fort . . ."

"Detrick?" said Susan. "Was that it?"

"Detrick. That's right. My mother was married to him then. Though I was only a teenager, I knew what was going on. Not that he'll admit it, even now."

"What do you mean 'going on'? What was he doing?" said Susan. She had the feeling maybe she was finally getting somewhere.

Kitty took a deep drag on her cigarette. "He's a biologist, right? Well, believe me, he wasn't trying to cure cancer. Probably trying to cause it, is more like it. Biological warfare. That's what he was into. Top-secret research. Only reason I know is because I overheard him discussing it once with a colleague. Like an asshole, I asked him about it later. That's one of the reasons he doesn't like me. He knows I see right through him and that I know all his talk of 'working for mankind' is a load of shit."

Susan felt a chill run down her spine. "Biological warfare. Jesus. What kind of research were they doing, exactly? Do you have any idea?"

"That I couldn't tell you," said Kitty, nervously crushing out one half-smoked cigarette and immediately lighting another. "Your guess is as good as mine. I think maybe it had to do with germ warfare. Stuff like that."

Susan stared down at the table, fidgeting with her spoon, trying to compose herself. This was it. It had to be. Biological warfare, she thought to herself. If what Kitty said was true, someone had to be after Nelson because of what he knew, some secret discovery he had made. But who? The Mafia? The Soviet Union? Jesus. Maybe Nelson wasn't kidding there in his office. But then what did all this have to do with the murder of Gloria, back in Greenwich?

"Tell me, Kitty, do you by any chance remember some of the other people working at Fort Detrick? I know it was a long time ago, but it really might help."

"Let me think." She puffed on the cigarette. "The Army brass in charge was a Colonel Tomly . . . no, wait . . . *Thompson*, that's it. I remember, because it was the year Bobby Thompson hit that famous home run against the Dodgers. I was something of a baseball fan, a real tomboy, if you can believe it."

For a moment Susan was unable to speak. She wasn't sure whether it was from excitement or fear. She swallowed hard. She needed something to calm her nerves. "Can I bum a cigarette?" she said.

"Sure." Kitty handed her the pack. "I didn't think you smoked."

"Usually I don't." Susan fumbled with a cigarette, lit it, and coughed. "Anyone else that you can remember?"

"Yeah. There was this one guy who came over for dinner a lot. He worked with my stepfather. I think he was a doctor."

"Can you remember his name?"

Kitty thought for a second. She smiled. "You know, you're really in luck."

"Why's that?"

"Sometimes I can hardly remember my *own* name."

Susan nodded.

"The man who came over for dinner. His name was Dr. Martin Greene."

Mike waited for Susan to leave before coming out of the subway station. Let her think he was going to a movie. He didn't want her to worry unnecessarily. God knows she would raise a stink if she knew what he was really up to. He could just hear her. "What the hell do you need with *that*? Talk about asking for trouble. That's *begging* for it." Susan was a spunky girl, but there were some things she would never understand. No reason for her to know anyway. Self-protection was his own business, and nobody else's.

In a phone booth on the corner, Mike looked up the number of Stanley Stoneman, a friend of his from Walkill. Fortunately there was only one Stanley Stoneman in the directory. Even more fortunately, Stanley was home. Mike recognized the heavy Boston accent as soon as he answered.

"Hey, Stanley. You old son of a bitch. This is Mike Ross."

"Michael Boy. How the hell are ya? Where the fuck are ya?"

"I'm in Boston, of course. Think I'd call you long distance?"

"Whacha doin' up here? Besides comin' over to see me?"

"I'm not here going to Harvard. That's for sure. Listen, Stanley. I need your help."

"You ain't in no trouble, I hope?"

"I'll tell you when I see you. Can we meet someplace?" Mike told him the subway stop he was near.

"How's I pick you up in my car? You ain't but a short ride from here."

"Great. Just make it fast, will ya? I don't like hanging around on the streets."

"Keep it in your pants, Michael Boy. I'll be right with you."

Mike stood in front of a bookstore, looking at the titles in the window. He could see the street reflected in the glass. Ten minutes later a blue station wagon pulled to a stop. The bald head behind the wheel was unmistakable, as was the broad toothless smile. Mike hurried out into the street and jumped inside.

Stanley Stoneman was old enough to be Mike's father. A longtime burglar who had risen to become a fence, he had spent much of his sixty-two years behind various state bars. His three-year stretch at Walkill had been for receiving a truckload of stolen mink coats. They had left the New York City garment center bound for Bonwit Teller, only to end up in Stanley's Boston warehouse. Stanley claimed he was set up by the driver, whose name was Dietrich and who was "obviously a Jew-hating Kraut."

Stanley had taken a paternal interest in Mike as soon as he discovered that he too was a Jew. "Can't always tell with a name like Ross," he said. "Could also be a goy."

"Not when you're from the Lower East Side," said Mike. "I'm bona fide. Bar mitzvahed, even. For all it's worth in here."

Stanley was delighted to see him. He threw his arms around Mike's shoulder and squeezed him tightly. Mike gave him an affectionate punch in the ribs.

"Michael Boy. Just look at you." He winked. "Bet you're knocking the dames dead out there."

Mike shrugged. "I'm doin' okay. You don't look bad yourself, for an old man."

Stanley was wearing a lime-green car coat with a fur collar, on top of a mustard-yellow V-neck sweater. "Old man, huh? Well, the broads ain't complainin'."

"I thought you were married," said Mike.

"I am. Wait'll you meet Sadie. Makes potato latkes like you'd never believe." Stanley grinned. "You also gotta see the little honey I got over in Newton. Pair of tits on her would knock your eyes out. Shiksa, that one. Know what she calls me?"

"I can imagine."

Stanley ran a hand over his bald head. "A Jewish Kojak. Just wait'll you lose *your* hair. You'll do even better."

"That's the least of my problems," said Mike. "C'mon. Let's move this thing. I'll tell you why I'm here. And how you can help me."

As Stanley drove down Massachusetts Avenue, Mike told him about Gloria's murder, how the police were after him, and how desperate he was to try to clear himself. Stanley's joviality immediately disappeared. Lines of concern showed along his endless forehead. They deepened when Mike told him about his betrayal by fellow inmate Joey Demarko.

"He oughta be strung up by the balls for that. You shoulda known better, Michael Boy. You never listened to me. Didn't I tell ya, ya can't trust the goyim. Given half a chance, they'll screw a kike every time." Stanley again squeezed Mike's arm. "Why do you think you and me stuck together? We needed one another. There weren't many of us there."

Mike nodded. "That's for sure."

Stanley looked uncertain. "I think one of the guards was a Heb. Wiley. Cell block six. Changed his name, but he couldn't fool me."

"I need your help," said Mike, to change the subject.

"You can trust me, Michael Boy. Shoulda come to me in the first place. I'll do anything I can for ya. You know that."

"I need a gun," said Mike directly.

Stanley frowned. "What for? Don't tell me you're gonna shoot it out with the cops?"

"It's not the cops I'm worried about. Like I told you, there may be some organization muscle behind this. You remember them hit men inside. Fucking animals, all of 'em. Hell if I'm gonna go against them unarmed."

"You're right," said Stanley. "Those schmucks'll blow you away soon as look at you."

"Whadda you say? You know where I can get a piece? I was afraid to try in New York. Thought maybe the dealers would sell *me* along with the rod."

Stanley sighed. "I don't like to see you packing heat, Michael Boy. But I see your need. . . . Sure, I know where you can get one. It's my business, ain't it? Give me a second. I'll just do a little 'reaching out,' as we say in the trade."

Stanley stopped alongside a phone booth and got out to make a call. A minute later he was back in the car. He smiled, snapping his fingers. "I told you, you came to the right place. Stick with me, Michael Boy. I'll take care of ya."

"What does he have?"

"Don't worry about it. This guy will fix you up with anything you want."

They took Storrow Drive by the Museum of Science, then along past North Station in the direction of the harbor. Stanley drove down Atlantic Avenue, parking outside of what looked like a deserted warehouse. Mike followed him up to the loading dock. Stanley rang the doorbell three times.

"Let me do the talking. It'll be cheaper that way."

"You're the boss," said Mike.

Stanley patted him on the back. " 'Bout time you realized that."

A black man wearing an Afro and shades came to the door. He nodded at Stanley, then looked suspiciously at Mike. "You sure he's all right?" he asked.

" 'Course he's all right. He's with me, ain't he?"

"Can't never be too sure," said the black.

"C'mon. C'mon. Let's see what you got. We don't have all day."

The black led them inside past piles of packing crates and assorted junk to a large corner table that was covered with canvas. Underneath the canvas was a locked trunk. He unlocked it and threw open the top.

"Jesus!" said Mike, staring at the collection of rifles, pistols, and knives. "You could outfit an army here."

Stanley smiled. "Only if it's profitable. Ain't that right, Jackson?"

"This ain't a lending library, if that's what you mean. What are you looking for, my man?" he said to Mike. "You name it. I got it."

Though Mike had never actually owned a gun, he knew enough about them, both from running with the Angels as a kid and from all the talk in prison. Guns were as popular a topic as women. "Man, the piece I had me," someone would say in the shower. "Black and lean. Butt felt like it was part of your hand. Good action, too. Real smooth." It was only when they described the trigger or the barrel that you knew exactly what was being discussed.

"Colt and Llama. Smith & Wesson. Bernadelli." Jackson pointed out the various models. "Buntline Special. Centennial Airweight. .357 Magnum. They're all cleaned, oiled, ready for use. How much you fixin' on spending?"

"How about that Smith & Wesson?" Stanley asked Mike. "That looks about right, doesn't it?"

Mike nodded.

"Smith & Wesson," said Jackson, picking up the slim pocket-sized pistol. "A good choice. Thirty-two caliber. Four-inch barrel. Walnut grip. I'll give it to you for sixty-nine-fifty."

"Sixty-nine-fifty!" exclaimed Stanley. "You gotta be outta your skull. That gun's forty bucks in a shop."

"Street price is usually close to a hundred," said Jackson calmly. "I'm making an exception 'count of he's a friend of yours, Stoneman. Even throw in two boxes of cartridges *on the house*."

"How generous of you! Remind me to come see you next time I'm collecting for Hadassah."

"Sixty-nine-fifty," said Jackson firmly. "Take it or leave it."

Stanley motioned Mike aside. "How much you got on you?" he asked.

"Less than thirty, I'm afraid." Just what Susan had loaned him for the day.

"I'll take care of it," said Stanley. Mike started to complain, but Stanley raised his hand. "It's the least I can do, Michael Boy."

Stanley paid Jackson in full. Jackson beamed, counting out the bills. "Happy hunting, my man," he said to Mike. "Come back and see us again."

"Don't count on it," said Stanley. "C'mon, Michael. Let's get the hell out of here. Before we get charged for parking."

Mike hid the gun and the shells in a side pocket of his army jacket. They returned to the car and started back toward Cambridge.

"Thanks a lot," said Mike. "I'll repay you first chance I get."

"Forget it. It's a gift. Say, why don't you come out to the house for dinner? You can meet Sadie."

Mike explained who was waiting for him.

"You mean that honey from Vassar used to come visit? Sure, I remember her. You're in good hands, Michael Boy. She's all right. Give her a kiss for me. Better yet, give her a . . ." Stanley grinned, punching Mike's arm.

He stopped in Harvard Square, in front of the Coop. "You be careful with that present," Stanley said, squeezing Mike's hand. "And get yourself out of this mess. Whatever you do, don't get caught. You know as well as I, prison ain't no place for a Jew."

"Take care, Stanley. I'll keep in touch. And thanks again."

Stanley grinned like Kojak. "Mazel, baby."

The Casablanca was filled with students who Mike assumed were from Harvard and Radcliffe. Susan was sitting at a back table waiting for him. She smiled when he approached.

"What'd you see?"

Mike thought fast. *"Exodus,"* he said. "You know. The one about the Jews."

"I've seen it," said Susan.

"And you? What did you learn? Anything?"

"You're not gonna believe this," she said.

"Oh, no?" Mike lit a cigarette. "Try me."

21

Markham kept seeing the eyes. Wide with fear. And those lips twisted in the anticipation of pain. The vision of James Nelson dying. It soothed him when he lay down to sleep. Inspired him when he shaved in the morning. And amused him when he hurried along the streets. Not since he was sixteen, and had his first woman, did an image linger so long. James Nelson's face was a source of continual satisfaction. It brought a gleam to Markham's eyes at odd hours of the day and night.

Markham was not blind. He realized how much he had changed. He originally intended to hurt the five men who had so callously hurt him. Killing their loved ones was merely a means to that end. The murders themselves were designed to be painless affairs. Simple and direct. Angela Nash, like a bump in the road. Gloria Thompson, down with a shot. But with Nelson, Markham had dragged it out, purposely inflicting pain, making him suffer before he died. He couldn't help himself. Thinking about it even now, Markham felt his chest contract and his knees quiver. He felt a tightness in his groin. It was true, what cops said, that killing became easier in time. What they never said was that it felt so good.

"What's so funny?" said Jennifer, looking up from her dictating pad. "You're grinning like a Cheshire cat."

Markham rubbed his eyes and yawned. He had forgotten where he was. Don't mind me, Jennifer, he thought of saying. I'm just laughing 'count of a guy I killed up in Boston. He's the third in less than a month. You've got quite a sense of humor, she would reply. Ever think of being a comedian? No. Only an actor. I'm very good at that.

"Really?" she insisted. "What's the big joke?"

Markham thought for a moment. "To be perfectly honest, I was thinking about how nice it would be to get out of this office for a while. Go someplace far away. Someplace where I can relax."

"I think that's a great idea, Mr. Markham. When's the last time you took a vacation?"

"Not since before the Connolly case."

"That's been close to two years."

"Really? Has it been that long?"

"Sure has. I was just reading over the report yesterday. You started working on that—"

"Pardon me, Jennifer. I'm sorry to interrupt. But could you please excuse me for a few minutes?"

"Sure. But don't we have more to do?"

"It'll wait," said Markham. "There're a few calls I'd like to make."

Jennifer stood up from the chair by his desk. She smiled. "One of them couldn't be to a travel agent, could it?"

Markham chuckled. "What possibly gave you that idea?"

"Mexico is fabulous this time of year. So's Puerto Rico."

"Jennifer, I didn't say anything about taking a vacation. At least not yet. So do me a favor, and don't mention it to anyone. Believe me, if I'm planning to go away, everyone here will find out soon enough."

"I understand," said Jennifer, turning and starting across the room. "Buzz when you need me."

Markham watched as she left the office, closing the door behind her. Not bad, he thought to himself. It had been a spur-of-the-moment idea, hinting about his trip. But if he knew Jennifer, she would soon be whispering to Cheryl, the secretary down the hall: Now this is just between you and me. The boss told me not to tell anyone. But . . .

Within minutes the story would make the rounds of the office. By the time he called them together to make the official announcement, they'd all be prepared for the idea. Not that it mattered much. He could pick up and go this very second without raising suspicion. However, it was always best to plan, even for something as minor as announcing his forthcoming vacation.

So far, planning had been the key to his success. He'd planned for Angela Nash. He'd planned for Gloria Thompson. And he'd planned for James Nelson. All with perfect results. Only in the case of Gloria were the police actively pursuing a lead. They were after some kid with a record, a kid whose picture had been distributed throughout the force. Markham had a copy right here on his desk. He picked it up, and leaned back in his chair, studying the face. The eyes suggested the kid was bright, and the nose that he was no stranger to the streets. He looked like a tough little scrapper. Markham saw that he was still on parole. Too bad, kid, he said to himself, shaking his head. Better not get caught. He tossed the photo into his wastepaper basket and reached for the phone.

Markham spent the better part of an hour making calls. Most of the calls were long distance, and none of them was to a travel agent. He didn't need one. At least not yet. He had to know where he was going, before he could book a flight.

After lunch, Markham called a meeting of his staff. Assistants, investigators, and secretaries, about forty in all, crowded in the hall outside his office. They smiled and whispered among themselves.

Markham stood in front of his door. "May I have your attention, please," he said. "I have a little announcement to make."

"You're running for the presidency," quipped Sherman, his assistant. "I *knew* it."

Everyone laughed, including Markham. It was funny how little they knew him.

"Right. And I'm taking you all with me to the White House. But that's in the future. What I'm about to tell you now will sadden you deeply, I'm afraid." He paused for impact. "Starting the day after tomorrow I will be out of the office . . ." Markham put on one of his best smiles. ". . . on a two-week vacation."

They started to applaud, but Markham raised his hand to quiet them down. "As you know, I have not been away for a while. I want this to be a *real* vacation. With no reports to write, no court strategy to consider, and no decisions of any kind. Frankly, the less I have to think about, the more I'm going to like it. I suggest that those of you with any problems, anything you need me for that won't wait until I come back, better have it on my desk by nine o'clock tomorrow morning. After tomorrow, you'll have to handle it yourself." His smile broadened. "I'm afraid I'll be unreachable."

"Where are you going?" asked Sherman.

"Someplace where no reporters can pester me about my future. And where I won't need a bodyguard." Markham laughed. Damn right, he thought to himself. Those bastards from Chicago will never find me. "Someplace secret. Right now it's even a secret from me. . . . Are there any other questions?"

There was a shuffling of feet and clearing of throats.

"Excuse me," said Sherman loudly. "I think Jennifer has something to say. Don't you, Jennifer?"

Jennifer stepped up next to Markham. She was smiling, and her hands were behind her back. "I don't know how it happened, sir. But somehow it got out that you might be taking some time off, and . . . well, we all got together to get you a little going-away present." She handed him the gift. Judging from the shape, it was obviously a bottle of wine.

"You really shouldn't have," said Markham.

"Well, in that case," said Sherman, "maybe we . . ."

"But I'm glad you did. Should I open it now?"

Jennifer and the others nodded.

Markham tore off the wrapping. It was a bottle of Dom Perignon.

"It's a great champagne," said Sherman. "I hope you don't mind, but I opened it and took a little sip."

"And it went well with your Big Mac?" said Markham.

Everyone laughed.

"Why don't we all have some?" said Markham. "And I'll send down for some more. I think we deserve a little break. Thank you again. And just remember what I said. Tomorrow will be my last day here for two weeks. All the crooks are in your hands." He smiled. "I expect the prisons to be overflowing by the time I return."

After the impromptu party, Markham cleared off his desk. Jennifer came into his office. "Thank you for organizing that," he said. "I appreciate it."

"I'm glad." She stood with hands on hips, accentuating the thrust of her breasts against her unbuttoned blouse. "Listen . . . any chance we might get together before you go?"

"I'd love to, Jennifer. But I'm afraid there's no time. I've got so much to do before I leave. Tell you what," he said, finding it easy to sound sincere. "The minute I get back, I'll give you a ring. We'll get together for dinner. How's that?"

Jennifer smiled. "You promise?"

"Scout's honor."

"I'm going to hold you to it." She stepped closer to the desk. "Seriously. Where are you going?" she asked softly. "You can tell *me*."

Markham continued to clear off his desk.

"At least give me a hint. Is the place hot or cold?"

"You know something," said Markham, looking her straight in the eye. "I honestly haven't made up my mind yet."

"No?" Jennifer was surprised.

"No. I'm still looking into it. I have to do a little more research before I decide."

"Well, wherever you go, have a good time."

Markham grinned. "I intend to."

Nugent and Howard were in a New York City hotel room. They were both in their shirt sleeves. Nugent lay on a bed reading *Sports Illustrated*. Howard sat at the desk playing solitaire.

"Dammit!" he said, throwing down the card in his hand.

"Still losing to yourself, huh?" said Nugent, lowering the magazine. "Looks like our luck's bad across the board."

"You can say that again. How much longer we gonna sit here?"

"Till the boss tells us otherwise."

"He must be shitting bricks," said Howard.

"I wouldn't be surprised."

The phone rang.

"That must be him now," said Nugent, jumping up off the bed. He sighed, walking over to the phone. "This ain't gonna be easy." He picked up the receiver. "Yes, sir, this is Nugent. . . . No, I'm afraid we haven't had any luck. . . . We checked everywhere, sir. His secretary. A couple of his assistants. Even the wife he hasn't lived with for over a year. . . . No one seems to know where he went. They say he kept it a secret, so he wouldn't be bothered by reporters. . . . I don't know what to believe. . . . You're right about one thing, sir. I didn't think so at first, but since Boston, there isn't much doubt. Of course, he could be finished now, and really be on vacation. . . . Well, in that case, do you have any idea where he might go next? . . . *That* many people? We could never keep tabs on all of them. Not unless we had more men. . . . Yes, sir, I understand why that's impossible. Just Howard and I. . . . I don't know what else to suggest, sir. If that happens, maybe we'll see some kind of pattern. . . . Don't worry, sir. We'll get him long before that. . . . I'll make contact if anything develops. . . . Good-bye, sir."

Nugent hung up the phone. He breathed deeply.

"Was he angry?" said Howard.

"He wasn't pleased."

"What'd he suggest? Anything?"

"Not much he could. He agreed all we can do is wait until something else develops."

"How worried did he sound?"

"*Very* worried," said Nugent, lighting his pipe. "Wouldn't you be?"

"Goddamn right. Especially if I were in his position."

"We've got to find Markham before he gets to the boss."

"Yeah. But how?"

"It'll take one more hit," said Nugent. "Then we'll get him."

"We should've gotten him that time in the car," said Howard.

"I know. And next time, we better not miss. Otherwise . . ."

"Otherwise what?"

Nugent puffed on his pipe. "We're all going to go down together."

22

Susan called her apartment from a pay phone on Forty-second Street. "Guess what?" she said excitedly when Mike answered. "I found out where Martin Greene lives."

"You mean that doctor from Fort Detrick?" said Mike. "The one Nelson's stepdaughter told you about?"

"That's him," said Susan. "The one we've been looking for."

"Fantastic. How the hell'd you do that? Take out an ad?"

"Soon as I got to the office this morning, I called the AMA. I told them I was doing an article on cancer research and was trying to track down a particular doctor for an interview. There're twenty-two Dr. Martin Greenes across the country, but only nine of them are spelled with a final 'e,' which is how Kitty remembers it being spelled."

"Very clever," said Mike.

"Hold your praise. I'm not through yet. Next thing I did was eliminate five of the nine by age. Either too old or too young. According to Kitty, the Martin Greene we want should be in his late sixties by now. I checked through our files, and none of the four was listed. They're not particularly prominent, but that doesn't mean anything. No one said he was famous."

"Go on," said Mike impatiently.

"I called one of our Washington correspondents, who's got good contacts in the Pentagon. He gave me a big song and dance, but I was able to convince him to see if any of the four had a military record and was stationed you-know-where."

"Isn't that stuff secret?" said Mike.

"It's not available to just anyone. That's for sure."

"So how'd you convince him to check it out?"

Susan hesitated. "He made me promise..."

"Promise what?"

"That I'd go out with him next time he comes to New York. I hope you don't mind."

"Mind? Are you kidding? I'd sell myself on the streets if it would help to clear me. So he checked it out, right?"

"Absolutely. The Martin Greene we want is an internist out on Long Island."

"Fantastic," said Mike. "Listen, you better be real good to that guy when he comes to New York."

"I see you're not the jealous type," said Susan.

"No reason *to* be."

"No? Why not?"

Mike laughed. "You couldn't do any better than me if you tried."

"Pardon me," said Susan. "I'm gonna hang up before I get ill. Smug men upset my stomach."

"Take an Alka-Seltzer. But before you do, what time are we going out to see Greene?"

"*We're* not going anywhere," said Susan firmly.

"Oh yes we are."

"We've been through this already. Up in Boston. Remember. It's better if one of us goes alone. Fact, it was your idea."

"That was Boston. This is New York. Things are different."

"Listen, Michael. I think we may be getting close to something. It'll all be a waste, if you get arrested now."

"So far my luck's been pretty good," said Mike. "No reason for it to change."

Susan sighed. "I didn't want to tell you this. But I may as well. You'll see it in tomorrow's paper anyway."

"See what?" said Mike.

"Your picture. The paper's had a flier on you for more than a week. It's a slow news day, so the editors are planning on running it along with an update of the murder."

"And here I thought the heat was dying down."

"It'll never die down," said Susan. "Not until we have solid proof that it wasn't you. So do both of us a favor. Sit tight. I'll see you later. Okay?"

"All right," said Mike finally, sounding depressed. "Guess it's back to the soaps."

"Mike . . ." said Susan tentatively.

"Yeah? What is it?"

"I miss you."

"I miss you too, dammit," he said so loudly that Susan held the phone away from her ear. "Why the hell'd you think I wanted to go with you?"

"So that's the reason," said Susan.

"Just hurry the hell back here."

Dr. Martin Greene lived in Manhasset, a small town on the North Shore of Long Island, about forty-five minutes' drive from New York. He conducted his practice from a white brick professional building located downtown. Susan parked her car in the adjacent lot.

She took her time walking through the halls to his office. She wanted to be as relaxed as possible, so she would remember the approach she had devised. "We're planning a feature article on suburban physicians," she would say. "I've heard some good things about you, and I'd like to do a brief interview, if you don't mind." Properly flattered, Greene should be more than willing to comply. Susan knew from experience that few people turned down the opportunity to see their names in print. She just had to be careful during the interview not to dwell on Fort Detrick. Otherwise Greene might become suspicious as to her true intent.

She didn't want to make the same mistake she had with Nelson. Mike was relying on her, and she hoped to have more good news for him when she returned that night. Crossing her fingers, she opened the door.

There were two people in the small waiting room, a middle-aged man and a woman not much older than herself. A nurse smiled at her from behind a glass partition.

"May I help you, miss?"

"Yes. I'd like to see the doctor."

"Do you have an appointment?"

"No. My name is Susan Draper. I'm with the *Daily News*." Susan was about to go into her planned speech on the article featuring the doctor. However, before she could begin, a man's voice sounded from somewhere behind the partition.

"Did I hear someone say the *Daily News?*"

"Yes, doctor," the nurse said over her shoulder, speaking to an open door in the rear. "One of their reporters is here."

"Show her into my office, Miss Russell. Tell her I'll be right with her."

The nurse turned back to face Susan. "The doctor will see you right away," she said. "Go through that door and straight down the hall. His office is on your left."

"Thank you," said Susan. She was pleased by the reception, although a bit surprised. She hadn't even said what she was there for. Who knows? Maybe the doctor always treated reporters so specially. Never underestimate the desire for publicity, Susan told herself, heading for his private office. Vanity was a reporter's secret weapon.

Greene's brown, dimly lit office was dominated by a bookcase on one wall and a collection of framed diplomas, awards, and photographs on the other. The room looked like it could use a good dusting. Susan took a seat on the green corduroy couch. She stood up when the doctor entered.

He was small, with thinning gray hair and a pale complexion that was emphasized by his dark, rumpled suit. His eyes looked tired behind his rimless glasses, making him appear ten years older than his sixty-seven.

"How thoughtful of you to come," he said, smiling, shaking Susan's hand. "Miss . . ."

"Draper. Susan Draper."

"Can I get you anything?" he asked, moving his seat out in front of his desk. "A cup of coffee or tea?"

"No, thank you." Susan smiled. This guy was sure nice. The interview was going to be a snap.

The doctor sat with feet flat on the floor, his hands folded together on his thighs, as if in prayer. He sighed. "Okay," he said softly. "I'm ready to hear it. What have you learned?"

"About what?" said Susan. *Don't tell me* . . . She was caught off guard, shocked that he had somehow learned of her inquiries.

"About Angela, of course."

"Angela?" *What was he talking about?*

"My sister," he said, his voice gaining strength. "That *is* why you're here?"

"I'm not sure what you mean," said Susan hesitantly, more confused than ever. "What *about* your sister?"

"That's what I thought *you* would tell me," he said firmly. "After all, it was someone from your paper who informed me of her death. Called me even before the police. Why, that was more than a month ago. By now they must have some idea who was responsible for that hit-and-run accident. Either from tire marks or however else they go about it."

Susan now understood the doctor's mistake. So that's why he was so cordial. He wanted information. Evidently his sister had died, been killed in an accident. Susan felt a knot growing in her throat. Twice she started to speak, but the words wouldn't come. She looked away, then back at Greene. "Of course," she said finally. "Where was she killed again?" she asked, as if the details had momentarily slipped her mind. She didn't want him to suspect her ignorance.

The doctor leaned forward in his chair. He looked at her over his glasses. "Edgewater, New Jersey," he said hesitantly. "On her way to school. . . . Wait a minute," he said coldly, sitting upright, hands on hips. "You're learning all this for the first time. You didn't even know about my sister. Then what are you doing here?"

Susan took a deep breath. She had no choice but to tell it straight. "You're right, Dr. Greene. I didn't know about your sister, although what I came for *does* concern her death. I just didn't realize it until now." She plowed ahead, before he could interrupt. "Dr. Greene, I want to ask you about the research you once did for the government."

Susan caught the surprise in the doctor's eyes. Along with more than a little fear. "Who told you I did research for the government?" he stammered.

"You were at Fort Detrick, Maryland," said Susan. "I know all about it."

His mouth opened, although he didn't speak. He looked up at the photographs on the wall, then back at Susan. His eyes were hard. "What does this have to do with the death of my sister?" he asked sharply.

"I believe it may be directly connected."

Greene's lips were pressed tightly together. They were trembling. He stood up from his chair. "I suggest you leave now, Miss . . ."

"Draper. Susan Draper," she said firmly, studying his face.

"Please, Miss Draper. I want you to go. My sister's death has been very painful for me. Do you understand?"

"I believe I do. More than ever."

His voice was sad, his tone that of an appeal. "Please don't come around here bothering me again."

Susan nodded as she got up to go. She was nodding, not to the doctor, but to herself. After learning about his sister, and noting his alarm at the very mention of Fort Detrick, Susan was now convinced that they were on the right track. She could hardly wait to tell Mike.

23

As the plane began its descent, passing beneath the clouds, Markham stared out the window. For a moment he was surprised at how flat Denver was. And where was the snow? He had been told just yesterday that the slope conditions were "excellent," the best early-December skiing in years. Then he remembered that Denver was on the outskirts of the Rockies, several thousand feet lower than the ski area. Relax, he told himself. Everything's going to work out fine. He was concerned because good conditions at Vail were essential for his plan.

Once on the ground, he remained in his seat, facing the window, until all the other passengers had disembarked. He doubted whether anyone would recognize him in his sunglasses and cap—he wasn't *that* well known—yet it was best not to take chances. He had spent the three-hour flight hidden behind a newspaper, sleeping on his side, or looking out the window. Standing in line in the aisle would put him on display. He was in no hurry. He could afford to be the last one off, and even dawdle in the shops of Stapleton Airport, waiting until the others had picked up their baggage before going to claim his.

Though he would have preferred to rent a car for the hundred-mile trip to Vail, that would have required producing his license for Avis or Hertz, and his name going down on their permanent records. He intended to remain as anonymous as possible. What did he need a car for anyway? From all he had read, Vail was so small you could walk from the slopes to any hotel or restaurant in town. He took the shuttle bus instead.

Two hours later the bus pulled into the Vail parking lot. The first thing he noticed, getting off, was the snow piled up in four-foot drifts around the edge of the lot. More than three inches of fresh powder covered the streets and weighed down the branches of the firs. The snow looked excellent, just like the man from the Chamber of Commerce had said. The sun was shining in a blue, cloudless sky. It was warm, somewhere in the high twenties. You couldn't ask for better ski conditions.

Vail looked exactly like it did in the pictures. The town had been created out of wilderness only fourteen years before, and had been deliberately designed to look like a Swiss village. All the buildings resembled chalets, with overhanging roofs and dark-stained wooden balconies. It was a bit tacky for Markham's tastes, with a "ye olde" covered bridge leading from the parking lot into town, and a big steeplelike clock in the center of the square. "Plastic Bavaria," he had read somewhere. It was a perfect description. No wonder the resort was so popular with oil-rich Texans, whose money had helped build it. Vail was just their style.

The ambience was of little concern to Markham. What was most important was that Vail, being the closest major ski resort to Denver, three hours closer than Aspen, attracted many of the college students from the Denver-Boulder area. Hundreds of them came to ski on the weekends. Markham knew there was one college student in particular who rarely missed a Saturday or Sunday on the Vail slopes. It was because of her that he had come to Vail in the first place.

Markham remembered the act he had put on for Jennifer and his staff. All that crap about a quiet, relaxing vacation. But now that he thought of it, he'd actually been telling the truth. This *was* a kind of vacation. Sure. He was away from the office and the people who were out to kill him in New York. He loved to ski. And he was looking forward to his encounter with Beverly Douglas.

He carried his one bag into the lobby of the Mountain Haus Lodge. "I believe you have a room for me," he told the clerk. "I made a reservation last week."

"Your name, please?"

"Thacher," Markham replied. "Steven Thacher. From Philadelphia."

The clerk smiled. "Mr. Thacher. Welcome to Vail. We've been expecting you."

"Thanks. Snow sure looks fabulous."

"You bet. Had another five inches just last night."

Markham smiled. "Can't wait to get out there."

"If you'll kindly sign this register, I'll have a boy show you to your room."

His room had a large double bed, a portable refrigerator-freezer, and a balcony overlooking the slopes. After unpacking his bag, Markham stood out on the balcony. He watched the gondola, snaking its way slowly up the mountain, and a pair of skiers, one following the other, carving graceful S-turns on the way down. The slopes looked almost deserted. That was the beauty of skiing on a weekday. There were no lines for the lifts, and no crowds on the trails. Markham looked at his watch. It was three-fifteen, and the lifts closed at three-thirty. He'd have to wait until tomorrow, Tuesday, to take his first run. Just as well, he told himself. He could spend the rest of the day getting ready.

Markham had not wanted even his doorman to know where he was going. So rather than bring his skis along with him, he had decided to rent all the equipment here. That proved to be no problem at all. He found everything he needed in the Gondola Ski Shop. He selected a pair of Rossignol skis with Salmon "step-in" bindings, aluminum poles, and fiberglass boots. He had the bindings adjusted for the boots, so they would release in the event of a fall. Though he was an expert skier, he had not gone skiing in over a year, and he did not want to risk breaking a leg. Markham bought himself gloves, goggles, a reversible blue-red nylon windbreaker, and a pair of navy-blue ski pants with a yellow racing stripe down the side. He had packed a woolen turtleneck sweater, three cotten turtlenecks to wear underneath, and all the changes of thermal underwear and socks he would need.

He left his purchases at the shop while he went to the Vail Ski Center. There he bought a lift ticket good for the remainder of the week, and obtained a map of the mountain. The map included all the different slopes and trails, with symbols indicating their relative difficulty. He would carry it with him in his pocket.

Picking up his equipment, he returned to his room. He laid out the clothing he would wear in the morning, attaching the lift ticket to the zipper of the windbreaker. He was now completely prepared. He did some stretching exercises to loosen his legs, and took a steaming hot shower.

That evening Markham dined on venison at the Antler Room of the Gasthof Gramshammer Lodge. He lingered over his bottle of Beaujolais, enjoying the solitude, feeling a peace of mind he had not experienced since Boston. It was snowing outside, and he took a brief walk through the village before heading back to the hotel. It had been a long day, and he was sound asleep by ten-thirty.

He arose at seven the next morning, and was waiting by the gondola when it opened at eight-thirty. He rode the lift clear to the summit, while studying his map. Deciding it was best to start out slow, he made his first run down Ramshorn, an intermediate trail that was wide enough to traverse, and ideal for practicing his turns.

He felt slightly awkward at first. He had to keep reminding himself to lean forward over the skis and to let his legs do the work. But Markham had been skiing since college, and he knew exactly how to get back in shape. By the third run from the top he sensed a rhythm returning to his linked parallel turns, and rather than traversing the trails, he began skiing straight down the fall line, turning every few yards to check his speed. He felt well under control, and he spent the rest of the morning gradually increasing his speed.

He ate lunch at the mid-mountain cafeteria. Then it was right back to the slopes, this time on "expert" trails: Headwall Ridge, First Step, and Northstar. All the awkwardness was gone now. He didn't have to concentrate so hard. His skis were like an extension of his feet. By three o'clock he was executing sweeping wedeln turns, and though his form was not yet up to par, he could stop suddenly to avoid a fallen skier, and take high jumps off moguls without losing his balance.

He took the last run of the day down Riva Ridge, which was narrow and steep. Putting on his goggles as protection against the wind, he shot straight down, as though in a race, without once stopping to catch his breath. He skidded to a halt at the bottom, his face flushed, exhilarated from the speed. Not bad, he congratulated himself, looking back up the mountain. At this rate he'd be able to keep up with anyone by the weekend. Even a girl who was born and raised in Colorado and who spent every winter weekend on skis.

Markham skied for the next three days. He was invariably one of the first up in the gondola and one of the last to ski down in the afternoon.

It was more than the simple delight of skiing in near-perfect conditions that kept him going with hardly a break. It was the knowledge that Beverly Douglas was herself an expert skier that compelled him. If he intended to kill her like the others, he could do so without setting foot on the slopes. He could follow her in the evening or sneak into her lodge room at night. But that was too easy, and too impersonal. There would be no satisfaction.

Of the five people Markham had felt duty-bound to kill, Beverly Douglas was the one he had thought about the most. Seeing her on the television news, leaving for Europe with her senator father, had initiated this mission of revenge. She looked so damn happy standing by her father's side, reminding him of how he too had once felt, before the good times were so abruptly cut short. What right did she have to be so carefree? The worst she had probably ever suffered was being runner-up for prom queen at school. The spoiled bitch.

The image of her, blond and smiling, had stayed with him ever since. He wasn't sure why, but he felt drawn to get as close to her as possible. He wanted to possess her. Only then would he destroy her.

Markham continued to perfect his form, while exploring new and more challenging trails. On Thursday he discovered the back bowls. Located on the south side of the mountain, they were a wide-open, virtually treeless area, offering deep, unpacked powder snow and steep, ungroomed slopes. Signs at the top advise nonexpert skiers to stay away. Because of their difficulty, the bowls are the least crowded section of Vail. The few skiers visible on the wide slopes resemble flies against a white wall.

Markham took a run down the Sundown Bowl, making smooth eights in the virgin snow. He realized during his next run that the ungroomed bowls were no place to relax. You had to be constantly alert for large rocks and bushes camouflaged by the snow. Schussing down the Headwall of the Sun-Up Bowl, he barely missed falling into a ravine. He had not noticed the posted sign warning skiers to stay clear. Jesus, thought Markham, peering over the edge. Someone could easily get killed here. He turned and looked back up the hill. Even an expert, if she wasn't careful. Still flushed and a bit breathless, he marked the spot on his map, then skied slowly to the bottom.

On Saturday morning Markham was up at his regular hour. He went to extra pains with his appearance, wearing a blue-and-white kerchief over his white cotton turtleneck and splashing on some Givenchy Gentleman cologne. Rather than heading immediately for the gondola, he now carried his skis and poles to a rack near the lift center. Leaning against the rack, he watched arriving skiers purchase their tickets. It was like Grand Central Station at rush hour, with skiers adjusting their bindings, assembling with friends, and poling across to the lift lines. Amidst the congestion, Markham was perfectly inconspicuous.

Several times he thought a particular woman might be Beverly Douglas. Blond-haired twenty-one-year-olds were not all that uncommon at Vail. But Markham had obtained a current photo of Beverly from her college directory, and closer examination of the women in question revealed either a nose that was too big, or eyes that were not blue, or front teeth that lacked a gap in the middle. He continued his search.

At last all doubt was gone. There she was, standing in line for her ticket, talking to a friend. She was wearing brown ski pants and a striped yellow-and-gold sweater. The sun played on her shoulder-length hair. She was much prettier than her picture and from how he remembered her on television several months before. Her face was tanned from the sun, and she looked healthy and vital, just the way he had imagined her.

Markham saw she was here with two other girls, obviously fellow students from the University of Colorado at Boulder. He knew that it was their regular routine to ski all weekend, returning to school late Sunday afternoon. That gave him two days to somehow get her alone.

Markham knew that the easiest way to meet someone while skiing was to try to take the same lift up the mountain. Sitting side by side for a fifteen-minute ride, you can become acquaintances by the time you reach the top. Share a run down the mountain together, then another ride up, and you're friends. However, Markham thought it wise not to ride the gondola up with Beverly. Each car held four skiers, and that meant he would also be accompanying her friends. He wanted her two classmates to notice him as little as possible. It was best if he took a separate gondola to the top, then followed the three at a discreet distance until they skied to one of the many chair lifts servicing the upper part of the mountain. As the chairs were designed for only two, he might, by some maneuvering, be able to ride alone with Beverly.

Markham stood two places behind them in the gondola line. He shared his car with a talkative couple from Texas and their teenage daughter, who stared at him through heavily mascaraed eyes. Markham ignored her, keeping his mind on the car directly ahead. At the top, he quickly put on his skis, just in time to follow Beverly and her friends down Zot, a narrow expert trail through the trees.

It was obvious, even from fifty yards behind, that Beverly was a damn good skier. She looked like a racer, the way she crouched forward to increase her speed, turning sharply in between moguls as though they were gates in a giant slalom. Markham did not have to worry about their noticing him. They never looked back, and it was all he could do to keep up with them.

Zot ended up at the mid-mountain station, and rather than continue to the bottom, Beverly and her friends got in line for the number-three chair. Markham hurried to get behind them. However, he was cut off by a ski instructor and his three private pupils, and he ended up two chairs back. Riding to the top, he could see Beverly up ahead talking animatedly to one of her friends.

He followed them for the rest of the morning. He skied far enough behind so he would not be obvious. And to be extra careful, he stopped once to reverse his windbreaker from blue to red. Beverly and her friends skied both expert and some intermediate trails, many of which Markham had not taken before. They knew the mountain intimately, judging from the way they switched from one trail to another in an apparent effort to maximize their runs and avoid the inevitably long weekend lines at the lifts.

However, eventually they had to go back up, and whenever they got in line, Markham tried to position himself so that he and Beverly would go up on the same chair. Twice the pairing almost worked out. But the first time he had to defer to a member of the ski patrol who was carrying a stretcher to an injured skier above, and the second time he was paired with one of Beverly's two friends. She started talking about the marvelous powder snow, and wasn't it a great day for a tan. Markham answered her in monosyllables, keeping his head turned away until she was discouraged from further conversation.

He stopped for lunch when they did, keeping an eye on them from a table across the cafeteria. His luck was no better in the afternoon. By now the mountain was even more crowded, and unless he skied two feet behind them to the chair lift, he was invariably five or six places back in line. Frustrated with this approach, Markham thought about skiing right up to Beverly on the slopes, introducing himself as a travel writer who wished to talk to some of the regulars on the mountain. However, he rejected the idea as foolish, knowing that her friends would then have more time to study and remember him.

He decided to forget about meeting her while on skis, and he let the three of them go off by themselves. He would just have to wait until evening.

Catering as it does to a predominantly family crowd, Vail has very few night spots, and so his search was relatively easy. He remembered reading in her college directory that Beverly liked to dance. He had a strong feeling she might be at the only good discotheque in town.

Garton's was a large multistoried barn that offered drinking, dancing, and shuffleboard. It was crowded as usual with ski instructors, locals, weekend visitors. Beverly and her friends were sitting at a table near the door, nursing beers, listening to the music, and nonchalantly observing everyone who entered. And that included Markham, dressed in a rust-red cashmere turtleneck, tight French-cut jeans, and Gucci shoes. His elegance immediately caught Beverly's eye. He noticed her glancing at him as he passed, though feigning lack of interest. He ordered a beer at the bar, then casually turned around and surveyed the crowd, positioning himself in full view of her.

Beverly could not help but note the striking blond man observing her from across the room. He reminded her of Paul, that French actor she had met in Nice during the summer, the one with the soft voice and the beautiful eyes. Her father thought he was a gigolo, and had tried to discourage her from seeing him. He was always doing things like that, whether on vacation in Europe or home in either Denver or Washington, D.C. Her father was overprotective, constantly subjecting her boyfriends to embarrassing interrogations, questioning them about their careers, ambitions, even incomes.

Well, thank God her father wasn't here and she was free to do as she pleased. Here at Vail she was even more free than at school. That was part of the fun of these weekend trips. If she found someone attractive and wanted to get involved for a night, why, there was no one to stop her. Certainly not Joanie or Karen. They were out for a good time as much as she was.

The handsome blond man was smiling at her. He was the best-looking man she had seen all night. He looked to be in his thirties, just like the French actor. She remembered how charming Paul had been, and how confident of himself. He was so relaxed and gentle, especially in bed, as though he had all the time in the world. How different from the four or five fellow students she'd been to bed with since. They always seemed so nervous and intense, like they were desperate to prove something about themselves. "Was it good?" they asked afterward. Paul hadn't needed to ask.

She wondered if most older men were that sure of themselves, that natural with women. It would be interesting to find out. She felt a slight shiver run down her back. Why not experiment? What did she have to lose? Anything? If he turned out to be a drag, she could always politely excuse herself. Besides, he reminded her so much of Paul, she couldn't pass it up. Go ahead, she decided. Turning in her seat, Beverly met the man's eyes. He was still smiling, and she smiled back.

Okay, thought Markham to himself. That's all the come-on you're gonna get. Time to make your move before someone else does. Gulping down his beer, he sauntered over to where Beverly was sitting.

"Would you like to dance?" he asked.

Beverly noticed his long eyelashes. His voice was soft, just like Paul's. "Why, yes. I'd love to."

Markham led her to the dance floor. It was crowded with

couples moving to the disco soul music blaring from the speakers. Markham was a good dancer. He started off slow, keeping his eyes on Beverly and matching his movements with hers, so that, though they were dancing apart, they still had a feeling of togetherness.

"You dance very well," he shouted above the music.

"Thanks. So do you."

"I bet you're a good skier," he said.

"How can you tell?"

"By the way you move. You're very graceful."

Beverly shrugged. "What can I say?"

"You don't have to say anything."

They danced three fast dances in a row. Markham could tell by the sparkle in her eyes that she was enjoying herself. When a slow record came on, he immediately took her in his arms. He held her firmly, and led her through an intricate series of dips and turns.

Beverly's face was flushed from the fancy footwork. "I take it back," she said. "You're not just good. You're fantastic."

Markham smiled. "Only when I have a good partner. How about a drink?"

She nodded. "I could use a beer after that."

"Why don't you take a seat over there?" he said, pointing to a table on the far side of the room, away from the inquisitive eyes of her friends. "I'll go get us a couple of steins."

Beverly was excited, waiting for the blond man to return. God, was he a good dancer. And, she had to admit, he was even better-looking than Paul. This could easily turn out to be one fabulous night.

Markham returned with the beers. It was quieter here, and they could talk without raising their voices. "My name's Steven," he said. "What's yours?"

"Beverly."

He told her he was a criminal lawyer from Philadelphia. Assuming that Beverly's attitudes, like her senator father's, were extremely liberal, Markham proceeded to tell her stories of unfairly charged defendants he had gotten acquitted, district attorneys he had embarrassed in court, and all the work he had done for the American Civil Liberties Union. He could tell by her enrapt attention that Beverly was impressed.

"Tell me about yourself," he asked warmly, knowing that

the next step to winning her affection was to show his interest in *her*. He listened intently as she talked about growing up in Colorado, skiing for the first time at age six, and later winning a closetful of trophies as a junior downhill racer.

"Do you still race?" he asked.

"Not competitively. I'm too busy at school."

"I gather you've always lived in Colorado?"

"Yes." Beverly made no mention of her years in Washington, D.C.

Several times Markham brought the conversation around to politics, discussing his experience with federal prosecutors and the fact that ex-President Ford still skied at Vail. Try as he did, Markham could not get Beverly to talk about her father. She stubbornly refused to reveal that she was the daughter of a senator. She obviously preferred remaining anonymous.

That bothered Markham at first, taking away some of the anticipated tension of their meeting. He wanted to think of her as her father's daughter. He was tempted to ask her if she knew what her father had once done. But of course she didn't. She hadn't been born yet. She knew absolutely nothing about his role in the Defense Department, the research, the testing, or the death of a certain scientist in Maryland. She was innocent, untouched by Markham's pain. The blue eyes were bright and unguarded, like his had once been. He would have loved to tell her the whole story, every last detail, watching the eyes gradually change, the horror settle in. And see the expression on her face when he said, "You see, we're related, you and I. Your father killed mine. We're bound by blood."

But maybe this was even better, manipulating her, toying with her the way her father had toyed with his. Like Markham's father, she had no idea what was awaiting her. He smiled. "Let's dance some more," he said.

They danced for more than an hour, fast dances which they began to perform like experienced partners, and slow dances, during which Markham held her closer and closer to him. His right arm moved from midway across her waist up to the back of her neck. Beverly responded easily to his embrace. He could feel her breasts against his chest, her cheek next to his own, even her breath in his ear. At the end of a particularly long dance, he took her hand, and when he squeezed, she squeezed back.

"How about getting some fresh air?" Markham suggested.

She grinned knowingly. "You mean on the way back to your room?"

Markham laughed. "You said it. I didn't."

"Why didn't you?" she teased.

Markham shrugged. "Maybe I hadn't thought of it."

"Why not? Afraid of being alone with me?" Beverly was not usually this aggressive. But it was fun for a change. And wasn't this the best way to act with older men? Didn't want him to think she was a kid. She was eager to go back to Steven's room, and to see if he made love as well as Paul. She wouldn't be surprised if he was even better. She had decided that he was not only better-looking than Paul, but he was also much brighter. And certainly more accomplished.

She laughed to herself, thinking that Steven Thacher was exactly the kind of man her father would like. Liberal, and a lawyer to boot. Of course, that had nothing to do with her interest in him. The whole thing was a lark. She would probably never see him again. And who would be any the wiser? Surely not Doug, her new boyfriend at school. Unless of course Joanie or Karen decided to talk. There was always that possibility. You could never be too sure with girlfriends.

"Okay," said Markham. "You've convinced me. Let's go."

"Why don't *you* go? I'll meet you later."

"Change your mind all of a sudden?"

"My friends," she said, motioning across the room. "The two I was sitting with. They've got a habit of minding my business." She grinned. "I'd prefer to keep you to myself."

"What are you suggesting?"

"Slipping out after they go to sleep."

Just as well, thought Markham. If he left alone, they'd be less apt to connect him to her later. "Here. Let me give you my room number." He wrote it down on a napkin. He folded it up, then without taking his eyes off hers, he gently placed the napkin in the breast pocket of her blouse. Neither spoke as his hand briefly cupped her breast. He could tell she was not wearing a bra.

"Hurry up," he whispered.

"I'll make it as fast as I can."

Beverly got up to rejoin her friends. Markham waited for her to disappear across the dance floor before he stood up from the table. He then left the discotheque. On his way back to the hotel, he bought a bottle of chablis, which, upon returning to his room, he put in the refrigerator.

It occurred to him that maybe she was just flirting with him, feeding him a line. Perhaps she had no intention of coming at all. In that case, he would have to . . . Stop being so nervous, he told himself. Give her a chance. He took a hot shower to try to relax. He put on his silk robe and lay on the bed to read.

But it was hard to concentrate on *Time*. Every few pages, he looked over at the clock. He put down the magazine and closed his eyes, visualizing what Beverly would look like undressed. He wondered if she was blond all the way down.

Beverly could hardly wait for Joanie and Karen to go to sleep. She lay awake thinking of what she should wear to Thacher's room. Certainly something more provocative than a blouse and pants. She listened for the sounds of even breathing before she tiptoed to the closet.

Markham must have dozed off, because the knock on the door startled him. He shook his head to clear it, straightened out his robe, and went to open the door.

Beverly had on high boots and a long fur coat that looked like it was bought in a thrift shop. "I'm sorry I'm late," she said. "They stayed dancing longer than I expected."

"That's okay," said Markham, closing the door behind her. "It gave the wine time to get chilled. Here, let me take your coat."

Underneath the coat, Beverly was wearing a dark green cocktail dress. It was cut low, and showed off her breasts. Markham could hardly contain himself. Silently he reached for her hand and led her to the bed. "Make yourself comfortable. I'll pour you some wine."

Beverly took off her boots and lay back on the bed. "Thanks. I'd love some."

Markham was right. She was blond all over. Beverly also was right. Slow and gentle, Markham was an even better lover than Paul. She cried out when she came, her nails digging into his back. Her moans brought a smile to Markham's lips. He had looked forward to this moment. Here she was, under his control. He possessed her. He couldn't have been more pleased with himself.

It was dawn when the alarm clock sounded. Sitting up in bed, Markham reached over and shut it off. He looked down at Beverly lying beside him. The sheet had fallen to her waist, and he stared with cold detachment at her breasts. Whereas last night he could not get enough of them, devouring them with his hands and mouth, he now felt repelled by the sight of her rounded flesh. Her hair now looked stringy and limp, and her deep breathing got on his nerves. He couldn't wait to get rid of her.

Markham tapped her on the shoulder. "C'mon. It's time to get up."

She sighed dreamily and reached for him. "What's the hurry?"

"Your friends. Remember."

"The hell with them," she said, snuggling closer.

Markham crawled away from her embrace and jumped out of bed. He leaned down and slapped her lightly on the ass. "I don't want you to get into trouble. C'mon. Get up and get dressed."

"You sound like you're trying to get rid of me."

Markham immediately changed his tone. "Are you kidding?" he said softly. "I'd like you to stay here all day. I'm just afraid your friends'll start to blab."

Beverly yawned. "You're probably right," she said, sitting up and stretching. "I better get going."

Markham went into the bathroom and closed the door. He dawdled, so he would not have to talk to her as she dressed. When he emerged, a towel wrapped around his waist, she was in her fur coat, ready to leave.

"Don't forget. We're going skiing together later."

Markham smiled. "I'm looking forward to it."

"Where do you want to meet?" she asked.

"Do you know where the Sundown Bowl is?"

"Of course. I ski there all the time."

"I'll meet you at the top. By the sign for Morningside Ridge."

"Great. Just tell me what time."

"One o'clock," said Markham. "You'll be coming alone, right?"

Beverly put her arms around him. "Would you prefer it that way?"

"What do you think?" Markham forced himself to hug her back.

"I'll do my best." She raised her head to kiss him.

After a few seconds Markham pulled away. "You're hard to resist," he said. "Maybe we'll come back here after a few runs."

"Good idea."

Smiling, he unlocked the door. "See you later."

"One o'clock," she said.

Markham let her out, then closed and locked the door behind her. His smile abruptly vanished. Wiping his mouth off, he went to take a shower.

Beverly was waiting for him at the top of the bowl. She kissed him hello. "I see I'm not the only one who arrives places late."

"I'm sorry," he said. He had taken one final run down the Headwall, and been stuck in a line for the lift.

"That's okay. Where do you want to ski?"

"How about beginning right here?"

"Fine with me."

They took several runs up and down the bowl. Markham's practice paid off, for he had little difficulty keeping up with her.

"You're very good," she said, riding the lift to the top.

"So are you."

She smiled. "You're also not bad on skis."

Markham was pleased, both by his skiing and by how the entire bowl area remained semideserted as the afternoon progressed. It was three o'clock, with time for one last run from the top, when he suggested they race to the bottom.

"You don't really think you can beat me?" she said. "You're good. But not *that* good."

"We'll see about that. I know just the place to find out. You ever been down Headwall?"

"Not this year. But what difference does it make? I'll beat you anywhere. Just tell me what I get for winning."

"Whatever you want. Name it. Back in my room."

Beverly grinned lasciviously. "Great. I know just what to ask for."

"What's that?"

"You'll find out soon enough."

They skied across to the top of Headwall. Markham pointed out the course they should follow. "We'll go straight down, and around that first tree on the right. See which one I mean?"

Beverly nodded.

"Then across to the left." He pointed to a tree barely within view, on the extreme far side of the bowl. "We go around that tree, and then all the way down."

"Okay by me," said Beverly. "I'll wait for you at the bottom."

"Don't be so sure," said Markham. "Get ready. Get set. *Go.*"

They were neck and neck from the start to the right side of the bowl. During the traverse to the left, Beverly pulled into the lead. However, she was still close enough to hear Markham calling from behind.

"Remember. You have to go *around* the tree."

He watched closely as Beverly headed for the far side of the slope. He had removed the warning sign on his last run before meeting her. But he wanted to make doubly sure she was not alert. He timed his fall for the point when she was just reaching the tree. It was actually less of a fall than a slide, as Markham was totally in control. However, he did not look it.

"Shit!" he yelled, pretending to be in pain.

As expected, the shout was just enough to distract Beverly from her course. Instinctively she turned her head. He could see her eyes. It was only for a second, but by the time she turned back around, she was too close to the edge to avoid it. There was not even time to scream.

Anyone watching from the bowl would think she had just disappeared behind a ridge. It looked that way even from where Markham was lying. He knew better. He got up from his fall and skied over to the tree. He could barely make out Beverly's striped sweater some two hundred feet down the ravine.

Though the sun was beginning to go down, the sky was still deep blue. The air felt crisp and clean in his lungs. It was a beautiful day. Markham skied slowly to the bottom. He was in a hurry to leave Vail, yet he wanted to be extra careful. This had been a glorious vacation, and he didn't want to spoil it with an accident.

24

It was Tuesday afternoon, and Mike was doing sit-ups on the living-room floor when the phone rang. He assumed it was Susan calling to tell him what time she'd be home. Yet he couldn't be sure. He paused to catch his breath before answering.

"Susan Draper's residence," he said in his most professional voice.

"Is Miss Draper there?" It was a man, and there was a definite urgency in his voice. Probably someone Susan had written about, calling to complain.

"Who's calling, please?"

"Dr. Martin Greene. It's important that I speak to her. Is she there?"

Dr. Martin Greene. The name flashed through Mike's mind. Given to Susan by Frederick Nelson's daughter in Boston. The man she had tracked to Manhasset, and then gone to see. He had a sister killed by a car. A week before the murder of Gloria. Three weeks before the death of James Nelson. Like Arthur Thompson, and Frederick Nelson, Greene had been stationed at Fort Detrick. And like the others, he too was now bereaved.

Why was he calling? Mike felt a racing in his chest. He tried his best to sound calm. "I'm afraid Miss Draper's out just now, Dr. Greene. May I take a message?"

"Whom am I speaking to?" he asked, sounding unusually suspicious.

"This is her answering service," said Mike.

"Tell Miss Draper to call me," said the doctor. "As quickly

250

as possible. Tell her I want to see her. It's extremely important."

"I'll give her the message," said Mike, struggling to hide his excitement. "Does she have your number?"

"Let me give it to you. I'll be at home for the rest of the day."

Mike waited for Susan to return home before he told her of the call. "Dr. Greene wants to see you," he said, meeting her at the door. "He called more than an hour ago."

"Fantastic. That means he must want to talk."

"Here's his home number. He's waiting to hear from you."

Susan kept her coat on as she went to the phone. She smiled at Mike as she dialed. Mike's face was without expression. He stood with his arms crossed, leaning against the door.

"Dr. Greene? . . . Yes, this is Susan Draper. I got your message. . . . Right away, if it's all right with you. . . . Great. Give me your address. . . . Okay, I'll be there within the hour." She hung up. "Looks like this may be it," she said, turning to Mike.

"I'm going with you," he said firmly.

"So that's why you didn't tell me at the office. Afraid I'd go straight out there by myself?"

"Something like that."

"You're right," said Susan. "And that's exactly what I'm doing." She started for the door.

"Don't count on it," said Mike, barring her way.

"Are you going to move? Or do I have to . . . ?"

"What? Call the cops?" he said, eyes flashing.

"Don't be silly. You know it's not safe for you to leave here, Michael. Your picture's been all over the papers."

"I don't give a shit. I'm going. That's all there is to it."

"What are you trying to do? Screw it up for yourself? Just when we're getting a break? You know, whatever he has to tell me, he might not say in front of someone else."

"You just tell him I'm your assistant," Mike said firmly.

Susan sighed impatiently. "Be reasonable, Michael. It's for your own good."

"It is, huh? You know, I'm damn tired playing helpless victim while you run around trying to clear me. I've had it with all of this bullshit."

She put a hand on his shoulder. "I understand, baby. But that's the way it has to be."

Mike threw off her hand. "Don't call me baby!" he shouted.

"I'm sorry," she said, backing away, surprised by his sudden display of temper. "I didn't mean anything."

" 'Course not. You just listen to me, Susan. And listen good. I'm going with you to see Greene. I don't care if my picture's been on every front page, television screen, and billboard in town. This is my life we're talking about. Mine. Not yours. And if I want to risk it by leaving this apartment, well, then it's my business. Goddammit! And not you or anyone else is gonna stop me. You understand? Do you?"

Looking at the intensity in Mike's eyes, his red face and jutting jaw, Susan was at a loss for words. This was the first time she had seen the full extent of his rage. She could see how he was capable of killing someone with his bare hands. She wasn't frightened. Yet she was intimidated enough not to argue further.

"You tell the doctor that you and I are a team," continued Mike. "He talks to both of us or not at all."

Susan meekly nodded her head. "Okay, Michael. You're the boss."

"Now, find something to help make me look like a reporter."

Martin Greene looked terrible when he came to the door. His face was drawn from obvious lack of sleep, his eyes were dim, and his hair was uncombed.

"Dr. Greene," said Susan, "I hope you don't mind, but I've brought my colleague along. Roger Mann. We work together."

Mike was dressed in a baggy plaid suit that had once belonged to Susan's husband. His hair was slicked down on his head, and he wore rimless glasses. He carried a notebook in his hand.

Greene nodded stiffly. He was so preoccupied that he did not look twice at Mike. He led the two of them into his living room. The blinds were drawn on the windows. He turned on a lamp and motioned for them to sit. Susan and Mike took a seat on the couch. The doctor remained standing by the mantel.

"I'm going to come right to the point," he said. "What you asked me the other day, Miss Draper, has been on my mind ever since. Frankly, I haven't slept a wink. I decided it was time to talk. You were right about my doing research for the government. And it *was* at Fort Detrick. I spent three years there, back in the early fifties."

"What kind of research were you doing?" asked Susan. "Did it have anything to do with biological warfare?"

Greene looked down into the unlit fireplace. He nodded. "Precisely. And I'm sure I don't have to tell you, it was all top-secret."

"Then why are you telling us now?" asked Mike.

Greene turned to face them. "For one thing, I've become very disillusioned by the government in recent years. I was opposed to the Vietnam war. And of course Watergate made me sick to my stomach. You see, it was very different in the early fifties. We had just won World War Two. Everyone was proud of America. And we all believed the stories of a Communist conspiracy that was said to be threatening us. Naturally we doctors and scientists were willing to assist the government in any way possible. I was no different from many of my colleagues. It wasn't until later that I realized what a terrible mistake I had made."

"Tell us about Fort Detrick," urged Susan.

Collapsing into a chair, Martin Greene gave Mike and Susan a full description of the work done at Fort Detrick. He described the different germs, poisons, and disabling chemicals that were tested by scientists and doctors like himself. "I can't begin to tell you how terrible some of these weapons were. Fortunately, few of the destructive things we developed were ever used. I am thankful for that."

"Dr. Greene," said Mike, "we believe there's a connection between your sister's death and the work you did for the government."

Greene nodded. "Miss Draper said that the other day. That's also why I called."

"You didn't give me a chance to finish," said Susan. "What I didn't explain was that you're not the only one from Fort Detrick who's recently lost a loved one. Do you remember Arthur Thompson?"

"Colonel Arthur Thompson? Of course. He was in charge of the base."

"His wife was murdered a week after your sister," said Mike.

"I recall reading about it. I just never connected the two."

"And Frederick Nelson," added Susan. "A biologist from MIT. *His* brother was killed two weeks later."

"Fred? Him too?"

"It was in the papers," said Mike.

Greene took off his glasses and rubbed his eyes. "My God. You may be right."

"We think someone may be trying to frighten all of you. Possibly to find out about some of the weapons you developed. Organized crime, perhaps. Or even the Soviets."

"But that doesn't make sense," said Greene. "Why in the world would they bother? It was more than twenty years ago. The stuff we developed is harmless compared to some of the weapons they have now. Neutron bombs, for example, which can kill millions."

"It's not just coincidence," insisted Susan. "Not with all three of you involved. Someone is definitely out to frighten you."

Greene sighed. "Or perhaps make us pay for the work we did. How better to hurt us than to kill someone we love? Whoever's responsible surely succeeded with me," he said sadly.

"But who?" asked Susan. "Your germs, your chemicals, the plagues you all developed. You said they were never used."

"That's right," said Greene. "All we did was research."

"If no one died, then," said Mike, "why are so many dying now?"

Greene was silent. He slumped lower in his chair, his head down, staring at the floor. When finally he spoke, his voice was weak. "There *was* a death. An accident. But it was in the family. One of the men working at the base."

"An accident?" said Mike. "What kind?"

"One of the chemicals we were testing at Fort Detrick was LSD. Not much was known about the drug in the fifties. We conducted a series of research tests on local volunteers, checking to see how it affected them." He paused, running a hand through his thin hair. "I don't remember who thought of it," he continued softly. "It was a stupid idea. But several men on the base were given the drug without their knowing it."

"You mean no one told them?" said Susan.

Greene shook his head. "As you can imagine, one of the men suffered badly. He evidently experienced tremendous anxiety, the proverbial 'bad trip' we now know can occur on LSD. But at the time, no one knew what to expect. And because he himself was in the dark, the man lost control."

"What do you mean 'lost control'?" asked Susan. "What happened?"

Greene cleared his throat. "He committed suicide. He jumped from the Chesapeake Bay Bridge."

"Jesus Christ!" said Mike.

"How did the guy's family react?" asked Susan.

"That's even worse," said Greene. "The government lied to the family. They never even told them that the man had been chosen as a guinea pig, a human victim for our research. As far as I know, they haven't told them to this day. The family still thinks it was suicide."

"That's terrible," said Susan. "How could they have done that?"

"I quit shortly after that," said Greene, once again staring at the floor. "I've tried to forget about it all these years. It's been hard. You see," he said sadly, "I was the one who administered the drug."

Mike stood up from the couch. "You know something. I think you just explained it. Your sister's death, as well as the others. If what you say is true, then what we're seeing may be revenge for that man's death."

"Of course," said Susan, getting up and joining Mike. "That has to be it. Some member of his family must have found out about it. Now he's out to make you suffer the way he did."

"What makes you think it's a 'he'?" said Mike.

"Doesn't have to be. Could very well be a wife, or a daughter even."

"What was the victim's name?" said Mike, approaching Greene's chair. "Once we know that, we have our man. Or woman."

"I only wish it were that simple," said Greene. "You see, all the testing victims came from a different division of the base. They were known only by code names. I never knew the man's real name."

"Someone must know it," said Susan. "I mean, there's gotta be records."

"Sure. But believe me, the Army doesn't want this to get out. Any records would be so classified you'd have to be almost head of the Joint Chiefs in order to see them."

Mike looked at Susan. "You got any contacts that high up?"

Susan sighed. "I'm afraid not."

"If it's any consolation," said Greene, "I believe your theory about the deaths is correct. I just didn't want to admit it. Have you seen today's paper?"

"Why? What was in the paper?" asked Mike. He had tired of his previous routine, and skipped reading it for several days.

Greene got up from his chair and picked up the *Times* from a nearby table. He opened it to the second section and pointed to a small article about the "suspicious skiing death" of Beverly Douglas, daughter of the senior senator from Colorado.

"Seeing this is what finally convinced me to call you, and to find out what you knew. You're probably unaware of this," said Greene, "but Senator Stuart Douglas is the former assistant Secretary of Defense. When this accident occurred, he was the second in command. Ultimately, he was as responsible as I."

"You think he knew about it?" said Susan.

Greene nodded. "I wouldn't be surprised. The decision to cover it up had to come from upstairs."

"In that case," asked Mike, "who was the first in command? Who was Secretary of Defense then?"

"You don't know?" Greene asked in surprise.

"No," said Mike. "Why should I? I was a baby."

"I just assumed everybody knew. I mean, it's current history. His rising from a cabinet post more than twenty years later."

Susan and Mike both looked confused.

"The secretary of defense at that time," continued Greene, "was none other than Andrew Talcott."

Susan and Mike both spoke at the same time. *"Andrew Talcott!"* they said in amazement.

"That's right. *The Vice-President of the United States.*"

25

Susan drove her Audi Fox down Constitution Avenue. Mike stared out the window at the Washington Monument and, in the distance, the Capitol.

"You know, it's still hard to believe," he said.

"What's that?" asked Susan.

"This whole mess. Here I am trying to clear myself from a bum rap, and where do we end up? Washington, D.C., for Christ's sake. I've never even been here before."

Susan smiled. "Maybe you want to take a little tour while you're here? See the White House?"

"Yeah. Right. As if we got nothing better to do. I still don't know how we're gonna handle this. Hang around the Vice-President's wife until someone goes gunning for her? Then jump on the bastard, whoever he is?"

"It won't be his wife," said Susan.

"Why not?" said Mike, sounding surprised.

Susan stopped for a red light. "Whoever's behind this is obviously no dummy. He wants these men to suffer the same way he did. That's why he's going after the people they care about most."

"So?"

"So with Talcott, it's not his wife. I did some checking at the paper just before we left. Apparently their marriage has been on the rocks for years. They stay together out of necessity. A divorce would hurt his career. You know, he's planning to run for the presidency in the upcoming election."

"I know that," said Mike. "But how'd you learn about his wife?"

Susan grinned. "I'm a budding gossip columnist, remember."

"All right, then, who's gonna be the target?"

The light turned to green, Susan pulled out of the intersection, continuing down Constitution Avenue. "Talcott's sister," she said. "Without a doubt, she's his closest relative. They were raised together in a foster home. Later on, she helped put him through school. He's absolutely crazy about her."

"She have a name?"

"Mrs. Mildred Walker. She's fifty-eight years old. And an official in a private international development agency. Spends most of her time traveling around the world. For the last six months she's been living in Africa."

Mike nodded in admiration. "You really *have* done your homework, haven't you?"

"Another thing. Are you ready for this? Mrs. Walker just returned to the United States two weeks ago. She's here for another few days."

"You think our vengeful friend knows that?"

"I wouldn't be surprised," said Susan. "There's been a good amount of publicity concerning her visit. Lot of people are interested in her because of her closeness to Talcott. Especially now that he's got eyes on the presidency."

"You've convinced me," said Mike. "Where do we find this Mrs. Walker?"

"That I don't know," said Susan. "She could be staying anywhere in Washington. Or in the suburbs, for that matter."

"Great. So what are we supposed to do? Keep our eyes on the obituary page? For that I could've stayed in New York." With a sigh Mike turned to look at the Capitol dome.

"Take it easy," said Susan. "I doubt if our friend knows where she is either. Whoever he is, his contacts couldn't be much better than mine. Anyway, there's more."

"Go ahead. I'm listening."

"Two days from now, the development agency she works for is holding a huge fund-raising luncheon here in Washington. That's why she's here in the first place. Mrs. Walker is to be the honored guest."

Mike turned back to face Susan. He looked at her closely. "Wait a minute. Are you saying that—?"

"The person we're after," she interrupted before he could finish. "I wouldn't be surprised if he makes his move right then and there."

"At the luncheon?"

"He may not have any other choice. Especially if he doesn't know where else she'll be. You see, it's been reported that Mrs. Walker is planning to leave town that very night."

"How big is this affair?"

"They're holding it at the Capital Hilton. Anybody who buys a ticket can go. Your guess is as good as mine. But I'll bet there'll be at least five hundred people there."

"Just our luck," said Mike. Shaking his head, he reached in his pocket for a cigarette. "Hey, why did you wait until we got here before you told me all this?"

Susan shrugged, looking straight ahead.

"I know why. You're paying me back for not telling you right away about Greene. That's it, isn't it?"

"You think I'd stoop to such pettiness?" said Susan, swerving to avoid a bicyclist.

"Damn right."

She couldn't suppress a smile. "Well, you're absolutely right. And now that we've resolved that, where do you want to stay?"

"How about the Hilton?"

"It's too expensive. Besides, you'll be there soon enough."

"Yeah," said Mike pessimistically. "I can hardly wait."

"Before then," said Susan, "I think we should find out all we can about Mrs. Mildred Walker."

"Like maybe what she looks like?" said Mike.

"That'll be good for starters."

"Yeah. That and a good lawyer, and I'll be back in prison."

Susan shook her head. "You know what I love about you? You're always so optimistic."

"Give me a good reason *to* be," said Mike.

"Easy." Susan reached over and squeezed Mike's hand. "You got me helping you. You could do a lot worse."

"Announcing Trans World Airlines' flight 563 nonstop from Denver, arriving at Gate 17."

Nugent put down his paper and looked at his watch. The flight was right on time. Here we go again, he thought, glancing up at the door from Gate 17 straight across the terminal hallway. He was seated in the waiting area for Gate 16, surrounded by some fifty passengers preparing to board a flight for Chicago. From here he was not only inconspicuous, but he would also be able to see everyone getting off the plane from Denver. Maybe this time he'd finally be in luck.

Working in shifts, Nugent and Howard had been staking out Washington's Dulles Airport for the last two days, ever since they'd learned of the death of Beverly Douglas in Vail. "That confirms it," Nugent's boss had said over the phone. "Vacation, my ass. The creep's working his way up. And I don't have to tell you where he's going next. It's your job to find him. I don't care how the hell you do it. But find the bastard, and stop him, you understand me. I don't want any foul-ups this time. Do it right."

It was tedious work, hanging around the airport looking for Markham on every flight from Denver. But there was no choice in the matter. He had to be stopped. And if Markham was now coming to Washington, as certainly seemed likely, then this was obviously how he'd come. Nugent turned and faced the adjacent gate. The disembarking passengers were just starting through.

Frank Markham felt a mix of emotions landing in Washington. On one hand, he was thrilled. He was coming home. Dulles Airport was less than thirty miles from where he had last lived with his father, and this was the first time he had been here since learning the truth of his father's death. Coming here was also the final step of his mission, his obligation both to his father and to himself. Soon he would feel the joy of completion, a release from the burden that had preoccupied him for so many months.

Yet he had no illusions about this last phase of his commitment. Considering his target, he knew this would be harder than anything he had done before. The men who had tried to assassinate him in New York would no doubt be gunning for him, and he would have to be constantly on his toes. But he was not deterred. He had given careful thought to the killing of Mrs. Mildred Walker, and he had every intention of carrying out his plan.

Unlike before, when he landed in Vail, Markham now made a point of leaving along with all the other passengers. If there was someone looking for him at the airport, then hopefully he could slip by in the midst of a crowd. He pulled the collar up on his overcoat, pushed his hat down over his forehead, and joined the line inching toward the exit.

Nugent kept his eyes trained on Gate 17. He knew all it took was a slight lapse of attention, a momentary glance at a pretty stewardess walking by, and he could lose his man. He was being well paid for this job, and he was determined to do it right. Of course there was no guarantee this was the flight Markham would be on. There were four others throughout the rest of the day. Still, he had to give each one his full attention. Otherwise...

Nugent stiffened. He bit down hard on his pipe. There he was. No doubt about it. The one in the overcoat and hat. If he wasn't so alert, he might have missed him. He was standing so close to that woman in red, you'd think they were husband and wife. Pretty clever, thought Nugent. Trying to lose himself in the crowd. But not clever enough. Slowly Nugent got up from his seat. With the casualness of a passenger strolling to the men's room or the water fountain, he followed Markham down the hall. He was careful to keep his distance. He didn't want Markham to feel the slightest bit alarmed.

Mingling with the other passengers from the plane, Markham proceeded quickly through the terminal. While waiting for his suitcase to arrive, he tried to notice if anyone was watching him. It was hard to tell. If so many of these people seemed familiar, it could always be because they'd been traveling together for several hours. Besides, looking all around would only attract the very attention he was hoping to avoid. Stay calm, he told himself. You're in the clear. Finally his bag came. He picked it up, handed his stub to the security officer at the door, and hurried outside to the taxi line.

Through the window Nugent saw Markham get into line for a cab. Smiling to himself, he watched as Markham spoke to the dispatcher and disappeared into a cab. As soon as the cab drove away, Nugent rushed outside. Flashing a badge that his boss had made up, and which looked as official as anything carried by agents of the Secret Service or the FBI, Nugent motioned the dispatcher aside. He looked at him hard.

"That man who just left in a cab," he ordered. "Where did he go?"

Without hesitation the dispatcher gave him the name of a Washington hotel. Nugent nodded curtly and hurried back inside. He quickly made a call from a phone booth. "We got him," he said confidently. "He's staying at the Hay-Adams.

He just left, so you have plenty of time. Pick him up in the lobby, and find out his room number. . . . Right. I'll meet you there. And remember what I said. We're going to do this as quietly as possible." Nugent hung up. He contentedly lit his pipe before heading outside for a cab.

Markham relaxed during the forty-minute ride into the city. Driving through the outlying Maryland suburbs, he couldn't help thinking of his years spent growing up nearby. He remembered the hikes he had taken with his father along the banks of the Potomac, and their visit to the Great Falls, during which they'd been caught in a rainstorm and had to huddle together under a tree until the storm had passed.

He wondered if the house they had lived in was still painted white, and if their next-door neighbor, Mrs. Bailey, was still alive. He'd love to go visit his old home. He hadn't seen it in more than twenty years. Maybe when his business in Washington was through, he'd take a ride over there.

"Hay-Adams."

Markham's thoughts were broken by the cabdriver speaking to him from the front seat. "Hay-Adams," he repeated. "We're here, sir."

Markham yawned. "Excuse me. How much is that?"

"Sixteen dollars."

He handed him a twenty. "Keep the change."

"Thanks."

Markham got out and stood on the sidewalk in front of the hotel. He pretended to check the lock on his suitcase until the cab drove off with another passenger. A bellboy came over to carry his luggage.

"No, thank you," he said. "I can manage by myself."

Markham picked up his suitcase, and rather than entering the Hay-Adams, he walked quickly down H Street and around the corner. On Sixteenth Street he hailed another cab. He made a point of getting inside and closing the door before speaking to the driver.

"Where to, buddy?"

"The Capital Hilton, please."

The driver looked surprised. "You can walk there from here."

"I know. I want you to circle around a bit."

"Whatever you say. You're the boss."

Markham had no idea whether or not he was being followed. But one thing was for sure. He did not want to take any chances.

Checking to see that the driver's eyes were on the road, Nugent loaded his pistol. He then screwed a silencer onto the front of the barrel and returned the gun to his pocket. He was now ready. Assuming Howard had gotten the room number, the job was as good as done. All it would take was a matter of seconds. A knock on the door. A forced entry when Markham answered. Then, well, it was all over but the shouting. Or should he say screaming? Too bad he couldn't allow any of that. He would love to see Markham die slowly. After what he had put them through, he deserved to suffer, like with a bullet in the stomach or the groin, something that would have him moaning in agony. But no. The boss wanted the job neatly done, and so, neatly done it would be. He might even make it look like suicide, as with Wilson in Chicago. The boss had been pleased with that. Nugent was eager to please the boss again.

When the cab pulled up in front of the Hay-Adams, Nugent paid the driver and rushed inside. He went immediately to the right side of the lobby, where Howard was sitting alone behind a magazine. Howard lowered the magazine at his partner's approach. He shook his head.

"What's that supposed to mean?" said Nugent.

"Exactly what it says. He didn't show."

"Didn't show? What the hell are you talking about? The dispatcher told me distinctly it was the Hay-Adams. He *must* be here."

"Well, he's not," said Howard. "All the cabs stop right in front of that door. I've seen everyone who's arrived in the last half hour."

"You're sure of that?" said Nugent angrily.

"That's what I said, didn't I? Don't start blaming me. Maybe the dispatcher was lying to you."

"No way. I scared him so much he would've betrayed his old lady."

"All right. So he hasn't gotten here yet."

"Shit!" Nugent clenched his fists. "He's gotten here, all right. He's obviously staying somewhere else."

"You mean—"

"I mean he's screwed us again."

"So what are we going to do?" said Howard, rising from the chair.

"God knows. But I'll tell you one thing. If we thought the boss was angry before, we ain't seen nothing yet."

"Maybe we shouldn't call him."

"We have to. He expects to hear from us. Only, he's counting on *good* news."

"What are you going to tell him?" said Howard.

"I don't have much choice, do I?" Nugent turned and wearily headed for the phone booth across the lobby.

Five minutes later Nugent left the hotel. He took a cab to the Lincoln Memorial and walked immediately to the reflecting pool on the adjoining mall. He was sitting on an isolated bench, nervously puffing on his pipe, when he was joined by a man dressed in an expensive camel's hair overcoat. The man was in his late fifties, with dark hair, a strong masculine face, and deep-set eyes that were even deeper in anger.

"So he got away, huh?" the man said, staring coldly at Nugent. "How the hell could you have let it happen?"

"He must have tricked us, sir," said Nugent. "Given the dispatcher a false address."

"That's just wonderful," said the man caustically. "And you have no idea where he is?"

"I'm afraid not, sir."

"Let me remind you, Nugent, that after Chicago, you and Howard are implicated as deeply as I. If this story ever gets out, we're all going to lose. Understand?"

"I'm aware of that, sir."

"That man *must* be eliminated. Do you hear me? He gets more dangerous by the minute. There's no telling what he might do."

"We've got to find him," said Nugent. "I only wish I knew how."

"There is one way," said the man thoughtfully. "But I was hoping it wouldn't be necessary."

"What do you have in mind?" said Nugent.

"We know why he's here," the man said firmly. "And it's obvious by now that this guy'll stop at nothing to hurt me. Knowing that, maybe we can set a little trap for him. Just leave it up to me. Don't worry. I'll let you know what to do.

And this time, you better not fail. Understand? Now, get out of here before my guards get a good look at you."

Nugent got up to leave.

"Just remember what I told you," his boss said quietly. "And you can remind Howard of this too. If this story ever gets out, you're gonna suffer even more than I. All I stand to lose is an election." The deep-set eyes were cruel. "If it's revealed who killed Charlie Wilson, you'll lose a lot more than that."

Nugent noded grimly. "We'll get Markham, sir."

"We better. For all of our sakes."

Nugent turned and walked quickly away. When he was out of sight, the man in the camel's hair coat got up from the bench and took a brief walk along the mall. Tall men in dark glasses observed him from a distance. But the man paid them no attention. He returned to his limousine, parked in front of the steps of the memorial. His driver hurried around to open the door.

"Where to now, Mr. Vice-President?"

"Back to the office, please, William. The fresh air was exactly what I needed."

26

It was noon when Markham left his eighth-floor room at the Capital Hilton. He rode the elevator to the second floor and crossed the hall to the Madison Room. It was one of the hotel's largest ballrooms, capable of seating over seven hundred people comfortably, with room left for bars at either end. With its dark blue walls and crystal chandeliers, it was ideally suited for convention meetings, formal wedding receptions, and elegant luncheons.

Markham saw that the workmen had already set up most of the tables for tomorrow's affair. The men were gone now, obviously on their lunch hour. That's why he had chosen this time to come. Alone in the room, he was free to study the layout of the large hall and the position of the different tables scattered around the floor. As expected, the table for the guest of honor was up in the front.

Visualizing all the people who would be here tomorrow, Markham realized he had assumed no small task for himself, trying to kill the Vice-President's sister in the midst of a crowded hall. But he had no choice. Try as he did, he was unable to find out where she was staying here in Washington. And the fact that she was leaving tomorrow had been in all the papers. What was he supposed to do? Follow her back to Africa? It was here or nowhere.

Markham laughed. Who was he trying to kid? He was delighted that Mrs. Walker was approachable only in this room. It was much more of a challenge this way, more of a thrill. He could just see the Vice-President's face when he learned that his sister was killed in full view of hundreds of people, and right in front of her bodyguards. Even worse, the man who killed her had gotten away. It could be done. He was sure of it. Like everything else so far, all it took was a well-conceived plan.

He was interested in the various doors that led into the room. Besides the main door, which he had entered, there were two doors in the back and two along the side. Markham opened them all. He saw that the two in the back led to an adjoining kitchen. They would no doubt be jammed tomorrow with waiters rushing to and from the ballroom. The door on the right opened onto a main corridor, which made it also of little use. Anyone looking for him would certainly position a man there.

But what about the side door on the left? It was an emergency exit, and opening it, Markham saw that it led onto fire stairs. The stairs led down to what was obviously a side exit of the building. They also continued upward, most probably to the roof. Standing in the stairwell, Markham closed the door behind him. He then tried to open it from the outside. He was in luck. The snap lock was weak, and with a slight push he was able to reenter the room. No need for adhesive tape to hold down the latch. Just as well. He was no dumb Watergate burglar, risking getting caught because of a piece of tape. He could enter the hall this way, and no one, not the men who had shot at him in New York, nor anyone else assigned by the Vice-President to find him, would be any the wiser.

Markham remained in the stairwell. As there was no marking on the door, he used his room key to scratch a large X on the black paint. That way he would be able to distinguish it from the others. Satisfied that the X was noticeable, he started up the stairs. It was a long climb up the six flights, but he was in good condition from Vail and was not the slightest bit winded when he reached the eighth floor.

The lock on this door was firmer than the one below. Yet it yielded when Markham slid an American Express credit card between the door frame and the door and pushed gently against the latch. He looked both ways before emerging into the corridor. He discovered he was in front of Room 803. His own room was 808, right around the corner. He smiled as he put his key in the lock. He couldn't have designed a better setup.

Markham sat on the edge of the bed and went over his plan. He was now confident he would be able to enter the hall unobserved. Once inside, he should easily be able to lose himself in the crowd. The woman who had sold him his ticket said they were expecting more than five hundred people. Just to be on the safe side, however, he would buy himself a dark-colored wig this afternoon. And a pair of horn-rim glasses. That way, no matter how many people Talcott had working for him, they'd have to be awfully alert to pick him out in the crowd.

The only question remaining was how he would shoot Mrs. Walker and still get away. An idea had occurred to him yesterday that struck him as having tremendous potential. But he would have to try it out. He was in no hurry. He had all afternoon to practice, as well as most of tomorrow morning. By this time tomorrow, he would be fully prepared to kill the Vice-President's sister.

Markham felt a pleasant shiver at the thought of his mission coming to an end. All his preparation had paid off. He could already anticipate the overwhelming joy that would follow the shooting. The sense of peace and satisfaction. Markham made up his mind. Immediately afterward, he would indeed drive over to his childhood home. Somehow it seemed a most fitting reward. He walked over and picked up the telephone.

"May I help you?" said the hotel operator.

"Yes. This is Mr. Thacher in Room 808. Can you give me the number of the nearest Hertz office? I want to rent a car for tomorrow afternoon."

Susan and Mike sat in the front barroom at the Palm, a fashionable restaurant at Nineteenth Street and Jefferson Place. The bar was crowded with men in expensive suits and women who were caught on their every word.

"Recognize anyone?" asked Susan, putting down her white wine to lean across the table.

"Should I?" said Mike, cradling his mug of beer.

"This is the 'in' place in town. All the congressmen come here."

Mike looked around the crowded room. "Looks like any Third Avenue bar to me. I wouldn't know a congressman if I was standing next to him in the men's room."

"Well, Arlene Hudson knows them all. Though I doubt that's where she meets them. I told you, her column in the *Washington Post* is considered one of the best gossip columns in the business."

"I gathered she had some clout by the way the guy at the door perked up when you mentioned her name."

"There she is now," said Susan, noticing the maitre d' pointing out their table to a woman who had just entered. The woman looked to be in her early forties. She was tall, almost six feet, and elegantly slim, with flaming red hair piled on top of her head. She wore a Halston ultrasuede suit with a silk cream-colored blouse and an Elsa Peretti pendant around her neck. She smiled widely as she hurried over to the table. Susan and Mike both stood to greet her.

"You must be Susan Draper," she said, taking Susan's hand. "It's a pleasure to meet you." She had a deep Southern accent, and she spoke very quickly, like someone with a great deal of nervous energy.

"It's a thrill meeting you, Miss Hudson."

"Arlene, darling. Call me Arlene."

"This is my friend Roger Mann," said Susan. They had decided to continue the alias, just in case Miss Hudson was familiar with the police investigation in New York.

Her blue eyes sparkled as she turned to Mike. "I always enjoy meeting handsome young men."

Mike smiled, pulling out a chair so she could sit down. "What would you like to drink?" he asked.

"I'll take care of it." She raised her hand, and one of the waiters immediately rushed over to the table. "I'll have my usual, Charles."

"One Lillet on the rocks, with a slice of lemon. Very good, Miss Hudson."

"I see they know you here quite well," said Susan.

"They better. I mention them in my column four, five times a week. That's why I told you not to worry about getting a table."

"It's awfully nice of you to see us," said Susan. "We really appreciate your taking the time."

"No bother at all, darling. Dorothea from the *News* may be a rival of mine. But she is a bosom friend. She called me about you this morning, and I'm delighted to see you." She winked at Mike. "Both of you."

A couple walked past the table on their way to the restaurant in back. Miss Hudson instinctively turned to study them. "I wonder who that woman is with Senator Manly," she said to herself. Then, as quickly as she was distracted, she turned back to Mike and Susan. "So, what can I do for you? Dorothea said something about an article you're writing."

"I'm doing an article for the *News* on Vice-President Talcott," said Susan directly, comfortable with the story she and Mike had agreed on. "I'm trying to learn more about his sister, Mrs. Mildred Walker. Talcott's apparently very close to her, and if he's elected to the presidency she could become very influential."

"Now, that *is* a coincidence," said Miss Hudson, fidgeting with the pendant around her neck.

"Why's that?" asked Mike.

"Why, just this morning I was discussing Mrs. Walker with the Vice-President himself. I called Andy to find out if there was any truth to that rumor I'd heard."

"What rumor?" asked Susan.

"Well, I'm not supposed to say anything, but"—turning from one to the other—"if you promise not to tell Dorothea . . ."

"I promise," said Susan. "Whatever you tell us won't leave this room."

"Scout's honor," said Mike.

Miss Hudson paused while the waiter arrived with her drink. "Thank you, Charles." She took a sip, then put down her glass. "Well," she said, turning back and forth from Susan to Mike, "you know Mrs. Walker, the Vice-President's sister. She's up here from Africa to raise money for that development agency she works for."

"That's right," said Mike. "And she's gonna be a guest at that luncheon tomorrow."

Miss Hudson leaned forward over the table. "That's what they want people to *think*," she whispered. "You see, the rumor I heard was that Mrs. Walker has taken sick and was checked into a private hospital in Georgetown. Of course, the hospital won't tell you, so I called Andy myself."

"What did he say?" asked Mike. "Did he deny it?"

Miss Hudson took a sip of her drink. She smiled. "You see, darling, I know some things about Andy that he'd just as soon I forget. Especially with the election and all coming up next year. So he tried his best to cooperate. Well, anyway, he told me it was true about his sister feeling under the weather, and how terrible it was, since lots of folks were coming to that luncheon just to get a peek at her. You understand, she's not what you'd call a household face. But being the Vice-President's sister, and coming all the way up here from Africa, well, I don't have to tell you, that's some kind of news."

"So she won't be coming? Is that right?" said Susan, sounding concerned. "I was hoping to talk to her at the luncheon."

"I was too. I haven't met her yet myself. It's too bad, really. But don't go telling anybody," insisted Miss Hudson. "At least not until after the luncheon. I promised Andy, and I think it's only right, even though I would love to print it. After all, they want a crowd at the affair so they can make lots of money for Africa. I've never been to Africa, have you? They tell me parts of it are like Georgia. I'd just love to go."

"Tell me," said Mike. "By any chance do you have a picture of Mrs. Walker? Susan's been unable to find one taken in the last ten years."

"Nine years back is as good as I've done," said Miss Hudson. "There just aren't any recent shots available. Evidently Mrs. Walker doesn't fancy having her picture taken. I'd give anything for a current photo. Especially one taken in Africa, like on safari maybe. Wouldn't that be just divine for my column?"

"What you're saying is that even you don't know what she looks like? Is that right?" said Mike. Mrs. Walker's obvious obscurity, along with the columnist's dramatic way of speaking, was giving him an idea.

"That's right, darling." She scanned the bar. "She could be sitting right here without me knowing it."

"I see what you mean," said Mike, smiling to himself.

Miss Hudson soon left to chat with an ambassador, leaving Mike and Susan alone at the table.

"Now what are we going to do?" said Susan, sounding discouraged.

"Exactly as we planned," said Mike, nodding his head confidently.

"But how? You heard her. Mrs. Walker's not going to be there."

"That's right," said Mike. "But our friend, whoever he is,

doesn't know that. What's more, he doesn't know what she looks like, either. There's no way he could."

Susan looked at him closely. "What are you driving at? Would you please tell me?"

"You tell me," said Mike. "What do they do on Broadway when a leading lady gets sick and can't make an appearance?"

"Why, they get a stand-in, of course," said Susan.

"Precisely. And I have just the person in mind."

"Who?" asked Susan.

Mike smiled. "The best actress I know. It'll be dangerous for her, but if anyone will do it, she will."

"Who are you talking about?"

"A close friend of mine. Don't worry. You'll meet her soon enough. Get the check," said Mike, rising to his feet. "I have some phone calls to make."

27

Markham adjusted the wig and stepped back from the mirror. Not bad, he thought, admiring the dark curls that fell to just above the collar of his shirt. He hardly recognized himself. Amazing what a change of hair color and style would do for your appearance. He had bought the wig in Garfinckel's, along with a pair of horn-rim glasses containing nonprescription glass. He put on the glasses and took another look in the mirror; the face staring back at him could easily be that of a journalist. He knew there'd be lots of reporters at the luncheon. And with a notebook conspicuously displayed in his outside coat pocket, he'd completely fit the bill. No one would look at him twice as he circulated in the ballroom.

He was wearing gray suit pants, a white shirt, and a dull blue tie, a purposely innocuous outfit. It was essential to his plan that he blend in as best he could.

Markham got the pistol out of his suitcase. He loaded it with six shells, screwed on the silencer, and fitted the gun into his holster. He adjusted one strap of the holster around his left shoulder. Another strap around his chest held the pistol firmly to his side, so that the gun barrel pointed directly to the rear. Even with the silencer, the gun fit neatly into his armpit. The barrel protruded less than an inch behind his back. Markham put on an old sport coat, and standing sideways, checked himself in the mirror. There was now no sign of the gun, nor of the barrel pointing to the rear.

Markham removed the phone book from the bottom drawer of the dresser. Though the Washington yellow pages were filled with holes from yesterday's practice, they were intact enough for one more dry run. He placed the phone book upright on the headboard of the bed. He had determined that was approximately chest level of a medium-sized woman, the precise target he would be aiming for. Leaning the directory against the wall, he then walked across the room. Glancing over his shoulder, he lined himself up with the book. He had secured the holster so that when standing roughly ten feet away the gun was pointed straight at the target. In yesterday's practice session his aim had been sure ten out of thirteen times. That was certainly a good enough percentage, especially since Mrs. Walker's back was twice the size of the book.

His jacket was closed and buttoned, and when he reached with his right hand to his chest, it looked like he was reaching for a cigarette. He pulled the trigger.

Pffft! The silenced shot made very little sound. It would be unnoticeable in a noisy ballroom. Markham went over and checked the phone book. His aim was true once again. The bullet had penetrated three quarters of the way through the directory. Pleased with himself, Markham now took off his jacket and inspected the hole in the back. Though visible, such a hole would never be seen in a crowded hall. Besides, when he fired the gun at Mrs. Mildred Walker, he would be facing in the opposite direction. As the Vice-President's sister fell to the floor, he would be on his way out of the room.

Markham grinned. It was the simplicity of the plan that appealed to him. He had no need for long-range rifles, telescopic sights, or noisy machine guns. They were for mindless assassins, like those guys who had shot at him in New York, and would be looking for him here. Unlike them, he was clever. He knew no one would connect a man whose back was turned with a woman collapsing by her chair. And by the time anyone realized she'd been murdered, why, he'd be on his way back to the room.

Markham replaced the spent cartridge with a new one. He double-checked the tightness of his holster, then put on his suit jacket. He took a final look in the mirror, patting his wig into place, before leaving the room.

Nugent and Howard entered the Hilton. They were dressed in dark suits, and each had a small silver pin in his left lapel.

"All right," said Nugent. "You know what to do. Remember, let's try to get him before he goes upstairs. The less risk to Janie, the better."

"What time's she getting here?"

"Don't worry," said Nugent. "She'll be here soon enough."

They took positions on the opposite side of the lobby. Nodding to one another, they watched the ticket holders heading upstairs for the luncheon.

A black limousine parked amidst the cabs in front of the hotel. The driver was Mike's friend Hardy, dressed in a chauffeur's uniform. Sitting in the back were Mike, Susan, and Miss Helen Wild. Mike was wearing a blue suit, and Susan and Miss Wild were in dresses. Miss Wild's was red.

Mike squeezed her arm. "You know, I really appreciate your doing this for me."

"Do we have to go through that again? I told you on the phone I'd be willing to help you out. You've missed enough classes as is."

"Are you nervous?" Mike asked.

Miss Wild frowned. "You know how many times I've played Washington before opening in New York? I was doing it before you were born. No one gets nervous in this hick town. I don't care *who's* in the audience."

"You're fantastic," said Susan. "It's not just anyone who'd expose herself this way."

"My dear," said Miss Wild, "I'm not just anyone. Now, are we going to sit here, or are we going inside?"

Mike nodded. "Let's go." He turned to Susan. "You got the tickets?"

Susan held them in her hand. "My contribution to international development. And to getting you back on the streets."

Hardy got out to open the door for them. He doffed his hat ceremoniously as they passed. "I shall be waiting for you here, sir," he said stiffly, hamming it up.

"You too," said Mike seriously. "Thanks a lot."

Hardy winked. "Good luck."

Mike took Miss Wild's right arm. Susan took her left. The three of them entered the hotel. They walked through the lobby and up the steps to the ballroom, past an oblivious Nugent and Howard.

Markham waited until the maid went into Room 802. Seeing there was no one else in the hall, he quickly opened the door to the fire stairs. His heart was beating rapidly as he made his descent, not so much from exertion as from the realization that this was it, the conclusion to months of preparation. As in New Jersey, Greenwich, Boston, and Vail, he felt assured he had considered everything that could possibly go wrong, and had planned accordingly. Now it was merely a matter of seeing it through. Standing outside of the door marked with an X, Markham took a deep breath. He pushed open the door and passed through to the ballroom.

He was immediately swallowed up in the crowd. The woman from the development agency had not exaggerated. There were easily three or four hundred people here already, and more still arriving through the front door. The lines were five deep at the two bars on either side of the room. It was obviously, at least by Washington standards, a very social affair. Many of the men were in three-piece suits. And the women, all smartly dressed, greeted each other enthusiastically, kissing the air by one another's cheeks, so as not to disturb their makeup. Markham wandered slowly around the room, looking for Mildred Walker. He'd had to pull some strings to get it, but from the passport photo, obtained through his office, he knew generally what she looked like. Of course, spotting her in such a crowd was not going to be easy.

Nugent was worried. Where the hell was Markham? The flow of people up the stairs was thinning out now, and yet there was still no sign of him. He looked across the lobby at Howard, who shook his head with a shrug. Don't tell me he got by us. Not again. He motioned for Howard to join him by the banister.

"I didn't see him," said Howard.

"Neither did I."

"Maybe he's not coming."

"Or maybe he figured some other way to get in. We better go upstairs."

"Janie's here," said Howard. "She's wearing a green dress."

"I know. I saw her," said Nugent. "C'mon. Hurry up. We gotta find him before they sit down."

Mike, Susan, and Helen Wild circulated slowly around the room.

"Our work is going on in thirty-five countries," said Miss Wild loudly. "Fifteen of them are in Africa. We build schools, hospitals, whatever is needed in the local communities. Of course, you understand, it's only a beginning."

She was playing a marvelous Mildred Walker, thought Mike, shielding her on the left. He'd had no doubt she could do it. After all, she was one of the best actresses in the business. But what a performance! My God! It was worth an Academy Award. Susan too was playing her role perfectly. Notepad in hand, she was a reporter, pretending to take down Mrs. Walker's words. But she was actually just scribbling. She was protecting her from the right, and like Mike, she had her eyes peeled for anyone paying unhealthy attention to the apparent Mrs. Walker. Despite her protests to the contrary, Miss Wild's offering to act as the Vice-President's sister involved considerable risk, and Mike was poised, ready to jump on anyone making a move.

The problem was, he didn't know whom to look for. Who exactly was a threat? What about that guy with the red mustache who was staring at them? Or that man in the green vest approaching so quickly from across the room? Was either of them the man who had killed Gloria, and was now after Mrs. Walker? Slowly, just to be safe, Mike reached into the right-hand pocket of his coat.

He hadn't told Susan that he was carrying a .32 pistol, although he had hinted at it to Miss Wild over the phone. "I'll be covering you every step of the way." He hoped he didn't have to use it. He wanted Gloria's killer alive so that he could clear him with the police. But he felt more confident with the gun in his hand. It was fully loaded, and if necessary, he was ready to shoot.

The red mustache had now looked away. But the green vest was still approaching, coming closer by the second. Mike tightened his grip on the gun. His finger was on the trigger. If worse came to worst, he could shoot right through his pocket.

The man was reaching into his own pocket. Oh, Jesus! thought Mike. Maybe this *was* it. He hadn't even seen the man's face. He was looking only at his right hand, hidden from view. His gun still in his pocket, he pointed it in the man's direction. Should he fire first, and risk being wrong? Or wait for the other man to shoot, at a risk to Miss Wild? Better make up his mind fast. The man was now only five feet away. And stopping, most probably to steady his aim.

Abruptly Mike stepped in front of Miss Wild. He was just about to shoot when the man's hand came out of his pocket. He was holding a Bic lighter. The would-be killer in the green vest calmly lit the cigarette planted between his lips.

Mike closed his eyes. He didn't want to think about what he had almost done.

"What's wrong?" said Susan, reacting to his blocking their way.

"Nothing. Just hold it a second." Mike's hand was shaking as he reached into his chest pocket for a cigarette. He put the cigarette in his mouth, and was searching for a match when the man he had almost shot extended his lighter.

"Here. Allow me."

"Thanks," said Mike, avoiding the man's eyes. He quickly turned away. "C'mon," he said weakly to Susan and Miss Wild. "Let's keep moving."

Nugent and Howard separately circled the room in search of Markham. They both knew it was going to be harder now, whisking him out of a crowded hall without making a scene. But they had no other choice. Somehow he had eluded them again, and was now inside, stalking the Vice-President's sister. He was in here somewhere. He had to be. Only where?

Nugent checked out both bars before moving among the group standing by the tables. He saw no sign of Markham.

Howard spied a man standing off by himself. Even from behind, he recognized Markham's blond hair. Okay, smartass. The game's over. He would take him by surprise, and lead him from the room. His eyes fixed on the blond hair, Howard threaded his way through the crowd. He kept Markham's back toward him. That way he'd have no chance to escape. Not this time. Howard could hardly wait to pay the bastard back for humiliating him and Nugent. He'd teach him a lesson he'd never forget, at least for the short time he remained alive.

He wondered where Nugent was. Probably all the way over on the other side of the room. What did it matter, in any case? He could take Markham by himself. No problem. Markham was still standing with his back toward him.

Howard waited until he was directly behind him. "Come quietly," he ordered softly, "and you won't get hurt."

Markham turned around. "I beg your pardon," said the unfamiliar voice coming from the equally unfamiliar face.

This wasn't Markham. Howard had never seen this man before. "Ah . . . excuse me," he stammered, turning and hurrying away, hoping to disappear in the crowd. And he'd been so sure of it, too. Fuming, he looked around the room. Where the hell was he?

Markham was sitting up front by the wall. After working his way around the room, systematically going from one side to the other, he had despaired of finding Mildred Walker in the midst of the crowd. Twice he had seen women who closely resembled the passport photo back in his room. Each time he had maneuvered close enough to overhear their conversation. The first talked of her daughter's private school in Georgetown, the other of her husband's "hearings on the Hill." The Vice-President's sister didn't have children, and her ex-husband was a stockbroker in New York. Even if one of the women had been Mrs. Walker, he could not have carried out his plan. There was too much movement in the room. By the time he could have positioned himself and been ready to shoot, either Mrs. Walker would have moved or there'd have been someone blocking his line of fire.

Rather than frustrate himself, Markham waited. He knew that in a few moments Mrs. Walker would be starting for her table, the head table up front. He knew exactly where she was supposed to sit. Markham was standing nearby.

There was a podium behind the head table, with a microphone screwed to the top. Seeing a man, who was obviously the master of ceremonies begin to tap the mike, Markham reached his right hand under his jacket, as though for a cigarette. The gun felt damp against his fingers. Training his eyes on the table, he removed his hand and blew on it softly. He was ready.

"May I have your attention, please?" announced the man at the podium. "If you'd all kindly take your seats, we're ready to begin serving."

Mike had been dreading this announcement. He hoped his nervousness didn't show. He knew that Miss Wild would be most vulnerable when she approached the table reserved for Mrs. Walker. He was worried for her, thinking he never should have gotten her involved. Unfortunately, it was too late now.

"What are we waiting for?" said Miss Wild. "You heard the man. Time to take our seats."

Susan caught Mike's eyes. She nodded in support.

"Okay," said Mike firmly. "Let's go."

Nugent and Howard stood by the main entrance to the hall. They watched the crowd begin to move toward their seats.

"This is it," said Nugent. "It's up to Janie now. I'll cover her up close. You stay here by the door. Remember, don't try to stop him if he comes through."

"Don't worry," said Howard. "I know what to do."

Nugent nodded, and hurried up front.

There she was, thought Markham. The tall woman in the red dress. She was just now approaching the head table. That *had* to be her. So she looked different from her photo. What did he expect? The photo was taken years ago. In any event, who else here would be talking to a reporter? And walking with an obvious bodyguard, that young man in the blue suit with the roaming eyes. He had a crooked nose, and he looked tough. Talcott was apparently taking no chances with his beloved sister.

If Markham had the slightest remaining doubt that this was Mildred Walker, it dissolved when he saw that she was headed for the chair at the end, the chair designated for her on the card.

Now was the time. He had to get Mrs. Walker while she was still standing, a much better target than once she sat down. As if moving toward his own nearby table, he positioned himself in line with her, less than ten feet away. He slowly turned his back in her direction.

As casually as possible, he unbuttoned his jacket and slipped his hand underneath. He was exceptionally calm. The gun no longer felt damp. It was like part of his hand.

He glanced briefly over his shoulder. Mrs. Walker hadn't moved. She was still standing behind her chair. But other people were beginning to sit, and the sound of chair legs scraping against the floor was a perfect cover for his fire. He put his finger on the trigger.

"Pardon me," said the high-pitched voice coming from directly behind.

Markham hesitated. Don't tell me someone's gotten in the way. He looked once again over his shoulder. Another woman was now standing alongside Mrs. Walker. She was wearing a green dress, and was roughly the same age.

"This is *my* chair," said the woman. "I believe you've made a mistake."

"No mistake at all," said Miss Wild firmly, picking up the card from the table. "Would you care to read this for yourself?"

The woman in the green dress looked at the card. "See," she said triumphantly. "Mrs. Mildred Walker. That's *me!*"

"My dear," declared Miss Wild forcefully, as if on the stage, "*I* am Mildred Walker."

What the hell was going on here? thought Mike, standing next to the two quarreling women. Hadn't Miss Hudson told them the Vice-President's sister was sick? Why, he never would have called on Miss Wild if he'd thought the real Mrs. Walker was going to be there. Good going, asshole. Let's see you get out of this one.

Markham looked at the two women, hands on hips, trying to stare one another down. Which one should he shoot? The woman in green? Or the woman in red? Which one was Mildred Walker? Or was either of them the one he was after? A sickening thought suddenly came to mind. How could he be so stupid? If Talcott was on to his threat, and there was no doubt he was, would he really put his sister on the line? Of course not. But what he might do was . . . Damn if he hadn't been tricked. The whole thing was a setup.

But it was not too late. No one had seen him, at least not yet. Markham removed his hand from under his coat. He had to get out of there. And quickly. He looked around the room. The door to the fire stairs was out of the question. He'd be much too conspicuous. There was no choice. As casually as possible, he started toward the front door.

Nugent didn't know what to make of the woman in red. Talcott had told him only about Janie. So who was this other broad pretending to be Mrs. Walker? He was standing nearby, not quite sure what to do, when he noticed the man, whose back was turned toward them, heading for the door. Since everyone else was sitting, where was this guy going? He couldn't be Markham. He had the wrong color hair. Unless, of course . . . Oh, Jesus! No wonder they hadn't seen him. But there was still time. Nugent hurried across the room.

Mike too saw the man with the dark hair picking his way

281

through the tables toward the door. Who knows? Maybe the scene at the head table had scared away Mrs. Walker's would-be assailant? It certainly seemed likely. Then what was he waiting for? That was *him*, the man he was after. Get going. There's the bastard who's gonna clear you. There was no time to tell Susan or Miss Wild. He had to hurry before the guy got away. He almost tripped over a chair in his eagerness to follow him.

Markham recognized the man standing by the doorway as one of the men who had tried to kill him. He was about to go for his gun, before he remembered he was wearing a wig. Relax. Act natural, he told himself. He'll never recognize you.

He was right. Howard paid him no mind as he breezed past toward the stairs. He had decided not to go back to his room. At least not yet. They were out to trap him, and it was not safe. For the time being, he wanted to put some distance between himself and the hotel.

Markham was halfway across the lobby when Nugent rushed up to Howard. "Did you see the guy who just passed?"

"Dark hair and glasses?"

"That's him. I'm sure of it."

Howard didn't hesitate. He pulled up his lapel so that the small silver pin was next to his mouth. "He's on his way, Fred," he said sharply. "Dark hair and glasses. Pick him up."

Nugent spoke into his own pocket transmitter. "Proceed as planned. We'll follow you." The two of them rushed down the stairs.

"Cab, sir?" said the doorman.

"Yes, please," said Markham. "Right away."

The doorman blew his whistle. The cabdriver in the front of the line, who had paid twenty-five dollars to be allowed to stay there all afternoon, now decided to work. He pulled up to the curb. Markham jumped in the cab.

"Where to?" asked the driver.

"Just go straight," said Markham. "I'll tell you where to turn."

"Sure thing."

The cab started off.

Nugent and Howard saw the cab halfway down the block. They ran in the opposite direction, toward their parked car.

"Cab, sir?"

Mike ignored the doorman. He raced to the curb, and waved for Hardy to bring up the limousine. Before Hardy had even braked to a complete stop, he jumped inside and slammed the door.

"Don't tell me," said Hardy. "Follow that cab."

"You guessed it. Our man's in the back."

Hardy peeled out from the hotel, leaving the doorman aghast and cutting off Nugent and Howard, who were directly behind them.

"Shit!" said Nugent. "Who's that nigger think he is?"

"Don't worry," said Howard, who was driving. "We'll pass them."

The cab was stopped at a light on the corner of Sixteenth Street and I.

"Turn left here," said Markham. "And head back toward the Hilton."

When the light turned green, the cabdriver continued straight down Sixteenth Street.

"Didn't you hear me?" said Markham, raising his voice to be heard through the partition. "I told you to turn."

The driver ignored him. He continued going straight.

What was wrong with this guy? Didn't he want a tip? Something terrible suddenly occurred to Markham. No, it couldn't be. He reached to open the door. Try as he might, the latch wouldn't budge. It was locked from the front. His worst fears were confirmed.

He pulled out his gun and pointed it through the partition at the driver. "Stop this car, or I'll blow your fucking head off."

The driver turned around. He grinned. "Try it."

Markham could see the partition was bulletproof plastic. Out of rage, he pounded it with his fist. There was no getting around it. He was trapped.

The driver, a colleague of Nugent and Howard's, had instructions to take Markham to an out-of-the-way farmhouse in Maryland. He knew what would happen to his passenger as soon as they arrived. That was no concern of his. It was his responsibility merely to get him there. Nugent and Howard, who were following them, would finish the job.

He looked in his rearview mirror. Where were they? All he could see was a large black limousine.

"What are you waiting for?" said Nugent. "Pass that goddamn thing."

"I'm trying," said Howard, honking the horn.

"Probably some fucking senator. Just be careful of cops. There're lots of them around here, and we don't want to get stopped."

It was on Sixteenth Street, between H and I, that Howard made his move. He swung into the other lane, pulled up alongside the limousine, and started to pass it. He could see the taxi with Markham stopped at the intersection immediately ahead. "Here we go," he said to Nugent.

Howard expected the limousine to allow him to pass. He was unprepared when the black car speeded up as well. "What the fuck's that nigger..."

The car plowed into the side of the limousine. Both cars were going so fast that the limousine, in turn, was propelled ahead, into the back of the taxicab, still stopped at the light.

Markham, slumped in the back, was all of a sudden thrown forward against the partition. He didn't know what happened. But he heard a loud cracking noise, and he thought for a second it might be his skull.

The horn was sounding from the driver bent over the wheel. Even through the partition Markham could see the blood dripping down the back of his neck. He turned around and saw the two cars piled up behind. Jesus, what an accident! How come he wasn't hurt? He felt his head, fully expecting to find half of it gone. Something felt strange. It was the wig. So that's what had cushioned his blow. He had some luck left after all.

And how. He suddenly noticed that the windows in the back were shattered. And here he was just sitting there. Wasting time. There were probably cops already on the way. He quickly reached out through the broken glass to open the door. He was in such a hurry to leave that the wig got caught in the glass. No problem, thought Markham, running from the car. It had saved his life. And he had no further use for it.

Mike didn't know what hit him. One minute he was leaning over the back of the front seat staring at the man in the taxicab ahead, and now he was facedown on the floor, eating carpet. His head hurt, and he had the feeling that his left arm was broken.

"You all right, baby?"

He looked up to see Hardy gazing down at him. Hardy had a deep gash across his forehead. "What happened?"

"Bastard tried to cut me off." In spite of his injury, Hardy grinned. "I didn't let him."

Mike picked himself up. Even if his arm wasn't broken, it sure as hell hurt. The pain seemed to clear his head. "Hey, where's that guy in the cab?"

Hardy looked out through the shattered front window. "Hurry, baby. He's taking off."

The back door was bent from the impact of the crash. Mike pushed against it with his good shoulder. On the third shove, he forced it open. He staggered out of the limousine. The first thing he noticed was the wig hanging from the door of the cab. Apparently the man just now entering Lafayette Park had something to hide. Mike had to catch him, no matter what. It was now or never. Ignoring the pain in his arm, he started to run.

Nugent and Howard were merely shaken up by the crash.

"Look what you did," shouted Nugent, holding his head.

"It wasn't my fault," said Howard. "It was the goddamn nigger."

"Where's Markham? Fuck! He's getting away." Nugent fumbled with the latch on the door. When he had finally opened it and was climbing out, he found himself staring at a blue jacket with a silver badge.

"Going someplace, mister?" said the Washington cop.

"Why, of course not, officer."

"Tell your friend there I'd like to see his license and registration, please."

Nugent sighed. He could see Markham disappearing into the park. What in the world was he gonna tell Talcott?

Out the corner of his eyes Markham saw the young man get out of the limousine. Damn if he wasn't following him. Where had he seen that broken nose before? That's right. He was the bodyguard to the alleged Mrs. Walker. No, wait a minute. Wasn't there someplace else as well?

What difference did it make? The kid was working for Talcott, and was after him. He had to get away.

Markham picked up speed. He tried to lose him in Lafayette Park. But aside from a lot of statues, there was no place here to hide. Emerging on the other side, across the street from the White House, he looked over his shoulder. The kid was about fifty yards back. Though holding his left arm, he was still coming on strong.

Markham crossed Pennsylvania Avenue onto E Street. What should he do? He couldn't just continue to run. He was bound to get stopped by a cop. He needed someplace to hide.

He got an idea. Why not? If the timing worked out, he'd lose the kid for sure. At least it was worth a chance.

Straight ahead of Markham was the line for the guided tour of the White House. And it was just this minute moving through the gate.

28

Mike could hardly believe his eyes. The White House? *He's going in there?* My God! He picked up speed, hoping to overtake him before the tour line passed completely through the gate.

He was too late. By the time he got there, the guard was just closing it. Mike rushed up to him.

"Yes? Can I help you?"

Mike was about to explain, when he caught himself. What was he gonna tell him? That the man at the back of the line was a murderer, and had to be stopped? That he was trying to kill the Vice-President's sister? He could hear the guard now. "Sure thing, buddy. Tell me about it. And about the Russians who just landed on the South Lawn."

They'd think he was crazy. They'd never let him onto the grounds. Then he'd lose the guy for good. There was only one way to follow him.

"How long do the tours last?" he asked.

"Thirty minutes," said the guard.

"When's the next one ready to leave?"

"Fifteen minutes. You best get on line, if you're fixing to go."

Looking through the bars in the fence, Mike could see the man he was after just now disappearing into the building. It was the first chance he'd had to take a good look at him. Was it his imagination, or did he know him from somewhere? The blond hair looked strangely familiar. Chalking it up to nerves and the pain riddling his arm, he got into line.

Glancing over his shoulder, Markham saw the kid who had been following him stuck behind the bars. He smiled. It had worked exactly as he'd hoped. Bye-bye, fella. Ain't much you can do about me now.

Fifteen minutes seemed like a week. Mike was lighting up his fifth cigarette in a row when the guard opened the gate. Mike looked behind him down the line. December was obviously a slow month for tourists, as there were only about thirty other people waiting to go in. Most of them were families. He'd expected longer lines for the White House.

"May I have your attention, please," said a perky blond woman standing alongside the fence. "My name is Alice, and I'm your guide this afternoon through one of the most famous buildings in the world. For most of you, I'm sure, the White House needs little introduction."

Right, thought Mike. So hurry it up.

"It is the oldest public building in Washington, and it's been the home to every president of the United States except George Washington. There are a hundred and seven rooms in the White House, though I'm afraid you'll only be able to see five of them."

"Good," said Mike under his breath.

"However, if you keep your eyes open, and you're lucky, you might just see the man who lives there. He *is* in the building at the moment, and you never know when he might wander through. So if you'll follow me up the walk, we'll begin our tour."

Gritting his teeth against the pain in his arm, Mike passed through the gate onto the grounds. Susan was right after all. Like it or not, he was going sightseeing.

He stayed in the front of the line as the group entered the building.

"The White House was designed by an Irishman named James Hoban," said the guide. "In fact, the building is very similar to the house of the Duke of Leinster in Dublin. The cornerstone was laid in 1792. The South Portico was added in 1824 . . ."

Mike peered down the hall. He was hoping for a glimpse of the tour up ahead.

"This is the East Room. It's where many of the presidential receptions you read about are held. Dances. Marriages of daughters. And alas, even funerals. Services for presidents Lincoln, Harding, Roosevelt, and Kennedy were held here. That portrait of George Washington on the east wall is by Gilbert Stuart. We owe it to Dolly Madison, who saved it from the fire set by the British in 1814 . . ."

Mike was not hearing a word. "Excuse me, miss," he interrupted, pointing down the hall. "What room is that over there?"

"That's the Blue Room. We'll be ending up there."

Mike could see the previous tour moving through the room. Gloria's murderer was somewhere in that crowd. He looked at the red ropes blocking his way, and the uniformed guard standing by the wall. Dashing down the hall would just get him arrested. And the man he was after would then get away for sure. Be patient, he told himself. Don't blow it now.

Markham was breathing easier now. Even if the kid were still waiting outside when the tour was through, Markham felt sure he could handle him. If worse came to worst, he figured he could always identify himself to one of the White House officials. Make up a story about how he was being followed by some crook he once sent to prison. Ask them for a ride back to his hotel. Who were they gonna believe? Some long-haired punk, or him, the district attorney of New York?

"As you can see," said Dorothy, his guide, "the Blue Room is not blue. The walls were changed to white silk by Mrs. John Kennedy. The beige picot design you see now was introduced by Mrs. Nixon. Why, then, is it called the Blue Room? Well, because that's the color it was in the days of President Van Buren."

Where had he seen that young man before? It was still nagging at him. Was it here in Washington, or in New York?

"That concludes our tour of the public rooms. If you want to see some of the other hundred and two rooms," added the guide with a smile, "you'll have to see about getting yourself invited. Now, if you'll follow me down the hall, we'll pass across the South Lawn on our way back to the gate."

"This is the State Dining Room," said Mike's guide. "This is where all the foreign dignitaries take their meals when they're in town."

The group laughed. All except Mike. He could hardly contain himself. He knew now he'd made a mistake following him in here. God knows where he was by now. There'd been no sign of the other tour since leaving the East Room. Here he was stuck in this group, and with two rooms to go. He should have just waited by the gate for the guy to come out.

Exasperated with himself, Mike glanced out the window of the dining room. It looked over the lawn. There was a group going past. And it was the one he was searching for. Sure enough. The blond guy was up by the front. He was about fifty feet from the window, and Mike could study him much better than he had earlier. He was convinced of it now. He had seen him somewhere before.

But so what? He was halfway to the gate. Within seconds he'd be outside, gone for good. Mike had to act fast.

Impulsively he threw open the window. "Hey, you!" he heard someone yell. He ignored it as he climbed onto the ledge and squeezed under the sill. It was a six-foot drop to the ground. The commotion behind him was getting louder, so there was no time to hesitate. He jumped. Misjudging the distance, he tripped, falling onto his bad arm.

A thousand hot needles pierced his arm from shoulder to fingers. But he had to get up. The man he was after must be nearing the gate. And any second now the guard would begin shooting, thinking he was after the President. That was obviously his voice shouting at him to stop.

Mike picked himself up. Grabbing the gun out of his pocket, he sprinted across the lawn.

"What's *with* that guy?"

The tour guide was looking over her shoulder toward the White House. "Is he crazy?"

Markham turned around to see who she meant. So he had followed him inside, that kid with the dark hair and the broken . . . It suddenly flashed through his mind where he had seen him before. Of course. On the police circular regarding the murder of Gloria Thompson. That's why he was chasing him. He wasn't working for the Vice-President at all.

It was time to reveal who he was, and to ask for help. Markham turned and bolted toward the front door.

"Stop!" yelled Mike.

"Oh, my God!" shrieked the tour guide. "He's got a gun."

Abruptly Mike stopped running and took aim. He didn't want to kill him. Only bring him down. Just as he fired, he heard another shot somewhere behind him. Then there was an explosion in his left shoulder that made the earlier pain seem like nothing. He pitched forward, landing on his knees.

Markham was just reaching the gate when he felt a hot tearing sensation deep in his neck. Then he was falling. His legs were like rubber, and the ground was coming up fast. He hit the gravel driveway hard. He expected pain. But there wasn't any. Not in his legs. His chest. Nowhere. All feeling was gone. He was lying on his back, staring up at the afternoon sky, when he died. The last thing he remembered was that he had rented a car for that afternoon, and he had better hurry to pick it up, for it was suddenly getting dark.

Mike was sprawled out on the ground. He knew he'd been shot. But not before he had seen him, the man he'd been after for so long. It was that district attorney from New York, the one who was always in the papers. Who would ever believe it!

Epilogue

"One more load ought to do it," said Mike, putting down the box in Susan's hallway. Susan was right behind him with a suitcase. "Here, let me help you with that," he added, taking it from her.

"Put that in the bedroom," she said. "Then let's get downstairs for the rest of it, before you change your mind."

Mike was grinning as he came back in the hall. "What are you worried about? I've been in prison before. Second time's always easier."

Susan poked him in the chest. "Watch yourself, Mike, or I'll deny all those articles I wrote. I'll say you forced me to write them just to get you off parole."

Mike held up his hands. "Okay, you win. Anything you want, babe. It's yours."

She put her hands on her hips. "Hey, Michael, I thought we both wanted this?"

"Come on, Susan," he said, sidling up to her. "You know I always play tough. I never do anything I don't want to do." He gave her a quick kiss on the cheek. "C'mon. I thought you were in a hurry."

Susan sighed, following him down the stairs. "You're too much, Michael."

He shrugged. "What can I say?"

"Guess what?" Susan said as she reached the first landing.

"What?"

"It's about Vice-President Talcott."

"Ex-Vice-President Talcott, you mean. Let me guess. He's suing you for libel? Claiming you cost him the nomination?"

"Hardly. He's had enough scandal for a while. His sentencing comes up next week. Anyway, his political days are over. He's found himself a whole new racket."

"What's he into now?" said Mike. "Drugs? Murder? Espionage?"

Susan laughed, joining him at the bottom. "Probably all of them. He's writing a novel."

It was four o'clock when Billy Markham left the apartment.

"You better hurry," said his mother from the doorway. "Mrs. Stone said you were late for the last two lessons. That's no way to pick up your grades. You have all your books?"

Billy nodded, pointing to the book bag slung over his shoulder.

The elevator door opened, and Billy stepped inside.

"Cheer up," called his mother, waving good-bye. "It's for your own good."

Billy forced a smile that abruptly faded as soon as the door closed. God, how he hated going to tutoring. You'd think he was a dummy the way Mrs. Stone went over his algebra and grammar. Who needed her help anyway? If his marks had gone down on his last two report cards, well, it was certainly understandable, considering all that had happened this last year.

It was cold for September, and Billy buttoned his coat as he headed up Riverside Drive.

Wasn't it bad enough that his father had died? After all, he was more than just a father. He was . . . well, sort of like his best friend. Billy missed him something awful, especially on days like this when they would have played together in the park.

But even worse were all the lies they told about him. Saying he was "sick" and . . . a criminal himself. If his father had killed those people like it said in the paper, well, there had to be a damn good reason for it. They must have done something really bad.

All too soon Billy arrived in front of Mrs. Stone's building. Reluctant to go inside, he looked across the street at the park. There was a group down on the playing field, tossing around a football. Billy hadn't played football for months. The memories were just too painful. But anything was better than

Mrs. Stone. Figuring he'd been late for his lessons before, and he could be late again, he wandered down the steps to the field.

The five players were high-school or college age, wearing jeans and old jerseys. Billy watched from the sidelines as they ran plays. On one of them, the wide receiver bobbled the ball, and it rolled right next to him.

"Hey, kid. Throw it here," yelled number seventy-six.

Billy stared down at the ball.

"C'mon, kid. Over here."

Slowly Billy took the book bag off his shoulder and flung it to the ground. He picked up the ball, gripped the laces as he'd been taught, and threw it as hard as he could. It was a high spiral pass right into the hands of seventy-six.

"Jesus, kid. Where'd you learn to pass like that?"

"I had a good coach," said Billy.

"Whadda you say? We're short a man. Wanna join us?"

"Sure," said Billy. He unbuttoned his jacket, threw it over his book bag, and sprinted out onto the field.

On the second play, he caught a fifty-yard pass for a touchdown. He only wished his father could have seen it. Boy, would he have been proud.

About the Author

TOM SELIGSON is the author of *The High School Revolutionaries* and *To Be Young In Babylon*. He has contributed to the *New York Times*, the *Village Voice*, and many magazines both here and abroad. Mr. Seligson lives in New York City. *Stalking* is his first novel.

More Bestsellers from SIGNET

- [ ] **PACIFIC HOSPITAL by Robert H. Curtis.** (#J9018—$1.95)*
- [ ] **SAVAGE SNOW by Will Holt.** (#E9019—$2.25)*
- [ ] **THE ETRUSCAN SMILE by Velda Johnston.** (#E9020—$2.25)
- [ ] **CALENDAR OF SINNERS by Moira Lord.** (#J9021—$1.95)*
- [ ] **SUNSET by Christopher Nicole.** (#E8948—$2.25)*
- [ ] **THE CRAZY LOVERS by Joyce Elbert.** (#E8917—$2.75)*
- [ ] **THE CRAZY LADIES by Joyce Elbert.** (#E8923—$2.75)
- [ ] **MAKING IT by Bryn Chandler.** (#E8756—$2.25)*
- [ ] **JO STERN by David Slavitt.** (#J8753—$1.95)*
- [ ] **THE HOUSE OF KINGSLEY MERRICK by Deborah Hill.** (#E8918—$2.50)*
- [ ] **THIS IS THE HOUSE by Deborah Hill.** (#E8877—$2.50)
- [ ] **EYE OF THE NEEDLE by Ken Follett.** (#E8746—$2.95)
- [ ] **A GARDEN OF SAND by Earl Thompson.** (#E9374—$2.95)
- [ ] **TATTOO by Earl Thompson.** (#E8989—$2.95)
- [ ] **CALDO LARGO by Earl Thompson.** (#E7737—$2.25)

*Price slightly higher in Canada

Buy them at your local bookstore or use this convenient coupon for ordering.

THE NEW AMERICAN LIBRARY, INC.,
P.O. Box 999, Bergenfield, New Jersey 07621

Please send me the SIGNET BOOKS I have checked above. I am enclosing $_____ (please add 50¢ to this order to cover postage and handling). Send check or money order—no cash or C.O.D.'s. Prices and numbers are subject to change without notice.

Name _____

Address _____

City_____ State_____ Zip Code_____
Allow 4-6 weeks for delivery.
This offer is subject to withdrawal without notice.

Recommended Reading from SIGNET

- [ ] **THE PASSIONATE SAVAGE** by Constance Gluyas.
  (#E9195—$2.50)*
- [ ] **MADAM TUDOR** by Constance Gluyas. (#J8953—$1.95)*
- [ ] **THE HOUSE ON TWYFORD STREET** by Constance Gluyas.
  (#E8924—$2.25)*
- [ ] **FLAME OF THE SOUTH** by Constance Gluyas.
  (#E8648—$2.50)*
- [ ] **SAVAGE EDEN** by Constance Gluyas. (#E9285—$2.50)
- [ ] **ROGUE'S MISTRESS** by Constance Gluyas. (#E8339—$2.25)
- [ ] **WOMAN OF FURY** by Constance Gluyas. (#E8075—$2.25)*
- [ ] **THE STAND** by Stephen King. (#E9013—$2.95)
- [ ] **NIGHT SHIFT** by Stephen King. (#E8510—$2.50)*
- [ ] **CARRIE** by Stephen King. (#E9223—$2.25)
- [ ] **'SALEM'S LOT** by Stephen King. (#E9231—$2.75)
- [ ] **THE SHINING** by Stephen King. (#E7872—$2.50)
- [ ] **ASPEN INCIDENT** by Tom Murphy. (#J8889—$1.95)
- [ ] **BALLET!** by Tom Murphy. (#E8112—$2.25)*
- [ ] **LILY CIGAR** by Tom Murphy. (#E8810—$2.75)*

*Price slightly higher in Canada

Buy them at your local
bookstore or use coupon
on next page for ordering.

SIGNET Books You'll Want to Read

- ☐ **THE DOUBLE-CROSS CIRCUIT by Michael Dorland.**
  (#J9065—$1.95)
- ☐ **THE ENIGMA by Michael Barak.** (#J8920—$1.95)*
- ☐ **THE NIGHT LETTER by Paul Spike.** (#E8947—$2.50)*
- ☐ **THE NIGHTTIME GUY by Tony Kenrick.** (#E9111—$2.75)*
- ☐ **INHERIT THE SEA by Janet Gregory.** (#E9113—$2.50)*
- ☐ **DELPHINE by Mel Arrighi.** (#E9066—$2.50)*
- ☐ **JOGGER'S MOON by Jon Messmann.** (#J9116—$1.95)*
- ☐ **THE PURPLE AND THE GOLD by Dorothy Daniels.**
  (#J9118—$1.95)*
- ☐ **THE LEGEND OF THE THIRTEENTH PILGRIM by Jessica North.** (#E9068—$2.25)*
- ☐ **THE AMULET OF FORTUNE by Susannah Broome.**
  (#J9134—$1.95)*
- ☐ **THIS BAND OF SPIRITS by Noël Vreeland Carter.**
  (#E9069—$2.25)*
- ☐ **THE SCOURGE by Nick Sharman.** (#E9114—$2.25)*
- ☐ **AN ACCOMPLISHED WOMAN by Nancy Price.**
  (#E9115—$2.50)*
- ☐ **FOOLS DIE by Mario Puzo.** (#E8881—$3.50)
- ☐ **TO SET THE RECORD STRAIGHT: The Break-in, the Tapes, the Conspirators, the Pardon by John J. Sirica.**
  (#E9156—$3.50)

*Price slightly higher in Canada

Buy them at your local bookstore or use this convenient coupon for ordering.

THE NEW AMERICAN LIBRARY, INC.,
P.O. Box 999, Bergenfield, New Jersey 07621

Please send me the SIGNET BOOKS I have checked above. I am enclosing $_____ (please add 50¢ to this order to cover postage and handling). Send check or money order—no cash or C.O.D.'s. Prices and numbers are subject to change without notice.

Name _____

Address _____

City_____ State_____ Zip Code_____

Allow 4-6 weeks for delivery.
This offer is subject to withdrawal without notice.